The 2024 NORTHWIND Treasury

Winners of the Northwind Writing Award

Edited by tara caribou
and Candice Louisa Daquin

Raw Earth Ink

2024

First paperback edition November 2024

Book concept and cover design by tara caribou
Edited by tara caribou & Candice Louisa Daquin

ISBN 978-1-960991-38-6 (paperback)

Published by Raw Earth Ink
PO Box 39332
Ninilchik, Alaska USA 99639
www.raw-earth-ink.com

TABLE OF CONTENTS

ABOUT THE AWARD

THE NORTHWIND WRITING AWARD, sponsored by Raw Earth Ink and facilitated by tara caribou, was created to shine light on little known yet exceptional writers across the United States, United Kingdom, Australia, and Canada.

THE AWARD WAS GRANTED by process of anonymous scoring by a panel of judges. The judges had no way of knowing who the authors were, so without any bias they were able to score impartially. Overall, we looked for writing which collectively stirs emotion, paints vivid imagery, is high-caliber or underappreciated, captures our attention, and lastly, is memorable.

A NOTE FROM THE EDITORS

WHEN I ORIGINALLY APPROACHED Candice with the idea to create an award for exceptional writers across multiple genres, immediately and enthusiastically she was all in. I often come across writers who are of such high caliber and yet don't recognize it for themselves just *how* outstanding they really are. I read. A lot. Much of it, especially in this day of social media and the desire for "everyone to feel like a winner," and with the market so flooded, can be difficult to spot the diamonds in the rough.

I want to showcase those diamonds.

The entries were vast and our judges wonderful. Since I wanted their judging to be completely impartial, no one but I knew who wrote what. I sent out the packets, hundreds of pages each with an alpha-numeric assignment on each entry, to each judge, who also did not know one another. Then came the task of adding up the tallies and comments and notes made by the judges, as well as a couple tie-breaker votes. Once the judging was complete, I read each entry and found myself nearly overwhelmed with excellent writing.

Every one of these winners which you now hold within your hands is to be commended and should be proud of the work they put out.

It has truly been my humble privilege and honor to read their work. I look forward to many more years of treasuries to come. *~tara caribou*

I LOVE READING AND WRITING. While I am by no means the most accomplished writer myself, I know good writing. I have read enough, and edited enough, that by now I can say this categorically: *Not all writing is equal.* There are outstanding writers who should be recognized. It was for this reason I really relished the opportunity to judge a writing competition.

I like the idea of a competition even as I myself am not competitive. I see it as more than merely *competing*, it is a chance to showcase the best writing submitted and for those who enter, a way to grow as a writer and hone one's craft. Not everyone can win but everyone who enters should feel like a winner for putting their best work out there.

Reading through the submissions was a huge undertaking and incredibly interesting. We all loved the variety of submissions and of course the best part was found in the variety of reading through different genres: fiction, poetry, longer poetry, and non-fiction. Having such a diverse range of writing styles available for the prize, as well as the wide variety of authors in terms of their writing style, made this a fascinating process.

Some of the pieces I read were outstanding. To the point where I was seriously impressed and slightly floored at how well written they were. This motivates me to keep going with the Northwind Writing Award, because it shows a need and a love for writing in our communities.

What was particularly interesting for me personally was how great the non-fiction entries were and many of my fellow judges agreed; I wasn't expecting that. I have unofficially judged writing submissions multiple times in my role as editor with several literary magazines, so it wasn't that different other than the quality of work, which showcased how hard everyone put their best foot forward.

I'm really excited to hold this treasury of that hard work in my hands and see the culmination of all this commitment to the craft of writing. There is no 'one way' of writing well, but there *is* definitely a type of writer who is seriously impressive and can hook you by the first paragraph. This is a collection of those writers. ~*Candice Louisa Daquin*

OUR JUDGES
Candice Louisa Daquin
Randy Easton
Jack "Shorty" Short
Rebecca Huston
Danielle M. Franklin
H. Graham

Tie-breaker/executive scores:
tara caribou

Non-fiction

1st Place

FROM THE EDITORS: *Winners are created when they write such original pieces that you literally haven't read anything like them before. An almost impossible feat, China Braekman's Peeling Tomatoes is a wholly original non-fiction, using the metaphor of a werewolf to describe a relationship, there's an entire book in this 4-page beauty. It stands out for its exquisite prose, intense language and impeccable pacing. Both ambitious and finely crafted, this is the definition of non-fiction at its finest; utilizing concepts from fiction to embroider a more vivid reality. -CLD*

PEELING TOMATOES
by China Braekman

In the ten years that I've known him, I've always relied on Tim to interpret poetry for me. A song comes on the radio, a poem emerges from the pages. *So, what do you think this means?* Ensues a well-rehearsed performance in which I oppose my rational analysis of words to his intuitive association of ideas. He talks about symbols while I focus on grammar. Eventually, after I've shut down all his suggestions on the basis that they are random, far-fetched, or plainly wrong, he smiles and concludes our little match by telling me that the poem is surely about one of three things: love, death or entropy. In reality, this whole act is an indulgence to which he graciously subjects himself, because he knows that I care less about the answer than I do about the answer being untethered. Some days, I need to know that my inability to trace the origin of meaning is shared. On those days, he articulates that for me. He speaks of love and death and the way an A minor chord stirs emotions, and I feel less alone.

* * * * * *

In her eponymous photobook, photographer Sam Contis documents life at Deep Springs, a small college tucked away on a cattle ranch in Bishop, California, near the border with Nevada. The college was founded in 1917 as an all-male institution which promised to forge the moral character of its students by combining a liberal arts curriculum with manual labor on the ranch, a form of self-government and a secluded lifestyle. Though the college has since become co-educational, all the students were young men at the time that Contis was photographing them. The book *Deep Springs* mixes color with black and white, Contis's own pictures with archival images taken by former students, intimate close-ups of young men with grandiose landscapes of the Sierra Nevada Mountains.

Through this amalgamation, Contis toes the line between softness and violence, offering a sensitive take on masculinity. One of the photographs is a close-up of a boy's chest, cropped right below the sternum, above the navel, and between the nipples, such that there's nothing else to see but hairless, pink, fragile skin. The only thing protecting this bare body from the lens is the boy's hand, which is tainted with dirt and delicately placed in the middle of the frame. Another photograph, also pink and fleshy, propels the viewer into layers of fat, inside an animal that is being cut open. The picture is all texture, with exploded blood vessels and animal fur reminding us of the death that just ensued. We only catch a glimpse of the blade which sliced the animal open in the top right corner of the image. In another picture, three men crowd around a dead animal hanging upside down, slit down the middle. Four indistinct hands are pressing into the animal to keep its guts from spilling out.

Set against the arid landscape of cowboy California, the photographs in *Deep Springs* offer a glimpse of vegetation – male bodies like we aren't used to seeing them: up close, amongst themselves, in that very liminal space of being both 'boy' and 'man'. Because the boys' faces are often concealed, their bodies speak on their behalf. One review of the book put it well: "[Contis] offers up an uncommonly tender view of masculine youth, ready and willing to be nurtured into useful purpose, as the land."

* * * * * *

The first time I slept in Tim's bed, our limbs intertwined like vines. It was the first time that I saw a man's body like that, that I let someone see mine like that. I was nineteen, he was five years older. He seemed a towering force, a lean but muscular body that only love prevented from crushing me. Our hands ran all over, fingers meshing, as we held each other closer and closer. Years before sex was even a reality to me, a precocious friend put it simply: *Sex? It's like a big hug.* We desire a person so much that our caress turns into an embrace, our embrace into a fusion. We pull them as close as we can, baffled that such a thin layer of skin, like that of a ripe tomato, encloses all the nutritious stuff that makes up our lover's soul and flesh. After our first night together, I woke up and saw Tim's back. He was seated on the bed, facing the window and, from the mattress where my head lay, I felt minuscule. The morning light streaked over his shoulders and through his armpits, revealing the constellation of raised freckles that I'd learned to read in the dark, as if I'd been deciphering Braille.

A decade later, and Tim's body is like an extension of my own. We've found all the latches: we lock into each other, and we breathe as if we shared the same reserve of oxygen. I pick at his scabs, run my fingers through his hair, and tend to his wounds as if they were mine. I collapse on top of him at the end of a long day and tuck into his sides when I need shelter, assuming that he feels my fear and my exhaustion – rather, that my fear and my exhaustion are *ours* – like two plants drawing from the same soil. In recent years, scientists have deepened our understanding of forest ecosystems, finding that trees communicate with each other via complex, underground fungal networks. They secrete chemicals into these networks to warn each other of danger, and they share nutrients to keep each other alive and healthy. I think of us as two trees but a single forest, free of language and dependent solely on an invisible, underground web to communicate.

And yet, sometimes I find myself staring at him, helpless, when I realize that I can't heal his wounds, that I don't understand exactly what he feels. I go to him to fill my cup, ignoring that sometimes his is empty too. In those moments, I'm reminded that what is shared in spirit remains separate in flesh, and that I am, in fact, not entitled to his body. It's an alienating feeling when you've played in a field for years and realize you were trespassing all along.

* * * * * *

I was walking home one summer night after dinner with friends. The roads were empty, other than a few food trucks scattered at street corners. It was that time of night when traffic was low and stop lights lost their meaning; I crossed without paying attention. At the intersection, a figure emerged ahead of me. It was Tim, I thought. He was walking in the same direction, only a few feet ahead. I was instinctively pulled forward and my mouth was half open, ready to call out his name, when I realized that the details didn't add up. Though my legs were already in motion, I forced them to slow down, and my steps gradually synchronized with his. We advanced silently in the dark and I observed him from a distance.

He was about Tim's height and had the same slouch, causing him to swing his arms in that characteristically loose way. Yet, where Tim's stride is steady, this man's was nervous, bouncing up and down as if he had springs under his feet. He kept twitching, fists clenched, muttering fury into the ground ahead of him. He wasn't simply walking but lunging forward, throwing his entire body at an invisible enemy. He was shirtless, only wearing a pair of black shorts that were ripped above the knees. Like a werewolf that had crawled out of his dwelling for metamorphosis. Intoxication, madness, starvation, the werewolf was on the hunt. In the summer heat, his back glistened with sweat, leaving a trace of past violence. Beneath what appeared to be soft skin was a weave of tense muscles. I saw them clench one by one as he rolled his shoulders, and I repressed the urge to get closer. Living in the city causes a degree of numbness – to eccentricity in the best case, to misery in the worst. This encounter, however, I wasn't immune to. I feared the werewolf would turn around and see me, or worse, that he would turn around and reveal Tim's face.

* * * * * *

A few years ago, Tim started studying his body like a scientist in a lab, dissecting the physical manifestations of fear. On several nights, he sat alone in the forest. He would go deep into the woods, far from the streetlights, where he could barely see a thing. There, he would keep his eyes open and wait – wait and see how long it took for his primal fear to kick in. Branches rustling, small animals scurrying, wind whistling. He would listen to the night sounds, repeating to himself, like an incantation, *You know there's nothing here, you know there's nothing to be afraid of.* He would drag this experiment out for as long as he could, until eventually his incantation lost its power, and fear would force him to get up and walk back to his car. Most often, there wasn't anything to be afraid of; one night, on his way out of the forest, he came face to face with a twelve-point buck. Those instincts are there for a reason, and he was trying to harness them. With time, he made the experiment last longer, but was never able to completely overcome the fear. He described it to me like, *it feels like you're getting kicked out of the driver's seat, and a more visceral version of you takes over.*

That kind of fear is not what animated me on that summer night. Only *I* could have been in the driver's seat, because my fear was somehow sitting atop a mountain of care. It was Tim and it wasn't him; I desired and I feared. It was unsettling. Here, it is helpful to consider Freud's description of the uncanny (*unheimlich* in German*)*. He finds that its opposite (*heimlich*) has two meanings – the first, of something that is intimate, familiar and belongs to the house; the second, of something that is secretive, hidden behind closed doors, precisely because it belongs to the most intimate space of the house. *Heimlich* ends up sharing the same meaning as its opposite, *unheimlich*: "What is *heimlich* thus comes to be *unheimlich*." Freud concludes, the uncanny is what happens when we can no longer tell apart reality from our imagination. It is what happens when both of these worlds burst at the seams, leaving us feeling exposed, vulnerable, doubtful – if not of the world, then of ourselves.

The werewolf was the spitting image of Tim. Brown hair, same build, long arms, lean back. On his shoulders I recognized a similar splatter of freckles. His backbone formed a deep crevice that split his back in half, evoking the familiar feeling of running my finger over the ridges and depressions on Tim's spine. I always release pressure on the last vertebra, because that is where he got injured in a snowboarding accident as a teenager. Since that first night, I learned to navigate Tim's scars, moles and bones like rock formations in the desert. I know his back like a treasure map that a kid stashes away, a plane of fantasy that no one else even knows exists. And I offer him my back, too, as uncharted land. It is literally on our backs that we first confessed our love to each other, tracing the letters I, L, O, V, and so on, shakily, in silence, in the dark. I often think of the front cover of *Deep Springs* – a grainy black and white photograph of a young man's back. You open the book and realize it may as well have been a picture of the valley itself, each freckle like a tumbleweed.

* * * * * *

Tim often used to tell me that there was a side of him he didn't want me to see. A side that carried pain and anger, both of which he feared would drive me away. As my love for him grew, so did my morbid desires to see that side of him unleashed. To be fully known, I thought, was to see what was beneath the skin, to be okay with your guts being spilled onto the floor. With time, I've learned that love will inevitably puncture you in places, and that it is unnecessary to slash yourself open all at once. I've learned that my own insistence about being fully known was half-hearted at best. As we've developed into what feels like a single organism, we've come to accept that each of us has a secret garden. That we both have the unrealized potential to be someone else, something else, is a risk we've been willing to take.

Eventually, the werewolf stopped in his tracks and sat on the ground, still staring into the distance and muttering, almost growling. I walked past him and discovered his face. It was a handsome face, but anonymous – like those faces you see on the subway and then forget. The pull that had kept me silently creeping behind him vanished in an instant, leaving me nonetheless with the reassurance that Tim was waiting for me at home.

FROM THE EDITORS: *A terribly challenging piece to love, because of its heartbreaking subject; suicide and the imprint people make in our lives, especially during our darkest times. However, this is a highly necessary subject, and one handled beautifully. With the motive of flowers throughout, the narrator recalls her own near death and how the friend who helped her through the worst of it, ended her own life some time later. There is no just sorrow here; there is the truth of love and caring and how as the writer repeats throughout, you never really know anyone, never fully. -CLD*

THE COLOR OF HEARTACHE
by Ann Kathryn Kelly

In my garden, one of the first of my summer plants to push up from the ground in late May, after the spring bulbs have gone by, is my "bleeding heart." My sister-in-law Jane Ann, an avid gardener, divided hers soon after I'd moved into my first home years ago. She'd whacked it down the middle of its root ball, after its flowers had dropped and its leaves had yellowed, and brought a large hunk of it in a plastic grocery bag to my door.

Fifteen years on, I've taken it with me to a new home. That piece of Jane Ann's bleeding heart—as close to her own as anything could be, given her devotion to plants—has landed in several of my friends' gardens, as I follow her lead of whacking and dividing. It propagates and charms grateful recipients with its delicate beauty.

My plant was in full bloom the first week of June when news broke from a French village that Anthony Bourdain—famed chef, author, and "Parts Unknown" star—had died from suicide. On June 8, 2018, a shocked world tried, as they do with tragedies, to make sense of it. Many of us had allowed ourselves to think we *knew* Bourdain because he showed up in our living rooms each week, all rugged good looks and real talk, to dish about exotic street food from the world's dustiest corners.

We don't know anyone, certainly not celebrities and often not even those in our families, fully. Their demons. Their fragility.

Never fully.

* * * * * *

The summer I was diagnosed with a bleeding brain tumor, Jane Ann would stop in every night to see me during those lost months as I weighed options. She and my brother, Pat, lived several streets away. I'd hear a knock at my door after the dinner hour. There she'd be, holding her Shih Tzu, Penny, whose toy legs had given out again during their walk because Penny was more doll than dog. It was easier, Jane Ann would explain with a wave of her hand, to carry her. Penny seemed to agree, her chocolate eyes radiating gratitude, a cream-and-tawny powder puff panting between yawns.

That summer, Jane Ann bore many offerings to my door. Tupperware containers of homemade soup. Lasagna in aluminum-foiled trays. Flowers cut within the hour, that spilled over the fence running the length of her Victorian. Peonies. Daisies. Roses.

Deep red roses.

Her daily visits kept me engaged when all I wanted was to come home from work, pull the shades, ignore the phone, and escape into the TV or my bed. If I didn't see anyone, I wouldn't have to talk about what was going on. I wouldn't have to work up my courage to schedule the surgery I needed to save my life; a surgery that would turn into almost twelve hours face down in the OR between a head vice as my skull was sliced open.

Jane Ann, a registered nurse, watched with my family my decline across June. July. August. I felt her eyes on me each night as we visited. The only thing she pushed those evenings was Penny, into my lap, and fistfuls of flowers, into my hands. Bright spots were few that summer, but what glimpses of light I grasped for often included Jane Ann somewhere in the frame, among those who surrounded and lifted me.

As my strength flagged, my surgery date loomed, and fear engulfed me, she drove back the dark with flowers vibrant and voluminous. Ruffled blooms—purple, pink, white—exploded from her grip. In a fresh-cut bouquet of dahlias, one flower, dwarfing the others, sprang from the middle. Butterscotch center, surrounded by a band of sunshine yellow and tipped in white.

"That's gorgeous," I said, pointing. "And huge. What is it?"

"Dinner plate dahlia." Jane Ann smiled and leaned in for a whiff.

Her centerpiece lived up to its name, large enough to hold a salad. Smaller dahlia varieties surrounded it. She removed wilted roses from a vase on the dining room table that she'd brought a week earlier and plopped in the latest selection with fresh water. Jane Ann was happiest when doing for others.

I'd developed "foot drop" from my brain tumor, a neuromuscular disorder that starts out as weakness and leads to muscle paralysis, as nerve signal communication from the brain to the foot is hijacked. I couldn't lift and flex my left foot. I dragged my toes.

I'd gotten a brace, bulky and impossible to get my shoes or sneakers over. Jane Ann stopped by one evening soon after I'd gotten it and dropped a shoebox on my dining room table. I'd told my family I was considering not wearing a shoe at all on my left foot: a risky choice. If I didn't fall from foot drop, chances were great I'd land on the floor as I swayed around shoeless, the brace's plastic sole like a banana peel.

"I saw these at Walmart, Annie." She flipped the lid open, while Penny panted patiently by a table leg.

My face fell when I pulled the sneakers from the box. They were bright white, vinyl, extra wide, with two Velcro straps. A thick rocker heel. The size of pontoons.

"It's bad, I know," Jane Ann said. "But, look, you only need to wear one. Wear your regular sneaker on the other foot."

The sound of ripping Velcro, as I tightened and retightened straps, filled my dining room. Penny's ears flicked and turned with each rip, like radar antennas.

I'd had a pre-op procedure weeks before my surgery. Called a cerebral angiogram, a catheter was inserted into my femoral artery and snaked up my body to my neck. Contrast dye was injected to show any abnormalities in my brain's blood vessels, giving my surgeon the full picture he needed prior to surgery. Following the procedure, I was not allowed to climb stairs for three days. My house had a bathroom only on the second floor, but Jane Ann and Pat had one off their kitchen. Springing into action, they converted their dining room into a temporary first floor bedroom. Jane Ann pushed their dining room table into a corner, had a bed brought in, carried a TV into the room, and kept me fed and watered until I could climb stairs again.

She took me to a hairdresser days before my surgery, after she and my mother agreed a pixie cut might be nice. There was no reason why I couldn't have style, they said, though it would be shaved seventy-two hours later.

I recovered in a rehabilitation hospital, learning to walk, swallow, and grasp objects again. While I was away for the month of October, Jane Ann planted rows of tulip bulbs along my driveway before she left for her winter in Florida. When spring returned and I was again living independently in my house, my driveway erupted into a palette of pastel splendor. I had a Monet watercolor outside my door. She'd never mentioned to me she had planted them the previous autumn.

"I wanted you to see a rainbow when you got settled in your house again," she later said.

The tulips bloom and re-bloom. Year in. Year out.

* * * * * *

Days after Bourdain's suicide, my news feed was crowded with reminders that it was a bathrobe belt, that the world had lost a legend, that his body was stuck in France due to bureaucratic red tape.

After a battle with French officials over his remains, Anthony Bourdain's body has reportedly been cremated and his ashes will be flown home Friday.

My stomach churned as my eyes moved down the page. This man, who meant something to so many, flown home in pieces. Like cargo.

Like Jane Ann.

One year and thirty-seven days after a neurosurgeon returned my life to me, after my family buoyed me above lashing waves that pulled me toward its undertow, after Jane Ann used up everything in her garden and her heart to bolster me through what I was sure would end me, she ended her time with us.

On Thanksgiving Day, 2010, we boarded a plane: Pat, my mother, and me. In Pat's suitcase, stowed in the overhead bin, an urn with Jane Ann's ashes sat tucked between shirts. We were flying back from Pat and Jane Ann's winter home on Florida's Gulf Coast to their primary residence in southern New Hampshire, to bury her in her girlhood hometown where her elderly father still lived.

Our generous Jane Ann, reserved until she knew you, until she trusted you, but then opened her house, wallet, heart to anyone. Jane Ann, friend to all animals. Our princess of perennials. She hadn't left a note.

We don't know anyone, fully. Their demons. Their fragility.

Never fully.

* * * * * *

I had my bathroom gutted to the studs last winter. My carpenter stopped in on a spring day to wrap up. While I had him, I asked him to hang a framed, stained-glass window from a chain. I'd gone with vintage black and white tiles on floor and walls, chrome fixtures, and lots of frameless beveled glass. A splash of color, I felt, would finish it.

Ruby red, royal blue, pear green, violet, gold. Jeweled pieces splay across the window in a mosaic, creating a vase-filled flower arrangement, each bloom outlined in lead.

When he finished, we stepped back. A spot in the middle of my chest started to ache. It was Jane Ann's window, one she'd bought in an antique store years earlier. The center flower, a rose, glows scarlet when sunlight streams in.

It's the color of a heart. Of heartache.

Of knowing we once had Jane Ann in our lives, and recognizing that we have pieces of her, still. Like when the rainbow of tulips push through the earth each spring, or the bleeding heart blossoms in my garden, its red, heart-shaped flowers ending in teardrop petals that drip from arched stems and nod to me on a breeze. Like when the sun shines through the stained-glass window, Jane Ann's window, with its riotous burst of flowers.

* * * * * *

A plant's stalk, strong enough to carry the weight of blooms—some small, but others at times as big as a dinner plate—can be easily broken. Sometimes, from a battering rain. Sometimes, rough handling is all it takes.

Certain flowers are too fragile to last. They break, and they're gone.

When we've had them in our gardens, however briefly they bloom, the space they leave behind is never filled the same way, even as other varieties open their petals to the sun.

Previously published in *The Coachella Review* in 2019

FROM THE EDITORS: *A very classic style portraying the existential angst of loneliness, in our modern world, where the protagonist comes to see his own isolation through the creatures on the sea front. There is something very clean and emotionally redolent in this author's writing style, where you directly feel the experience and understand why we become so detached from our world and how we perhaps can change that. -CLD*

BEACH CLEANED EYES
by Joe Labriola

There's this man at the gym—a middle aged "bro"—who says to his fellow bro, "I made two-hundred-grand last year. And I got *no* savings. Freakin' ridiculous. Nevah enough. It's nevah enough."

His friend sighs a quivering chuckle, then grunts. "Eh, that's the way it is," he says, and goes on huffing and puffing as he pumps his bicep cords like a sailor bailing out a sinking ship.

That's the way it goes, I think, sitting there at my own machine. *But going where?*

I leave the gym, thinking about those bros. Not so much *what* they said as *how* they said it: shoulders hunched, jaws grating. I hop in my Chevy, but where to go? I live on an island, after all. A pretty big one, but an island all the same. You go north, you hit water. South, water. West, traffic and heat, and eventually water. East, more of the same. In fact, it's pretty much all traffic. It's pretty much all heat. It's pretty much all traffic, heat, and water when you boil it down.

Wherever you go these days.

But I know, really, where I *want* to go. *The day's still young,* I tell myself, even though it's almost three p.m. I head north, toward the water. *It's still early.* I'm still young.

The beach is surprisingly bustling for a Monday in early June, although the forecast does tout continued postcard perfect weather today, tomorrow, and probably even the day after. Maybe a third of the spots in the main blacktop lot are full. I wait on line for my seasonal parking sticker. It feels strange. I've been coming here to beach clean all year. In the wind, and the rain, sleet, and snow. But I need a pass. For fifteen dollars, plus proof of residency. Proof: license and registration. But I've got plenty of beach clean gear: reusable bags, trash pickers, bins, gloves, hats, and more. What more proof is there?

"All we need is license and registration, please."

So I show them my documents and get my sticker, and now I'm finally a renewed member. Like a family, of sorts. *That's funny,* I think, finding a spot. *The deer know me better.*

The seagulls. Better than the summer lackeys manning the guard stand. Better than the belly-bloated day-drinkers plopped at the bar. And the teenage waitstaff at the beachside

restaurant. Reverse zombies, I think of them, not quite sure what I mean as I turn off my car. The AC only half-works. Even with the windows pressed all the way down, it's still hot as hell.

The deer and the gulls and even the crabs know me better. They *see* me. And I see them. Watching each other. And I tell them with a nod and a blink: "Hey guys! Uh, just cleaning more trash! Sorry for my people. Um. Sorry for me. They don't mean to make a mess. Uh, I don't either. They just—we just—don't know any better. You know? You understand."

But all the animals do is stare right back, even after I move on.

I start down the beach, drifting toward the private residences. I do this because there's too many mouth-breathers at the public part. I don't want to clean their crap. I don't want them to yap, "Hey! That's mine! I ain't done with that!"

I'll get their trash later.

There's a short, wood-and-wire fence at the "border" that only extends to the high tide line. A plastic placard dangles in the middle. "PRIVATE PROPERTY" it screams in big red letters plastered on the white square, and then in smaller font below cries: "ABSOLUTELY NO PETS. YOU KNOW WHAT WE MEAN—*WHO* WE MEAN." That last part is only implied. But it's there all the same.

I weave around the stringed barrier. The public beachgoers dare not tread here. Most of them. The fence and its sign warns, and scolds in advance. There's trouble to be found on this other side—for those who don't belong. But there's also trash—and now a man with a bag and a squeaky picker, wearing a hat and a modest but honest smile.

Yet most homeowners are thrilled—if sometimes confused—by my presence. One time, an aggressively gray-haired man stumped up to me from out of his beach chair. "What're ya doin'?" he demanded.

"Just picking up trash," I said, simply.

"*Shells?*" he whipped back, mishearing profit in my purported purpose. "No... Beach trash," I answered politely.

"Oh," he said, rolling his shoulders as if trying to release a landslide of stockpiled stress. "That's good then."

Another time, a mother and father and son paused amidst their sea glass hunting to thank me. "So the town pays ya for this?" one of them asked.

"No."

"Oh, so...you're volunteering then?" "No. Just here cleaning."

They stared blankly, not too unlike the deer and their ilk.

I find sea glass too. I found a chunk here once, unlike anything before, or since. And I've found thousands of bits of broken bottles over the years, smoothed over by time and salt and sun and surf. But this one was a big old palmful of wave-polished cobalt. Deep and dark. Dense.

Rare. Beautiful. One-of-a-shine, glimmering under the still, strong sun.

Maybe it means something? I wondered, tilting the pentagonal piece under the blaring light. *Maybe it means nothing.* But it was here and now, and so was I. And something about that was simply lovely as hell.

* * * * * *

There are fisherfolk here of all varieties. Many spend their weekends on the main public beach—either near the parking lot or on the pier: set back in their chairs next to coolers of bait, their rods wedged in plastic stands, which sometimes wiggle with the heft of a porgy, sea robin, or flounder. For some, this is a lovely weekend diversion from their normal workweek routine, AKA: heat and traffic. For them, their weekend is, finally, *water*.

For others, fishing is a way of life. Sustenance. As much a cultural-familial outing as the most practical way to win dinner. To survive. I see these families often during my weekday beach cleans—both at the public beaches and farther down along the homes and stock photo cliffs.

Sadly, sometimes I find more fishing debris left behind than anything else.

"We don't even botha cawling the cops no more," one of the cliffside home dwellers lectures to me. She shakes her head. "They're outta control... And then the kids come at night. Leave all their trash. What's the purpose? It nevah stops."

"I guess they just don't realize," I say with a shrug. "We used to party at the beach in high school, but I like to think we cleaned up after ourselves. And you would think that the people fishing at least, they'd be the last ones who'd want plastic in their fish. But I don't think they know. I don't think anyone's really explained it. They are fishing for dinner, after all."

She stares at me blankly. "Yeah, it's a real mess."

* * * * * *

A few years ago, I participated in my first art gallery. I never thought of myself as an "artist" in the sense of visual work—at least not until my friend texted me that she was curating a trash-themed exhibit of pieces wrought from reclaimed material. She proposed that I create something to highlight my ongoing beach cleaning efforts.

And so I cleaned, and crafted.

I ended up with a two-fold design. The first: a pedestal-propped poster board featuring beach clean photos, statistics, and information on *"HOW YOU CAN HELP!"* The second: a lean, semi-translucent plastic tower; packed to the top—about six feet— with beach clean treasures: cans, bottle caps, pens, caution tape, etc. etc. etc.

"So, how long have you been doing eco-art?" one observer asked me as I stood next to my display.

"Oh, I'm not an artist," I said with a mild chuckle. "Just a guy who likes to clean the beach. So many people don't really realize how much plastic is leaching into fish, hurting ecosystems—especially with other climate change that's already happening. I just wanted to make something to help show that, you know?"

"Hm," she grunted, tilting her head at my display. "You sure seem like an artist to me."

* * * * * *

Nevah enough, I think with an internal laugh, remembering the gym bros as I pluck wrapper after wrapper out from the tideline seaweed. I suppose it's kinda like doing weights. Certainly feels like it's going someplace, even if I don't know where.

And then I see it—maybe fifty meters ahead: a glossy brown baseball helmet shining in the sand. *These freaking kids' toys...*, I think, suddenly feeling twice my age. I sourly take my time getting there. It's far from the first out-of-place item I've stumbled across. Balloons and Barbies, golf balls and grease cans, condoms and cocaine bags. The list rolls on and on and on and on, just like the roiling surf itself...

A mile-long hike can easily yield a bulging garbage bag. Mine is nearly full. I ignore some of the smaller scraps, trudging on toward the helmet. The stupid thing probably weighs as much as a hundred wrappers. A thousand. Sure, those add up too, but something big (like a single cracked white lounge chair) will eventually break down into a hundred thousand wrappers worth of microplastics.

I pause as I near the upright helmet. I pause, because that's when I realize that it's *not* a helmet, but the upright shell of a big, lone, *horseshoe crab...*

Coming closer, I see its underbelly facing the sky, briny legs crinkling under the June sun.

It's stuck, I realize. How could it not be? Its pointed tail wags helplessly on the sand like an overworked windshield wiper.

It's dying, I think, wondering why I just stare.

I step up next to the creature, blocking the direct light with my shadow. I wonder if it knows I'm here. If it wonders what I am. Who I am.

I bend down to flip the head-sized being over. It immediately turns around, skittering toward the mellow waves. Almost as if it *knows* where to go. What to do. Who to be. Who it is.

The rest of my cleaning goes by as normal. Plenty of strange trash. Confused stares by critters and coastal homeowners alike. Friendly "thank you!" waves from passersby. Yet the whole time I have this sinking feeling in my gut. And I don't know why. *Maybe it's the tupperwares*, I think, sensing the residual stench from the abandoned bait containers that waft from my bag.

Maybe it's me, I wonder. *Us.*

But then there's a saying that comes to mind, for some reason; it rings me like a bell. And it goes something like, "Critical mass is a hell of a thing."

That sounds about right. Certainly feels it, at least.

* * * * * *

Sunset "arrives" as I reach the parking lot. Sunsets, like time, are fleeting. Always on their way out. More of a movement. More of a spectrum than any sort of ever-solid thing. The daytime tanners have already departed, replaced by scenic gawkers, phones all raised in unspoken synchronicity. They need to capture what will soon be gone.

But there's something else here...

They don't notice me as I load my day's work into the back of my car—although I too pause to enjoy this uniting scene: the prom couples, tired commuters, and fisher families all sharing a thought, even if just for one moment.

I snap a picture too. I love a good sunset like anyone else. I'm only human, after all. But even so, I can't help but remember that horseshoe crab flipped alone on its back.

Except now, I imagine where it might be. What it might feel. Clear in its purpose, however clear that might be. Flowing with the tides. Going where time takes it.

I wonder if it ever says to itself, "Nevah enough"?

At least now I think that I understand why we stare at each other.

FIDELTY
by Charlotte Crowder

For Austrians, vociferous argument is a national sport, a regular spleen-cleansing exercise regimen. The ground rules dictate that only half of what is shouted is meant in earnest. That nuance, however, got lost in translation. In the States, where my mother landed after the upheaval of the war, her anger was volatile and high-pitched. My Mid-Western father never learned to duel with harsh words. Lacking a verbal foil, my mother's grew vicious. My father fought off each barrage of her ire with a silence far more violent, withdrawing more deeply and aggressively until the two were poisoned with hatred. So as not to witness their final dissolution, the summer I turned eight, I was sent away to stay with my grandparents in England.

As soon as I unpacked my bags and took possession of the narrow room that was my grandmother's sewing room, the very air of the semi-detached house on Fernhurst Gardens grew static with my grandfather's jealousy. He was my mother's stepfather, and I became a stepchild as we fought for the attention of my grandmother. The fights were stand-offs, silent struggles for power. I had learned to fight in silence—like my father. I withdrew from the noisy confrontations that characterized the Viennese branch of the family. In silence, I stole my grandmother's affections, taking for my own her adoring words, her caresses. Though capable of clamorous argumentativeness, my grandfather sensed in me a true opponent, against whom querulous half-truths were an inadequate defense. He too, fought silently.

Each morning by the umbrella stand, we offered each other our cheeks, mine soft with childish down, his equally soft, scraped smooth with a straight-edge razor. His steel-gray hair was oiled slick. Fascinated by the regularity of the comb tracks, I stared across his head and breathed in the smell of horehound, so pungent it pulled my nostrils together. After the prescribed goodbye kiss, Opa said, "Now be a help to your grandmother. Try not to get in the way." He donned his bowler and strode down Fernhurst Gardens toward the train station, looking like the impeccable Englishman he aspired to be.

Then I was alone with my love. I dogged her about the house through the rooms crammed tight with European antiques, intricately inlaid Biedermeier furniture and elaborate china figurines that had replaced objects left behind in a hurry.

Comfortable in the envelope of my grandmother's love, I sat by her footstool and studied the porcelain folds of the Rosenthal shepherdess's dress and the dainty lace on the edges of her pantaloons. The shepherd leaned across a fence with a bouquet of wildflowers for her. His lips were pursed in expectation of a kiss. I squeezed my eyes tight and opened them quick, again and again, each time hoping to catch them in an embrace, each time disappointed.

Oma, her ample roundness settled deep in her easy chair, stitched a rag doll for me out of cast-off nylon stockings. Made of thick fabric like so many elastic bands woven together, they were different from my mother's stockings. They did not shimmer like my mother's, which showed the gentle curve of her calf. Oma's were opaque. They obliterated the shape of her legs, making thick posts of them. But they provided a good casing for my rag doll, which had a round dimpled face, sturdy legs and arms, blue button eyes, and a quirky smile cross-stitched with red embroidery floss. Oma finished her off with a head of yellow wool hair, fashioned of scraps from the yarn basket.

As Oma worked, I pulled photo albums from the bottom shelf of the bookcase. On days when the homesickness, a tight clamp around my heart, was strongest, I chose the newer vinyl-covered ones with gold-embossed curlicues. These documented my life from babyhood in garish colors and I took solace in the recorded smiles of my then still-happy parents. Other days, I reached for the old album with the cloth cover, cardboard poking through at the frayed corners. The stiff, black pages were bound together with a heavy cord. Brittle fragments broke off as I turned them. The black and white photos of my mother as a child slid off the page, exposing dried glue. Each was painstakingly labeled and dated in my grandmother's perfect hand. The album ended in the middle. The last photo, labeled "Vienna—March 1938," showed my mother as a young girl standing between Oma and Opa in a park or a garden. They all wore overcoats and Opa had an armband on one sleeve.

It was the doll, or rather her clothes, that caused the problem. For weeks Oma worked on her wardrobe, knitting miniature cable-knit sweaters and argyle socks, sewing tiny quilted bathrobes and floral-print sunsuits.

When the sewing machine was set up, my narrow bedroom was impassable. The machine and Oma's chair filled the space between the wall and my bed. The bay window became an island at one end of the room. I sat there, secure in the small circle of love formed by the space, dressing and undressing my doll. The damp air brought the scent of roses up from the front garden. Oma, with her mouth full of pins, pushed the tiny pieces of fabric under the sewing machine's presser foot.

An hour or two before Opa was to return home from work, Oma packed up the machine and pushed it against the wall.

In the kitchen, I stood at her elbow as she prepared a three-course dinner for Opa. When he arrived home, the only sign of our infidelity was a plate of crescent cookies my grandmother baked just for me. But we were discreet; we left them in the kitchen where Opa rarely ventured.

He gave us each a gruff peck on the cheek. His face was no longer soft, but scratchy with stubble, the scent of horehound barely perceptible. He reclaimed my grandmother, insisting she sit in the living room. Although Oma seemed more eager to tend to the dinner than to sit, and Opa immediately disappeared behind his newspaper, I granted him that and retreated to my bedroom.

This time, I grabbed a roll of tape on the way. I amused myself before dinner playing window dresser, taping the rag doll's clothes and crayoned signs with prices in pounds and shillings to the panes of the bay window. I ran down the narrow stairs and out the front door to view my display. The effect was perfect—an upstairs doll boutique. Except, the argyle socks didn't show well. I ran upstairs and moved them to the center of the window, ran down again to see the result. What the design needed was something to tie it together. Upstairs again, I rummaged through the fabric scraps in Oma's work basket and found a long piece of red satin. I made a valance with it, draping it above the doll clothes. Downstairs from the front path, I could see it hung a little crooked, but it would have to do. Oma stood in the doorway, folding her apron; dinner was ready.

Oma ladled soup and dumplings from the tureen.

"It looks thin, Trude."

"Nonsense, it's a good cream soup. Taste it before you complain."

My grandfather lifted his spoon to his lips. "It lacks salt."

Oma bustled to the kitchen for the salt cellar. It was a daily ritual, performed grudgingly, but with no lasting bad humor.

"What have you been doing, running up and down the stairs all evening?" His tone was softer than the admonishing words. His curiosity about my childish industry was genuine.

"Playing shop."

"And what are you selling?"

"Doll clothes."

"Ah ha." He tried hard to understand me, but I could not believe he had ever been a child and he seemed not to remember if he had been.

At bedtime, I proudly showed off my work to Oma. She cooed, admiring the display, and kissed my forehead as she tucked me into bed.

The explosion did not happen until the next morning: Saturday. I was in my room fashioning a cash register out of a shirt box, sorting scraps of colored paper and paper clips for money. I was ready for business.

"Trud---E!" Opa bellowed. He stood in the front hall. Oma rushed from the kitchen. "Tell the child she has to clear out the window right now."

I stepped into the stairwell and listened. What could I have done? At home, I never did anything wrong. Here, it seemed I was bad all the time, bad without knowing it.

"But Max, it's just a child's game. What harm could it possibly..."

"We are not zoned for commercial enterprises. The authorities will come. Someone will report us."

"Max, really."

"Trude."

From the hall below, they heard my sobs. "Now look what you've done," Oma hurried up the stairs and enveloped me with a hug. She tried to console me, "There, there, now."

My grandfather followed her up the stairs, "Trude, tell her the clothes must come down now. Before someone notices."

I clung to my grandmother, crying harder now. "I was just playing. It looks so nice. I don't want to take the clothes down. I don't want to."

"Now, now." Oma patted my head. Opa stood over us, glowering. "I know what we'll do. You can hang your display in the back room, overlooking the back garden."

"But it won't be the same. It won't look like a shop."

Opa paced back and forth. Oma caught his eye with an accusing look. He looked back, resolute. "It's what we'll have to do." She smoothed my hair. "I can help you. Come on then."

"I'll do it myself." I pulled away from her, for this was her betrayal, proof that her love for me could never overpower hers for Opa. I shut the door of my bedroom behind me. As I removed the tape from the windowpanes, I could hear them shouting back and forth, drowning each other out in a jumble of English and German. It was not just the language that was beyond my childish comprehension.

"It's long over, Max," Oma said. "You're in England now."

WITH THE TIME LEFT
by Heidi Lasher

I had my first Tarot reading several years ago in Mexico. The reader had me cut the deck and pick a card with my left hand. I turned it over with great anticipation.

Disenchanted with my consulting job, worried that maybe I was considering an irresponsible and potentially harmful decision, I went home after the reading, quit my job, and told my kids to pack their own lunches. Soon thereafter, I met Lee and started paddling the river.

* * * * * *

Already October, it hadn't rained more than a handful of times since, what, May? June? A long time. Lee and I climbed out of the car and peered over the high bank to the river below. The water level, controlled by the dam, had risen slightly since Labor Day and, according to Lee, looked fine for canoeing.

We lifted Lee's navy-blue fiberglass canoe off the car and carried it down a steep trail to the water. I confessed that I'd been in a hurry that morning. I hadn't packed a change of clothes or gloves or boots, and in the dark, I had grabbed my mother-in-law's life jacket, a size smaller than mine. "I remembered a water bottle, at least, and a bag of trail mix," I said, holding up both as evidence.

She looked me up and down, waded into the water, and pushed the canoe onto the beach so I could climb in without soaking my running shoes.

A nearby fisherman asked how far we were going. We had left my truck at Sullivan Bridge, a more enterprising float than Lee had originally planned. I hesitated to admit this to a stranger, particularly to someone who may have known more about distances than I did. I had a history of miscalculating paddling distances. But Lee interpreted his question generally. "We're paddling the whole river," she answered. We waved and floated away.

* * * * * *

My family used to spend a week or two in Idaho every year. We owned a share in a small condo along the Little Big Wood River and visited in winter to ski and in summer to hike. I had brought my friend Becky one summer. We did all the stuff twelve-year-olds might do. We spent long days at the pool, took the free bus to town, bought hot pretzels, tried tennis lessons, tagged along on family hikes, and attempted ice skating, all the while complaining that there was *nothing to do*. My mom proposed we recruit a third friend and take an afternoon float down the Little Big Wood. The next day, she rented three inflated truck tires, stuffed five bucks in my hand, and waved us off from the condo balcony. We wore cut off shorts, one-piece suits, flip flops, and SPF 6 Sea 'n Ski Suntan Lotion. The plan was to float a few hours and catch the free bus home.

Not long into our trip, I announced a more ambitious plan. We would float the river to its confluence with the Big Wood River. I pictured a long, lazy afternoon sitting on inner-tubes atop sparkling mountain runoff, culminating in a short jounce on bigger water. I assured my friends that the float would be straightforward, which is how it looked from the road.

We learned over the course of the day that rivers aren't like roads. They twist, flatten, and drop. The Little Big Wood narrowed into deep channels and widened into shallow braids that snagged our tubes. At times, fallen trees blocked our passage. We bushwhacked through overgrown thorns and willow. By sunset, we had lost flip flops, portaged around trees, slipped on rocks, and scratched our bare, sunburnt skin. My friends shivered in their tubes, mute with fear. I insisted we carry on. The sun had set by the time we dragged our inner tubes across the Big Wood River. My mom and dad found us with flashlights. They hugged us, draped us in wool blankets, and promised us we'd never to do *that* again.

I understood the sentiment. It was foolish of me to take my friends so far down the river. I'd been irresponsible to continue past dark. Someone could have been hurt. We could have drowned. *But we didn't,* a small voice inside me insisted. I put the memory in my pocket and tried to make better choices.

* * * * * *

The river paraded Lee and me around a sharp bend. We commented on the unusual rock formations along the river. A modern, angular house peered down on us from a cliff on our right, and a simple shingled cabin lazed on a pebbly beach to our left. A great blue heron stood on a rock ahead, tall as an exclamation point. Lee said it was a beautiful stretch of river.

"Aren't all rivers beautiful?" I asked.

"No," Lee said. "Not all rivers are beautiful."

Lee had been on more rivers than anyone I knew and had lamented that the Spokane River had been reduced to a disappointing series of "ponds" impounded by dams. But on this stretch, the river ran free from its concrete enclosures. I wondered if the river's beauty emerged from its lack of obligations, its few responsibilities. Water carried us easily downstream, past willows, pine trees, and a telephone pole from which an osprey glared down. Beyond the willows, Interstate-90 blazed past an outlet mall, a Cabela's, and an abandoned greyhound racetrack. We bobbed along and admired ourselves in the water's reflection.

We scouted sections of turbulent water. The rapids weren't big, but our canoe, with its open cockpit couldn't handle waves. At our first rapid, Lee suggested we dodge the center wave train and stay right. I nodded assent. We executed the plan without incident. The current carried us downstream, and Lee offered her customary praise of canoes. Canoes, she said, are "more sporting" than rafts. This made me smile. I pictured Lee on horseback, holding forth among aristocrats about the virtues of a sport like fox hunting.

"Sporting, indeed." I said in my best high British accent.

* * * * * *

While it's okay to be young and foolish, it's embarrassing to be old and foolish. Old people are supposed to be wise, thoughtful, and reliable.

I didn't intend to get old. One day I was drinking beers on the back deck, chasing toddlers around the yard, and the next day I was in bed before dark, wondering how I might find cheaper auto insurance. This was not a gradual change. It was sudden. It felt like I got old only about five years ago and have been so ever since.

It's not that I yearn to be young again. To re-do all the piano lessons and soccer games. To endure another high school lunch or drag myself out on a blind date or negotiate condoms. I'll be fine if I never have to attend another college party or cram for another final exam or drink beer through a funnel. I do not long for those early-twenties work environments, sitting quietly through meetings and transcribing memos. I do not want to nurse an infant or argue with a toddler about socks or attend a PTA meeting. But I can't help but feel a twinge of dread when I anticipate the second half of my life. I worry that maybe the fun parts are over.

* * * * * *

Lee was a good pilot. I trusted her judgement on the river, and she seemed to trust mine. Over many miles on the river, we'd become unlikely friends. We shared a common goal and paddled well together. We looked alike: tall and slender, cropped hair, sun-cracked lips. But she had ten years on me and no kids. Her heart beat with righteous passion; mine with eager naivete. We both liked to talk about things like landfills and combined sewer overflows and invasive species. To me, it was all new. To Lee, it was what mattered.

We stopped for lunch on a gravel bar opposite a row of unimaginative 1980s houses. The roar of wheels from the freeway filled the silence. I asked Lee about her mountaineering experience with her ex-husband. "I had a husband for ten years," she said in typical Lee parlance. Never that she'd been "married" and "divorced." She simply "had a husband" until she didn't. "We climbed Denali twice, three 18,000-plus peaks in Nepal, the Grand Tetons, and a lot of peaks in the Cascades." I nodded to my sandwich. I had climbed Mt Rainier and several smaller peaks before I had kids. "Then my hips gave out," she added. "And I started canoeing more."

I peeked over at Lee's gray hair, gimpy hip, and sun-speckled skin. She wore a faded red lifejacket and loose-khaki pants tucked into tall rubber boots. Sipping coffee from a green thermos, she looked somewhere near 60. But as she yammered something about private property signs and setback violations, the years fell away. I hugged my knees to my chest ate trail mix from a Ziplock bag. The day had transported us: a lazy afternoon, sparkling mountain runoff, cut-off shorts, one-piece swimsuits. I gathered some rocks to skip.

After a few minutes, Lee waded into the water and edged the canoe to shore. I stepped in, dry as Queen Elizabeth. We paddled under the bridge where Lee had originally suggested we leave a car. The bridge came and went overhead, a reasonable offer, politely deferred. We fixed our eyes downstream and paddled toward destiny.

* * * * * *

A few years ago, I was involved in a five-car pile-up on an icy road on the north side of town. My daughter, a middle-schooler at the time, sat in the passenger seat. We had wisely pulled over when a white sedan slid into incoming traffic. The sedan hit the car in front of us—which slid into our car—and then ricochet back into its lane and hit two more cars before coming to a stop. In slow motion, each driver emerged (unscathed) from banged-up cars and took stock of the situation. My car suffered minimal damage, and yet my arms found my hips, and I bent forward like one of those birds tipping its beak to drink. It wasn't dizziness I felt, but the exhausting realization that I was the oldest person on scene. *What*, they asked me with their bright eyes and plump cheeks, *do we do now?*

Jesus, I thought, *when did I become the oldest person in the room?*

With great effort, I guided the other drivers through the unwritten rules of accident protocol. First, we make sure no one is hurt. Next, we inspect our cars for damage. Now we exchange information and call the authorities. With logistics out of the way, we place our hands on our heads, rock side to side, and imagine how much this will cost and who will pay.

I tend to play the role society asks me to play. As a middle-aged, white, mother of teenagers, my job is to show up, serve snacks, and wear low-heeled shoes. We are molded by experiences and by the people who teach us what we'll never do again. I'll never drive 55 mph through the airport, never wear a white swimsuit to the community pool, and never forget to pay my insurance premiums. I eat on a predictable schedule, pack wipes, tie shoes, pay my bills, return calls, and arrive on time to pick up my kids from school. I know that, in the coming week, I should deal with the maintenance light, take the cat to the vet, and buy a pair of pants with a higher waistline.

But when, I wonder, did life became such an effort to avoid failure?

* * * * * *

We found ourselves in a long set of riffles that curved left. The waves intensified as we rounded the bend turning to whitecaps. With no time to maneuver, we headed straight down the tongue of the rapid. The canoe teetered bow to stern. The first wave sloshed in, saturating my shoes and socks. The second wave filled the boat to my thighs. The third sunk us to the gunnels. I turned to look at Lee, thinking she might know what to do.

We flipped.

My bag floated a few feet downstream, along with some garbage we'd gathered along the way. I reached for it and bobbed downstream in my too-small lifejacket, gasping for air. Fed by the aquifer, the water in the Spokane River registers about twelve degrees above freezing in some places. "We must be in a gaining reach," shouted Lee, referring to the cold. I kicked, pulling the boat with me, and swam with one arm toward shore. "It's weird" I shouted back, my lips too numb to function, "I don't feel cold."

But my mouth swallowed the c.

On land, we snapped selfies in our wet gear and sat on sun-warmed rocks. Lee shook her head in disbelief. "We didn't do anything wrong," she said, "we just swamped." She changed into a dry shirt and scanned the river for her lost paddle. "Maybe we could have steered to the right and missed the waves," she went on. "Or maybe, if we had hit the waves with more speed, we'd have taken on less water." I blew on my wet phone and smiled.

* * * * * *

In a Tarot deck there are 22 numbered trump cards known as the Major Arcana. The Fool is number 0—some say, "the number of unlimited potential"—and can be played high or low. He is depicted wearing brambles in his hair and carries a small bundle that hangs from a stick. His eyes gaze upward at the sky as he walks off a great precipice, oblivious to his fate. The card symbolizes naïve beginnings, bold and baseless decisions, stupid trust. It both warns against and encourages excitement for the adventure ahead.

When I was young, I assumed people my age were complete. Adults developed evenly and possessed a ripe, round, knowledge of the world. I believed that people waxed like moons into their forties and waned after fifty. Now, I wonder if we develop like clouds, appearing and disappearing in form and substance as we move across a sky of time. Each new season teaches us to learn again who we are and what we might become, our morphography changing with the weather.

* * * * * *

We lined the next rapid, a strategy that required us to stumble along, chest deep in water, and guide the canoe with ropes.

"This is such a better idea than canoeing," I yelled back at her.

"I am one with the river!" Lee shouted up to me.

Drenched and short on time, we hopped back in the canoe and navigated the final rapid before the take-out. We maneuvered it expertly. Hardly a gallon of water came aboard. We pulled to shore, grinning like champions.

At the take-out, a guy in the parking lot leaned against his car and gave us a long, concerned look. Biceps bulging, shoes sloshing, hair dripping wet, we carried the boat to my truck. He watched us heave the boat over our heads, over top of the truck, and strap it down, our strong hands dappled in sunspots and wrinkles.

I pealed the truck out of the lot and draped my arm out the open window before giving him a wave. Lee hung her arm out the other window. A crackly silence settled upon us. We gazed onto separate horizons, held by our private thoughts. Twice, I caught Lee's eyes and shared a wry smile, knowing the day had floated us over the precipice of age and safely across the sky.

ONLY TWO SIDES
by Devon Jeffers Valdes

Outside the back door of the house where I grew up was a narrow path. It was a quaint footpath with spots of grass that were missing from years of use. The bare feet of my sister and I running and chasing one another, my mom walking to and from the clothesline to air dry our laundry, and my dad walking to and from his car to go to work every day were the cause of the missing spots of grass. When I followed this path for about a quarter of a mile, it led to an old, clay, dirt road where I would eventually end up on Garden Lane. This area was not a highly traveled area. Actually, there was hardly any traffic at all. A few neighbors used it as a back road to cut through to the main highway, but other than that, Garden Lane was simplistic and minimally maintained by the county. No flash or flare, it provided just enough space for a single car to travel. When a car did pass by, it'd take minutes for the dust to settle back down into the earth. It was almost as if the cars that did come down the road were unwelcome, in a way, and the dust that settled in the car's wake reminded the road of its intruder.

Running alongside the dirt road was a ditch that lined either side. When I was little, this was a treasured spot I loved to frequent. It may seem highly unusual that one of my favorite places to visit as a seven-year-old girl was an old ditch that bred mosquitoes with black and white striped legs, but it was somewhere that I could experience freedom and go on adventures of my own.

While the adventures that awaited me were the reason I visited the ditch, the aspects of serenity and peacefulness by seeking refuge in nature were all too appealing for me to resist. On a hot summer day, or sometimes on a weekend in the early fall, which was never really fall at all in coastal Georgia, I would travel down this dirt road just so I could experience freedom and solitude. No parents, no teachers, or even friends for that matter. No rules or regulations. This allure is what drew me to the ditch time and time again.

Walking to the ditch as the scalding sun penetrated through my cotton tank top, I often reflected on how hot it was, but I didn't care because I was alone. I enjoyed the five-minute walk from my house to the ditch as much as I enjoyed the ditch itself. The regal pines would provide much appreciated shade on a hot day, sacrificing themselves to the sun in order to protect the life that existed below its needles and limbs. Mother Nature in all her glory, outstretching her arms to provide a safe haven for the creatures who needed it most. The smell of the pines was so pungent and distinct that it would linger with me for hours, even after I returned home. Sometimes the wind picked up the scents of pine and carried them away like a soft melody. The perfect combination of shade and fresh air; this was my immediate reward for enduring such an intense journey.

The ditch was shaded, for the most part, and it ran the full length of Garden Lane. It was steep and usually filled with brackish water due to the summertime thunderstorms we experienced almost every evening. The edges were also covered with brown stickers and underbrush, daring to torture anyone who may enter, like a warning sign to a haunted house, "Beware" or "Enter at your own risk." Despite the warnings from the local flora, this ditch was where I spent plenty of afternoons.

When I arrived at my hiding place, I would get down into the ditch and allow my eyes to peer over the embankment. My small hands would then clasp the top of the red earth as my feet burrowed into the side in order to strive to stay atop the murky water. Sometimes, when feeling an extraordinary sense of exploration, I would loosen my shoestrings, strip my feet of my red, Georgia clay-stained socks, thanks to a season spent on the softball fields, and allow my toes to burrow in the bottom of the soft, brown earth that lies underneath the ditch's almost opaque waters. During these times when I did take my shoes off, it almost seemed as if my feet and the earth were engaging in a special kind of matrimony; intertwining with one another, discovering and learning everything about what makes the other whole.

Some days there would be tadpoles in the ditch, and they would swim furiously about with no schema at all. While I tried to identify with them, all I came away with were feelings of resentment and jealousy. Their sole existence was to experience nothing other than absolute freedom. They swam around without any restraint or any kind of governance to hold them back. However, I quickly forgave them when I realized that the tadpoles were confined to this ditch much like I was confined to my house. The juxtaposition between child and amphibian, each waiting to break free of their temporary homes, but only allowed to do so after its metamorphosis is complete.

When the tadpoles finally took notice of my feet in their waters, they gazed at this new, movable figure in their home. Some would even show their bravery by coming closer. They would do this until I flinched because of the tickling sensation my ankles were feeling from their even braver counterparts that chose to examine me further by seeing if I would make a new home for them or figuring out if I could potentially be their dinner.

When I bored of the tadpoles, I cast my attention towards the crawdads that also resided in the ecosystem of the ditch. They tunneled their way into the thick, muddy substrate and searched around trying to either find food, a home, or both. It intrigued me as I watched them because they seemed so simplistic, yet their sole purpose in life is survival, which is not so simplistic to them. They fumbled around with no rhyme or reason, yet they knew exactly what to do to survive. The crawdads were the most menacing thing to watch in this ditch of mine, so I continued to observe even more intently as they slowly moved about.

Sometimes I'd muster up my own bravery from somewhere deep inside and make myself pick up a crawdad. My intrigue of them overrode my fear. Nevertheless, I was still frightened by the claws of this creature. I clutched its slippery, black abdomen and hesitated, but carefully grabbed it, with my forefinger and thumb, quickly examined it, and then dropped it after about a minute due to fear for my petite fingers. Its pincers would show no mercy to human flesh, and while I meant them no harm, they could not tell. I would eventually let them go, and they would use their lobster-like claws to edge themselves back into the water. I only liked catching them for the thrill of it and examining them like some amateur scientist. Making mental notes about how slowly they moved and how they writhed around in my fingers trying to escape, I felt as if I were right in the middle of being the narrator of a Discovery Channel documentary, or even better, a less-intensified, female version of Steve Erwin "Crawdad Hunter," may he rest.

When I decided not to amuse myself in the water, sometimes all I did was sit on a dry spot on the bank and throw small, smooth rocks or dried lumps of clay into the standing water. I likened the sense of peacefulness I felt when observing my ditch, much like a watchmaker spinning the gears of the hands of time to see what happened next. While sitting on the bank, I often tried to be as inconspicuous as possible to the few, surrounding neighbors who happened to be in their yards burning leaves, pine straw, and branches. Knowing that they saw me, I still pretended to remain innocuous. The train of gray smoke rising high from the incendiary piles of debris in their yards would often destroy the delicate scent the pines provided that I enjoyed so much. The smoke typically weaved and meandered until it found its resting place underneath my nose. It never failed to find me.

Towards the end of my journey, if not before, I would scan the area of the ditch where the blackberries tended to grow. If it was the wrong time of year, I would be highly disappointed, because the only evidence of blackberries would be dried leaves and shriveled vines from where these blackberries used to sprout. However, if it was the right time of year I would be overjoyed and enthused to find these charming berries, plentiful enough for me to feast on for the afternoon. Picking them straight from the vines, I would shove them in my mouth and enjoy the sweet and sour juices they produced. Without hesitation, and without thinking twice that my mother would disapprove of me eating a foreign berry without properly identifying it, it would become a secret just between the ditch and myself. The innocence of a secret borne by nature and bounded by a promise. Only the ditch saw this exchange but agreed not to tell.

Walking back home barefoot as the pine straw itched the bottom of my feet, I watched the yellow and orange sunset glisten through the tops of the pine trees. Sometimes the sound of the rustling leaves that had fallen early, grazed effortlessly across the ground. It was the most beautiful sound of all because it meant fall was coming. The heat would soon subside, the tadpoles would grow into young frogs, the crawdads would begin to burrow in preparation of the cold weather, and the blackberries would yield produce no more. When I turned off of Garden Lane and back onto the footpath that led back to my house, I realized that the ditch was always there when I needed it and would always be just as reliable. It was only during certain times of the year that I would visit this unlikely place, but when I did, I always felt refreshed and at ease with myself, partly because I was alone and partly due to the fact that I did have freedom, much like the tadpoles, even if it was only an afternoon.

MY MOTHER'S KEEPER:
ONE FAMILY'S JOURNEY THROUGH DEMENTIA
by S.G. Benson

One: A Dangerous Road

Thursday, July 10, 2014. This isn't exactly what I'd envisioned for the first entry in my new journal. Today I traveled a familiar prairie highway in my gray, Forest Service work truck at sixty-five miles an hour. As the road dipped into the winding, wooded Long Pine canyon, I slowed to round the first curve.

An elderly man in a battered, blue pickup pulled out from a side road and I slammed the brakes. I sighed and followed him, drumming my fingers on the steering wheel, not daring to cross the double yellow line to pass on that treacherous stretch of road.

I checked my rear-view mirror and saw four more vehicles stacked behind me. Then, a silver sedan. Something about it looked familiar.

Our line of vehicles reached the bottom of the ravine and started up the other side. I glanced in the mirror again and gasped as the silver car pulled out, careened across the centerline, and sped up to pass us all—just as we approached another sharp curve.

"Geez—what an idiot!" I muttered. As the car drew even with me, I looked at the driver. Then my annoyance turned to fear.

Good God, I thought. *That's my mother!*

Eighty-five years old, pedal to the metal, she flew by. My ninety-year-old father sat in her passenger seat, pale as a ghost, white knuckles visible as he gripped the panic bar. Mom seemed oblivious to everything as she zipped around the old blue pickup in front of me and swung back into the right lane just as a semi-truck rounded the curve coming toward them. I saw the driver's face, wide-eyed, as he swerved into the shoulder, missing my parents by mere feet.

* * * * * *

A Love Affair with Driving

Mom loved to drive, and for most of her life she'd been very good at it. She got her first license in 1943 at the age of fourteen—and she'd been behind the wheel almost daily for the next seventy years. After retiring, she taught the American Automobile Association's '55-Alive' driver safety class to senior citizens in the town where she lived.

Driving meant freedom to her. It allowed her to be on the go, on her own terms, independent of others. My mother possessed a take-charge personality, and self-mobility helped make that possible.

As I was growing up, I noticed that when my parents argued, Mom often gave Dad a loud piece of her mind before storming to her car and heading for places unknown. When she returned—sometimes hours later—her demeanor seemed calm. She acted as if nothing had happened. Dad didn't say anything to her about the argument or her departure.

When my parents went on long car trips together, they took turns behind the wheel, but my mother usually claimed the first shift to retain tight rein over the route and itinerary. Dad good-naturedly laughed it off, saying that was a battle he didn't want to fight. I didn't even try to get a learner's permit until after I turned seventeen because I knew she'd take me wherever I needed to go. Driving me kept her largely in charge of my comings and goings until I left home.

Cars

I remember every car Mom had since I was a toddler. She handled her vehicles like a pro, and I always felt safe—even before seat belts. My mother had an instinct to reach out her arm to keep me from flying into the windshield when she hit the brakes.

In the days before air conditioning and interstate highways, she'd drive with the windows down and a colorful scarf on her head to keep every hair in place. I remember the scent of the fresh air and the look of pure joy on her face when I accompanied her on the open road.

Her early cars were utilitarian, but she had a hankering for a really nice ride— one to match the high life she vigorously pursued. The brand new 1968 black Ford LTD fitted the bill, and I imagine it stretched the limits of her pocketbook as much as it did our little garage. But my parents upgraded to a bigger home in a better neighborhood shortly thereafter, and Mom enjoyed travelling to high-class social events in style.

Years later, my mother actually <u>won</u> a BMW in a "Guess the Secret Sound" radio competition. The secret sound was a Ronald Reagan campaign pin sliding into a lapel, and Mom was so proud she figured it out. I remember once, when I came home from college, she allowed me behind the wheel of the BMW—but she never let me start the engine. After I got out of the car, she went in with a polishing cloth and carefully wiped down the steering wheel and dashboard. She didn't want Dad to drive the Beemer, either.

About the time my folks retired, frugality replaced extravagance in their automotive choices, and they went through a series of more economical cars. But all of her vehicles were spotless, impeccably detailed, and ding-free.

Two: Something's Amiss

Friday, July 11, 2014. I went to my parents' house after work. Mom's dangerous passing of the line of vehicles on that winding road yesterday worried me, and I wanted to find a non-confrontational way to discuss her actions.

"Did you see me when you passed me on the Long Pine hill yesterday?" I knew I had to be careful because my mother is likely to take offense at any suggestion that her driving isn't up to snuff.

She shook her head.

I took a deep breath. "It scared me when I saw that big truck come around the curve toward you, while you passed so many vehicles."

She glared at me, but softened, probably because she could detect no malice in my facial expression. Then she laughed.

"I've been driving a lot longer than you have, Sandy. I have everything under control. There's no need to worry."

I glanced at Dad, who raised his eyebrows at me but said nothing.

Monday, July 14, 2014. I ran into Dad at the post office and he pulled me aside. "I'm worried about your mom," he said. "It scared me, too, the other day when we passed all those vehicles on the highway. She's been taking a lot more risks on the road lately, and her temper has gotten much shorter. She yells at me all the time."

He looked from side to side, shuffling his feet as if fearing being overheard. "I've gotta go," he said. "She's waiting for me."

* * * * * *

Foundations

My mother was born in 1929, at the beginning of the Great Depression, and she came of age as the Second World War wound down. Her parents held prominent social standing in St. Cloud, Minnesota. Her father, a well-known dentist, and her mother, a dental hygienist until they started a family, enjoyed the advantages of high society, including a live-in maid.

My mom, Lucy, was the youngest of their three children. She and her sister, Virginia, were young teens when their brother, George, left home to fight in World War II. Mom admired her big brother and when I was small, she sometimes told me stories of his adventures.

Tales, like the following one, dominated what Mom related about problems growing up with her sister, with whom she'd shared a bedroom.

"You keep away from my side," said Virginia, scowling at her sister, who stood in the doorway.

Little Lucy, then maybe six or seven, feared her big sister. The younger girl sniffled, fighting back tears as she eyed the route she'd have to run to reach her own territory. Virginia had built a barrier between their beds, using books and toys to separate her tidy living space from Lucy's cluttered mess.

Lucy waited until Virginia looked away, and then scampered as fast as her little legs would carry her across her sister's domain to the safety of her own bed.

"Don't be such a cry-baby," Virginia said with a sneer. "And clean up that pigsty!"

My mother's feelings of discomfort and unhappiness toward her sister continued for the rest of her life. Years later, Mom told me she did a good job learning to "keep my pigsty clean." I can testify that I never saw anything out of place in my childhood home.

Mom told me that when Uncle George came back from the war, he entered dental school and eventually joined his father's practice. She said their parents were dismayed when she announced plans to go into dentistry, too. My grandmother, the picture of poise and gentility, insisted that their youngest daughter learn all the social graces. They sent her to finishing school in Missouri. Lucy hated it, but endured two years there before returning home to attend the University of Minnesota, where she earned a degree in dental hygiene. This breadth of background prepared her well for what she later termed the best of both worlds.

Three: Her Own Particular Way

Saturday, July 19, 2014. While visiting my parents this afternoon, I paused to admire Mom's taste in decor. Beautiful paintings by well-known western artists hung on the walls, accented by colorful, hand-loomed Navajo rugs. Rare Hopi Kachina dolls sat carefully arranged on well-polished antique tables. Not ostentatious; it just made a subtle statement. The room sparkled from the sunlight streaming in the window. I didn't see a speck of dust anywhere.

I followed the aroma of peach pie and found Mom in the kitchen, peeking into the oven. She smiled. "I invited our priest and a few other people from church over for dinner tomorrow evening. Father Randy loves home-baked pies."

I glanced at a piece of paper on the counter—a menu carefully written in her tidy cursive: four-bean salad, Viva la Chicken on wild rice, dinner rolls, pie with whipped cream. "Mmmm . . . looks yummy," I said. "I know they'll love it."

She still has a knack for entertaining, I thought as I headed for home.

Sunday, July 27, 2014. Today after church, Father Randy pulled me aside. "Sandy, I'm concerned about your mother," he said.

"Your parents invited Paul, Donna, Chris, and me for supper last Sunday, and something just didn't seem right.

"The food tasted delicious, but throughout the meal your mom continually jumped up and down from her chair—scurrying back and forth to the kitchen, where we could hear her bustling with dishes. I've never seen her do that before.

"Once we finished the main course, Donna got up to help take dishes to the kitchen before I could catch her eye. I remembered that your mother has her own particular way of clearing the table, and I knew she wouldn't welcome the assistance. Sure enough, your mom returned from the kitchen to find Donna holding a stack of dirty plates, and Lucy came unglued. She sternly reprimanded Donna as she took the plates from her hands and marched with them back into the kitchen. Donna looked bewildered and hurt.

We guests all felt pretty uncomfortable during the rest of the meal and—I'm not certain—but I think your dad did, too. Right after dessert, we thanked your parents and left."

"Poor Donna," I said. "I'm so sorry that happened."

Earlier in Mom's life, while she would not have liked having guests help clear the table, she would have had the grace to smile and thank them for the gesture.

* * * * * *

Mom often said she liked to have me assist her, but doing so proved nearly impossible. A micromanager with a 'Type A' personality, she never seemed satisfied with the efforts of others.

I was my mother's best and only kitchen helper throughout my childhood. She taught me to set the table according to her standards, and anything even slightly off earned me a redo. Mom instructed me to place three ice cubes in each water glass. If I put in four, she made me fish one out.

Only I could help my mother clear the dinner table because she'd trained me to do it the 'right' way. She said that when people stack soiled plates one on top of the other, the bottoms of them get dirty. Mom scrubbed the plates before placing them in the dishwasher. She hand-washed the most fragile pieces, and when I dried them, she inspected to ensure I didn't leave behind any moisture. I learned to put the clean dishes gently in their correct places, facing the proper direction. After I left the nest, she trained Dad to help her acceptably, but whenever I came to visit, I got my old job back.

Mom's pickiness wasn't confined to the kitchen. Often, she'd have a list of jobs for me to do in the yard, garage, or the laundry room. But I waited for her to orchestrate every bit of it because, if I just proceeded with the work on my own, she'd stop me and want it done differently. I distinctly remember performing these chores in increments—completing the first part according to her directions, then pausing and standing stock still until she provided the next set of instructions.

I never thought a thing about it until many years later—that's just the way things were done at our house.

Four: Balancing

Sunday, August 3, 2014: "I'm sure feeling my age," Dad said when I stopped by my parents' house to reconcile their checkbook this afternoon. I've been doing this accounting for them since January, when Dad asked for my help with it. He told me he just couldn't handle it anymore; by age ninety he'd suffered a series of health scares, and he needed cataract surgery.

Initially, Mom didn't like the idea of my taking over the checkbook duties from Dad, who had always kept track of my parents' finances.

"Why don't you take charge of paying the bills and maintaining the register?" I suggested to her. "I can come by monthly and put everything into the banking program on Dad's computer."

"I guess that would be okay," Mom said. "I don't like using a computer to balance the checkbook, so you can do that part of it."

Mom did a pretty good job with her new task, at first. On the rare occasions I found arithmetic mistakes in the checkbook, I quietly corrected them without saying anything to her. As time passed, though, math errors increased. Once in a while I'd find questionable purchases, but the expenditures were small and I didn't mention them to her.

While I worked on Dad's computer today, my parents sat in chairs nearby. Mom played a game of solitaire, and Dad just watched me and chatted.

"I wear out so easily these days," he said with a sigh, "even though I go to bed early, eat right, and try to exercise. I can barely enjoy a drink before dinner like I used to, because it makes me woozy. I don't like getting old."

Mom looked up and made a face at Dad. "George, stop griping. If anyone should be complaining, it's me. I'm eighty-five. I do all the work around here, and I take excellent care of you."

Yes, Mom has indeed taken good care of my father during his medical issues, and I admire her for that. After Dad suffered a botched bladder-cancer surgery, she chauffeured him to a series of urologist appointments a day's drive from home. She learned to catheterize him and perform other nursing duties that aren't for the faint of heart.

But I'm not so sure about the other ways she 'takes care' of him. I remember last winter, when she insisted he shovel the driveway immediately after a snowstorm, before my husband, Barry, and I had time to dig ourselves out so we could help them. Overexertion drained Dad to the point he ended up in bed, and she accused him of being a slacker. And this summer she forced him to weed in the yard with her during the hottest part of the day until heat exhaustion nearly claimed him.

* * * * * *

After college, my mother married, had a child (me), and two years later our little family moved from Minnesota to California. At five, I saw my parents' divorce, and Mom and I lived on our own until I turned eleven, when she married George, the man she'd been dating. A wonderful gentleman, he adopted and raised me as his own child. I called him Dad.

Our family lived comfortably, with Dad managing a savings and loan and Mom working as a dental hygienist. They were active in their community, volunteering for their church and several charities. They had a vibrant social life. The etiquette my mother learned early served her well. I remember my parents' fashionable dress as they hosted and attended countless elaborate dinner parties.

Mom and Dad retired in the mid-1980s and moved to Prescott, Arizona, where they quickly made friends and a mark on their new community with their volunteerism.

Dad had a serious bout of bladder cancer in 2003. After a series of operations, my parents and I worried that my mother would soon become a widow. No family members lived near them in Arizona. As an only child, I felt responsible for caring for them. I visited them from Nebraska as often as I could, but between my demanding forestry job and raising a house full of foster children, I found it difficult to get away.

On several occasions, I suggested my parents consider moving closer to us, but I never really expected them to do that. Deep inside, I knew the culture shock might prove too much for them. I wrestled with the idea of leaving my job, uprooting my family, and moving to Arizona to care for them—but ultimately, I couldn't make that happen. And so, in 2005, Mom and Dad relocated to Nebraska, which for them was the beginning of the end.

TRAVELLING HOME
by Fiona Ritchie Walker

I watched Jeanette's face light up as she listened to her son, Charles, on the phone. Her reply was in French and while I understood a few words, the only thing I really knew was that she was happy. After returning the phone to its cradle on the wall, Jeanette came back to the kitchen table where I was sitting.

"He said you met on the bus — how amazing! And now we get to meet you too. Doug and I have friends coming for a lobster dinner tonight. Please say you can stay."

I looked at my empty plate, stained with blueberries from my breakfast pancakes. An hour ago this woman had picked me up from the bus station — a complete stranger. I wondered what I should reply. Before I could say anything, Jeanette disappeared, then came back with a bulging photo album. She opened the cover and I saw younger versions of her, the same smile, arms full of baby.

"I've waited a long time to show these to a girl," she said, touching my arm.

At the other side of the table lay the letter I'd given her; the one Charles wrote and sealed when we were in the little café on our journey down from the Canadian north. Maybe I should have read it first, or left it in my pocket and continued my journey to Toronto. Or perhaps, if I wanted to, I could forget about my plans to return to Scotland, pick up everything I'd left five months before. Something new, different was within my grasp. I glanced in the mirror by the door and a more sophisticated, French-speaking version of myself seemed to appear. Then I picked up the photo album and began studying the black and white snaps of the boy I'd met on the bus.

It was when the lake iced over and days shrunk to perpetual dark and dusk that I'd decided it was time to leave Snowdrift (which would later be known as Lutsel K'e), the tiny community on the eastern arm of the Great Slave Lake where I'd been volunteering since June. As there were no roads, we'd arrived on a float plane when the last of the ice was just melting, the sun hardly kissing the horizon every night.

We were a small international team of volunteers — teens and twenties — working for Frontiers Foundation, a charity which helped build houses in remote settlements and towns. Many headed home at the end of summer, but a few, like me, stayed on until the work ran out, defeated by the weather. Now I was leaving the remote setting of the Northwest Territories and heading home for Christmas, before deciding what the new year of 1982 would bring.

I was definitely not the urbanised 24-year-old journalist who had left Scotland that summer, travelling in style from Southampton to New York on the QE2, then heading up to Toronto for a week's training in health and safety, how to survive in remote locations.

After months of eating dried caribou and duck in porridge, I was several sizes bigger while my outdoor work meant I had muscles that no gym sessions at home had ever achieved. My winter clothes, essential in Snowdrift, also began attracting the attention of other bus passengers the further south I travelled.

"Hey, mind if I sit next to you?"

I'd looked up to see a guy, dark hair, beard, about my age, with his backpack ready to load onto the luggage rack above my seat.

"Sure."

"Looks like you've been pretty far north." He pointed to my beaded, fur-lined slippers peeking out of the rubber over boots which I was wearing on top.

"I got on the bus in Yellowknife, but I've been working in Snowdrift. The family I was living with after ice-up gave me the slippers for my birthday. Plus the mitts." I pointed to the enormous red felt mittens on my lap, with their beadwork flowers and dark fur trim. I'd eaten that bear when we cooked our share of it over a camp fire in the summer. Sweet and sour. Delicious.

I didn't mention that if he looked in the rack above, he would see my matching red and white felt embroidered parka with a hood big enough to accommodate a chunky woolen hat.

He nodded. "Nice." Held out his hand. "I'm Charles."

"Fiona."

There's something about a bus journey that if you have the right travelling companion, instantly turns them into a friend. That's how it was with us. I noticed nothing of the countryside as we journeyed south and the endless snowscape began to break up, the roads became busier, wider.

Two hours later, I knew that Charles was travelling with a group. Like me, they'd been volunteering, but in a proper town with running water, flushing toilets, phones. Now they were heading to another project, then a break for Christmas, before Charles decided whether to return to the world of paid work, regular hours.

"What will you do long-term?" he asked when we were sitting in the bus station café on our lunchtime break.

"Maybe return to journalism. I was offered a job in Yellowknife, but I'd need to sort out a work permit. Anyway, my main thing now is to get used to all this." I swept my arm round, taking in the bustling café, the busy street outside, then stood up and pointed to the restroom sign. "Right now I'm still enjoying the novelty of a flushing toilet."

By the time I returned, Charles had a notebook on the table and was busy writing.

"You go through Winnipeg on your way to Toronto, right?"

I nodded.

"So, take this letter." He ripped out the page, pushed it into an envelope and sealed it, then wrote a name and telephone number on the front. "This is my mom. Ring her when you get to the bus station. She'll pick you up. They'd love to meet you."

Back on the bus, the hours slipped by. We chatted and laughed, discovered we'd been in the same places on our teenage tours round Europe, imagined it had been within days of each other. We spoke of the restlessness in our guts some days and then the other times when we craved stability, something normal, and how quickly it could change.

"Where have you been all my life?" he said, jokingly, his hands clasped over his heart.

"Waiting to meet you," I gushed, with as much drama as I could muster.

And then his group leader announced it was half an hour until their stop. Suddenly we were two awkward strangers again.

"How about," he began scribbling in the notebook he'd pulled from his pocket. "Christmas cards. The worst ones we can find."

I nodded and took the slip with his address, then wrote my own one on the pad and returned it. "Just warning you. My ability to find awful cards is amazing."

There was a silence, then Charles spoke.

"You know, I'm sure it wouldn't be too hard to join our project. It's not as remote as where you've been, but you'd still be helping people. And you know me already."

"Thanks," I said. "I'll keep it in mind."

On the other side of the window outskirts of the town were starting to appear. Streets and houses, then a school, shops. The bus pulled in where a line of people was waiting.

"This is it." Charles stood up and pulled down his backpack from the rack above us. He leaned towards me and we hugged. I breathed in clean lemon, then he was gone.

Don't ask me to remember which town it was or where to find it on a map of Canada. I was in long-distance travelling mode with vast winter wheat plains, towns and provinces rolling by without me noticing.

Companions arrived, then left, while I changed like a chameleon to match each person who sat next to me. The elderly lady who loved my accent and wanted to tell me about her Scottish ancestors. The man born in Glasgow who left forty years ago, never wanting to return. The girl going on a first date. Her scent lingered long after her seat was empty. Then evening and only a few silent travellers remained. We stretched out across our double seats to catch some sleep or watch the stars.

Sometime in the middle of the night we stopped and the bright lights of the café drew me in. It reminded me of service station stops when I'd got the overnight bus from Scotland to London, those first forays into travelling on my own. My eyes felt gritty and I knew the coffee would taste wrong-time-of-the-day bitter in my mouth, but still ordered one. Then, for good measure, one of the rolls which the waitress said had arrived from the bakery ten minutes before and would taste delicious. She was right.

When the driver announced we'd be leaving soon, I headed for the washroom, marvelling at how my vocabulary had changed, just so I could be understood. Bin bags had become garbage sacks, disinfectant was Lysol, but I had no idea where I'd picked up the words washroom and restroom. After all, I'd spent my summer living in a tent and we'd dug a hole for what I called a loo, put a wooden outhouse on top. Then, when everything iced up, I'd learned the delights of living in a house with a honey bucket — a toilet seat on a plastic bucket lined with a garbage sack, plus plenty of Lysol.

As I locked the door of the bus station cubicle, I remembered the first time I'd used a honey bucket in a neighbour's house when we were playing cards one night. Such a strange sensation, disappearing behind a thin piece of curtain in the corner of the room where we were all sitting, and how our conversation continued as if I were still at the table.

Now, something I'd taken for granted at home was like a Christmas gift I couldn't stop playing with. I smiled every time I made the water flush. It was the same with turning on taps, which I never got round to calling faucets as I'd spent five months without any. Instead we'd washed in the lake and brought buckets of water back to our tents for boiling over our open fire, ready to make drinks or wash dishes.

There was no running water in the community and most houses had an old oil drum with a lid on it. Each week a truck came along the dirt track and a long hose was used to fill the drums with water.

It took ages for me to get used to washing dishes. When it grew too cold to sleep in the tent, I'd moved in with a family, sleeping on the other side of a curtain from the couple and their two children. Their house had a proper stainless-steel sink but instead of pipes in the cupboard below, waste water ran into a black bucket, which had to be emptied regularly. More than once, I'd flooded the kitchen floor.

I let my fingers dance with the scalding water pouring out from the bus station taps, then jumped at the unfamiliar noise of the air dryer. Yawning, I headed back to the bus, where I fell asleep as soon as it started moving again.

"Okay if I sit here?"

We had stopped again, somewhere bigger, with well-lit buildings and neon signs. Now the seats were filling up with local commuters and long-distance travellers who, like me, were heading towards Winnipeg, where the bus would terminate. A huge man with unruly hair and a big beard stood in the aisle, pointing to the empty seat beside me.

"Of course." I shuffled closer to the window and he sat down with a sigh.

"Going to be a long journey."

Within minutes, I knew Jake worked on a mining project and was on his way south after being told his father was to undergo emergency surgery. It was touch and go whether he'd survive.

Jake put his head in his huge, gnarled hands then rubbed his face and when he looked up again, I saw what he must have looked like when he was a boy, 25 years ago.

"I don't know what I'll do without him," he said. "I need something else to think about."

And so my one-woman entertainment show began as I tried to tell Jake anything and everything which I thought would keep his mind off his ill father, his eyes from checking his watch.

We arrived in Winnipeg late that night and I was brain-drunk from talking. The connecting bus south was early the next morning, so Jake and I walked to a nearby hotel, where he went to book in first while I extracted my cash from various purses and pockets. When Jake turned round with his key and saw the notes in my hand, he frowned.

"Are you sure you've enough money? These rooms aren't cheap."

"I'm fine, but thanks for asking."

Then it was my turn at the counter. The man behind the desk glanced at Jake, then me.

"Are you sure you want to pay for a single?" he said in a low voice. "The guy you're with just booked a double room." I spun round.

Jake's face was bright red. "I just thought, since we got on so well...."

"Well," I said, trying to make light of it. "I'm going to make the most of having a room all to myself for the first time in months."

Jake nodded. "Are we still OKAY for dinner?"

Up in my room, I ironed the crumpled shirt I'd pulled from my rucksack. Should I eat on my own? Order room service?

The restaurant was next door and right in the centre of the city with plenty of people around. I had my own room and key. Eventually, I decided the best thing was to eat with Jake, not mention anything about the room bookings. He obviously felt the same way, but it was all a bit forced as we joked and laughed our way through the evening.

"Well, let's hope we get the same seats tomorrow," Jake said, as we walked back to the hotel. I thought of the many hours until the bus would arrive in Toronto and remembered the letter in my bag.

"Actually, I'm going to meet up with someone tomorrow."

And so I found myself feeding coins into the hotel lobby payphone the next morning, then waiting half an hour until Jeanette's car pulled up and she ran out to embrace me.

"Charles said to expect your call," she said, as she drove me home.

In the end I went shopping with Jeanette for the lobsters, but didn't stay for dinner, although I did meet her husband, Doug, who was just as welcoming and keen to hear about my time in the Northwest Territories.

Before lunch, Jeanette had shown me a little bedroom, said I was welcome to stay as long as I liked. Perhaps the next morning I'd like to join her on a trip into town, then in the afternoon she was meeting up with a group of friends and was sure they'd love to meet me.

The other life on offer was taking shape, but I knew it was time to continue my journey, explained there was an early evening bus and I needed to be in Toronto, so couldn't stay.

Jeanette hugged me, said she understood. But when would Charles and I meet up again? When would I return to Canada? Please would I stay longer next time.

I spent the next week exploring Toronto and sleeping on the floor of the charity's offices before boarding my Heathrow flight. The last leg of my journey north to Scotland was by train and the seat next to me was empty all the way. I didn't sleep once, watching the countryside change, towns and cities appear, disappear until the familiar rumble of the train crossing the Tay Bridge told me I was almost home.

"Who are Jeanette and Doug?" my mother asked, not long after I'd arrived. Then she showed me the Christmas card, addressed to her and my dad. I read the message, took a sip of my coffee and began my reply.

BARN SWALLOWS AND THISTLE
by Tom Wade

What I remembered exceeded what was in front of me. The buildings (or ruins) and environs seemed too small. While visiting my aunt and two cousins in the mid-2010s, I gave in to a yearning to stop by where I lived from age three to seventeen. When asked, "Where are you from?" I think of this place in its pre-derelict days of the 1950s to mid-1960s, as I answered, "Just north of Kansas City." I pulled into the gravel driveway in my Honda Civic, driving over thick, green thistle, six to ten inches high, that sprouted from a raised mound running the length of the thirty-yard lane. I carefully guided the vehicle, listening to the dense weeds scrape and thump the undercarriage. I worried it would damage the oil pan. And I fretted that a suspicious neighbor would report me for encroachment.

I first passed the slab foundation and stub of a fireplace of the erstwhile Rabb house—a large white house with a wrap-around porch that burned down in 1960, give or take a few years. The elderly Rabbs' son owned the property my dad farmed. I stopped at a no-trespassing sign posted on a gate to the field surrounding the little house that sheltered my family and me. Beyond the gate, I saw the barn with a skeletal milkhouse still attached. The last time I stood on that spot, five decades before, a cattleguard lay in place.

Ignoring the warning, I clambered over the gate and approached another wire fence enclosing the barn and livestock pens. I had envisioned an enormous structure but beheld what looked like a weather-worn A-frame cabin that was diminutive compared to the mountainous presence in my mind. Staring at the hay door under a gable induced an itchy flashback of the rash blanketing my fourteen-year-old face—poison ivy— after camping in the hayloft on a winter night.

The milkhouse, where a stainless-steel cooling tank held milk from the herd of twenty or so cows, was attached to the barn by a short walkway. I recalled a clean room smelling of antiseptic soap and the metallic odor of the cool-to-the-touch tank. A Purina calendar hung by the door opening to the field I was standing in. The walls were pearly white, and the floor was polished concrete. Leaning against the fence, I gazed at the boxy structure that time and weather had wrecked. Weeds taller than me obscured the empty window frames.

I hiked the hundred-plus yards to the shell of the home where I lived for fourteen years. Like the barn, it was smaller than what I had recollected. Much smaller. The remnants of a hog wire fence surrounded it, but I managed to peek through the broken windows, getting a glimpse of rooms that appeared to be about ten by ten but which I remembered as half again as large or even double that size. The gaping entrance to the cellar on the east side of the dwelling evoked the damp, claustrophobic room where the washing machine churned next to shelves for canned vegetables. An oak tree I used to climb stood near the fence. The lowest limb, six feet up and covered in dark bark, stuck out, parallel to the ground. In the third or fourth grade, I learned to sit on it with my hands grasping the branch on each side of me as I let myself fall backward, somersaulting in the air and landing on my feet.

I thought about an impromptu race when I was about eight with my six-year-old sister on the path between the outbuildings and our house—she beat and humbled me, and I reacted with an outburst. From behind the screen door to the big front porch, I heard her whisper to our mother, "Why is he like that?"

A quarter-mile to the south, Interstate 435 grumbled with speeding cars and semis through what were pasture and hay fields forty years earlier. The Kansas City

International Airport was three miles away, its runways and decentralized terminals spanning thousands of acres where soybeans and corn formerly grew. For a moment, I considered that during the time I lived there, I often felt isolated.

My dad was a dairy farmer, tenanting two hundred and forty acres of land. When I was six, he gave me the chore of getting up the cows every afternoon at around 4:00. Sometimes, they would be grazing in a field adjacent to the barn and sometimes in pastures a good half-of-a-mile away. I would tramp to their location and round them up, sporadically yelling, "Hey," as I ushered the black and white cows toward the barn. About half to two-thirds of them lumbered along in single file, with the rest moving in one or two clusters of three or four.

Although herding the slow-moving Holsteins was tedious, I found something about the large, gentle animals and their leggy offspring alluring. By the time I turned ten, I had wanted to take up dairy farming when I reached adulthood. I joined the 4-H club and browsed a couple of trade journals my dad got. I asked Dad about getting a calf, and he gave me a choice of two that were a few weeks old. Studying them in an empty lot on a cold winter evening, I saw one was a little bigger and less jumpy when I approached them. I chose her and named her Candy. During stray moments, caring for or thinking about Candy transformed my mood. I would lose myself in training her to walk with me on a lead or grooming her, overcoming the diffidence that shadowed me.

Yet, raising a heifer only partially satisfied my desire to become a genuine farmer. I asked Dad to show me how to use the milking machines. He demonstrated how to start the device that held five to six gallons and put suction cups on the teats after washing the cow's udder. I pored over the monthly Hoard's Dairyman magazines my dad subscribed to that generated daydreams of having a herd of my own, milking them in a modern facility, and raising grain crops, hay, and silage for feed. I had hoped he would ask me to assist him in the afternoons, undertaking such tasks as situating cows in the milking parlor, feeding them, and putting on milking machines. But he didn't ask, and I didn't request more involvement, apprehensive I'd try his patience. Still, I hung around, pretending I was helping by occasionally driving a cow into the barn. For the most part, however, I wandered along the edge of the holding pen, fantasizing while he worked.

By the time I turned seventeen, my career interests had evolved from farming to indoor jobs with free weekends: first, engineering, then teaching, and then to working for a corporation. I wanted a clean break from this place. Forty-eight years later, standing by dilapidated buildings and pens, I reminisced about the barn swallows darting in crazy circles on the north side of the barn, catching insects in a graceful spectacle that left me breathless. As an intruder, I couldn't stay. Departing on the rough lane reminded me about the wayfaring woman who came to our door asking for food, and my mom, flustered because we were on our way out, gave her a glass of water to drink and a bunch of saltine crackers with peanut butter on them wrapped in wax paper. Minutes later, we passed her sitting on the road bank by the end of this driveway, eating her meal.

LOOK BACK BIG SAVAGE
by David Summerfield

When I look back, the happiest time of my life was the nearly decade long period I spent on Big Savage Mountain and Backbone Ridge, in the scenic wildlands surrounding the Savage River Dam and Big Run State Park, in the mountains of western Maryland. I owned nothing but a dog and an old Ford pick-up truck, and if I had five dollars for gas, it was enough to get there and back. From the bridge over the lower Savage River I'd unconsciously hold my breath to the crest of the dam then gasp at the beauty that stabbed me in the eyes there every time, an expanse of blue-green water, fjord-like in its containment by steep mountain walls and cliffs of green forest, Backbone Ridge on one side, Big Savage on the other.

I lived in the back room of a small country store where along with my mother we sold pop, candy, and cigarettes, homemade sandwiches, cinnamon buns, pies, and fudge. My only requirement, to relieve my mother at three, tend the store until ten, take five dollars from the register, and at dusk head back into the beauty, permanence, and inspiration of the wilderness.

We'd left Big Savage when my father died. Widowed young, my mother went to find work in the city. Leaving Big Savage, growing up on city streets, Big Savage never left me. After high school I entered the Marines, while in the Marine Corps my mother retired and returned to Westernport, about ten miles from the crest of the dam where we'd lived years earlier. She'd bought a trailer that had an old, abandoned storefront from where she could make and sell her wares. When I left the Marine Corps, I was not sure I could return there myself and find work. To avoid going to work at all, I stayed in the city and went to college on the GI Bill, then drifted through a series of jobs, always an ache in my heart to return to Big Savage. In a hasty and defeated withdrawal one day I opted to make my retreat, left the city to join my mother and in the manner of the prodigal (or so it was in my private vision) return to the wilderness, an opportunity regained to think and wander in introverted isolation and solitude over endless miles of rugged forbidding landscape.

* * * * * *

Across from Big Savage the six-mile drive around the reservoir along Backbone Ridge was nirvana. From the crest of the dam the road went to the bridge over the first of five tributaries, Crabtree Creek, then wound around to the bridge over Middle Fork, from Middle Fork the road went three-quarters of a mile to the top of Swisher Hill, then down the same distance to the bridge over Dry Fork, then finally snaked its way to the bridge over Big Run. Towering above the park at Big Run was the south end of Big Savage Mountain bright green and the upper Savage River running silvery below it, a splendid park with clean water, big trees, and a good breeze where I ran, hiked, camped, and explored unencumbered in a sweet sort of ignorant bliss, losing track of time, the future only the next day when I could return free and untroubled.

I camped everywhere and all the time. Along the tracks of the Western Maryland that cut along Backbone Ridge, I gathered old railroad ties for campfires that baked thick black creosote sooty and acrid into my skin and nostrils. Occasionally old friends would come. We'd pour Yukon Jack into paper cups under Hemlock and Spruce that blunted the wind and rain. Crowded around the firelight, we'd talk, laugh, shout, and reminisce. In the morning after farm eggs and black coffee we'd fish the reservoir or plumb caves above Crabtree Creek. But such occasions were rare. My friends from the city had obligations that kept them there. Once, we'd hiked the seventeen-mile trail from the north end of Big Savage Mountain and were camped near the bridge over the lower Savage River, when Ann and I wandered off, we sat on the railing over the bridge under a full moon listening to water whisper softly over the rocks.

"You've been here several years now, educated, approaching thirty, and you've never found your niche," she said.

"It is what it is," I answered, "I don't give a shit about that."

"Okay, Mister I-don't-give-a-shit, but you left a good job in the city to live with your mother, she has nada, and all you have is an old pick-up truck and a brown dog, you contribute nothing."

"The city was a predator. It ate me up from outside in, its charm, if any, diminished by hazards that appeared and reappeared like pop-up targets on a rifle range. I found myself in a constant combative stance—catlike, cornered with back arched whirling on all fours to face the 'enemy,' whether it be rush hour, crowds, or the endless assault from crooks, kooks, and punks waiting to rip me off or to take me out, living dead in that cubicle I came to inhabit, trapped in a tall building and dead-end career watching younger people, less senior, less talented rise above me, another horse in a stable of broken-down horses. I can still feel the pull and jerk of the bit in my teeth. To feel alive and inspired again, I had to unbridle myself, and return to Big Savage, where I sat and listened to the ripple of water over rocks and breezes through trees, learned to see stillness in the flow of the water, sought my own truth, letting the worst of society go, waste, greed, pollution, numbing consumerism, started to explore again, found some wisdom and authenticity, honed an instinct for survival, refined my understanding of the earth."

Unconvinced by this soliloquy I thought I believed in myself Ann left but I'd been guilted by her words, 'you never found your niche and contribute nothing' echoed in my subconscious. But, I thought, who was she to call out my years long experiment in simplicity and self-reliance, when she and the rest lived dead in the city, eyes dim breath shallowed by the meaningless of it, swimming against a torrent of disappointment and dying illusions, never considering swapping out logic and practicality for a life with heart because as voracious consumers that would never sustain them, as if she'd found her own purpose. But internally her comment generated a seismic event that caused my knees to buckle. I was conflicted, not knowing what would become of me, one mind saying go, another saying no.

* * * * * *

I stood atop the view tower on Swisher Hill to see the one best image where everything had always combined to create in me a spell, a state of enchantment that allowed escape from everything else, the one best image I would take with me. The vast and utter indifference of the silence there offered no response to my decision except for the long, lovely wail of a Loon. I thought how all my life I'd been chasing illusions, too, that perhaps that's all Big Savage was, or had been. It was time to give up the beauty, and inspiration of the wilds, to give up the innocent bliss of isolation and solitude, return to a world of mindless iPhone zombies, deconstruct and rebridle myself, to again become a contributing member of society, and in a sudden wind, came the voice of the loon, this time its long rising wail a laughing crazy cackle reverberating like a primal scream throughout the entire chasm of ridge and slope water and dark forest in front of me.

On a visit now to Big Run I was three-quarters of the way in my new truck driving from the city when I pulled over. I couldn't go any further. It didn't feel the same and I didn't know why. Had the magic of my coming there worn off I wondered or was I suddenly overwhelmed with regret at having left and reburdened myself with old aggravations. Never stalwart, or unmalleable as I'd believed, influenced by guilt I'd traded away what I thought to have been my only loyalty, life in the wilds was where I evaded death only temporarily, unaware our final appointment was always going to be in the city. Listening to an oncoming train struggle through the fog along Backbone Ridge, squealing sparks of existential wailing fused images and recollections of silvery apparitions flashed in front of me, angrily I tossed the empty flask of Yukon, Who the hell am I, I shouted. But the train itself had only been a memory, absorbed into the primal mist until dimly lit its taillamp winked farewell then barely flickered. I got to Big Run, stood in the rain--along with a profound sadness let it pour over me as the breath pulled from my body. Through this collage of disorientation, I realized what was true, like Indian summer my time there had shined briefly but flickered out as only another dying illusion.

I could feel the day coming, about to appear as if under glass or outside a picture window, the kind of rare day that would come only once or twice a year, almost always in early autumn, a day that would be like living in a great hall of still-life, with no weather--no wind, no clouds, the air rarified, leaves on the trees hushed and unmoving, not with the normal silence, but with the stillness heard after a great crash, that in its wake leaves only a faint, lazy, hypnotic buzz. It would be a day when spelunkers would soon the fill caves, climbers would scale cliffs, with wildflowers ablaze hikers would scan overlooks, out of the corner of my eye, and at every turn, under each shady tree, in the wavy grass and among the ferns I could see the brown dog, where the wind blows steady and unobstructed I'd buried her on top of the mountain, still running, still leaping, low to the ground, ears perked, stopping to sniff my scent in the brush, she had been waiting, I'd watched her look for me then disappear into the wood. When one tear was about to fall, I looked up at the mountain, red, yellow, and orange splotches of autumn on the trees then to the river undulating in the coming daylight below, ensconced in my failures and disappointment, I had to smile instead, as this thick melancholy ebbed away covertly as it came to reveal for one moment a knowing and intense happiness, at where I was, where once removed from duty and obligation, I'd been joyful and free.

TORN BETWEEN TWO CULTURES
by Kim Kiedaisch

As I am running errands, driving on all the familiar streets, I pass the spot where the Dunkin' Donuts used to be. Further up, a new retail outlet occupies the space where the old Carvel once stood. *I hope the Indian restaurant is still open,* I think to myself. All these places bring back memories of our first date, almost 23 years ago. That evening, I took a chance that would lead to intense love and pain, followed by acceptance and healing.

Our story began on an unseasonably, cool May evening as I waited for my car service to pick me up at JFK. I was smarting after a whirlwind business weekend in Las Vegas, filled with too much eating and drinking. Historically unreliable, it was no surprise to not see my driver in baggage claim. After several pleading calls, I was finally told he broke down; another car was enroute. With the quick trip between time zones, lack of sleep and over-indulgences, I was not happy to hear this.

Standing on the curb with the masses, I waited for him to arrive. Spotting my name in the window of an approaching car, I waved for the driver to slow down. He pulled over, popped the trunk, quickly exiting the car. I had all this pent-up frustration and was ready to unleash it. As he emerged from the car, with the biggest smile, our eyes met. I immediately thought, *Ooh, he is handsome.* He was definitely not my usual type; I thought he was either Indian or Arabic. He had dark hair and a mustache, which was common among the Italian or Latin men I was typically attracted to at the time.

Quickly tossing my bag in the trunk, he snapped it shut as I let myself in the backseat. With the traffic whirling around us, formalities were forgotten; I just wanted out of there. The minute I got in the car I let go, venting my frustrations about the car service. He politely listened, letting me babble on, inserting comments where appropriate. He continued to smile at me in the rearview mirror. When we got to my apartment, he handed me a business card for another car service he also worked for, telling me they are more organized. "When you call, tell them I gave you a card. Ask them to send me. My name is Jay." I thanked him for the recommendation and the rescue. Little did I know, the company I was bad-mouthing was managed by his family.

As I exited the car that evening, I didn't give him a second thought. That summer, I saw him a few times, using the new service for business. During the rides, Jay and I chatted casually. I learned he is Muslim, originally from the Pakistani area of Kashmir. Again, each time I left the car, I didn't give him a second thought, never mentioning him to anyone.

In August I went to Italy on vacation. Jay didn't drive me to the airport, but was there when I returned. Sporting a Mediterranean tan, I noticed he stared at me a bit more. Our conversation turned more personal, as he asked about my trip and my thoughts about Italian men. Call me stupid, but it didn't occur to me that he might be fishing for information. When I asked about his situation, he stated, "My family wants to set me up with girls."

Always one to share my opinion, I told him I thought it was a great idea, having your family do all the leg-work; I could use some help with the luck I had been having. At this point I must've been feeling more comfortable around him, or maybe just delirious from traveling through time zones. I offered my opinion about marriage, saying it was not necessarily a goal of mine. *Oh my, what is that saying? Green light, come and get me. I'm available with no strings attached. Great!*

We didn't see each other again until September when I left for another business trip. I was flying to Chicago for a week; it was September 7, 2001. As I settled in the backseat, I jokingly asked, "Are you engaged yet?" He laughed, looked in the rearview mirror and said, "No, I really like you." Despite our conversations, I was still shocked by this revelation, very grateful to be wearing sunglasses to hide my stunned reaction. Gathering my thoughts, I responded, "Well, I am sorry I am not Pakistani or Muslim." Jay assured me it didn't matter to him, saying he wanted to take me out for Indian food, which he already knew I liked from our conversations. He told me he "liked my personality". *Hmm?*

At the airport, we chatted at the curb. He said we could discuss our date when he picked me up upon my return. Not knowing what to say, I thanked Jay for the ride and said good-bye.

Flattered, I felt at that point I wasn't going to date him. Everything inside of me was saying I shouldn't. Then, four days later, 9/11 occurred.

With all planes grounded, I drove from Chicago with my colleagues in a rented van. After a sixteen-hour journey, a weekend of rest, and news watching, I couldn't help but worry about Jay and his family; Americans focused their hate on all Muslims. The following weekend, he called, getting my number from the service. He expressed concern about me, while I was very happy to hear he and his family were okay. Still talking about getting together, we made plans to speak again.

True to his word, he called the following week and left a message. I will admit, I fell prey to the negative news from the media regarding 9/11, plus some friends were less than encouraging. After speaking with Mom and taking her advice to "go for it," I called him back. I really enjoyed speaking with Jay for hours about everything and anything. However, other than our love of Indian food, I did fear we had zero in common. Apprehensive and nervous, I agreed to go out with him the following week.

When Jay picked me up that evening, he showered me with compliments; it was the first time he saw me dressed up, wearing make-up, with my hair down. During our dinner at the Indian restaurant, conversation flowed easily. From there we went to Carvel for dessert, followed by a coffee at Dunkin' Donuts. There, in the parking lot, we shared our first kiss. When he dropped me off, I didn't want to get out of the car, I was sad to see the evening end.

From that point, our relationship took off quickly; it was a plethora of emotions. There was fear on both our parts; mine caused by past bad choices and his by insecurity. It didn't help that, as a defense, my sarcasm emerged, causing numerous misunderstandings. In the beginning, Jay broke up with me many times, coming back after a day or two. The longest breakup painfully lasted a week. When he did come back, there were no other breakups, only talks of them due to family loyalty. The romantic in me thought our love for each other would be strong enough to overcome that. After all, we weren't kids, both of us in our late 30s.

My job, at the time, kept me busy, traveling a lot. I was content seeing Jay whenever time allowed. I had fun introducing him to many new things; a Yankee game, a Broadway play, a Knick game, and many concerts. We even managed to get away a few days to Cape May in NJ one summer. All the while, everything was kept a secret from his family. He had an aunt, uncle and several cousins living here. They smothered him, calling him incessantly. His driving job allowed him to easily "disappear", he could tell them he was busy or had an out-of-town job.

Six years into our relationship, he opened an auto service garage with his uncle. Jay ran the office, while still driving. I brought my car there for service as needed. One day I met his aunt and uncle, spending an hour speaking with his aunt in the office. Other times, cousins would stop in when I was there. I never let on who I was, but I have a feeling they suspected something. When he met my mom, she gave him a big, warm Italian hug. After the meeting, she said to me, "I can see why you are attracted to him!"

From the start, I knew Jay didn't have a green card, leading to speculation by friends and family he might be trying to use me to get one. In back of my mind, that fear lurked because of comments he made. A few years into our relationship, Jay obtained a sponsor in Virginia who assisted him with the process. He had to move there for a while, which was difficult for us. We spoke daily and he visited most weekends. In hindsight, I wish we had spoken more about this; things might've taken a different direction.

When he finally obtained his green card, I had mixed feelings; I was happy for him, but also nervous. I knew, after being here 9 years, he could now travel back home. Of course I wanted him to see his family, but I was really scared. My thoughts went back to our first conversations. *Is there someone back home they want him to marry? Will he tell them about us?*

Sure enough, that summer Jay went home. Before leaving, we discussed my fear and he assured me everything would be okay. Even so, I told him to be strong, to call me if something happened. I had a gut-feeling, but I put it aside, thinking our love would prevail. He called a few times, telling me everything was just fine. One Friday in August, I brought my car to his garage. While waiting, his employee said to me, "You know Jay is getting married this Sunday." I could instantly feel my insides drop to the floor, but without missing a beat, I said, "Of course I know."

I am surprised he did not feel the pain emanating through me, as my body shook. Backing my car out to leave, I hit a fire hydrant; I couldn't get out of there fast enough. I drove home in a daze. Once in my apartment, I let loose, wailing so loud and hard, the sound was almost primal. My body ached from the emotional and physical pain of crying.

The remainder of that summer was a nightmare, as I lived through the day of his wedding, imagining Jay making love to another. When he finally called, he said nothing, acting as if everything was fine. I didn't want to confront him on the phone. I also had no idea if she would be coming back with him. When he got back, he arrived at my apartment looking as thin as I did, though happy to see me. Giving him every chance to tell me what happened, he didn't say a word until I asked, "So, what happened on August 12?"

Shocked by my knowledge, he asked how I found out, which really didn't matter. What mattered was if he was ever going to tell me. He said eventually he would, but not at that moment. Jay explained he had no choice; he was pressured by his entire family. As the second oldest, next in line to marry, he had to comply so his sisters could marry. Why couldn't he tell me this before he left? Why couldn't he tell them he had someone here? He said he was outnumbered and couldn't do anything. Bottom-line, he did what he had to do and he came back without her.

Those first weeks were difficult for me as I struggled, crying a lot, trying to decide what to do. Content to continue our relationship, Jay lived in the moment, while I had many questions and fears about the future. Once I too started living in the moment and realized he chose me when he asked me out and she was forced upon him, things settled down a little. He even referred to me as his "first wife", which gave me little solace.

During the next few years, Jay traveled back home, sending me into a depression each time; I was on the worst emotional roller coaster ride imaginable. Two of the trips resulted in pregnancies and two sons. He stayed a few months, calling me several times during each trip. When he returned, things would just resume back to normal for him, while I struggled with the knowledge that he now had a family that could one day come here.

I also had to deal with the heart-wrenching fact that our relationship never produced a child. Early on, I thought I might've been pregnant; I had two positive home tests. My doctor said I could've been but sadly, it didn't take. She determined if I wanted to have a baby, I needed medication. We spoke about this, but Jay never agreed so I did nothing. I am confident if I had been pregnant, he would've done the honorable thing. There were times I felt he was hoping I would get pregnant.

Then in 2013, I was diagnosed with breast cancer. That year I asked him not to go home while I went through chemo and radiation; he agreed. Jay supported me through everything, while I successfully beat the disease. At this point, I had been keeping him a secret from my family as well. Since his marriage and annual trips home, I found it much easier to not have to explain our situation to anyone; only a few friends knew. It alleviated a lot of stress off of me and the situation.

The following year, he went home. Before leaving, Jay said he was certain they would be coming back. *This will be the end for sure*, I thought. Returning a few months later, they were with him. It was not the end, but it took time to develop a new routine for our relationship. It killed me to know that he would leave me to go home to be with them/her. He assured me that in their culture, husbands and wives did not sleep together. I found it hard to believe, since we slept together all the time. Then again, through the years, he experienced many new things with me.

We were 13 years in when baby number three arrived. Jay was hoping for a girl, which in their culture was important. When she arrived, he was happy and relieved. I started to realize a strange phenomenon about his culture; women take care of all things inside the home, while men do all things outside. He handled the shopping, the kid's schooling, medical appointments. Most of the time he was calling me for assistance and advice, which angered me at first, until I got used to it.

Several times we talked about breaking up; I think it was just Jay feeling guilty. He said he wanted me to meet someone, have a normal relationship. However, he would not get out of my life completely for this to happen. My feelings for him were still intense, my love so strong. How could I meet someone new? I explained that I needed to get over him and heal before moving on.

We continued on for the next few years until COVID hit. The last time we were physically together was January 2020. During COVID, Jay did not want to take any chances because of his family. We spoke on the phone a lot. Because my feelings were still so strong, this was very hard for me; I became angry and passive-aggressive. Through the years he grew accustomed to my sarcasm; I unleashed my best work on him.

Towards the end of COVID, we saw each other a few times, meeting in the lobby of my building or at my workplace. Within two years' time, Jay lost his mom and his sister to two different illnesses, returning home to see his mom before she passed. There has been a definite change in him since the loss of these two important women. I tell him he has become "more Muslim," praying every day now, adhering to all holidays, giving up drinking wine and being alone with me.

It has been an intense struggle for me, a slow death so to speak. Just talking on the phone was so painful at first; I wanted to see him. I'd beg him to leave me alone, stop calling so I could move on. At first, he did not listen, but then he would call less until it got easier for me. I just didn't understand what our relationship had become; I was so hurt and confused.

Now, almost twenty-three years later, we speak a few times a week. Am I over Jay? Not completely, but the feelings are not the same. I care for him and love him, but I am not in love as I was. I do wonder what would happen if he did come over. From past experience, I know it is best he doesn't; it will ruin the wonderful memories. I believe my heart is open and ready to let someone new in if and when the time comes.

It is ironic how two major events are responsible for our relationship; 9/11 brought us together and COVID broke us up. We overcame so much during our years together, then COVID killed us. I know he struggled between his family loyalty and his feelings for me, hoping to adapt to life here in America. In the end, he made a choice and, sadly, his allegiance ultimately lies with his family and culture.

SHE WHO HEARS THE CRIES OF THE WORLD

by Winter Ross

It was not a good day to die – It was too beautiful. The Denver smog was behind us. Before us was the pass, it's peaks snow-capped even in July. I'd driven 1,200 miles to deliver my two children to their father for a summer visit. The Boyfriend, along for the ride, had entertained the kids in exchange for an opportunity to get away from the humidity of the East Coast. My sadness and anxiety about being separated from my little ones had motivated me to schedule a retreat at a Zen Center within a day's drive of them.

We drove by a group of people on the side of the road. *A flat tire,* I thought, as I glanced in the rear-view mirror. But the reversed image reflected the truth. Startled, I recognized the posture of a man performing CPR and braked. Boyfriend, who'd been keeping his eyes closed against the sting of gritty contact lenses, looked over at me from the passenger seat in surprise. It was no time to slow down. The van needed momentum to climb through the thin air.

"Someone's hurt back there," I explained.

"Nothing we can do about it." He pulled at his beard.

"You know I was an EMT. I'm going back."

He shrugged, "It's up to you."

Taking a deep breath, I swung the wheel of the van hard to the right to gain extra road for a U-turn. Still, the wide turning radius of the vehicle brought it close to the mountain's edge.

The complaining tires flung sandstone into the canyon below but the van obeyed. I pulled into a wide space across from the gathering and got out. Brushing the hair out of my face, I glanced both ways for traffic and ran across the road to the fallen figure.

He was a big man in his late 50's, stretched out on his back in the red soil. I took in the twisted bike on the ground nearby. *Too old and out of shape to be biking up a mountain,* I thought. *Should've known better...probably a heart attack.*

A young man, blond hair obscuring his face, knelt at the bicyclist's head, breathing for him through a plastic mouth guard. A middle-aged man in a Department of Wildlife uniform, leaned hard into the bicyclist's chest. I bent between them. "I'm an EMT if you need help." Both men hesitated. The younger stopped for the count and looked up as if to make way for me. "No. Don't stop!" I said, "Unless you have to. You're doing fine."

I'd come from sea level and could barely breathe for one. I knew I couldn't put air into those dying lungs as effectively as the twenty-year-old across from me. The body on the ground was heavy and solid. I could see it took all the government man's weight and strength to reach his heart. I wasn't strong enough to help much in that position either.

I slid my palm beneath the bicyclist's neck, made sure the airway was open, then felt along the soft jowls for the carotid artery. "I think I can feel what you're doing, but no pulse," I murmured to the man grunting beside me. He glanced sideways and nodded. Sweat trickled through his thinning hair and down into the collar of his uniform. The broad chest beneath his hands barely rose between compressions.

"You need to breathe a little harder," I coached Younger. "That's good. If you get dizzy, stop and I'll take over, okay?"

"Thanks, I'm alright." he whispered over the bloated face between us.

So I just crouched there between the struggling men, trying to be helpful, my fingers on the bicyclist's damp wrist. I never felt a pulse. I could have checked his pupils but I didn't. I didn't have to. I didn't want to look into a dead man's eyes.

I found myself looking, instead, up into a sky of such deep blue that I could sense the stars behind it. A chill came over me as I imagined the bicyclist looking down on us: three strangers kneeling in the desert dirt around his body, agonizing over our inept attempts to bring him back. Was his lingering consciousness comforted by the compassion of these strangers?

Forcing myself to take a breath of my own, I looked around. Vehicles were parked haphazardly; I noticed another bike flung on the ground. A thin man, watching through tears, twisted his biking hat between his hands; a man in jeans stood with a ten-year-old boy squatting near his patched knee. I looked for Boyfriend. He leaned against a stray U-Haul trailer with his arms folded, a spectator. Bluejeans picked up the bikes and put them in the trunk of an old Buick where a woman waited behind the wheel. The boy didn't move.

"Ambulance and sheriff are coming," the wildlife officer gasped, nodding toward his green pickup. Its radio antennas shone in the sun. "It won't be long."

Almost as he spoke, a white truck with a gold star laminated on the side swerved into the pull-off. Clouds of dust and gravel tore from the wheels. The sheriff banged open the truck door and ran toward us. "Hey, Bob! Let me take over for you, there."

Wildlife shook his head, sweat spinning into the dry air. He had a grimace of irony on his face. "No, man. I have so much adrenalin going, I'd explode if I quit."

"You sure?"

"I'm sure."

"You okay, son?"

Younger nodded and kept breathing.

The sheriff noticed my fingers on the bicyclist's wrist and raised his eyebrows. I shook my head.

He turned back to the truck to report to the ambulance coming along behind him somewhere in the rough forest at the bottom of the pass.

The ambulance crew, two men and a woman, were from the village. Although they toted high-tech equipment and wore orange jumpsuits, it was clear they weren't used to handling life or death situations every day. An IV had to be inserted twice by hands that were visibly shaking. Their patient vomited reflexively and the tube pressed down his throat had to be readjusted. Electrodes hastily taped to his skin wired him to a red box full of gauges.

"Everybody back! Clear!"

The big body stretched out stiffly, convulsing. I looked away. I saw the ten-year-old, his eyes wide and face as white as the dead man's, still sitting in the dirt unattended. I moved to block his view and caught the kid's eyes with my own. I heard the next "Clear!" behind me.

"This is not something you need to watch. Go back to your mom and dad."

With a look of relief, the boy got up and headed toward the Buick without a word. I watched him, wondering at parents who'd leave their child to witness this and thinking how amazingly easy it was to order someone else's kid around and get an unquestioning response. My own would have ignored me.

"Clear!"

From the corner of my eye, I saw Younger, standing now, sway. Both hands covered his face. I walked over to him, put my arm around his back to steady him. We stood together silently, averting our faces at the next "Clear!"

"What am I going to tell his family?" the thin man moaned. "What am I going to say to his wife? It was my idea to ride today. How can I face them? The ambulance was too late! It's taking too long!" He turned a tear-streaked face to me. "He's dead, isn't he? Don't you think he's dead?"

"I think so." I answered hesitantly, trying to soften the obvious. "Don't blame yourself. It's not your fault."

One of the paramedics shot me a hard look. "There will be a counselor at the hospital to talk to him," he said in a tone that told me to shut up. "Let's get the gurney."

It took six of us, straining, to lift the bicyclist's body onto the gurney, the gurney onto the ambulance. We almost lost him once, tipping at the step up to the wide orange doors. The body rolled toward me, the blue-white lips brushing my arm. Finally, the gurney slid in. I gave one paramedic a hand up into the back and slammed the doors after her while the other two climbed into the front. The ambulance arced onto the road, its' siren screaming down the mountain air. The sheriff, his yellow lights whirling, drove after, followed by the tearful man and the family in the Buick.

After the echo faded, Younger wandered the turnout, stooping to pick up bloody pieces of gauze, bits of white tape, strewn tubing. His companion, who had waited quietly in their Volvo, packed up their first aid kit. Younger looked at me, then up at the sky. "All this...and for nothing. What good did we do?"

"You did the best you could do. That's good enough."

"Yeah, I guess you're right. Thanks." He'd removed all evidence of the tragedy. The pull-off was pristine as an environmentalist's campsite. He ducked into the Volvo and waved as they headed on over the pass.

I scuffed across the road to the van where Boyfriend had resettled himself. Mica twinkled in the black asphalt at the road edge. I walked around the van and skidded down the bank toward a low wall of willow. Puffs of red earth drifted away from my feet; rabbit brush scratched at my knees. I couldn't see the stream but knew willow grew only beside water in this dry country. I pushed my way through the narrow-leaved branches and squatted as close to an eddy as I could. With my hiking boots sinking into the sand, I washed the dead man's drying vomit from the back of my hand and forearm. The shallow water was fast, clear, and cold enough to numb. Beyond my reddening fingertips, fool's gold sparkled in the sandy bed. I reached to touch it, but wavelets caught the sun and threw painful shards of light into my eyes. I turned stiffly, shook my hands. Rainbow prism droplets flew, evaporating before they hit the ground. I ran my palms across my eyelids and into my tangled hair. Sighing, I lurched back up the bank and hauled myself into the driver's seat.

Boyfriend sprawled on the passenger side, head back, eyelids clamped. "My eyes are killing me," he whined, opening one a fraction to regard me. I ignored him, reached for the keys in the ignition, and glanced in the rearview mirror. The road and turnout beyond were eerily empty – as if the past had been a mirage. Already it seemed a shimmering dream in the day's heat. *It had to have happened,* I told myself. The van was facing the valley we'd already traveled. I cranked the wheel laboriously to turn back uphill.

At the top of the pass, I looked out across the plain below to another mountain range: the Sangre de Cristos. Legend has it that two hundred years ago, a priest, mortally wounded by natives, took refuge on a raft in some lake down there. He had watched the snow on the peaks turn deep pink with alpenglow as the sun set behind him. "Sangre de Cristo", Blood of Christ, were his dying words.

Down valley, we drove past a pink stucco cafe and I spotted a pay phone on the outside wall. "Do you wanna stop for breakfast?" Boyfriend prodded. *Eat? Is it still morning?* My shoulders ached; my hands gripped the wheel as if they were melted on.

"No. I need to talk to my kids. I need to hear their voices."

"What do you mean, 'No'? I'm starving!" Boyfriend glared at me from his eye slits.

"We're expected for lunch at the Zen Center," I reminded him. "You can wait." I parked in front of the phone. I dropped a quarter in, but all I got was the ex's voice on an answering machine.

Up in the Sangres, junipers and ponderosa pine stretched out their arms and waved alongside the four-wheel track to the center. I knew this road. I'd dreamed about years ago. A carved wooden sign said, "Welcome to Dharma Sangha". We left the van in a small parking lot, climbed the path, unlatched a gate, crossed a tiny lawn and opened a rusty screen door to the back entry. Low shelves were lined with shoes and sandals. We slipped out of our boots and padded into the kitchen.

"Welcome! Welcome! Come in and sit down!" A monk in T-shirt and shorts bowed formally, giggled, then gave us both hugs. His shirt was decorated with a portrait of Yoda, the wise little master from *Star Wars*, and the words, "May the Force Be With You." I couldn't imagine him in a long black robe. He rubbed his shaved head. "Is something wrong?"

"Put me to work!" I pleaded. "Give me something to do. I can't sit."

"Sorry, hon. That's what we do here!"

I tried to laugh, but I felt too dried out.

"You won't believe the morning we had!" Boyfriend interrupted cheerfully. "This woman is a hero!" The other two monks in the kitchen put down their knives and hurried around the counter to hear his story. Their salad preparations would be postponed by speculations of exactly which mountain pass had claimed the life of the bicyclist. Surrounded by craggy peaks that regularly took the lives of climbers and hikers, they were keeping score. Boyfriend had hooked his audience. "They musta shocked the guy five times…"

I backed out of the kitchen, left the performance behind, and entered the open space of the monastery's main hall. Giant ponderosa logs formed the ceiling vigas. The vigas supported a long room that jutted from an earth berm to the open hillside. I blinked in the white light coming in through the windows. The entire southern wall was glass. Black paper cutouts of swallows were taped high on each pane to warn real birds away. A painful crack, running from ceiling to floor in one panel, was either testament to the futility of communicating with nature or a memorial to a pre-cutout casualty. I could see past the lawn, beyond a tangled garden of herbs and poppies, to the sagebrush floor of the valley. If I squinted off into the distance, I could just make out the Great Sand Dunes nestled at the foot of the mountains.

Silent children. Seas of sand. Corridors of dreams. Bleeding mountains. Gold for fools. A dead man's kiss. Suddenly I felt like a bird hitting the window, feathers scattered, stunned. The light flared in rhythm with my pounding head. I had to shut my eyes and turn away.

When I opened them again, I saw a figure begin to emerge from the shadow of the north wall. It seemed to move toward me as my eyes became accustomed to the dimness. It took my complete attention, finally, and filled my frame of vision. Before me stood a life-sized statue poised on a low pedestal. Kuan Yin, the Buddhist goddess of compassion, gazed serenely at me from the darkness. The lustrous eyes were not heavy-lidded and inward looking like those of the Buddha. Instead, she stared steadily out from the shade to the harsh landscape beyond the monastery. The flowing robes, cast in black patina bronze, glowed with polished detail. Her left hand held a budding lotus. Prayer beads trailed down the folds of her gown and ornate hems lapped like waves around one bare foot. Her right hand held a small pouch from which flowed a stream of water. Slender fingers opened gracefully toward the ground in a gesture that suggested both offering and acceptance. She seemed to be waiting patiently for whatever the desert brings. Waiting, with water, for whoever crosses the pass.

I felt the peace of this Bodhisattva flow over me like a cool wave. The images of the panting wildlife officer, the little boy wide-eyed with horror, the trembling hands of the paramedic, the young man swooning in my arms, and the tears of the thin man, faded as I met the deep gaze of the goddess known as "She Who Hears the Cries of the World." I brought my palms together before my face and bowed. The taste of salt tears brought me back to myself.

When Yoda-monk entered the hall with a vase of flowers for the table, I straightened and quickly brushed at my cheeks, embarrassed.

"May I help?" I asked.

"Sure, sweetie. Come back to the kitchen. You can grab the kettle and cups. We'll make tea.

Versions of this memoir were published in "Pilgrimage: Story, Place, Spirit, Witness"
Volume 31, Issue 1 (2006) and "What We Talk About When We Talk About It" Vol 1 (2020)

OVER THE RAINBOW
by Harvey Silverman

Sometime after it became clear that my best friend was going to die within the next couple of years – I had been there the night he had his initial episode of pulmonary edema – I began a casual conversation with him so far as any thought of something beyond this life.

His childhood Catholic faith, even nourished by a time as head altar boy, had long disappeared. Neither of us had any belief in the Biblical heaven or of any sort of anthropomorphic afterlife. I remained open to the possibility, however improbable, that there was something – a something beyond human comprehension – that might follow this mortal existence. A few odd occurrences that were likely wishful thinking on my part and dismissed as "cosmic serendipity" by my friend had left me open to the idea. He would have none of it and was clear in his belief that beyond this life there was nothing.

My best friend. Yes, he was that; more than fifty years earlier I sat in a classroom that was nearly full with about fifty freshman students in the Honors Chemistry course as the professor, standing behind a typically black topped laboratory desk, the chalkboard at his back, lectured on in a particularly dull performance. Finally, the signal of the period's end sounded but the diminutive lecturer, seemingly oblivious to the sound, continued on. After a minute or two slowly increasing background noise in the room, the result of closing books, shuffling papers, and fidgeting students, grew loud. Still, he continued as I turned to my friend sitting next to me on my left and instructed him, "Carl, tell him to shut up, would you?"

It was a facetious request but he was as impatient at that point as I. Just as he spoke the background noise without reason suddenly ceased and my friend's voice which would have otherwise been lost in the din was clearly heard.

"Shut up, you dink."

I hunched down in my seat trying to hide and at the same time stifle my laughter but my friend was unfazed as he sat straight with his arms crossed in front of his chest and a defiant expression on his face while the professor, apparently oblivious to this sound as well, continued on. At last, having made whatever point in the lecture he intended, the professor dismissed the class.

I had seen that expression on my friend's face before. Weeks earlier, sitting in an English class of a dozen students, a young lady asked my friend about the paper he had written for the assignment we all had. It was early in the first year of the advanced program when some of us were apparently trying to impress one another. With a look of serious concern she inquired, "Didn't you double footnote?"

He sat up straight, slowly crossed his arms in front of his chest, stared at her with an expression that combined annoyance with disgust, and said nothing. After a few moments she turned away, a victim of this marvelous countenance I would see many times over the next half century.

All had begun at the end of August, 1964, a week before most students arrived, when nearly forty young men – or were we really still boys? – moved into a wing on the seventh floor of the old dormitory, a residential hotel in an earlier time, the walls painted institutional dull and the faded charm of old fixtures still in the suites. The early week was required for an orientation to the accelerated academic program to which we thought ourselves fortunate to have been accepted. Beyond orientation, this first week allowed us to meet our classmates with whom we would presumably spend the next six years which would culminate, each of us hoped, with the awarding of an

MD degree.

It was easy for Carl and me to become friends. He had traveled the furthest distance to be in Boston and spoke in the easy and friendly manner of his home in small town Ohio, so unlike many east coast classmates who were somewhat louder, somewhat more brash. The differences between us - he was Catholic, Midwestern, and confident, I was Jewish, New Englander, and insecure – were unimportant. We soon became friends, and had in common other things, an independent outlook, a bit of stubbornness, underlying honesty. An appreciation and joy found in intramural football and occasional beer as well.

But more than anything it was the conversation that was so much a part of our enduring and lifelong friendship, a long running exchange about life which meant about everything and so went off in various directions - religion, politics, sports, family, work and play. As time went on, as the conversation created its own history, it never became old or dull. There were always, for me, new things to be learned, new opinions to consider, different perspectives to ponder. It was a guy's conversation, a sharing more of ideas and thoughts than feelings. There were insights and hopes, expectations, and disappointments. As the decades passed it noted the surprises, the unexpected twists and turns life takes. It was that ongoing conversation I most enjoyed, and easily, as we understood each other, being pretty simple and uncomplicated individuals.

Carl became a radiologist, comfortably happy in the dim light of his field, proud of his efficiency, good at what he did. I became an emergency physician when the specialty was in its earliest stages and had practiced it for fifteen years until age and family led me to an easier life with the regular hours of primary care.

Emergency medicine had exposed me to many episodes of pulmonary edema in which the failing heart cannot pump well enough to keep up with the returning circulation which then backs up and fills the lungs with fluid. It is an extremely uncomfortable and frightening experience for a patient; it occurs rapidly and produces the sense of drowning. Untreated it is usually fatal but the treatment is generally straightforward and most patients improve rapidly, going from a struggle for air, thrashing anxiety, and wild-eyed panic to restful smiles and thankful words.

After school had ended, we followed our own paths thousands of miles apart, visiting each other every few years when opportunity allowed. Later, having become parents, we managed to twice, years apart, cross paths in the middle of the country on family motorhome trips beginning on opposite coasts. Later still and children grown I was visiting him and his wife in Salem, Oregon, the night of the pulmonary edema.

By then the party times were long passed. He had become physically disabled, wheelchair bound because of failed hips. I had been doing the travelling, the visiting, for more than a decade. In 2002 my wife and I flew from our New Hampshire home for the reunion with our dear friends. Five years later she and I spent a delightful meandering month in our micro-mini motorhome on a cross-country trip with Salem the destination, another happy visit.

Two years after that I began to visit yearly, flying to Portland and driving on to Salem. By then he was newly diagnosed with heart failure. Heart failure - why? There are a number of possible causes but he showed little interest in further evaluation or investigation. He accepted, he chose, minimal care. My advice, my encouragement, my pleading to look further, to go further was politely ignored. He seemed comfortable from the cardiac standpoint, more distressed by his hips.

During a night in May, 2012, I was asleep in the Salem guestroom when his wife rushed in to ask me to look at my friend who had awakened acutely short of breath. In a moment it was clear he was, as he himself had thought, in pulmonary edema. There he was, struggling for air, wild eyed, panicked. I was helpless, without equipment or medicines, unable to treat a life-threatening condition in my best friend, a condition I had treated successfully many times. The best I could do was to get him upright, to encourage him to breathe deeply, and to reassure him while we waited for the arrival of the EMTs I had instructed his wife to call.

An hour later he was sitting comfortably in bed in the ER, feeling well, having responded to standard treatment. We spoke for a bit, I promised to return later in the day to watch a basketball game with him, and left him with his wife. My visit was extended for a few days while he remained hospitalized, no longer able to deny his heart condition or to avoid the necessary and long evaded evaluation.

Disease of the heart muscle, myocardiopathy, progressive and essentially untreatable was the diagnosis. I returned home with the hope I would see him again and the expectation of no more than a year or two, at best, of life for my friend.

For more than a dozen years our conversation had been in part continued by means of email. He had been more the listener – or the reader – faithfully, perhaps at times dutifully, reading my sendings which at times were long meandering thoughts, ponderings, and reminiscences. He might reply in some detail or briefly with such as, "That's really interesting" or, "You're an idiot!" In a certain way my emails had been like keeping a journal that recorded thoughts and ideas as well as prompting more than superficial contemplation. I thought that upon my best friend's death I would miss our exchanges most of all.

A few months after that visit my wife and I traveled west to Salem to visit him and her. We happily found him remarkably well and had a pleasant time. I resumed my annual visits the following spring, still happy to see him, still anticipating his death.

Health complication followed complication. The powerful diuretics required to eliminate the fluid his heart could not pump destroyed his kidneys; he required thrice weekly hemodialysis. He was in the ICU a number of times for gastrointestinal bleeding, gall bladder surgery, cardiac tamponade, and worsened heart failure. He was within hours of death several times but always survived. The year or two of life I had expected turned to three and then four.

Our email exchanges continued, my long musings continued while his responses became shorter and shorter, finally, when they occurred at all, a single sentence. In response to one in which among other topics I concluded that our particular friendship had been a special one he replied with a thanks for having been such a great friend for so long. Short, to the point, the way we liked it.

When I visited in May, 2016, four years after I had been helpless to deal with the pulmonary edema and well after the period for which I had predicted his death I found him again in the ICU. Our ongoing conversation was nearly over. Discussions of any existence beyond this one had concluded the year before with his belief unchanged; my suggestion that even if wishful thinking it was somehow possible that our paths would cross in some future unknowable and unimaginable fashion had been rejected. He died at the end of October and so did not learn who had prevailed in the Presidential election, one of the few subjects about which he could still become energized.

There was no funeral. His wife instead planned a memorial gathering for family and friends at their home for early December. My wife and I arranged to fly from east coast to west to Portland and then an hour drive to Salem. As the plane began its descent the pilot announced freezing rain had closed the airport and we would divert to Seattle. It became clear soon enough after landing that we would not be able to fly that day from there to Portland and so rented a car to instead drive.

The storm that had closed the Portland airport was moving north along the coast and we began to experience blizzard-like conditions. "That's okay, we're New Englanders and used to this," we told each other but the many cars and trucks that slid off of the road soon muted our confidence. The drive was long and slow. Finally, well after midnight we arrived at our Salem hotel.

At the memorial we embraced his widow, our grieving friend. I told many stories about my friend to his younger brother who had travelled from Wisconsin, and a few to his younger sisters. Standing by one of several poster boards adorned with various photographs from my friend's life was a sweet young lady, a Physician's Assistant who had often attended my friend and who had learned just a day earlier of his death. She pointed to various pictures and I explained them, often with a brief story. Her eyes filled with tears. "He talked about you all the time."

The following morning the weather was as it had been in the days since the snowstorm; typical Pacific Northwest - overcast, rare snatches of sun, intermittent rain. A dreary end to a difficult visit. We had begun our drive north to Portland's airport, anxious to return home, I lost in thoughts about my buddy and concerned as to our widowed friend's future. Across the highway in a large field there appeared a full and seemingly perfect rainbow. We admired the beautiful spectacle as we continued, leaving Salem. The rainbow seemed to touch down in a far end of the field just up the road. Instead of the rainbow's landing place continuously moving further away as normally happens when driving we had instead the sense of getting closer and closer.

Suddenly, the rainbow's end touched the car, the full spectrum of colors dazzling, flashing brilliantly, a sparkling dance on the windshield, the road obscured. This lasted just seconds and then disappeared, the rainbow itself completely gone. We were silent for a few moments, then looked at each other and asked, "What just happened?"

MY GRANDMOTHER
by Ahona Dam

My grandmother and I walked hand in hand inside her old house, almost inspecting it, looking for any mistakes in how the new inhabitants had designed the interior. Slowly, step by step, we walked through the living room, to her old bedroom, the dining area, my grandfather's room where she took care of him when he was bedridden, and even the bathroom.

"This tiling doesn't look that great, don't you think?" she whispered to me, pointing at the tiled trim on the entranceway of the bathroom.

I thought the same thing but didn't dare say it out loud. I looked at her, smiling and nodding in mischievous agreement. It was her house after all. Built from the ground up, every architectural choice was made by my grandfather's and grandmother's creativity. Even though the house was eventually sold because of my grandmother's old age, the memories embedded into the walls transcend further than any structural change in tiling or interior design.

Sometimes when I can't sleep, I think about my grandmother's house and her presence in each room. The words she said, the sound of her voice, and her face with a loving smile were always invitations to play or converse. I remember, when I was younger, the mole on the upper right of my grandmother's nose always stood out to me. It was unique and caught my eye. My sister has my grandmother's nose — wide and prominent. My sister doesn't like her nose, but I remind her that it's our grandmother's, a maternal stamp from our mother's side. My grandmother's nose was beautifully curved and perfectly paralleled her lips which stretched wide when she would smile or laugh. Her skin was so soft and her wrinkles rippled like sand dunes.

Every afternoon when I would nap between my grandmother and mother, I would face my grandmother and notice her wrinkles, sometimes dragging her matrimonial bangles across her arm, noticing how they would get caught in the folds of her skin.

My grandmother was the most special person. I don't think I can describe her simply using adjectives but there's a beauty in just memories. In 2020, my mental health was not great and my mom told my grandmother that I was feeling down almost every day.

"You can always talk to me. Anytime you feel upset, you can call me and talk to me about anything," she told me 8000 miles away.

This was my grandmother. Bela Talukdar. A piece of my heart, a teacher, a storyteller, someone who had lived a thousand past lives, my blood.

April 17th, 2022 my body had woken up earlier than usual. I could hear my dad downstairs talking in a muffled voice. Something happened to someone. A distant relative, I thought. I went downstairs, and so did my mom. My sister came down shortly after.

"Who? What? Who?" my mom kept frantically asking my dad on the verge of tears.

My dad wanted my mom to calm down and told her to sit down. It was the first time, in my life, that I heard my dad's voice crack. My grandmother had suffered a hemorrhagic stroke. My mom's wail was her heart screaming across the ocean for her mother. My mom planned a trip to Kolkata in June to see my grandmother after 3 years, and now she was changing her flight to leave early that night to perform the last rituals.

I was so naive. I thought that a miracle would save my grandmother. It was laughable but still, a part of me believed that I would be able to see my grandmother again, talking, laughing, and playing Parcheesi with me. We got the call that night that my grandmother had passed away. My mom was on the plane, and she would know the news when she landed in Kolkata.

Why this news was even more shocking for me was that the day before, I had spoken to my grandmother. It was Bengali New Year and I had asked for her blessings for the new year. We all talked to her. When it was my turn to ask for her blessings, it felt different. Not in a bad way, instead it was beautiful and touching.

"*Amar shubho naboborshor pronam niyo.* Accept my respect and prayers for the new year," I told her through my mom's phone.

"*Amar onek, onek, onek, onek bhalobhasa niyo.* Accept my endless love," she repeated telling me how much of her love she was giving me for the new year.

How could I have lost someone who I had just talked to the day before? I've read stories and shocking events like this before but never imagined that I would be living it. My grandmother was my everything and now she was no longer someone I could talk to, ask questions regarding my mom as a kid, or laugh with.

I don't think I have ever cried the way that I did when I lost my grandmother. I felt the pit of my stomach become knotted and a release of a single sigh would send tears rushing down my face. At night, in the shower, and while I ate and spoke about her I could feel the pit unravel.

There isn't a single day, even now, that passes without me thinking about my grandmother. It was so difficult for me to understand that someone with no chronic health conditions, someone who had spoken to me less than 24 hours ago could suddenly be taken by God. That's how I imagined it. God had taken her away from me and my family and my grandmother had done nothing to deserve it. I was angry by the sheer audacity and power that God had to take her away in this perfect state of mind. My faith in religion started to crumble and I was now uncertain in my beliefs. I felt somewhat selfish in thinking that I should have had more time with my grandmother. But that's what I wanted. I wanted her to live longer and pass away when the time was right, but the time didn't feel right.

From time to time, I look through all the photos of my grandmother on my phone, and unique memories piece together in my mind like a mosaic. I'm scared of losing the sound of her voice, the feeling of her sari, the taste of her food, and the smell of her home. I long to go back to her house in Kolkata and have the chance to spend one last day with her. Nothing special, just the usual routine and banter. I will grudgingly make my way to the table for lunch as I see that we have fish again, but smile at the *aam chutney*, mango chutney, as a side. I will swing on the *dolna*, and call my grandmother to the veranda if a vendor asks if anyone is home because she is the head of the house. I will eat the sour *mushumbi*, sweet lime, and give a plate to my grandmother as we watch our current favorite Bengali serial. I will pester my mom to take me somewhere. Anywhere. But I will want to go in a rickshaw. For dinner, I will smear Kissan mixed fruit jam on my *roti* and watch the singing competition on Zee Bangla. My grandmother will join and at around 10:30 she will start snoring. We will go to bed to the barks of stray dogs and mutters of people across the field. Just one more day.

I'm grateful and so lucky to have known a person as kind-hearted, loving, and wise as my grandmother. She was my direct tie to Kolkata and the person I would go to for a laugh, advice, or funny stories. If I could spend just one more day with her, I would tell her: *Tumi o amar onek onek onek onek bhalobhasha niyo.* Accept my endless love.

Essay: SUN TZU AND ENTERTAINMENT:
THE LION KING'S FALL OF SCAR
by Andrew Nickerson

In the annals of military tactics/strategy, one name has long stood above the others in terms of influence and potency: Sun Tzu, author of *The Art of War*. This 2,000+-year-old masterpiece literally set the standard for wartime brilliance, both for its layman's approach to warfare and its unique goal: winning. Subsequently, generations of experts have continually sung its praises, their most constant refrain being this: if you listen to Sun Tzu, you'll win; if you ignore him, you'll lose. Furthermore, his knowledge is universally applicable, and is known to have been used by everyone from businessmen to politicians and even athletes to achieve victory.

However, there's one medium that remains untapped: pop culture plotlines. If Sun Tzu is universally applicable, why not here too? To better illustrate this, we're going to explore one such arc right now: the fall of Scar in the animated classic *The Lion King*. More specifically, we'll be analyzing it through the following Sun Tzu principles: morality, terrain, leadership, preparation, improv, foreknowledge, deception, direct-indirect acts, baiting foes, recklessness, cowardice, delicacy of honor, seizing an opening, and underestimation. One more note: for streamlining purposes, we're only going to look at moments directly involving Scar, thus excluding sequences like with Pumbaa and Timon.

In Africa lay the Pride Lands, ruled by mighty lion King Mufasa, who's just had a son, Simba, with his wife Sarabi. The rambunctious Simba, eager to make an impact, soon begins his education under Mufasa, who explains the value of maintaining balance and respecting all around so his son can rule properly. It's a wonderful display of four of Sun Tzu's Five Essential Victory Factors, morality[1], terrain[2], leadership[3], and preparation[4] as well as the principle, "What enables the wise sovereign and the good general to strike and conquer and achieve things beyond the reach of ordinary men is foreknowledge."[5]

Sadly, the entire time Mufasa has also violated two other principles, one of Sun Tzu's Five Fatal Failings of Leadership, recklessness[6], and never underestimate a foe[7], by neglecting one of the kingdom's worst threats: his younger brother, Scar. The latter had been next in line to rule, but was bumped in favor of Simba, leaving him extremely bitter toward brother/nephew alike, a shocking violation of another fatal failing, delicacy of honor[8]. Hence, he aims to usurp Mufasa and Simba by killing them both, a plan he puts into action by first using prep to secretly gather a mercenary army of hyenas, the lions' natural enemies; the term mercenary applies because they're not fighting for loyalty, but due to Scar's promise that they'll be allowed to live in the Pride Lands, something they've always longed for, making this a grand use of foreknowledge by their boss.

Later, Scar makes his first move on Simba by deliberately letting slip knowledge of an elephant graveyard just beyond the northern border, which he witnessed Mufasa not showing his nephew, even hinting "only the bravest lions go there", a subtle use of foreknowledge and two more principles: "all warfare is deception"[9] and "use baits to entice enemies."[10] Naturally, Simba naïvely goes there with BFF Nala, only to have Scar's top three hyena enforcers (Trio from now on), ambush them, a good use of prep by Scar. Yet, the Trio foolishly violate recklessness, underestimation, and another principle, if an opening comes to seize victory, take it[11], by not killing Simba and Nala immediately, allowing Mufasa's majordomo Zazu to inform the king, who swiftly overpowers the former and saves the day. In the aftermath, Scar chews out the Trio before organizing his massive force...but then makes a critical mistake: in a shocking violation of recklessness, leadership, and foreknowledge, he tells the hyenas, "Stick with me and you'll never be hungry again!" It's the first of many such moves, ones that'll cost him dearly.

The next day, Scar decides to use another pair of principles: "be flexible; according as circumstances are favorable, one should modify one's plans"[12], or improv, and "Direct methods can join battle, but indirect ones are needed to secure victory."[13] The direct act, in this case, is having Simba meet him in a nearby valley, where the Trio are waiting to initiate a stampede of wildebeests. When they move, Scar uses the indirect act by informing Mufasa, who swiftly goes there while using prep and foreknowledge by having Zazu fly in to locate Simba; upon doing so, Mufasa goes to the rescue, but then Scar uses seizing an opening by KO'ing Zazu. Mufasa's able to use improv and terrain to get Simba onto a ledge, but violates underestimation when a wildebeest knocks him down. However, in a thunderous display of strength, the former manages to leap onto a ledge and begin pulling himself out, only to violate recklessness and underestimation again when he begs Scar to help him. Instead, the latter uses seizing an opening by throwing Mufasa to his death, leaving Simba traumatized, and then employs direct-indirect acts once more by hinting the latter is to blame; he cruelly finishes this tactic by telling him, "Run away and never return," something the trusting prince quickly does...after which Scar uses seizing an opening again by ordering the Trio to kill him. However, all guilty parties violate underestimation for Simba, in a wonderful use of terrain and improv, manages to slip out through a section of thornbushes. Seeing that area, the Trio, blatantly violating seizing an opening, foreknowledge, and another Fatal Failing, cowardice[14] refuse to enter, ultimately writing off Simba as dead anyway, followed by making the second major mistake of the film when they violate recklessness by not telling Scar.

Either way, Scar assumes the throne, using deception by claiming Mufasa and Simba are both dead, and then has his massive army take over the Pride Lands. He then foolishly violates delicacy of honor and leadership by decreeing none are to mention Mufasa's name in his presence, a pointless move that only undermines his authority. It's the first stage of his fall, and the second comes after some time elapses, when the Trio arrives and drops a massive bomb: there's no food or water left. It's Scar's elephant graveyard decree coming back to haunt him, since he neglected a basic rule of army logistics: a big force has a big appetite. Also, unlike Mufasa's belief in keeping things balanced, Scar has been violating an important caveat of leadership, enforcing discipline[15], the whole time by not reining in the hyenas, who've all opted to take what they want, when they want, accelerating the collapse of the food chain; in short terms, he violated a rule anyone who's taken a check-writing class has heard, "Never write a check you can't cash." As if that weren't enough, he further violates leadership and foreknowledge by simply remarking, "It's the lionesses' job to do the hunting," only to have the Trio answer "Yeah, but they won't go hunt!" To add even more icing to this cake from hell, Scar violates those same principles again by dismissing the Trio without addressing the problem, the third dear mistake of the film.

Later, no doubt under pressure, Scar calls Sarabi to Pride Rock, whereupon he violates leadership and foreknowledge still again by demanding to know why her hunting party isn't working. The latter, in a wonderful display of morality, foreknowledge, and leadership, replies there's no food, only to have Scar angrily violate leadership and delicacy of honor by snapping "You're just not looking hard enough!" Instead, she uses those principles again by informing him there's nothing left and they must leave Pride Rock, only to have Scar, in an insane violation of morality, leadership, foreknowledge, recklessness, and delicacy of honor, not only declare they're not going anywhere, but actually strike Sarabi when she boldly brings up Mufasa's name. That move costs him when Simba, newly rehabilitated by his newly minted-sweetheart Nala's use of morality and leadership, appears, causing a major rift to form between Scar and the Trio due to the latter's lie being exposed.

Enraged, Simba confronts Scar, with the lionesses openly rejecting the latter's rule, only to have Scar use both deception and baiting by using a fake revelation that the former is responsible for Mufasa's death. This shatters Simba, allowing Scar to push him back Pride Rock until he nearly tumbles off the edge...just in time for lightning to strike the dry ground beneath, starting a wildfire. However, Scar now makes the film's fourth dear mistake: in a shameless violation of morality, leadership, seizing an opening, recklessness, and underestimation, he leans boasts of murdering Mufasa to a supposedly helpless Simba. This incredibly sloppy move eliminates Simba's guilt, the only thing holding him back, causing the now enraged prince to leap off the cliff and pin Scar down, yelling "Murderer!" The latter, hopelessly violating cowardice, tries to plea for his life, but Simba, in a potent use of leadership, literally chokes the truth out of him, eliminating any question of Scar's guilt.

Hence, the hyenas use seizing an opening to knock Simba off Scar, but fatally violate terrain, recklessness, and foreknowledge in the process, for they're currently on Pride Rock, a tall, narrow space whose only safe exit is at the rear. Furthermore, they're packed together like sardines, meaning they can't maneuver, and since they've been forcing the lionesses to do the hunting their physical combat skills have slipped. Meanwhile, the latter are in prime fighting condition, enraged, and have cut off the rear exit, an excellent use of terrain and improv that pays off when they begin knocking the trapped hyenas off Pride Rock into the wildfire below. Simba's other allies, namely warthog Pumbaa, meerkat Timon, and baboon Rafiki, now enter the fight too, a wonderful display of how morality and leadership can gain allies.

Still, Scar's the real target, and Simba quickly goes after him, the former desperately trying to flee, only to violate terrain, foreknowledge, and underestimation when his escape path is cut off by the wildfire. The latter then arrives, and Scar makes the film's fifth dear mistake: in a shameless violation of morality, leadership, recklessness, cowardice, and underestimation he tries to blame the hyenas for the entire plot, unaware the Trio can hear him...and it's all for naught, since Simba doesn't believe him. Yet, Simba displays admirable morality and leadership by not sinking to Scar's level, instead opting to exile him instead. Unfortunately, this move turns into a violation of underestimation when Scar, in a quick use of improv, seizing an opening, and deception swats an ember into Simba's face, blinding the latter before attacking and ultimately knocking him down. But the former now makes the film's final dear mistake: in a clumsy violation of recklessness, delicacy of honor, and underestimation, he leaps at Simba, only to have the latter, in a great display of improv, use a move he learned from his many wrestling matches with Nala and flip the former off a nearby ledge. Upon landing, Scar sees the hyenas approach and greets them as friends, only to have all his prior violations catch up to him when the latter, enraged at his betrayal, attack him instead, the entire lot soon being incinerated by the wildfire before rain extinguishes the blaze.

This was a breathtaking scenario, especially for a children's film but, as we all witnessed, Sun Tzu's guiding hand was there the entire time, ensuring an evil tyrant's fall even as he rose to power. Scar may have been clever with using *The Art of War*'s wisdom at first, but he turned his back on it once he felt secure and, as was said in the beginning, if you follow Sun Tzu, you'll win...but if you ignore him, you'll lose.

[1] Lionel Giles, *The Art of War* (New York, NY; Fall River Press, 2011), 3.
[2] Giles, *The Art of War*, 3.
[3] Giles, *The Art of War*, 3.
[4] Giles, *The Art of War*, 3.
[5] Giles, *The Art of War*, 50.
[6] Giles, *The Art of War*, 28.
[7] Giles, *The Art of War*, 33.
[8] Giles, *The Art of War*, 28.
[9] Giles, *The Art of War*, 5.
[10] Giles, *The Art of War*, 5.
[11] Giles, *The Art of War*, 46.
[12] Giles, *The Art of War*, 4.
[13] Giles, *The Art of War*, 15.
[14] Giles, *The Art of War*, 28.
[15] Giles, *The Art of War*, 4.

Bibliography

Allers, Roger and Minkoff, Rob, directors. *The Lion King: Diamond Edition*. 1994. Walt Disney Pictures, 2011. 85 min. Blu-Ray.

Sun Tzu. *The Art of War*. Translated by Lionel Giles. New York: Fall River Press, 2011.

Essay: FINDING NICK DRAKE:
RICHARD MORTON JACK'S NEW BIOGRAPHY
by Tyler Martinez

As we get older, the landscape of our memory is dotted with life's important moments. For those who love music, some of these moments include the first they heard their favorite artists: famously, Bruce Springsteen says about the first he heard Bob Dylan: "I was in the car with my mother, and we were listening to, I think, maybe WMCA, and on came that snare shot that sounded like somebody kicked open the door to your mind, from 'Like a Rolling Stone.'"[1] Jon Anderson, lead singer of Yes, says about hearing the Beatles song "Tomorrow Never Knows": "I was in a brothel in Hamburg ... It was when I put Revolver on in that brothel, and got to the end of side two and heard Tomorrow Never Knows, that I realized that The Beatles weren't just a rock'n'roll band. That song stands out as their most sonically and lyrically adventurous departure from everything I'd ever heard. It was like listening to music for the first time."[2]

In some ways, these epiphanous stories seem like things of the past – it's less often we're introduced to music via broadcast radio or by the originality of an album's artwork and more the case that we're recommended individual songs from carefully curated algorithms and playlists. Today, most people use streaming services[3] over analog recordings (like CDs, vinyl, and tapes) for their music listening and discovery (although this isn't to say one is better than the other – Spotify has seriously upgraded music as a *social* experience.)

That being said, I don't have a grand story about how I found Nick Drake's music. I wasn't at the house of an older relative-mentor whose music taste I was captivated by; I wasn't spellbound by something playing from the window of a stranger's house. Unceremoniously, it's more likely the case that at some point, *Pink Moon* made its way onto my curated Spotify feed as an album adjacent to my tastes and, being in a rare mood to listen to something new, I gave it a listen.

But while I can't tell for certain the story of *how* I found his music, I can tell the story of when.

It was sometime in 2020 after schools had "let out" for the summer after, ironically, being held entirely online. I had just graduated with my Associate's and was spending most of my time indoors, as everyone had, wondering whether life would ever be as normal as it apparently always was. I wasn't sure whether continuing college online was worth it given how "making connections" (which, I was told, was an invaluable skill pursuing a liberal arts degree) seemed nearly impossible without face-to-face contact.

At some point during the deliberation, two artists crept into my musical diet: Frank Zappa, whose sixty-two-album discography (and sixty-four album posthumous discography) constitutes a universe of its own, and Nick Drake, whose three-album discography was several times smaller, but conceptually, seemed several times larger. Both inadvertently complemented the spirit of a global pandemic: Zappa's music – highly-orchestrated and experimental progressive rock – represented the confusing and hallucinatory new world of deadly contagions, and Nick Drake's music – quieter, delicate, somber folk – represented the very real and disturbing reality of daily global death-tolls, family separation and eerily barren city-centers.

But today, I prefer not to pigeonhole either's music by associating it with a global catastrophe of which they and their music is unrelated. In 2021, after having escaped the pandemic vaccinated, Nick's music and story continued to resonate with me, so I endeavored to find any information about this increasingly enigmatic figure (unlike Zappa, to whom information and recordings abound.)

I picked up Amanda Petrusich's *Nick Drake's Pink Moon*[4] – catalog number fifty-one of the 33 ⅓ series – and, unfortunately, found much of it to be speculative, romantic, too often informed by opinion, and focused too much on the Volkswagen ad sometimes associated with Nick's posthumous popularity. This, though, is almost no fault of Petrusich – for decades, the public has had very little information about Nick Drake other than the information provided on record sleeves and in vintage music magazines (and in both of those places, still, there is very little to work with.) To make matters worse, in place of accurate information was often-erroneous fan estimations on how someone who committed suicide at twenty-six years old managed to create some of the greatest records of all time and slip under the mainstream radar.

After finishing Petrusich's book and still eager for information, I looked to join any and all music forums whose focus was Nick's work. I happily stumbled into a group on Facebook founded by Richard Morton Jack, whose purpose of the group was to post updates about *his* upcoming book *Nick Drake: The Life*, eventually scheduled for publication June 2023. He would also occasionally share interesting anecdotes about his writing process and respond to queries from ardent fans. The conversation in the group was alive with many sharing about the first they'd heard Nick's music, often accompanied by rare photos, articles, CD anthologies, and listening recommendations (Jack himself recommended the album "Time of the Last Persecution" by Bill Fay, which then ended up in my end-of-the-year "top tracks" in 2023.)

When Jack's book was published, I had the book shipped internationally and received my copy in July, and found that Nick's story is thoroughly and objectively told.

It was incredible to see how many people in the group had enjoyed Nick's music just as much as I had – many of them alive at the same time he was and remembering purchasing his records and uncovering what they rightfully believed to be popular music's diamond in the rough. Unfortunately, as Jack mentions in the biography, Nick's music wasn't so "popular" outside of Nick's immediate circle and the small (but fervent) English folk circuit (Nick himself, however, despite being described as somewhat reticent, *was* quite popular and many of his friends helped volunteer information for Jack's biography.) Despite accruing local fans through word-of-mouth and receiving many favorable reviews in music magazines (as Jack says in his blog, Galactic Ramble[5]), Nick's records sold poorly, which many cite as a significant factor contributing to his steep psychological decline beginning sometime in the early 70s and accelerating over the next few years:

> "Everyone who knew Nick agreed that he had become worryingly uncommunicative by the summer of 1970." (339)[6]

But what few had the opportunity to notice then is what many notice now about Nick's music: it is incredibly unique. In a studio discography of 108 minutes – shorter than most feature-length films – Nick demonstrates an incredible ear for melody, impressively introspective and observant lyrics, guitar playing and vocals wholly unique to itself, and a subtle but subversive attitude that keeps with the delicate beauty of music. Elements of classical music, jazz, and folk are reassembled into truly timeless collages of which imitation is nearly impossible. After each album, the sound is reinvented, but the music maintains an important and distinguishing orientation towards originality.

Nick's third and final album is what he is perhaps best known for. The stripped-down 28-minute *Pink Moon* was released in 1972, and mostly features only Nick with his acoustic guitar. This choice was a departure from the lush production on his previous two albums, *Bryter Layter* (1971) and *Five Leaves Left* (1969). As Jack describes, its recording was a comparatively brief process: "Nick's third album was recorded in Sound Techniques [in London, England] over two consecutive nights in the week of Monday, 25 October 1971 ... both sessions took place between 11PM and 2AM." (385)

Jack also offers insight about Nick's intention in keeping the album so bare and perfectly describes its musical depth:

> "The album's approach can be interpreted simply as a rejection of its predecessors' elaborateness, and some detected a streak of petulance in Nick's determination to keep it so plain." (389)

> "Another interpretation is that Nick perfectly understood his own artistry. The album not only holds attention throughout, it becomes more engrossing and more deeply mysterious upon repeated plays. His bearing is profoundly introspective, his lyrics more inscrutable than ever, yet the songs artfully bridge despair and hope, carrying a substantial emotional charge ...The album's overall economy and power is remarkable; Nick's genius was in full flower." (390)[7]

The tragedy of Nick's story, however, is that despite reaching creative anthesis, Nick was suffering from a mental illness that was somewhat difficult to understand, partially owing to Nick's irritability and indecision to accept help from family and medical professionals (which many incorrectly assume he hadn't received.) He would live only two years and nine months after *Pink Moon*'s release, unfortunately succumbing to what Dr. Gerald Dickens – one of Nick's psychiatrists – described in a letter to Nick's father as "simple schizophrenia," but adds

> "I think such labels are meaningless, and to a large extent cover our lack of understanding of such illnesses ... I can well understand your concern over the use of the word 'suicide', with all its implications. Again, I think that this is a meaningless word, part of an often-meaningless legal jargon. It would be quite impossible for anyone to understand what was in or on Nick's mind when he took the overdose of tablets ... People who have studied this illness all their lives have no better understanding of patients than you had of Nick." (507)[8]

I think what Dr. Dickens means is: firm diagnostic labels often fail to capture the complexity of psychological illnesses; for one to believe they have complete access to what "went wrong" in a person's life would be, at best, a theory-of-mind overstep, and at worst, a dangerous medical transgression. There were certainly obvious contributing factors (Nick's perception of himself as a "failed" musician being one of them), but ultimately, the complete and exact formula for Nick's disintegration is inaccessible.

It was somewhat heartening (if grimly) to read this letter from a psychiatrist whose responsibility was to assign words to Nick's fluctuating pattern of behavior (and whose profession is sometimes disparaged for its *inconsiderate* attitudes.) His letter does a good job of *humanizing* Nick, as does all of Jack's book, which is to say: let's not understand Nick as someone whose mind was overcome by a dark, otherworldly, metaphysical force, but as someone who suffered from a perplexing illness of the mind in the same way people suffer from illnesses of the body, one which complicated and ultimately ended his musical career, his relationship with friends and family, then his life. It robbed the public, too, of what more Nick had to contribute to our shared experience of art and music.

Jack's book made me realize: we should be able to acknowledge the relationship between Nick's story and his music while avoiding falling for what Stuart Jefferies at the Guardian describes as the "fetishised" version of Nick as a "depressives' pin-up"[9] – or, someone whose story is more *symbolic* than actual. By subtracting nuance from Nick's story by assigning a sort of glamor to his demise (or by assuming his illness was solely caused by something like LSD, his record company not tending to him, or a negligence in his support system, all of which Jack proves to be demonstrably false), we imply: Nick's death was something *meant* to happen as a fated consequence of being able to introspect and create at such a deep level – as if Nick were a sensitive folk messiah who, upon creating *Pink Moon*, was ultimately destroyed by the creative force it took to conceive it. This interpretation, I think, doesn't fully recognize the real and difficult realities of life that were made much more laborious given Nick's highly fluctuant (and oftentimes invisible) illness. Even worse, it disallows us a richer understanding of the fragility of life, the value of art, and how inseparable the two are.

I finished Jack's gorgeous book a few weeks ago. It not only provided me with the most information I've ever known about a singular person, but a ton of sympathy for the Drake family given the unique and painful situation they found themselves in. What a confusing situation to have a loved one pass away so young, leaving behind a small but significant body of work that saw its deserved praise only *after* its creator passed away; what a confusing experience to know and love a family member, then only after they've died, having the world learn to know and love them too. The ways in which Nick's family handled his death speaks volumes of them as caring and intelligent people: in one example, a fan named Melinda (twenty-one and from America) traveled to Nick's home to meet his parents after listening to *Pink Moon*. They immediately embraced her, allowing her to stay with them, listen to home recordings, and gave her "Nick's address book, watch and black jumper ..." (510)[10].

To me, Nick Drake was a brilliant artist. He was an artist who, despite a devastating illness, managed to create something wholly unique and meaningful, transcending many of his contemporaries whose discographies are oftentimes much larger. As fans, we sometimes rob ourselves of the privilege of knowing that our artists are painfully human – that despite their magnificent contributions to the world, they were of the same material as us, which, given how *time hurries on*, is sometimes the only lasting similarity.

Thankfully, this similarity is the most important one.

Works Cited

[1] Taysom, Joe. "When Bruce Springsteen Heard Bob Dylan for the First Time." *Far Out Magazine*, 16 July 2021, faroutmagazine.co.uk/bruce-springsteen-first-heard-bob-dylan/.

[2] Hasted, Nick. "The First Time I Heard The Beatles, by Jon Anderson." *Louder*, 28 Nov. 2023, www.loudersound.com/features/the-beatles-jon-anderson.

[3] Duarte, Fabio. "Music Streaming Services Stats (2023)." *Exploding Topics*, 10 Oct. 2023, explodingtopics.com/blog/music-streaming-stats.

[4] Petrusich, Amanda. *Nick Drake's Pink Moon*. Bloomsbury Academic & Professional, 2007.

[5] Jack, Richard Morton. "Nikipedia." *Galactic Ramble*, 3 July 2023, https://galacticramble.blogspot.com/2023/07/nikipedia.html. Accessed 7 Jan. 2024.

[6] Jack, Richard Morton. "A Different Nick." *Nick Drake: The Life*, John Murray, London, 2023, pp. 339.

[7] Jack, Richard Morton. "A Small Reel." *Nick Drake: The Life*, John Murray, London, 2023, pp. 389–390.

[8] Jack, Richard Morton. "A Very Special Person." *Nick Drake: The Life*, John Murray, London 2023, pp. 507.

[9] Jefferies, Stuart, and Gabrielle Drake. "Gabrielle Drake: 'I Want to Complicate the Nick Drake Story.'" *The Guardian*, Guardian News and Media, 15 Nov. 2014, www.theguardian.com/lifeandstyle/2014/nov/15/i-want-to-complicate-the-nick-drake-story.

[10] Jack, Richard Morton. "Epilogue." *Nick Drake: The Life*, John Murray, London, 2023, pp. 510.

Prose Poetry

FROM THE EDITORS: *The core of prose poetry is the rhythmic prose that distinguishes it from common prose, but has enough poetry in its heart to sustain a sound about it, like a song. Gray Baby Hairs, whilst not an appealing title, is a deftly composed short piece with a devastatingly powerful message. To convey this truism in such a short space, to move the reader hugely with so little, is surely a sign of mastering language and why this was a clear winner from all the judges. It literally is the definition of prose poetry and why the genre is so beloved. -CLD*

GRAY BABY HAIRS
by Summer Chambley

My breasts were still leaking milk when they told me my father was dead. In fact, little white drops for my dead baby appeared on my nipples for years, but on this day, it had only been a few weeks.

No baby. No father. No baby. No father.

Where do you turn first? I was buried in grief and shame. Saddened that I had deviated from our plan without even a grandchild to show for it. I was only halfway through law school.

You know you can tell me anything.

You were 21 when you found out I was coming. 22 when I made you a father. Yet, I was still too buried to see the irony of being afraid to tell you.

No baby. No degree. No baby.

You took care of me. Quietly. So I could recover. Paid all my bills. One by one. When your own blood seeped into the vacuous parts of your brain just three years before. You weren't the same, you said.

But I could only see my own face as blood poured from my insides and covered my crisp gray pants.

Is this my blood or the baby's? How strange that it could be both.

You think it can't get worse. You said it more than once.

But what could be worse than waiting for tiny fingers to appear on the shower floor. What could be worse than the contractions radiating through every cell of my being, signaling to the world that someone new is coming. The deliriously intoxicating hormones that trick your brain into thinking that you aren't just a daughter anymore, you are now a mother too. Bonding you to this person you will never hold. Where is my baby? Where is my baby?

Until suddenly you come up for air and you really aren't a mother. And you somehow aren't a daughter either. Air itself has ceased to exist.

How could it get worse?

I have always been a daughter.

I have always been your daughter.

How can I be your daughter if there is no you.

No baby. No you. Which is more unimaginable? I spoke at your funeral. My eyes bouncing from pitying gaze to pitying gaze. My friend called and said that he cried after

I told him. Sorry not for me, but for himself. Sorry for himself. Sorry for himself. because he would never know grief like mine.

I touched your hair. You couldn't bat my hand away. I counted every single gray hair. Over and over again. But the number never changed. Seven. Seven.

Seven.

Seven.

Does hair turn to ash or dust? Or whatever we become? Does my father still have seven gray hairs?

I put "loving father" on your headstone. Gold letters spelling out a name that I still felt like should be signing my field trip forms. You never knew about all the times you signed me out of class. Or did you know. Really, you were a grandfather too. If only for a blink of an eye. If only by loving your daughter through what felt like insurmountable pain. If only it was just for the tip of the never-ending iceberg.

Seven and an ancestor.

You knew that it could get worse. Maybe you knew that it would get worse. Maybe you know that I would be sitting here just like the morning that I began to bleed.

Cat curled up at my knee. Still waiting for the bleeding to stop.

FROM THE EDITORS: *Proof of high caliber writing is when an author wins two years in a row when the judging was blind. Trout's powerful prose and poetry writing is unparalleled and with dear entomophobic america, she wastes not a single word. In less than half a page she's reeled you into her intelligent, considered rebuke where her roar is a beautiful, uncompromised protest against erasure and faux politick. Exquisite wordplay is Trout's calling card, I suspect she has a powerful future as a writer because she possesses what few do; the guts to call it like it is.-CLD*

DEAR ENTOMOPHOBIC AMERICA
by Amanda Trout

—after "dear white america" *by Danez Smith*

i have left your surface in search of deeper soil, some root i can latch on and suckle until this shell grows too tight to stand. i have left in search of sustenance. i do not trust all the meals i have been served and have run out of insecticide taste-testers. i spent my summer scavenging spruce trees for sap, forgetting to wipe the sticky evidence from my mouth. at dawn i count my brothers and sisters in the sycamore tree and always count less. i keep a running tally as the day progresses; strike one for caesuras that never end, strike two for every pound of second-grader sneakers into wood chips, strike three for a human scream but add one back for a cicada song. i have left the surface. i am equal parts sick of your plague pathology, your misnaming, your carbon monoxide kill jars and your pinning rituals. i am sick of the necessity of swarming when i am stuck being a solitary species. i am sick of being solitary when i crave the comfort of a swarm but can't find one, and even when i can find some semblance of companionship i have to force myself not to scream in excitement. screams scare people. loud scares people. songs in a different key than the larger symphony scare people.

america, it was never the bugs you were afraid of.

3rd Place

FROM THE EDITORS: *Braeden Michael's prose is jaw-droppingly accomplished and beautiful. From his titles to the depth of his considerations, in this case in ¾ of a page, he's able to catapult the reader into his intense, poignant world of image-play much like a song. Quite simply, his writing is beautiful and intoxicating. You want to keep reading, you become addicted to the way he sees the world. This is the juxtaposition of gorgeous poetry in the medium of prose. -CLD*

ONCE UPON A RAIN, SHE BLOOMED
by Braeden Michaels

I took a bite of sorrow from the moment of birth. As an infant, I crawled on the floor with friction in my heart. I resided in a home that wore a facade like a virgin wearing a dress.

From the second I learned to walk, I was labeled a troublemaker, iron vixen, and a cynical curveball. I spoke when I was spoken to and screamed when I was screamed to. You call me an introvert and see myself as a spirit not knowing who I am or where I belong. I spit out the happiness you claimed to provide.

I fell in love with cradle rockers, pathological liars, water down evangelists, and the prince of persuasion. They pretended they could save my desperate soul. From rattlesnakes to men in charcoal suits I inhaled the scent from each of their manuscripts. I lie in my bed of careless decisions staring into the moonlight with agitation gnawing inside my veins. I can't see desirability beyond my skin. They offered me clothing, jewelry I never wore, decorated homes but never an ounce of unconditional love. The more I gave, the lonelier I became. Worth is just a snowflake falling from the sky that I will never feel. I need to feel something on my tongue other than lava and drops of emptiness.

I shrug my shoulders with instability engraved on my neck. I am filled with abandoned pauses, mouthful of spiders, and a head full of sermons. But I continue to seek for the shadow of my rain in the garden. I am invariably breathing in dissension and breathing out destructive tendencies. I am covered with secrecy sewn to my sensitive skin. But I continue to seek the outline of my rain in the garden.

As my presence started to fade, I found a delicate flower in the garden. Never have I felt the comfort of a gentle hand. Never have I witnessed unimaginable compassion. Never have I clutched on to words that reverberated. Never have I received unquestionable affection and kindness. Never could I see myself bloom in an oasis where I can't feel the sun.

MOUNTAIN BAPTISM
by Susan Mason Scott

for Caleb

Might be a mountain, she muses, staring at the red map above the bridge of my firstborn's nose. Her East Tennessee lilt and stitch bear a heritage not even her beloved could claim. It remains hers to affirm. A birthright in rows of tomatoes, carrots, lettuce, yellow onions, and red potatoes.

With my baby swathed in her stained apron smelling of fresh game and salt, she explains how some things grow from seed and others need help from cousins—how a garden abides. Then she lifts her eyes and my son to the unfolding trails of pine, scarlet oak, coal's black smoke, distant wisps measured in crows fly, and a smile so wide it wrinkles her every hard road. Her face like a bulldog, eyes, deep-set, divine a cross in motes of filtered light, the intersection of wood splintered and nails staked like fingers in Appalachian soil.

Her palm, a wizened cup, scoops a handful of peat and manure, holds it to his nose pink and pinched as a pig's snout, smears it across his forehead. His newborn blues wide as nickels, my womb still fat with his impression, she attaches him to my swollen breast to eat the vegetables she nurtured, and says, *lick his forehead, three times a day,* as if a prescription for gout or ache.

Last of Colorado's evening hugging the Front Range, my oldest son, twenty-seven, and his dog sit by my side. He recounts stories of his younger brother, Sam, born to that same Southern mountain, but gone now. I trace the fading birthmark, hear a familiar accent. *Might be,* I answer, notes of dust on my tongue.

JACKKNIFE CAFÉ
by Braeden Michaels

11:32am, situated on the corner of James Madison Boulevard and Whitman Street. I am sipping emptiness on the rocks in the scowling part of town, Jackknife Cafe. I'm sulking in the chestnut-colored booth throwing darts at the bombastic God I use to love. I continue to taste the kisses of my skeptical past and shake hands with the skeleton of my future. I raise my clenched fist, "Hey brother, can you pour me another? If it's not any trouble, make it a double."

A Marylin Chambers look-alike tapped me on the shoulders with an indecent proposal. I shook my head with a chuckle and a sleazy grin. "This isn't a joke; I can only pay by the minutes or the number of strokes." She disappeared like a magician with the smell of her perfume turning into an aphrodisiac. I swallow loneliness like an amber ale. Isolation is my best friend without a voice. I tend to make a midnight rendezvous with yours truly but my left-hand shouts, "I'm quite overzealous" and the right-hand whimpers "I'm quite jealous." I only tend to acquire sparks with jumper cables.

Between noontide and the teardrops of the moon, the carnival weaved in and out of the cavern. The hooligans are tapdancing next to the jukebox, the husbands are window shopping, the cutthroat whistle stoppers are juggling negotiations and plastic speeches. The jamboree was full of exaggeration, plagiarism, copycats, and Satan's storytellers. I could hear them drinking the tears more than the alcohol.

2:35pm, the regulars and bystanders strolled in with folktales dripping grief. Cigarette smoke reeked of melancholy and satire. The ambiance was filled with extravagant bar tabs, sobbing cliffhangers, romantic comedies with the mourning saxophone playing in your left ear. If you listen closely, the excuses and irritation can be heard in your right ear. A pint of desolation will taste sweet, and a shot of despair will run down your throat faster than a horse at the Kentucky derby. It is a relief and a head scratcher that we call happy hour.

5:45pm, the eyes are dry, and my stomach grumbles. The gin mill is as empty as my crooning soul. I can never make out the lyrics, but I get goosebumps when I hear the sorrowful piano. Harper Guthrie struts in with his graveyard black t-shirt with the phrase "You can get this body for $19.95 for one hour, but if you act now, I will make you as happy as a sunflower" printed on the front. Harper is jammed with acidic antidotes but will sell you antidepressants, antibiotics, and antisemitism. He talks with his wandering hands and pleads innocent until proven guilty. He will boast about his latest purchases, meaningless job titles, and the abundant cash flow problem. He serenades the audience that he drinks to happiness. Unfortunately, he's been charged with terrible humor and convicted of lying to himself.

7:15pm, Jackson Bryant fumbles in with his auburn acoustic guitar. He glances at the minimal crowd from the undersized stage and begins to strum. Out comes a raspy but a smooth sound "You can find me in the dark trying to grip the wind, you can find me feeling lost not knowing where to begin, you can shout from the depths of your lungs, you can point your fingers at me and forget the person you've become." Heads turn and faces become pale as if they see a reflection of themselves. The song ends with the spectators clapping their hands rapidly and shouting out their name. He continued to play his set as the crowd was quite allured by his presence.

As the night began to fade, the exchange had less of a bounce. Solitude was a fog prancing in front of our bloodshot pupils. I wrote "Goodbye, Goodnight" on a vanilla napkin and handed it to the gargoyle next to me. It was time for me to face the chorus in a song I didn't want to play. Thirty-five years ago on this melodic day, I married a ballerina that is still spinning on her tip toes of my crippled heart. The King of kings took my queen away. She was plagued with a disease that had no cure. I'm done praying to a God that doesn't listen. All I know how to do is to fill up my glass with destitution to try to take away the overwhelming misery.

NIGHT WANDERINGS
by K.S. Dearsley

Hauled from sleep by the dog, I wander outside to see the world dreaming under the winter stars. The moonlight is bright enough to cast shadows. I am not afraid of the night. I welcome the peace where I can hide from the harsh scrutiny of daylight where others are noisy in their need to prove they exist, and judge without seeing more than the surface.

I stand under the sable field strewn with stars searching for the few shapes I know– constellations and nebulae passing in a great wheel. Is it the world or the sky that turns? Gaze at it and see the things that matter.

Darkness brings other senses into play, revealing scents and sounds never noticed in the day. The snuffling of small animals sounds like dragons or bears going about their business unconcerned that I am there, sharing the communion of nocturnal wanderers' wonderings the world over.

My thoughts stray, trying to join the winking dots. I consider the phases of the moon, predictable only to sailors and astrologers. They faze me, so the moon arrives as a surprise guest with an 'Oh!' shaped mouth as if it is as startled as I, wherever it appears. A lone bird–maybe a blackbird or a robin, perhaps a wren–sings of love and loneliness while the day is still abed. Each note rises and becomes another star until the sky trails songs behind it.

I remember other nights when clouds scudded across the moon, their rims frilled with silver as they hid its face. They wiped out the stars as if an overzealous cleaner swept them out with a giant duster swiped across the indigo backdrop. Or driving through a summer night with the full moon plating the barley fields, and turning hedgerows to black ribbons.

It is cold, but I forget to shiver while the dog sniffs the moon on frosty grass that is sparkling diamond-adorned. The sky ought to be empty with so many of its stars fallen to earth, not crowded with constellations, sharp and clear as insect stings. The longer I stare, the more of them I see, and the night feels warm in their company. Unable to touch or move closer, they move in strict procession, without hierarchy. It is reassuring to know they are always there, processing in their allotted order, even if I don't know what it is.

Generation upon generation has stood, as I stand, whispering secret wishes, wondering where it all begins and where it ends. How insignificant an individual is–our turn will come and go and be forgotten; what we wished for, loved or fought against. The frantic day tempts us to deny our fears of blinking out without the world pausing to sigh. Is a lone star more valued than a galaxy? Am I a single point of light or an essential part of a constellation? How do we know our place in the sky unless there are other stars to be near or far from?

I notice two more luminous circles of light, twin moons reflected in the dog's eyes looking up at me. She doesn't know either. I take her back indoors to sleep on it.

MR. HANDSOME
by Anne Marie Wells

We've taken to calling him Mr. Handsome / or just Mister / or just Baby / He's taken / over our lives / with times and amounts he has eaten / Times and amounts he has pooped / Times and amounts he has slept / Each time / he does something brand new / or we do something brand new / say something brand new / *Let me wipe the breast milk out of your neck rolls for you / Mr. Handsome*

I've taken / to imagining other mothers / in my town / then in my country / then the world / Are they stalking their child / as they sleep in the almost dark / Do they feel for their baby / 's ribs searching for their baby / 's breath over and over and over again / Do they weep / when their babies don't nurse and their breasts ache as if wrapped in rubber bands / Do their babies not nurse / Do their breasts ache as if wrapped in rubber bands

Mr. Handsome came eight days early / My water broke three minutes after midnight / I woke to my pajamas sticking wet to my thighs / Eighteen hours later nurses shouted at me to push / and the epidural didn't take / and my labia split open / and then my clitoris / and I begged / for help / as if begging / for death / as my vulva stretched to impossible thinness to release his impossible skull

I was beautiful once / my mother used to say / And we'd say / *You're still beautiful, Mom* / And she'd smile at us to say / thank you / And now I feel that smile on myself when my husband refers to me as Mrs. Beautiful

Mr. Handsome wraps his tiny arms / around my neck / places his impossible skull on my collar bone / I kiss the side of his face as he chews on his fist / I can't help but bite his little ear / Later / he will lie / in his bassinet and I will reach / for him in the night over / and over / and over again / I will sleep / not sleep / in the same nursing bra and spandex shorts I slept / didn't sleep / in last night / the same ones I wore all day / and will wear tomorrow / This time / maybe I will shower first / before bed / Or maybe / brush my teeth / Maybe I won't weigh myself

WHERE TO PUT HENRY
by Shoshauna Shy

Crafting the obituary
for their widowed mother
in her final days,
the eldest daughter omits
mention of Henry, the gent
whom their mother accompanied
everywhere, and who passed
away the week before.
But the youngest son, who shot
pool with Henry on Sunday
afternoons in the community room,
insists Henry should be included.
The eldest son winces.
Sides with sister.
No way.
The youngest daughter sides
with younger brother; thinks
it's OK as long as the sentence
with Henry's name doesn't touch
the sentence that mentions Dad.
The middle daughter suggests tagging
Henry on at the end of the paragraph
listing great-grandchildren where it
won't stick out.

The youngest son says they could
call Henry her "boyfriend"
but somebody who's 90+ is many miles
from boyhood, so how about
"subsequent suitor"?
The middle son says nobody uses
"suitor" in this century, and besides,
Henry was not that either.
page 2 (no stanza break)

This makes the middle daughter blurt
did you not know Henry proposed
to Mom on her 97th birthday?
All jaws drop.
The eldest son insists Henry was simply
the neighbor.
The youngest shakes his head. Claims
he was more like "beloved companion."
The middle daughter points out
they can't say beloved; they mention Dad
and don't call *him* that.

The middle son says I know what
I can call him.
The eldest daughter says let's drop it,
OK? Mom won't know either way
and *The Aurora Sun Times* charges
by the inch.

She goes down the hall to check
on their mother in the far bedroom,
finds her fast asleep.
The framed 8x10 of a jovial Henry
in dapper cap and parka, once
positioned on her nightstand,
is folded to her breast with both hands.
Eyes burning, the daughter returns
to her sibs. Hearing her footfall,
they lift expectant faces.

Henry gets his own paragraph,
she announces.

FIRST SNOWFALL
by P.T. McAllister

When the first snow falls, it clears the dirt from the atmosphere. That's what my grandmother used to say.

'Picks it up on the way down. Filters the air, so it does.' She'd be up first thing, rubbing half a lemon on our windows to prevent condensation, reminding us to, 'Never eat snow until at least the second day.'

We'd smile, mouthing her warnings to each other behind her back as we pulled on our warm waterproofs and ran from the cottage she raised us in.

'And even then,' she'd shout after us from a gleaming Crittall window, 'you need to make sure you don't scoop too deep.'

It's funny. I don't remember any of us eating snow. Not ever. So perhaps her advice had the desired effect.

As I trudge from the cottage now, rugged vegetation skirting the dunes is weighted with a cool frosting that mirrors crashing waves and a growing band of gold assures me the tide is on its way out. The beach offers a direct route into town, much quicker than the cliff trail, so I should still make the last post.

'Never forage bladderwrack from the beach once the tide has turned.' Another questionable gem that makes me laugh to myself as I notice the seaweed shrivelling on the shoreline.

When she died, things changed quickly. It stopped snowing each winter. The familiar smell in the cottage of baking, mingled with her perfume and a touch of damp faded fast, changed. Even the air felt different – cooler, bitter somehow. I cleared her jewellery from the windowsill in a fit of desire to do something, anything; wrongly thought that hiding reminders of her would help us get through. I hadn't considered how the light used to catch her costume jewels and splay colours over the walls, making it feel like home. Later, I couldn't remember how it was arranged and didn't want to put it back wrong. It felt too painful to try. The others noticed too. Elizabeth cried in her bed each night for months, so I sang to Joel as I rocked him to sleep, hoping he wouldn't hear her through the walls.

When the priest came to say we were being split up – me bound for an aunt in America, Elizabeth to the workhouse and Joel to the orphanage – I told him no. He laughed.

'I promised to keep everyone together: promised our mother, then later our grandmother.'

'How can a sixteen-year-old support two young 'uns?' he'd sneered.

'Hopefully with your help,' I replied. We never saw him again.

I kept my twice-made promise. Now, as I think of Elizabeth finishing her nursing training, Joel starting at Trinity and this signed deed in my hand, I wonder where the years went – where I was all that time.

Maybe the new house will birth memories of its own. Maybe I just needed a fall of snow. And maybe it doesn't matter which way the jewellery goes up in the new window.

ON COLLAGIC MEMORIES
by Donna Myers

My father keeps telling me that in time, I'll forget most of the things that happened when I was 16. Maybe. But for now I still remember–

Waking up in the recovery room, blinking to evaporate the blur, thinking—*this is just like on TV*. Then immediately puking, thinking—*this part isn't like on TV.*

My grandparents presenting me with one of my late great grandma's board games while in the ICU. Wondering if that meant I'd have to play it right then, because I really didn't feel good, but did appreciate it, and didn't want to hurt their feelings.

Screaming in pain while rolled onto a metal cartridge to check for pneumonia. The mint green curtains surrounding my cubicle. Watching my heart rate and blood pressure digitally displayed on the monitor. Seeing if I could will my heart rate to change. Being able to and wondering if that made me special. Watching that other monitor with the green lines and wondering what they stood for. The incessant beeping. The guy next to me who'd broken his back in a motorcycle accident but was drunk and kept trying to get up to go to the bathroom.

The frustrated nurse who couldn't get my IV in but kept trying. The other nurse who came to help and refused to use any anesthetic. A small argument ensuing between the two. Silently siding with the one who wanted to use the anesthetic and deciding that the other one didn't know what she was talking about and was just mean. The mean one starting the IV in one try, using the underside of my wrist instead of the crook of my arm.

Playing with my surgical drain, amazed that the little circular see-thru pack was actually filled with my own blood. *Hema-vac.* Just—vacuums up the extra blood from inside you. Holding it in my palm, rolling it back and forth, mesmerized by the crimson ebb and flow.

A nurse motioning to the bag attached to my catheter, exclaiming "You pee like a racehorse!" Wondering why a racehorse peed more than a non-racehorse.

My mom sleeping in the orange chair beside my bed almost every night. Feigning sleep one evening as she cupped my hand in both of her own, drawing the ensemble to her lips and gently rocking, softly repeating, her voice quivering like a scream forced to whisper, "I wish it were me, I wish it were me."

My dad crying. And saying he loves me. Once. But that was enough.

Wondering if anyone was going to come change my IV bag when the alarm went off, and wondering what would happen if nobody did. Wondering if that lady who came in and turned off the alarm and then left without doing anything except having pushed a button to turn off the alarm, really knew what she was doing or was just trying to get rid of that damn alarm. Wondering if it's true that you die a painful death if an air bubble gets in your line, what it would feel like, and how an air bubble might get in your line in the first place.

Thinking how much it would hurt to actually pull out my IV in a fit of rage like I'd seen in movies. Wondering what angle would be best if I chose to do so. Thinking how stupid it would be because then it'd have to be put back in and the area would be really sore from having pulled it out.

The marvel in knowing there was a tube sticking out of my neck, running directly into my aorta, delivering morphine from the PCI pump. The satisfaction of having a little half-inch scar there as a reminder. The satisfaction of having a little white circular scar on my wrist. The eight-inch scars on my stomach and back, and knowing that my back is really three scars in one. The way the one on my stomach curves around my belly button and is still pink, like an earthworm dangling from an invisible line.

The sting of having staples removed that the skin has started growing around because they've been in too long. The sting of having staples removed by someone who is learning how to remove staples. Practicing patience because everyone needs someone to practice on.

The burning in my feet. The boredom. Personal injury attorney ads. The Summer Olympics. The discoveries at Jeffrey Dahmer's house on the morning, afternoon, evening, and late-night news.

The sting of a butterfly needle. The stickiness of paper tape. Senekot, valium, morphine, methadone, flexeril, composine, cipro, pepto through a nasal tube.

Dreaming I could fly and was floating cross-legged as the world whirred by in a slur of vibrant color; then slamming into a brick wall but it not hurting at all—back first, sliding down but not landing, suddenly standing.

Standing in the waiting room at the photography studio supported by a walker, clad in my bright peach body cast, waiting to have my senior pictures taken. Reclaiming a sliver of empowerment by staring back at the people staring at me until they looked away.

The game my little nephews played with my cast by putting their fingers in the ventilation holes, pulling them back out again, giggling "Ding dong!" then unleashing that kid laughter that refuses to be muted by sick-person etiquette. Wearing the body cast to school and wanting someone to unsuspectingly punch me in the stomach.

An acquaintance I hadn't seen since middle school approaching my family in a local restaurant and asking how I was. Me answering with a canned "fine" and her touching my arm and saying "No—really. I heard you had cancer and I thought to myself 'How horrible. She's the nicest girl I've ever met.'"

Learning a brilliant student had been in a car accident while I was gone. She'd suffered a brain injury and returned to school even more changed than I.

Thinking: *Give me an injury like mine over one like hers any day.*

HEBREW CHILDREN
VS. PHILISTINE GIANTS
by Robert B. Robeson

"And David...took thence a stone, and slang it, and smote the Philistine
in his forehead, that the stone sunk into his forehead, and he fell upon
his face to the earth."--1 Samuel 17:49, KJV.

This cataclysmic contest began in a remote Middle East valley a long time ago and everyone got in free. The two teams faced each other on either side of the ball field. It featured the Hebrew Children vs. the Philistine Giants. This would be a baseball game of grit and guts that would rewrite the record books. It was an unparalleled confrontation. A winner-take-all-event that would be written about by scribes for thousands of years.

The Philistine's franchise player was named Goliath, a proven All-Star standing over nine feet tall, who'd been playing the game for a long time. A champion of champions. Their super slugger. A veritable combined "Sultan of Swat," "Casey at the Bat," and the "Splendid Splinter" clumped into one mighty action figure for the ages.

The Hebrew Children had a brash young hurler, a rookie straight from the boondocks near Bethlehem directly to the big leagues. He was a phenomenon whose cannon for an arm could sling that old "stone" with the power of a tornado. Some of David's teammates told him Goliath was too big and intimidating to rely only on his "heater." But he replied, "Hey, this dude's so big, how can I possibly miss his strike zone? Let no man's heart fail because of this braggart. I intend to go out and cut him down to size."

Twice a day, for forty days before this ultimate confrontation, Goliath stood in the outfield humiliating the Hebrews in front of David's fellow teammates. He cursed and razzed an undersized David who ultimately came out to face him. "Am I a dog that thou comest to me?" David heard Goliath talking this smack over and over, and he'd finally had enough of it. Intending not to take this verbal abuse any longer, David stood on the mound, faced Goliath, and shouted back, "This day...I will smite thee with my best pitch and take thine head from thee. I think thine mouth is bigger than thine brain" It was like Ali calling out Liston centuries later.

Observers thought these were unusual fighting words for a rookie gunslinger with a whip-like windup who'd only competed previously against the Lions and Bears with his pitching magic on his family's practice field near Bethlehem. That's where he'd previously been tending his father's flock of sheep. It had been his responsibility to ensure that these animals kept the infield and outfield grass trimmed.

No umpires had arrived yet so there wasn't any threat either of them would face immediate ejection for their physical threats.

Goliath paced back and forth with a batting helmet on his head made of brass (before brass became a banned substance by the league's commissioner). His uniform was made of mail that tended to slow him down a bit on the base paths, but he was such a consistent home run hitter he didn't have to run that hard. He also had brass coverings on his legs, being a big-time catcher, and a brass chest protector that foul balls bounced off.

Teammates on both sides shouted encouragement and were anxious for the competition to begin.

Behind David, Hebrew chatter predicted that if he blew away this prodigious clean-up hitter he'd probably be rewarded with a hefty new contract by Jehovah, the Hebrew Children's owner.

Goliath strode from the outfield to home plate dragging his mighty wooden staff behind him. As the Hebrew players took their positions, Goliath took a few practice swings making a mini-tornado from the dust on the base paths. That's when David could be heard informing his infielders, "Don't sweat this over-hyped, uncircumcised, heathen home run hitter. I'll introduce myself by playing him a little 'chin music.'"

David turned and faced Goliath. The giant's staff he continued to wave was able to cover the entire home plate area and also reach halfway down either base path. What Goliath hadn't been warned about, by his team's scouts, was that David had a slingshot for an arm and could hurl that ol' rock over 100 mph. That was unheard of velocity in those days.

David's first and only pitch was a rocket shot that "beaned" that biblical, big-mouthed behemoth in the center of his forehead; an area his helmet failed to cover. Smack! Down! There it was! Flat on his over-sized face! One zinger and David became the ultimate Hebrew hero. It was the biggest win of the season for the Hebrew Children. That's when the umpires called the game, because the rest of the Giants had run from the field of play in headlong panic. Their big gun had just been gunned down by a rookie hurler.

There wasn't any need to worry about concussion protocol at that moment because emergency medical personnel couldn't find a pulse for this Giant. It took nearly the entire Hebrew team to cart Goliath's carcass off the playing field. David's rocket shot was embedded so far into his forehead that it remained permanently mounted there when he was buried.

After David "killed it" with his premier pitching performance against the league's biggest and toughest opponent, nobody in the commissioner's office had the nerve to fine or suspend him for any length of time. (He'd later enter politics and be chosen King of Israel, with the reward of being surrounded by a large retinue of wives and concubine groupies.)

Competitors in today's 21st century wouldn't have stood a chance against David or a team like the Hebrew Children. That diminutive pitching stud didn't mess around and always played for keeps. Whenever he talked about "cutting a head," back then, he wasn't referring to moving in front of someone. And David's harp version of the Hebrew National Anthem before games would often bring home town fans to tears.

WE HAVE CHICKENS IN OUR BACKYARD
by Vidyaroopini Nair

We have chickens in our backyard!
It's the first thing anyone learns
When they step into our home,
Sipping masala chai,
Munching on homemade fruitcake,
The conversation often interrupted
By the distant call of our feathery friends.

We have chickens in our backyard,
I tell my friends when they visit,
Watching for the twitch of facial muscles—
An upturned smile,
Or a swift raise of the eyebrows,
Disbelief or amusement,
At the randomness of it all.

We have chickens in our backyard,
A remnant of Singapore's kampung past,
I posit, pretending to sound smart,
Though it's not quite accurate.
For starters, they're wild fowls—
Acha's degree in ecology is of some value, it seems
And they showed up one day,
Years after we moved in,
Perhaps thanks to our neighbour's liberated pets,
Now the culprits of this feathery invasion. *Patient Zero?*

We have chickens in our backyard.
"It must be nice!"
Is usually the response,
Which triggers Amma's well-worn tirade,
About how they mess up the flowerbeds,
Shit everywhere, crow at 4 a.m.,
You know...typical wild beast behaviour,
When new condominiums encroach their land.
"If this were America," she sighs,
"Acha would have a shotgun by now."

We have chickens in our backyard.
My university friends from the UK
Are equally surprised,
Perhaps expecting *Crazy Rich Asians*
To be more than just a movie.
What about the casinos and infinity pools?

We have chickens in our backyard
And cats from Pasir Ris Park greet me loudly,

Their glossy eyes begging to be catnapped.
Neighbours hand me homemade pineapple tarts,
Even when it's not Chinese New Year.
The mist of sandalwood incense
Fills the air at the edge of dusk...
The shrill of our pooja bell follows,
And I know I'm home again.

BEANS FOR THOUGHT
by J.R. Woods

The doctor actually used the word Zombie when describing the side effects
and it was at that exact moment my parents decided
that I needn't be medicated after all...
They told me to chew coffee beans
because caffeine should have the opposite effect
than it does on a normal boy
but the problem with that is coffee tastes worse than dirt
unless the flavor is concealed by chocolate
but I wasn't allowed to have sugar because sugar made me hyper
and the more hyper I became the faster my mind would race
until it was impossible to communicate the endless stream of thought and soon I was
six branches high on a tree roughly adjacent to the track I was supposed to be following
and rarely could I find my way back to the roots without chopping down the evergreen
to make the sleepers for the rail...
and in the event I could navigate that incomprehensible yard
the words would pour forth from my mouth
disordered and incomplete—unorganized an unintelligible
stuttering and stumbling over each other until I froze.......................................
for much longer than was socially acceptable and sometimes so long that people would
assume that I was done and interject in an attempt to finish my convoluted thoughts
because clearly I was incapable of communicating them myself
but really I despised the taste of the beans
and it wasn't long before I refused to consume them at all
and I was resigned to eat my words instead...
which proved an impossible task...

ONE MORE THING
by Jessica Natasha Lawrence

I hold my dog's ears between my fingers, rub them gently, tell her she's in every memory. A month before she dies, I tell you...*if I lose one more thing, I will completely cease to function.*

I hit balloons off U-Haul boxes. I know how to make a fist so I can punch the bathroom tile without breaking my knuckles. The nail polish under my sink has separated into color and water, but it transforms into paint when I shake it, and that's what I'm asking you to do to me.

Maskless people cough in the grocery store while healthy people talk about COVID in the past tense. You say, "I'm so sorry," and I'm ten years old, biting into a soft cookie or swinging at the park near my house. I used to crawl under trees and pretend to be a cat and now I crawl under words and pretend to be a poet.

My life fits in the tip of a pencil and it's breaking. You'll brush my complaints off your sweater and find them in your car's center console for months, and I'll bruise my shoulders on your favorite books and good advice. You don't know that I know it's your birthday / I don't know if you know it's mine. Please reply.

I add a coat of pink glitter to my nails and fantasize about you telling me what meds you're on. I'll remember that sparkle months after it's chipped away, when my dog's heavy panting scores my nightmares, and I think of that sweaty, desperate email. *If I lose one more thing I will completely cease to function.*

SILENT ASSASSIN
by Brady Kent

We arrive and continue where we left off,
best friends for life and probably beyond
Now in our sixties, how did that happen?
But everyone can still recall and stargaze

Some are fallen and missing which seems
unbelievable, unfair and unbalanced
A silent assassin is amongst us, his aim to
conqueror us all, in tears of blood

Bear hugs and chatting, doing what
really makes us happy, banishing
any negative thought of others,
despite aches, tired legs and minds

Some need help to regain their balance
from a standing start, it's a mismatch
But let the games begin, with victory to
the bravest, thriving on the challenge

Skilled, mischievous, clever or none of the
above, it matters not, we are together,
laughing like ailing, hopeful artful dodgers,
in an earthly, gentle, magical walled garden

LEAP DAY AND THE SUMMER SUN
by Svetlana Litvinchuk

Among all the winter days, my favorites are the ones on which the sunlight sliding past me warms my hips. Even in January, the sun is powerful enough to bake the skin, to singe the damp retinas. Though I keep watching, my mind wandering snowblind praying not to fall off the mountain and though this forest has always been a time-forgotten island, what becomes of winter when summer refuses to take its leave of us? There are ominous sign this year that the winter is a culmination instead of the expected hibernating ebb. That summer isn't going anywhere. Between La Nina and the calendar's decadent addition of a Leap Day, there will be extra of my favorite kinds of days, but they will be mercilessly plucked from elsewhere in the year. No freezing nights ahead means no apples to gather in our baskets this October. Today's joy seems always to somehow borrow from tomorrow's happiness. This unseasonable warmth yet another finite resource borrowed from somewhere else. With this new future getting sparser and less, my love, what will we do with our time instead— with this extra day and all the ones of harvest? What will we gather into our baskets as we count the imponderable things? What joys will go extinct before our daughter's age can understand?

BYWATER BAY
by Deborrah Corr

Lucky there was a boat for crossing the bay,
a battered yellow rowboat you had to carry
down a rocky beach into freezing water
wishing the tide was high because you had
nine more trips back up to the car
and down that beach again with water jugs,
canvas clothing bags, banged-up cooler,
sleeping bags, and kids.

Lucky to find life jackets, two of them,
dirty and smelling of mold, to buckle
on the kids and perch them on the center plank.
One adult pushed off the boat, the other rowed,
aiming for the one smooth stretch of beach
on the other rocky shore, where the giant log
served as shelf for the tubs, jugs, bags, and kids
you carried up this beach.

Lucky the winter storms hadn't washed away
the wooden steps that rose up the bank
and into the woods and lucky the tree
fallen over the trail was easy to climb around.
Other fall-downs, covered now in ferns and moss,
like green walls bordered the path to the cabin
with the sagging roof there at the base of Douglas
firs so tall their tops were only visible
with an uncomfortable backward bend.

Lucky, in the dripping wet, to get a fire started
in the pit, cook oysters pried from rocks
at low tide, rocks that twisted your ankles
and made you wish you'd brought the other shoes.

Lucky to remember those days, the glint of sun
on wet leaves, pockets heavy with collected stones,
smell of smoke in the morning air, the four of you,
shoulders touching, pushing close to the fire's warmth,
the smoke lifting away to be lost in the highest branches.

A PICTURE OF THE LONDON DREAM
by Jonathan Chibuike Ukah

She was singing in the park,
eating her cake and having it
capped with ice, white cream and foam,
munching a bar of black chocolate,
smiling at everyone, in love,
though she didn't know what she loved.
Perhaps it was the iconic moments she had,
perched on the top of the Sightseeing Bus,
screening street air with her eyes closed;
perched on the plinth, overlooking the world
through the prism of the paradise of circuses;
perhaps the admiration on the faces of her listeners;
the air, though taut and icy,
cleansed the tears from her eyes;
the peace or silence around her,
despite the crowd watching her;
the birds that stopped and flew on;
the hums of the Thames nearby;
the expectation of chicken and chips,
white, flawless steak with brown bread;
or perhaps the minimal powder on her face.

After that, the miracle happened,
and she was not among the five wise virgins;
nor was she with the foolish ones;
when a surprise falling of spears from the oak tree,
took her body out and left her soul,
which had been still and quiet
all through the long hours of songs.
She saw the knives flying towards her,
and retreat was not among the hymns
which her genius had composed.
Her mouth parted, and her scream was muffled
and she learned how to die without practice.
There was a partition in her throat,
between what was and what was to come
but they never came together.
Instead, she found no inherent solace
in the similarity between dreams and nightmares,
and decided to die so that she could live
many, many years to come.

RESTORATION
by Colm O'Shea

first day of holidays me and the lads want to stomp around the haunted farmhouse but the old fart goes *foreigners restoring the place feck off out of it* yeahyeahyeah but it was all buildingsite signs and hardhatsmustbeworn *our* haunted farmhouse with the rotting piano flat on its back like a granny cant get up cant believe it a brand new door staring us in the face gleaming lock look found a gun found a glue gun just lying there in the sunshine easy as you like put that nozzle to the lock shoot the polymer jism right in the rape of the lock POP it goes sheep in the fields watch on helpless we kick the door in swarm the whole tribe of us through the farmhouse *our*house was a free-for-all at the start putting nails through the workmens cheap radio repainting surfaces with our opinions ripping wiring from walls sledging the sinks tiles cupboards gluing rubble to rubble burning carpet samples but the bathtub took teamwork twelve pairs of skinny arms straining to haul that big porcelain bastard along the upstairs landing to the edge then a good shove and the giant white dick crashes down through the body of the building cracking the staircase snapping the banister like twig that huge dust cloud better than scoring a goal better than scoring off ciara nelligan then madness comes fast and grunty like ciara nelligan hahahaha scarper skittering free to the outside sunshine holiday garden all peels of laughter I turn an afterthought to hurl a breezeblock through the kitchen window parting kiss for the lovely lady all tarted up she looks the same on the outside as before like nothings happened like weve never been inside her and made our mark shes been good to us give that kissing block a good hurl now heft   and   *hurl*

sucking sound	punctured vacuum	like inhalation
then shattering	stark as the first thunderclap	waking us to vivid glass rain

DARK GLEN
by Joyce Frohn

The arched darkness of trees along the road should have told me something, but I couldn't stop thinking that this was regrowth. The original vegetation was oak opening. I appreciate landscapes; even the ones scarred by man. I expected no more than meadows and deep woods having the shadow of their previous life lurking like a ghost at the feast. But instead, there were rock cliffs and layers of beauty. The thousand greens of moss, liverworts and lichen. The tree roots draped over rock, seeking a way in. The cross and initials carved into a great boulder. Speaking tales of unknown and unknowable martyrdoms. Concealed behind the life-green of all the plants was the old tale of the rocks. It took my eyes to see the layers of eroded beach stone pressed between layers of sand into the leaves of the book of time. This was what I had been looking for; something old enough and great enough that Human Time was but an eyeblink in its life. There is comfort in things like this. To know that when my bones are lime streaks in wet soil; this place will yet stand.

THE BLISS OF A GLITTERING HORIZON
by Rebel Brown

He was putting his small boat away
under the porch, and moving a few
of the logs from the woodpile
when a ground hornet flew into the tender
spot between his middle and index finger
jammed its barb, left him breathless

Then four more flew up, then 100
stung his elbow, forearm, bicep
he turned and ran, and hollered
slammed the door to the garage
looked at his stings, took a breath
leaned up against the lawn mower

A dizzy little bliss of a glittering horizon
came around him then, shimmering air
ring of sixteen or seventeen tiny bells
when he breathed it in, he winced, waited
then grinned to himself, at this surprise
that was pain first, but then something else

Poetry

FROM THE EDITORS: *Impossible not to be devastating and have this sheering poem affect you deeply. Writing on the death of one's child, is a near impossible feat. To do so in a way that proffers that experience to a reader without drowning them, but with the sincerity of that death, is equally impossible. Lind writes simply, beautifully, acknowledging a loss that is irreparable. This is why we write poetry; this is why we should read poetry. This is the life we may try to pretend does not occur, but it does, and a poet is the lighthouse for words to come, unsafe to shore. -CLD*

YEAR ONE
by Laurinda Lind

On Easter morning I fed
my seventeen-year-old son's
funeral cake to the yard crows.
We heard they were starving,
in this spring that came
and then uncame,
the same way my son and
reportedly Jesus did.

New snow smothered the green grass
and the crocuses, and iced
the backdoor steps
and ate down into cracked concrete.
The stones someone hauled here
a century and a half ago
lay flat and still under the slush.
He is gone and I can't help it.

The crows watched, or didn't,
from all our trees. The branches
went black with them,
the sky was full but waiting.
He is so brilliantly gone.
Spring is alive, over and over.
It just can't be alive enough.

Originally published in *Paterson Literary Review*

FROM THE EDITORS: *Such gorgeous classical language, it transcends genre again and again. This writer is a poet in all ways, his very way of existing is poetry, you can see this throughout the glorious stanzas he produces as naturally as if breathing. It's been a long time since I have read poetry that evokes such high regard and leaves so much beauty. I want to quote line after line rather than say anything myself, such is his art. "to that pale fire dancing in our dark-riven eyes. / Unscrolling there / Was the story of man." -CLD*

WE ENTERED STONE'S DOMINION
by Joseph William Vass

Descending through time.
      The unchinked seams of stacked rocks.
Each coiled-spring tremor of an age I had never inhabited
      but somehow still knew.
When long ago we left the oceans and walked
      the lifting land outside.
But somehow we kept the tide-worn sea
      remembered within our bodies.
Then one day we the last men
      discovered the first.
With hammers and chisels, klieg lights glaring
      hard against the curious dark
We entered stone's dominion. Where flint-chipped sparks
      first rose, lightning born
With the promise of fire. And hands worn hard
      like a prayer reaching out
To that pale fire dancing in our dark-riven eyes.
      Unscrolling there
Was the story of man.

          * * * * * *

Together we crawled unbidden
      into a darker dark.
Where cloddish and earthbound we saw
      the prodigal vision of beasts
Prancing in the soundless wind-skirl
      upon a high wall. Stallion and stag
Their soft eyes touching
      the timeless reach of the infinite.
Their shyness a treasure. In the dark
      shadows they trembled with light
Wherever the cave walls breathed. Sweat gathered
      upon us as we worked
To remember their age long forgotten.
      When a bison was born by a hand
Spit-ochre blown
      on a stone-canvassed wall.

          * * * * * *

What breath we draw from stone is old.
      Within the deep-held

Memory of caves, the creator grasped for something
        beyond himself. From earth arisen
A hand upon a wall became
        my hand. The breath inside my body swelled and held
Like dragon fire. My startled mouth
        from out of me expelled
In oxide reds the fur-ruffed grace
        of aurocks and deer. A cave bear
Lumbered in his dusky charcoal coat. And even past
        the echoes of his snorts and chuffs
Eyes burnt umber, beneath the elegant
        horns of an elk.
On calcite walls their story written
        in the holy script of fire.
And then came man, the hunter
        who descended from the stars.

               * * * * * *

From the pale riven ghosts of deep rivers
        bathed in unassailable light
Our flesh incandescent turned.
        Shape-shifting gods becoming
Something more than ourselves.
        Memories on a wall up-floating
From the cold collective reaches
        of the cells' long remembering.
Our bodies were ghost-walking back
        to the age of ice and stone.
But for the animal hides
        of the first men, we stepped
Longingly into our nakedness
        a birth cry howling
To be born. Becoming beyond
        blood-thirst and hunger. Beyond time. Becoming
Whatever it is that we are.
        Some great beast stalking, roving beyond
The snarling plains of the Serengeti.
        Through a spoor trail leading
To the dreamed shades of ibex and lion.
        And then something found us
Weightless as love
        on the frail skin of breath
Beneath the down-soaring dead.
        The conjugate dance eternal
Between the hunter and prey.
        Found us willing
To hold on to something
        we still had to lose.

               * * * * * *

Marveling in the dark we stood
        facing our own blind hunger. Hoping to escape
The fair notice of time. We recognized

       that far border in the torch glow
As we low-huddled down
         into a deeper dark. And there they all saw
Seared upon the face of my wonder
         the dun smudge of ash
From a far-distant fire.

* * * * *

The voices in the cave had stilled.
         I turned back to find them
But they had already
         dissolved into light.

LUMINOUS
by Teresa K. Burleson

Night shrouds
The symmetry
Of winter branches.
Yet the veil is rent
By pulsating Light,
Primeval Light.
Through these pinholes
Shines the Unspeakable.
Nothing is hidden
From the Choreographer
Of these starry hosts.
Here is my Bethel.

First published in Startled by Nature 2020.

THE VARIOUS
by Matt Dennison

When I was quite young, our neighbors' daughter
was going to school to be a teacher and had learned
from her parents I spent many hours alone
in the woods. Eager to find out what questions
an eight-year-old boy might have regarding
the natural world, I was summoned to their house,
made to sit, offered a cookie and the opportunity
to ask any and all questions I might have
but I had none. I was the woods-the streams,
the river, the trees, the skulls, bones and fossils,
the earth breaking from tree roots exposed above
stream beds, all creatures under rock, in soil and air—
the soft-spined hellgrammite, the various suckers
and snails, catfish and bass and dinosaur gar
from another world-turtles snapping and boxed,
snakes of water and land, insects under bark
and on carcasses, the dried skins of discarded
fish in the weeds, hornets under downed limbs,
soils both sandy and clay-like, the slick clay itself
and snake grass and arrowheads and Civil War bullets
and rusty old beer cans so empty it hurt and bridges
of wood and concrete with bad words layered
and scraped into each and sand caves under trestles
where wild boys died for being wild boys and springs
from hillsides with water so cool and reaching my hand
into holes in the riverbank, praying for fight or shaking
hands with God at the tug of a fish and the struggle to
catch, to have and to hold small creatures and save them
in dark places, lift them in bright spaces and look into
their eyes to see if I could see myself staring back from heaven—
but I had no questions for the teacher-to-be and I did not care,
for I had small monsters in alcohol pill bottles, spread across
pinboards, staring from shelves, whispering from walls
and sleep talking in drawers who had already told me
everything I would ever need to know.

Published in *Soundings East*

SECRET CONVERSATIONS
by Tom Conlan

To avoid misunderstanding
I talk to animals
Many often reply

Reminded by the magnificence of the red-tailed hawk
perched on a cedar rail
overlooking this year's sweet corn patch
loaded with ears but spindly
the soil weakened by twenty years of growing vegetables

A sign, the grand bird, regal in browns and white
came in the morning as dawn embers shown
above hills hiding the eastern horizon

A tree frog with a cobbled voice
lives in a hanging flower basket beneath
the porch eave

Hummingbirds come to the flowers as often as to the feeder
and particularly enjoy fruits of trumpeter vines boldly orange
three times the size of the gentle hovering bird

The old yellow barn cat comes when I call
or when he pleases for a bit of food
or a firm rub until his sharp, killing claws stretch
setting a hook into my soft skin.
I fear I will react with anger at the pain

A garbled meow
A muted whistle
A call to the sky
A scream to the heavens
Simply a look into another being's eyes

And flowers
The smile of a young sunflower
orbiting her glow to glimpse the sun

Bright red roses contrast
with daisies at the foot of a scarecrow
Yes, I talk to flowers, too

Butterflies of many hues
flitter about
briefly landing upon bushes
sparkling with sprinkled natural groundwater
as if called by a spirit

Tone matters most
A friendly inflection
A scolding squint
Stop mid-step, watch
Sit silent, wait

I favor trees like silver maple saplings with
slender bodies dancing in the wind
Sugar maples in the prime of life
speak while oozing sap
not seeming to mind

In old age when mammoth limbs fall in the wind
gnarled beauty remains like the sparkle in the eyes
of a greying couple paired still in old age

Listen to white oaks strong and true
grown tall and broad from solid trunks
I am told roots buried deep
keep the secrets of life
while firm shapely limbs stretch
spread their story afar
A quest for continuing life

Green grasses grow cool and tall
beneath the foliage
thankful for the shade

I whistle to the songbirds
though chickadee and finch already know
the feeder is full of sunflower seeds

Our wild but gentle rescue mutt
watches over the farm environs
poised like a sphinx beneath a rusted sundial
while three does with two fawns
carelessly chew alfalfa a stone's throw away

Neither deer nor dog move
as I push open the wooden screen door
to join in the secret conversation

THE HOUSE UPON THE HILL
by H Peters

Upon the hill, sits a house
It is large, it is hungry.
What goes inside, stays forever
The lonely walls are crying.
An empty shell, it wants more.
The floorboards creak under foot
Doors and windows lock behind.
You'll stay awhile, won't you? Please?
The house is always grasping.

Upon the hill, the house cries.
Trees wither and die again,
Carpet and wallpaper rot,
The windows break and shatter.
Thresholds are too empty now.
Shouts are locked in, far away.
An edifice of lost love.
The house is always sobbing.

Upon the hill, the house loves
It is a monument of
What was lost, but not found
Toys and photographs- loved things
Gone, eaten away by time.
Wanted, needed things, devoured.
The house is always reaching.

Upon the hill, the house waits.
It is lonely, it does know.
It cannot stop, it needs more.
To be loved, to live again.
Why are you trying to leave?
Incisors and molars close
The house is always eating.

LINES FOR PAINTING ON GRAINS OF RICE HARVESTED IN STARDEW VALLEY

by Kait Quinn

You are the kind of person who buys
a blue hat from a mouse. Your arctic
boots, your cornflower bonnet. You look
like an eskimo. Every kiss nose to nose.

Where do they come from, the soily
worms waving like umber flags for your
attention? Here are three piles of ochre
clay. Here is a winter yam, bright and blinding
as lightning when it fingers the rods.

Your preservers are always pulsing. For every jar
of pearly powdermelon jam, five salmonberries
you can't help plucking, raspberry blushed and
skin staining, off the bushes.

Where gold ore disguised as stone once rested,
a laddered crater to center of the earth.

Summer is a prose poem, ending and beginning
all at once. We could stay hazy here forever.
We couldn't crave pumpkin and breeze so crisp
you could bite it more.

I cannot bring myself to donate the opal panned
from the south pond's stream of stars to the town's
Museum of Artifacts. All day I have turned it over
in my palm, seen your eyes in its moon shine,
rivers of amber.

Running to town, encased in a green drizzle.
A snow globe filled with moss.

The ground was ripe with blackberries.
I spent 10,000g on a bigger backpack so I
could carry all twelve home. I gift one to the
mountain man. I save the rest for cobbler.

I bring you an amethyst from the mines.

Please buy me a horse so I can get home
to you faster. I have everywhere to be
and nowhere at all.

SLEF PROTRIAT
by Alex Baskin

I lie on the earth—I practice falling. Whenever I visit my mother, she insists, "You've lost weight." But I am exactly the size of my body. I don't wear baggy clothes anymore. I don't need to make myself as big as the other boys. Every story my father tells boils down to, "They tried to screw me, but don't you worry I screwed them." When a stranger gives me the side-eye, I pat myself down, search for my crime. When water dives up from the sink and splashes me, I take it personally. If you ask me, "What do you want, Alex?" I will faint. In my apartment there are several Buddha statues. One's neck is shiny from re-gluing. Sunday is laundry day. I refuse to find meaning in the coronavirus. I regret telling my therapist how beautiful I find him. Francis Bacon says that to be a painter you must not be afraid of making a fool of yourself. I wake up tangled in pillows and sheets. Vulnerability is not an identity.   Don't worry, all of your popcorn kernels won't pop at once.

published in *Rock & Sling*

SWALLOWS ON THE PORCH
by Rachael Ikins

Squeaks,
voice of another screen
door-hinge. Bass/tenor you could
pick yours from a hundred screen-songs.

Fledglings,
mosquitoes out of thin air to feed,
bomb the German Shepherd, spearing
parents. Rowed yellow yawns.
Nest sculpted to barn beams
daubed mud.
Females plain blue, screen,
iridescent males
covering,

swallows on the wire just outside.
She asked her father why
one bird hopped on top of another
the spring she was six.

* * * * * *

A thirteen-year-old grown.
Between her legs strange
dampness below the knot
that tied her to her mother.

Beautiful English teacher.

* * * * * *

Dad, grilling steaks/burgers,
flipped a math project,
not getting in the last word,
mother—staccato aftermath
a squeaky hinge slapping.
Too many beers, glowing cigarette eyes,
arguments dripping through.

Setting sun eyes dinner's bones.
Dark green bamboo lowers lid.
Dreams around the card table
Lilac fragrant porch, daughter's cheeks
redden.

Every May, Dad screwed feathers
to the porch frame, stacked
like folded wings,
like princesses
waiting for a ceremony.

MEDITATION
by Jack Harness

I hear your voice under the drip of water,
It lets my mind wander to a more simple time,
One where my peace did not rely on meditation,
And you allowed my diet to include berries and butter.

I dwindle and linger here,
My ghost spins webs to fill up the hollow space around my desolate form,
As though I would not recognize what it is doing,
As though I would not notice it waiting for you—
But still, I let my mind wander.

My body is lifeless and stiff sitting on the cold cave floor,
It does not think of you anymore—it only wants to return,
The way my body only wants to mourn,
My fingers dance about my skin—

Listless, waiting for the nerves to return once more,
Something callous and cold in my body, allowing my bones to move,
It makes them stop and stare, my form becoming duller like the sun turning into the moon.
I sit and wait for you—

A dog without its master,
A flower without its water,
I will sit hungry and rest-less waiting for you;
I close my eyes to evade the silence.

Otherwise my eyes would eat the world whole,
I have sores in my throat just from saying your name,
And now I remember why I promised myself to always be alone:
I wait for you to come—

To see my state and tenderly wrap me up,
Let your fingers skim across my bones in attempt to fill the cracks with warmth,
And wrap my collarbone with Jasmine.
I chuckle to myself, just thinking about your reaction to my words.

Because you know better than anyone,
That once I've begun to speak in metaphors,
I have begun to lose myself.

THE SMALLER PICTURE
by Jonathan Chibuike Ukah

We wrap up this evening of songs
seeking cold, lucid memories,
seeking the lyrical beauty of nothing,
eating fireflies crazed from the forest
into the bright light, a terror forgiven.

A thousand streams of memories in ripples,
like sticking a needle into open wounds,
or losing sight of the guiding star
searching for the moon in the wilderness;
staring at martyrdom in the middle of life.

I have grown into a catalogue of regrets,
crows humming at dawn, choking the air
with a waterfall of fusses and losses,
like a passenger on the beautiful Titanic
where all doors and windows are locked.

I create anarchy when I crave order,
war with the lunar molecules of peace;
the less I can imagine of a family feud
cast like a pebble into a pond,
unable to see the smaller picture.

Yet, I have come with a bottle of truth,
corked with the leaf of yesterday's lies,
to build a Molotov of anger at nothing
but the anxiety disorder of a panic world,
my phobia, my order, my beauty and pain.

RUINOUS
by Ahona Dam

How can I not feel anything (for you)?
There's so much to hate (about you), so that's an emotion I guess.
(You) stain my present with what happened in the past.
I am weak and obey the command.
It's so hard when I become blinded by the glimmers of hope.

(You) lure me in with vulnerable stories and I talk until I should go.
I keep looking at the time. The night ripens and fleshes out its darkness.
And I always come and lose my way.
It's my fault, honestly. I said I'm a bad person, (not you).
I'm sorry, I shared too much. (You) forget everything.

It's becoming bitter with every interaction.
How could I be so blind?
(You) make me feel so small yet heard at the same time.
Cunningly skillful, I must say.
Next time, I will not answer (your) prying questions.

I wonder what happened (to you).
I fell for the innocence that stayed stuck in the past,
that laugh, and that calm demeanor.
(You're) hurting, and I can see that.
Thank you for showing me what I should never have.

NORMAL HYDROCEPHALUS
by Suzette Bishop

He says he has to have the chip checked,
Send it up North,
Probably by train.
It's a problem, but we'll get it fixed.

Did I glimpse my dad working years ago,
Phoning a boss,
Spinning problems?
Some of what he had to keep secret
About nuclear submarines,
Some of the troubleshooting,
Some awareness of his dementia,
A jumbling of past and present?

We'd been comparing weather,
Mine in Texas, his in Florida,
Hot but not as humid,
And he asked if I'd heard from my sister.
Then out of nowhere,
He's apologizing about a malfunctioning machine,
Promising to get everything straightened out.
As if it's his fault,
As if he's holding everyone up.

His brain jumps tracks,
                And it jumps back from chips to weather just a quick.
        A few months ago, like this, he said he was moving North,
                        To New York City.
                                        He must want to be back there,
I think, back to his twenties, perhaps single,
        Ogling girls at the beach
Where he met my mom.

I act like track jumping is perfectly normal,
Trying to go with the conversation,
But there's nothing normal about it,
And I don't know if I'm peeking at something that happened
Or that's made up,
Or wished,
And if I'll see something I don't want to see,
Can't unsee,
Like sex with an old girlfriend
He wishes he'd married instead of Mom,
A Cold War warhead with a broken chip.
What I extract from faulty wiring
Is placating a boss about machines that don't work
According to plan,
At least one more move looming as he nears 98.

Those are real, something that did happen,
Something that will happen.

And from this inbetween, he asks,
Are you ok? Are you happy?
I nearly drop the phone,
The engineer so disappointed I was behind, labeled "slow",
No love for math, struggling with it,
The man who left for another woman
And engineer step-son,
Barely staying in touch,
Launching out of his damaged brain,
                              A normal fatherly hope.

PERSEPHONE'S FIRST SEASON IN HELL
by Alison Stone

That winter I learned what the animals know.
My hair thickened,
blood grew cold and slow,
and as the flowers had fallen
from my apron, so joy and memory
spilled from the sack of my skin.

Now that food was safe,
I would not eat.
The chewed heart
of pomegranate blocked my throat.

All I had cherished went on
above. Mother's tears watered my roof.
Armored in loneliness
I learned to love no one.
The dead scurried about
while my heart slept --
red seed beneath its tree of bone.

I learned to quicken my husband's pleasure
and to melt memories of his touch with tears.
My marriage lengthened and coiled.

Above the black walls of my world, Apollo
drifted in his ring of fire.
With half his journey done,
the ground above me split.
Like a child in the womb I felt
the tingle beneath the fingernails
that marks the end of death.

from *They Sing at Midnight*, Many Mountains Moving Press, (2003)

GOAT IN THE CORNER
by Deborrah Corr

I snapped that moment, my vision
extended through the camera lens,
my finger on the shutter, opening
the diaphragm for the light needed
to capture them.

He's on one knee, his arms around
a baby goat. Its white legs dangle,
its ears flatten back. Our little daughter
leans her weight into his side, her hand
on the back of the kid's neck.
Her whole body sings with delight.

My past is printed on glossy paper. Flat,
with only memory to inflate it. I reach in
and feel the rub of her corduroy pants,
the slippery nylon puff on his down vest,
how his mustache tickled my cheek.
Her soft braids. The tug of the purple sweater
when I pulled it over her hair.

The head of the mother goat enters
the lower right corner. White, almost
faded now, frozen as she moved
to free her baby. Stopped in the act

that goat and I, rendered impotent.
Cancer, the camera, its shutter snapping
closed, first on him, then on her.
They're pinned inside this frame.
And we are fixed forever
staring in from the corner.

SUCCESSION: THE TIME IT TAKES TO HEAL

by Erin Robertson

after the flames consume
and the heartwood is gone
the soil lies black
awaiting a seed

what comes next isn't the end -
the flashy fireweed
the jangling aspen
are just short stages, not the climax

not until the deep dark roots
of the quiet white spruce
knit the land back whole
does the earth recover from the burn

SEND ME
by Katie Moino

My eyes glistened with frozen
crystals as the river froze
over for winter. A mirror,

the way the broken ice reflected
the sky. A layer of skin, the way the sun echoed
on the river-glass in the figure of a woman.

The breeze pushed the pieces together,
knocked each other like wind chimes
for the ducks who walked on ice,

elegant as ice skaters sketch circles.
Icicles of winter's teeth hung low,
clung to the brush like fine dust

in a windpipe, set to bite down,
peel skin. If this surrounding city
disappeared,

had never been built,
the blue mountains beyond
would stand—their majesty

unquestioned
uninterrupted
by manmade weeds.

The river would flow
with no bridge to cross,
like a dream with no mind

to show when two black jaguars
leapt through my open
window while I slept.

When I heard a bird take his final breath
as the river cat slunk away
with wings between his teeth,

when my hair set on fire
twice from candlelight—
the first when my back turned

on a bar's patio, the second
20 minutes after telling the story
of the candle on the patio—

I don't want to believe in
coincidence anymore so please,
if you're out there and you're listening,

send a red flower,
while I'm no more than the magpie
passing by, or the water slides

down the tiles that hold up my mind.
Send a red flower to the depths
of the dirt where I muster

the courage to know my worth.
Send a red flower to the forest
of trees, beneath chandeliers

of branches that move apart
then together like lips that speak. Please,
if you're out there and you're listening,

send me a red flower in the cold
of this winter while dried-up leaves,
these crumpled crescent moons,

carry me all the way to June.

previously published in Isele Magazine

WITNESS
by Aimee R. Cervenka

Sitting that night by the fire, all she could think
was how the logs had segmented to look
like a spine. You were saying something
about your life, but the bones in the fire
glowed slow flashes of red,
she heard only their sighing breath.
Voice falling in the empty air, you saw
her eyes closed, hand reaching
for the graceful length. Her fingers
gentle and burning, like rest.

Previously published: *Ascent*

RECOVERY: on learning my recovered-alcoholic father secretly drank until his death

by Erin Robertson

y
and
more than one
allowing me in infrequently

ry
rye
whiskey and
no, just whiskey and ice
wry
dry summings up
the way he spoke

ery
Er
his mother's name for me
Éire
land of lost belonging
ultimate cause of our family's suffering
airy
antonym to the thick cloud of smoke in his den
the sad black plastic fan/filter feebly trying to swallow some
to clear the air

very
more than enough
I never was
veritas
truth, hacked in half

overy
ovary
mine in between us always
son of the fierce matriarch
he begrudged any other woman dignity, respect
too much given over to her already
overy
our postures in rotation
myelin laid in tracks we'd retreat to
feet falling into the same prints
whatever the weather

covery
cover
to protect from harm
cower

to hide behind
covering
something that cloaks, conceals

ecovery
discovery
to uncover, reveal, disturb the cloak
eco-very: me
eco-not: him
Buick and golf course and plastics plant
never venturing into the backyard
let alone Lake, woods, mountains, world

recovery
recovered memory
recovered story
with the truth of non-recovery I recover our relationship
finally understand the unending dysfunction
what happens when recovery doesn't: false acts and fury suffused with shame
our currency gone worthless
with the wound covered, not recovered, there's no resolution
you have to find a way home to the tonic
to get the poison out of your system
before you can heal

ARPEGGIOTIC
by Angela Cummings

Memory scales the surface
for the familiar ridge, correct key.
Your fingers playing
in the empty cathedral of my hands.
In your mouth, the dying
syllables still wanting
to tell me what it is that you know.

There was a time
when I too had no words,
when all you could do was look at me.
I know your love was orchestral.
You were the timpani and the harp.
String, reed and valve.

And then, your final recital
sightreading on my palms
melodies unknown to me;
your encore unlocking Memory's vault,
releasing an elegy of grief's great bounty—
a lucid lullaby for the child still.
Both of us.

I know it now.
I could not know it then.
And Mother, I remember
what you told me, what it was you knew:
music is someone else's memory
that we remember too.

SHIVERS DOWN MY SPINE
by Braeden Michaels

Once upon a tender kiss filled with tears...
Like a caterpillar in the midnight rain
Crawling through the hollow misery
Love departed in the chilling seams
Disappearing sentiments shriek
A Rendezvous slipping away in palms

Astonished by the copper leaves flying
Lakes drying up from the emptiness
Broken prayers misguided by the glare
Compromises thrown like pounds of dirt
Discomfort stuck in the tendons

Our love trembles and yowls

Agony settling like trampled dust
Gasping on the soaring affliction
heartache submerged in soot and spit
A romance ripped at the fingertips
Surrounded by the scalding temperatures

Violent cramps pricking rhythmically
Thickening torture runs down my throat
Weeping madly and in confusion
Seeking deadly faults within the glass
An illness dispersed in coarse veins

Our love shivers and screams

Clarity is a dark cloud dangling
in my sunken and insomniac eyes
Jumbled up words scribbled in my mind
Walking like a tormented disorder
Gripping on to the petals with my palm

Forever embroidered within my sleeves
Dropping it below my tattered knees
Falling to the distorted earth
Gazing up at the swollen apricot sky
Tears flooded like a waterfall

Our love bleeds and pulsates

Shadows of the gravestone widen
A fortress of preciousness clamped
Clutching adoration and admiration
Seeking answers from a growl
Tasting chunks of sorrow

Drinking melancholy from a flask
Elsewhere and gone in my pockets
A nickel has more value than my identity
Bitten by never ending and lasting scars
Latching onto oppression and misfortune

Our love flinches and grovels

Questioning faith and man-made religion
Cursing like a drunken sailor
Angry at the curved roads without signs
Cut hands raised in the fickle air
A flight of exasperation lingers

Waking up from vexation in my stomach
Anxiety and headaches twinkle like stars
Burden worn like an army jacket
Distress sinking in my teeth
Anguish and inward sketches touch

Our love is seeking answers in the mist of our hands

ACOUSTIC PUNK SAD SESTINA MIDNIGHT
by Amanda Trout

—You listened to <u>angst</u> and <u>love anxiety</u> at midnight. Here's some<u> homemade cd mixtape, stomp</u> <u>and holler, acoustic crying, yearning,</u> and <u>piano rock.</u>

Turn up that shuffle. I'll teach you to burn
bitten nails, ice cream on a compact disc,
track midnight hopeless romantic playlists
until your brain feeds only emo anthems,
endless alternative rage-ridden songs
queued back to back to back. Now backtrack

to a time when your liked tracks
were less lonesome wolf, more burning
phoenix, when your shower songs
performed fresh like undiscovered
talent, when the single woman anthems
didn't leave your self so listless.

Your coping mechanism music lists
have changed, and this change tracks
back to before wedding chrysanthemums
overtook your For You page, burned
your inner eyes to envious green discs.
You could imagine their partner songs,

their hand-in-hand moonlight date night songs
like acoustic guitars and renegade idealist
dreams could blind your status quo dissonance,
but when the song ends, it's just your tracks
on an empty dance floor. Love illusions burn
phlem down the back of your throat and theme

further hours with the same anthems:
you always choose now, sad songs
we catalogue "crying" and "yearning"
until every hours' newly titled daylist
is just old words and older tracks
in new formations. So let's disc

twenty voices in eighty minutes, risk
conversation between you and them
to wittle your near-daily crisis attacks
down to a Sunday song session.
You'll sit in the car and listen
like this status quo doesn't burn.

I would never discourage your lonely anthem
track your life to some prescribed anti-love list—
Burn for me, and I'll help you sing solo.

A WING-STROKED SPECTACLE
by Daniel Moreschi

Segmented sets of starlings sharply elevate
towards candescent skies, suspend, then circulate
in sync. Their wingspans whisper sunset symphonies
while manifesting silhouetted symmetries.

With poise, finesse and swiftness, they transform the air
into an ever-changing scape; this canvas where
each turn and swirl unfolds a painterly display:
a moving mural, rendered on a dying day.

The starlings coalesce to make a checkered veil.
They crown the clouds and skim across a seaside trail,
then separate as if surrendering to gusts,
and cover summits like a desert's storm-flung dust.

With tapered pace, their fevered flights revert to long
glissades of shimmering shades; a showy dance along
a latent stopgap stage. They stir, careen, decline,
retracing what remains of lofty lazuline,

before it all becomes a screen of red-specked gold.
The starlings falter in its wake; they cannot hold
their elegance in fading light. Their spirals wane
in streaming chains. They spill in spates of jet-black rain.

Published by the Society of Classical Poets in January 2024

SOUL IN ICE
by Lowell Klessig

July 23-24, 1977
Portage, Alaska

Like menthol t'was cool
Like sky it was blue.
Bluer even than sky
The blue thru and true.

Of heart it had none
10,000 years in a bowl,
But break now a piece
And peer into a soul.

Broken and melting
To sea goes the soul.
Sculptured by sun and wave
The soul is still whole.

Some in bergs have grown
Hoary in summer's stew.
Mustache of mountain black
But with soul still blue.

Portage they call it,
Tanaina Indians, Chugach Eskimoes
And Russian fur traders,
Glacier trail of no mosquitoes.

It's retreating now
Leaving a lake,
Where the icebergs float
Until small they break.

To and down the creek
They bob-bob and play,
Changing with every wave
A new sculpture every day.

While the big ones lay
Giant ships in blue bold,
Afraid to hardly move
Momentum in hold.

Giants slowly dying,
The icy bier not fully cold
Enough to save the soul
Till this story is told.

Previously published in the Postude section of *Words With My Father*

BLITZ OF GROWING
by Camille Hiltbrand

Growing up
Growing pains
Painful scrapes to the knee
Painful relationship breaks
Breaking my mother's lamp
Breaking a sobriety promise
Promising to go to bed
Promising I will stay clean
Cleaning my toy closet
Cleaning a wound I made
Making cookies at Nana's
Making out with everyone I see
Seeing the bright side every time
Seeing them walk out of my life
Living on the spur of the moment
Living off of the scraps I find
Finding rocks in my backyard
Finding out why they left
Leaving space for my dog to sleep
Leaving them on read for days on end
Endlessly biking around the block
Endlessly obsessing over accidents
Accidentally forgetting homework
Accidentally letting responsibilities slip
Slipping under a childhood blanket
Slipping away from everyone who cares
Caring about everything
Caring about nothing
Nothing was going to stop me
Nothing stopped me from crying
Crying over math with my dad
Crying over who I am becoming
Becoming what my parents had hoped
Becoming a shell waiting to die
Dying to see the next hit movie
Dying for them to answer my call
Calling my siblings childish names
Calling out for someone to notice
Noticing when my parents were tense
Noticing that I am no longer invited
Inviting the neighbors to come over and play
Inviting the cold to take over my presence
Presenting talents to crying mothers
Presenting only what they expect
Expecting that every day was adventure
Expecting to be the butt of a joke
Joking that I'll live forever
Joking that it is time for it all to end
End...
Forever...

AUTUMNAL WHISPERS
by Susan Mayer Brumel

Though in the midst of summer's thrust,
As August heat steals all of reason
Like conjurings of faerie dust,
Senses are stirred by coming season

On leafy greens red color glows,
And summer songbirds' feathers dull
Field grasses golden 'neath my toes,
As flowers, ebbing hours cull

Smoky breath of wildfires meet
With musky scent of first leaves' shed
From fallen fruits a fetid sweet
With savory whiff of earth is wed

Upon my tongue confection plays,
I taste the candied apple air
Across my lips warm spices graze,
Teasing flavors of harvest fare

Crickets of sleepy summer wake,
As geese fly south and honk farewell
And buzzy bees last honeys make,
While whirring winds begin to swell

Though August sun not yet shying,
And summer folly still abounds
Autumnal whispers 'round me sighing—
Stir sights, and scents, and tastes and sounds

YOU DO NOT HAVE TO BE GOOD
by Carolyn Martin

You do not have to be good.
 --Mary Oliver, "Wild Geese"

Ain't that a kick in the head!
After all the bunk about straights and narrows,
wrongs and rights, confessionals
where venial sins are laughable,
it's come down to this: we've been duped.
Friday fish, forty fasting days, crownings
in the Mary month of May; rosaries,
callused knees, indulgences that smudge
our sins: they don't add up to *good*.
Neither do tidy rooms, top grades in school,
nor mandatory modesty.

So let's delete the snake behind the apple tree
and every bite of stale theology.
Let's resurrect original wildness
and ramble through valleys scratched and scarred,
down unquiet streams, across raging fields
of blooms disguised as weeds.
Let's celebrate every fleshy flaw,
each mistaken thought that turns out true.
Let's race wild geese to the nearest star,
cheering on imperfect
nakedness with disheveled glee.

First published in the *Gyroscope Review* (2016)

QUOTH THE POET
by Patricia Doyne

Once upon an **iamb** (hanging
in a line with rhymes slam-banging)
suddenly there came a clanging,
stamping feet in groups of four.
"'Tis **quadrameter**, "I mutter,
scowling at the muddy floor.
"Verbal drumbeats, nothing more."

Ah, distinctly I remember
scribbling in my attic chamber,
hearing five matched-footsteps clamber
through the window, out the door.
"'Tis **pentamete**r," I mutter,
"Something we can all ignore.
Verbal drumbeats, nothing more."

Clock strikes midnight, as my raven—
croaking muse and mystic maven—
quoths some verses, quaintly graven
down the dusty corridor.
"Got to mop this place," I mutter,
"Sing-song verses I deplore.
Verbal drumbeats, nothing more."

There's one rule all Poe-clones ponder
when their words begin to wander—
make no sense, drift way out yonder,
floundering on a Classic shore.
"Just one bookish rule," I mutter,
watching words slam-dunk and score.
"Mind the form, but never bore."

THE STORM
by Neil Vincent Scott

the chaos of cancer
      the confusion
      the cruelty
      the chemo
with the winds of change blowing sideways
    like a cold driving rain
with bolts of lightening
    filled with lament
mixed with thunder
    and the darkness of reality
as the storm whistles
  like a drunken sailor
        dancing far into the night

the caustic nature of cancer
    obscuring all inner vision
      with coulds
      and shoulds
      maybes and mights
trying to nurture possibilities
      into probabilities
    with hope being the ring
    that we try to catch
knowing that hope
    without action
is but a four letter word
      as the merry go round
    goes round and round
one circle closer to tomorrow

cancer is the enemy within
    a stealth invasion
challenging
changing
    a formable foe
  with tentacles extended
as we fall
    face forward
into the unknown
  the unready
and power through the storm
walking together
    side by side
    heart by heart
through the deep darkness
into the bright light of healing

for love has no borders
    it is the engine of survival
and the light
    is not at the end of the tunnel
but in the sparkle of the eyes
as the journey toward tomorrow
    continues in the confusion of today
    with courage and confidence

RED DRESS
by Kelly J. Sullivan

I'm an aging woman in a red dress
Manifesting ghosts in my kitchen
My sixth cousin's gravy recipe steams on the stove
My third great-grandmother's corn bread stuffing is ready
Her brother was a surgeon in the Civil War
In the back of an album in the back of a closet
Is a photograph of him sitting outside a field tent
Next to President Abraham Lincoln.
Checkmarks on the calendar for the past month
Today is the day they come
Children who are not children anymore
And I've placed cards with their names on them next to each plate
Tied to pine cones with ribbons
Like they showed on the morning show I watch.
No matter what I ever was
I was a mother first
Recording first steps, first words, giggles and baby teeth
In three separate albums
Now in the back of my closet
Sharing a shelf with the faded image of Lincoln.
Colored gourds from the farm stand
Are arranged on the front step
Beside a pot of orange mums
A vase of cattails stands in the center of the table
The floors have been scrubbed and the curtains changed
New hand towels hang on the bathroom rack
A nice fall yellow.
The children who are not children anymore
Can be in ten places at one time
Without being present at any of them
They are seated at the table
Reaching through the room
Knocking over knick-knacks and memories
To grab hold of things far beyond the window T
hat looks out over the yard
Where a rusted swing set still stands.
Hands gripped to phones
They watch videos of co-workers
And comment on the photos of friends
International wars, celebrity weddings
The goings on at places they would much rather be
Are of more importance than pumpkin pie
Or their names attached to pine cones with ribbons.
No one cares who great-aunt Sophie is
Or that it's her scrawled list of ingredients
In the biscuits they are mindlessly spreading butter on
While looking back and forth
From table to the screen.

Everything in their lives that matters
Has been conveniently collected for them
A collection that doesn't include anything
I've had to offer
My grandmother's recipes
Like old bills and junk mail
Will be tossed when I am gone
They won't remember colored gourds
Or ribboned pine cones
Yet next month I am here in the kitchen
Reincarnating lost souls
I've cooked a roast and Aunt Petey's gingerbread
Under the tree, are presents for each of the children
Wrapped in leaf-stamped paper I learned how to make from
Brown shopping bags
On the morning show I watch.
They don't notice the paper
They don't notice I've made the tiny spiral cinnamon cookies
They used to love
I make them every year
They haven't noticed for years
They don't notice me
In this filled silent room
Staring out the window
Where the wind blows empty swings
I am an aging woman in a red dress
Who they don't see anymore.

Fiction

FROM THE EDITORS: *Fiction this year was filled with superb writers. The moment we read Like a Pearl; the judges were all separately convinced it was the winner. Usually it's impossible to truly say one story stands out when all the entries are good, but Like a Pearl possesses everything; it's a magnificent, deeply moving story of immigration, it doesn't lose the power of its message by being political. It has a simple story, unfolded in gorgeous vivid language. The tempo in 4 short pages speaks volumes, and the revealing of its core is excruciatingly emotive, where its resonance stays with you for weeks afterward. I found myself telling people about this story, because it's so powerful you feel a real urge to share it. I thought about it many times after reading despite how many stories I had read for the competition, it literally burned itself into my appreciation and stayed there. If there is any story that was literally written perfectly, it is Like a Pearl. This is a story everyone should read for multiple reasons, not least, its necessity at the heart of all things that matter. -CLD*

LIKE A PEARL
by Mei Davis

The worst part about it was that Má never let her sit on her lap anymore.

"Not enough room, Thi," Má would say, feet propped and her hands laid over her swollen belly. They were never given enough food for all of them, and Má had grown thinner and thinner. Her spindly legs could hardly walk with that big, big belly taking up so much room. Thi didn't hate the belly, not really, she just didn't like how instead of bustling over the stove, sneaking Thi little sips of *cahn chua*, or kneeling on the floor to play with her and Chau doll, Má just laid on the floor cushions and slept and cried. "Not enough room, Thi. There'll never be enough room again."

Maybe that's why Thi didn't mind getting on the boat. It wasn't very big, just a fishing skiff really, with two old motors and a sheet tied to a makeshift mast. "Just in case," the man at the front motor said.

"In case what?" Thi asked, but no one answered her question, just Ba whispered at her to be quiet and to hold onto Chau doll tighter. She was already holding on to Chau doll as tightly as she could, and she wished she could take off some of her clothes. "Too hot! Too hot!" The sun baked the faded, splintered wood of the boat, and Thi winced as she sat down on the sizzling planks. It rocked and creaked every time someone new stepped aboard, and after a while there were so many people stuffed into the boat that arms and legs spilled over the sides, and there seemed to be a knee or elbow just about everywhere she turned.

But it wasn't any more cramped than the little shanty they shared with two other families, and at least when they were on the boat, Má didn't cry as much or tell her "Not enough room." On the boat, Má looked out at the waters with eyes that glistened like a ripe longan. She let Thi cuddle into the sliver of lap not taken up by that big belly as much as she wanted, and Thi felt like her precious thing again.

"Malaysia would be better," the man at the motor said. He revved it up and the boat roared away from the sagging pier and the throng of waving, wailing people. "It's closer. Not as many days at sea."

"We decided Hong Kong," Ba spat. Her father was always spitting his words these days, ever since he came home early from work and the men with blunt faces and sharp tongues forced them out of their home, their nice, big home with plenty of room. "If we go there, we'll have a better chance at resettling in Britain or Australia. Maybe even America."

"You can't know that."

"I had a cousin write me from Los Angeles. Los Angeles!"

Thi snuggled into the loose fabric of Más shirt. She breathed into the familiar, sticky skin that smelled of salty fish sauce, saltier tears. Má stroked her hair. The long shadow cast by her upright frame shaded Thi from the blistering sun, and her salty scent became one with the sea. "This boat will take us to a brand-new home," Má said as the coastline dissolved into never ending streaks of blue, gently rolling waves that shone like Chau doll's marble eyes. "There'll be great big buildings that gleam like pearls in the sun, tables falling over with food, and no more fighting. A place where families like ours can find a place to fit."

"Not enough room for us in this country anymore," Ba spat. "Never enough room again."

Thi thought of wide streets trickling with bicycles, the clear glass panes of store fronts and her father's old register. Grassy parks and kitchen gardens blooming with lemongrass and basil. How could a country so big not have enough room for them? There weren't many of them, just Má, Ba, and herself.

And the big, round belly. Thi pushed against it to keep from sliding off Má's lap. "Stop squirming, Thi. It hurts." Were her parents right? Would there never again be enough room for them?

For her?

The boat plunged further into the open sea as a roof of grey clouds gathered above them.

Thi fell asleep to the sound of rain.

* * * * * *

The storms soaked them, the salt scrubbed them, the sun dried them. Thi lost count of the number of baths she'd had out on the boat, but it was after her brown skin peeled for the third time that the back motor broke, which Ba said later was why the bad men were able to catch them.

The man at the front motor saw them first, a little white dot bobbing on the water. He shouted, and then everyone else shouted, and even though there was no room to move, everyone seemed to be moving everywhere all at once. The boat rocked as they tried to speed away, but the bad men's boat was much smaller and faster. They zipped over the choppy waves as if they were sailing on air, and the closer they came, the more people moved and shouted and cried, their voices tangling together into one, shrieking knot.

Thi couldn't hear her voice when she asked, "What's wrong? Why are they so afraid?"

Má put her hands over Thi's round cheeks. "They want to take the precious things away." Thi couldn't hear Má's words either, but she felt their meaning. She watched Má's quivering lips and knew exactly what they said. "Be quiet and keep Chau doll close. Don't let her out of your sight, or out of your arms."

Thi shrank into her mother and hid Chau doll under her shirt. She didn't know why she did that, except she thought she might hide her the way Má hid her new precious thing. Precious things were always hidden away, weren't they? Jewels buried in mountains; pearls pressed between shells. Chau doll was a gift from *Ba Noi*, made with nice fabric and neat, dainty stitches. And the marble eyes. They were Thi's favorite part of Chau doll, and she knew the bad men would want her.

"We have no money," the man at the motor called to the bad men as they pulled up alongside their boat. "What wasn't taken was spent on exit papers, and the boat."

But the bad men came aboard anyway, with sharp knives which they shook in everyone's faces. They collected watches and jewelry out of shaking hands, and they growled things in a language Thi didn't understand, but at the same time also understood. They looked at her and her mother, and all the other women, and she understood they wanted other kinds of precious things, the kinds that aren't lucky enough to be hidden away all the time.

The men on the boat, all the fathers and brothers and sons, tried to fight against the bad men. Not Ba, who just stared out to sea with eyes full of silence and tears. But some of the others tried to fight them, but were stabbed or thrown overboard. Everyone stopped moving and shouting after that, and let the bad men do whatever they wanted. They grabbed some women, and left some others. They pushed Thi off Má's lap. Thi thought they might take her too, but Má rose up on her spindly legs, and wobbled away with them instead.

Thi didn't see what happened afterwards. She rolled herself into a ball, into a big, round belly with Chau doll stowed safely under her shirt.

When Má came back, she cried so much she threw up over the side of the boat. But Thi didn't mind the smell of the vomit, because the wind whisked it away so fast, and some of the other ma's never came back at all.

The bad men sputtered away with their treasures. Má leaned against the side of the boat. Her eyes were closed. Thi pulled Chau doll from under her shirt and held it up to her. "I kept her safe, Má. Just like you asked. I held her in my arms and never let her go."

Má opened her eyes. She pulled Thi onto her lap. She clutched Thi with one arm, her big, round belly with the other, and cried and cried, and even though there was more room on the boat, it didn't feel that way. Something else had come aboard. Something that took up more room than Má's big belly, or all the knees and elbows in the world.

* * * * * *

The day the big freighter glided into view, the last grains of *cơm* they had brought in the big brown pot, the kind used for plants and not for *cơm* at all, was scraped out and divided among them.

But Thi didn't mind. She didn't mind either that the fruit was all gone, gobbled up before it had a chance to spoil, or that the fat rolls of *chả lụa,* which she thought could never run out, had run out days ago, because the hunger wasn't half so bad as the thirst. Every hour or so they gave her a little spoonful of water, which seemed to be gone before it even hit her tongue. Sometimes she got two spoonfuls, and when Thi asked why, the woman in charge of the water cans told her to, "Be quiet and be grateful," and clucked something about hoarding treasures.

The sight of that big, red and grey freighter was almost like drinking another spoonful of water. It wasn't the first ship they'd seen out on the water. Other ships had passed them by, probably because there was not enough room aboard for them. But the freighter was big, so big the waves of its wake pushed against their boat and made it rock so hard she thought she might be thrown over the side. But no one else seemed to worry. They pointed and shouted at the man at the front motor. "Steer towards it! Steer towards it!" And everyone was taking off shirts and scarves, and waving all sorts of fabric in the air, and shouting even louder than when the bad men had come.

The freighter didn't slow. It slid past them as if they weren't there at all, and sank slowly into the horizon, and everyone put their shirts back on.

"There must not have been enough room for us after all," Thi said to Chau doll. She could only speak to Chau doll, because Ba had gone back to his silence and sea-staring, and Má wasn't often awake anymore. She didn't answer Thi anymore or pull her onto her lap. She laid on the boat bottom, where a puddle of ocean water lived, and moaned, and that morning, after the freighter decided there was not enough room for them, Má began moaning louder than ever, and shouting too.

There was a little bit of frenzy as the men took down the mast and pulled off the sheet, and draped it over her. The other women on board, the too-old ones and too-young ones left behind by the bad men, huddled around her. They pushed Thi further away from Má, crowded her out until Má was just a distant ripple under the sheet, like the tiny bit of wake that was the only thing left behind by the big freighter. So close, but out of reach.

Thi covered her ears because Má's screams were so loud. She shut her eyes because somehow, the people's faces were even louder than the screams, and she decided that she did mind coming on the boat after all.

* * * * * *

Má and baby Ngoc, which Ba told Thi was her name, stayed underneath the sheet all the next day, and the day after that, and the day after that. There was less room on the boat, and she never got two spoonfuls of water anymore.

But Thi didn't mind. For some reason she didn't know, she liked the soft cries and suckling sounds that came from beneath the sheet, and one day, after Má was strong enough to come out from under the sheet, she would get to sit on her lap without that big, round belly in the way.

More ships passed by. Nice ships, that would only pass them by, and not come aboard to take precious things away. The man at the motor said more ships passing by meant Hong Kong was not too far away anymore. He said they would be there any day now, but not before the day another ship pointed its prow straight at their little boat.

A ship filled with men and glinting things.

Everyone was shouting again. Shouting and moving. There was lots of room to move now, but not enough room to get away. Thi looked at the rippling sheet and the rippling waves. Chau doll's eyes gleamed more brightly than ever, and when the first man came aboard, she ran over to him and held her up.

"I'll give you my most precious thing, if you promise not to take anything else."

People were yelling at her to get away, and the bad man looked down at her like he wanted her to get away, too. That he would make her get away, if she didn't do it herself. But Thi stayed where she was. The soft cries and suckling sounds drifted from under the sheet, the same sounds she had listened to day after day, and a funny thing happened inside her chest. As if an egg had cracked inside of her, and the gooey parts were spilling out and spreading. All her insides were spreading and growing, bigger than the freighter, wider than the sea. It didn't matter anymore if there was no room in their country or room on Má's lap. Inside of her was enough room for them all to fit.

She lifted Chau doll up to the bad man. "My most precious thing. Please, take it."

Maybe the man didn't understand her, the way he cocked his head and frowned. Or maybe he did understand her, because he grabbed Chau doll out of her hands and laughed. Not a nice laugh, like when Ba told jokes and pinched her nose, but the kind of laugh that sounded almost like the sputtering motor of the boat. Rumbly and fierce and chop-you-to-bits. He took Chau doll in his hand and plucked out her marble eyes. It made Thi wince, and even though her lips quivered like Má's did sometimes, she said nothing. He took the glinting knife in his hand and sliced Chau doll's neat, dainty stitches open, poured out all the marble eyes, the extra ones that Má had sewn inside in case the ones on her face fell off, into his palm. The marbles spilled into the bad man's palm and he laughed and laughed, because anyone would be happy to get such a nice doll with such gleaming, marble eyes, and Thi didn't mind that Chau doll was gone forever, because afterwards the bad men piled back onto their boat and sped away without taking any other precious things with them.

"You gave her up," Ba yelled when they were gone. "We told you to keep her safe, to keep her in your arms no matter what, but you gave her up!"

"It's all right," Má said. She came out from under the sheet for the first time since she went in. "It's all right, Thi." Then she brought baby Ngoc out from under the sheet, too. She was bigger than Chau doll, but also littler at the same time, and Thi felt another egg cracking inside.

"You gave up your Chau doll, and now you'll have nothing," Ba said. "We'll have nothing!"

Nothing? Thi didn't think she had nothing, but maybe that was the trouble all along. With the country and the boat, and Má's lap, too. Making room for nothing, instead of making room for everything.

Thi patted the soft, dark mat of baby Ngoc's hair. "I don't mind." She took her from Má's outstretched arms and held her in her own. "You'll be my new Chau doll. My new precious thing."

The first beacon of coastline shone in the distance, gleaming bright as pearls, as bright as her sister's eyes.

First published in the Canadian literary magazine *prairiefire* in the fall of 2021.

FROM THE EDITORS: *The title made me smile, but this is so much more than a humorous title, which belies its deeply moral core from the fantastic opening lines to the perfect culminating ending, this short story possesses everything. Dark humor. Deep observation and unpredictability. Not easy to do in four pages. Only masterful writers can draw the reader into a kooky story that ends proving itself several times over. The sheer originality and layers beneath are astounding. It will make a believer out of a non-believer, for sure. This is short-story telling at its finest, the kind of story you'll find yourself impressed by even if you began with skepticism. -CLD*

GREEN TIGHTS
by Sherry Morris

I met Marianne lying face-down in a ditch. I'd pulled the car over to take a call from Jackass and was so busy cussing I didn't see her at first. Then I spotted these legs, cocooned in cucumber-green tights. They stood out in all that dirt-brown west-Texas wasteland. I was going through a colored footwear phase at the time and hung up on Jackass mid-sentence to investigate.

The tights (and legs) belonged to a woman who faced away from me. Long, curly black hair fanned chaotically from her twisted body. I wondered how she got there. The last road sign I'd seen had basically declared, *You are now entering The Fuck-Middle-of-Nowhere*. No buildings were in sight. I hadn't passed a vehicle for miles. Had she dropped out of the sky? Legs akimbo, arms outstretched and bent at odd angles—maybe this woman was dead. Should I touch her and find out? Maybe I should call an ambulance instead. Paramedics were trained to deal with this sort of thing. Not me. But how long would it take them to arrive? I had stuff to do. I could touch her just enough to find out if she was dead. If she was, I'd make the call from the road—it's not like she'd need company. If she wasn't dead, I'd get her medical attention. That seemed reasonable, so that was the deal.

I took a step towards her, snapping a twig. Her head jerked up and around.

"Stop!" she announced, attempting to push herself up. "My hair could kill you!"

Her sudden movement and odd message gave me pause. Blood oozed from a cut on her forehead.

"You're bleeding," I said.

She looked at me blankly. Shuddered. Struggled into a sitting position.

"Don't come any closer!"

"You're hurt," I said. "You need help."

"But my hair—,"

"Stay still," I told her. "I'll get some Kleenex."

On my way back to the car, I reviewed the situation. She wasn't dead. Incoherent maybe, probably in shock, but not dead. I could call for an ambulance and wait for it to arrive. Or I could take her to hospital myself. My decision was quick. I'm not a woman who dithers. Or waits. I'd take her to hospital. I'd be late, but so what. Let Jackass wait. I plucked a packet of tissues from the glove box, stuffed an unused trash bag into my back pocket—the closest I could get to a foil blanket.

She was out of the ditch now, sitting on stony ground and shivering. Her tights were spotless. Immaculate, somehow. Not a run, snag or tear anywhere. She was younger than me, scarecrow-thin, in a flimsy ill-fitting summer dress. At least she had nice tights. I wondered where she bought them.

"What's your name?" I asked, squatting in front of her with a tissue.

"Marianne," she answered, grabbing it and blowing her nose.

"Marianne, I'm Lilith. That tissue was for your head. You're bleeding."

Her eyes darted wildly, wanting to see everywhere all at once, as if expecting an attack.

"My hair is electrified," she rasped, scooting away from me. "Don't touch me, I could kill you."

I sighed. Getting her into the car was going to take longer than I anticipated. It was getting dark. I wanted to get going. Inspiration struck.

"Marianne, your hair won't hurt me. I've got this." I pulled the trash bag from my back pocket and waved it at her. "It's one of those neutralising capes of galvanised plastic. The kind that absorbs all electrical elements—it'll make your hair harmless."

I watched her consider my offering.

"It looks like a trash bag."

"It's the deluxe model. With a reinforced Teflon coating. You activate it by breaking the drawstrings, then fasten it around your shoulders. It deactivates everything."

There was a pause.

"Everything?"

"Absolutely everything."

"Has it been approved by the Catholic church?"

I didn't bat an eye.

"Yep. The certificate's in the car. Come on, I'll show you."

She wouldn't accept help to stand but after she fastened the trash bag cape around her shoulders, she took my offered arm. Slowly, we made our way to the car.

"My hair isn't hurting you?"

"Not in the slightest."

"Praise be." Her body relaxed.

"Marianne, how did you get here?"

"I was transported."

"How?"

"By Kit."

"Where's Kit now?"

"He's gone—far away. Breaking my heart like my head."

It sounded like she had her own Jackass to deal with. I buckled her into the passenger's seat. The gash on her head looked deep. Five dark purple marks circled her upper arm. Fading yellow smudges lassoed her neck. Maybe I'd stay on once I got her to hospital. Keep an eye out for this Kit in case he showed up.

"Marianne, what happened to you?"

"I've been touched by grace—seen Her face. My hair is electrified."

Maybe the hospital people would make sense of her gibberish while they'd sew up her head. Before setting off, I checked my phone—ten missed calls from Jackass. I put the ringer on silent. Google informed me the nearest hospital was two hours away. Plenty of time to hear her story. Little by little, it came out. Sometimes in whispers, sometimes with pauses so long I thought she'd fallen asleep...or unconscious. I don't feel bad telling her story. In a way, it's my story too.

She didn't talk much at first. I supposed she was gathering herself. Straightening her tights so to speak. The first half of the story was predictable. Some faux Prince Charming treated her like a princess until she moved into his place. Then he started criticizing and gaslighting. Proceeded to shout, shame and isolate. Escalated to grabbing, slapping, throwing plates and glasses that smashed inches from her face. I got the picture quick. A lot of women would.

She prattled on some more while I tuned out. I couldn't stop thinking about her tights. My legs would look fantastic in a similar pair. She probably bought them in a chain store. I'd be able to find them easily enough. All I needed to do was butt-in on her babble and ask. It's what I intended to do. Instead, I found myself listening as her story veered down a strange road. And when she finally finished talking, I needed a few miles of silence to digest what I'd heard.

"Let me get this straight," I said, taking a breath. "Your Not-So-Charming Prince smashed your head into the bathroom mirror. When you came to, the cracks in the mirror looked just like the Virgin Mary to you—that unfortunate woman who managed to get herself knocked up without the least bit of foreplay or hot-sex. Ms. Immaculate Conception tells you to pack a bag and get on a Greyhound bus. But Not-So-Charming catches you. Says if you're leaving him, you won't need a change of clothes. Ever. Hustles you to the car. Drives out here to the desert while you sit in the passenger's seat and pray. During your tenth Hail Mary he grabs your hair. You see a flash. There's a burning smell. You're propelled through the air. When you come to for the second time that day, you decide your deity gal-pal has answered your prayers—not only has she helped you escape, she's electrified your hair. Then I come along to pick you up."

I paused, out of breath and out of story. I glanced at her. Hoped that by hearing her own words back she'd acknowledge this was just some fantasy tale. The quiet built. I couldn't stay still.

"*That's* what you're saying happened to you?"

She produced this beatific smile. Looked me straight in the eye.

"Yes."

And then something weird happened.

Now my rational mind knows a halo of light didn't suddenly surround her head. I'm a practical woman who sees the world through fact-based eyes. Religious mind-melding doesn't work on me anymore.

But at that moment, I believed.

An electrical charge filled the air. The hairs on my arm stood on end. I wondered if we needed another trash bag.

I shook my head. The halo was simply sunlight streaming through the window at just the right angle. Her boyfriend had probably popped her a good one in the car and then chucked her out. Religious deities did not answer prayers by electrifying hair. Unless I missed that memo. I'd let my membership to the church lapse some time ago.

Still, when she said, "I'd like to go to church and pray for forgiveness", I didn't argue. Maybe by some miracle she had managed to cause Kit harm. Good for her, I thought. And taking her to church worked in my favor—there was bound to be a church before a hospital in this part of the world. I'd leave Marianne with some Catholics—they went in for all that Mary-Miracle stuff—and some wine would probably do her good. It was a win-win situation: she'd be where she wanted and I'd be on my way. I updated our destination on the satnav.

Even after all those years away, church was just how I remembered it: dark, cavernous, candle-lit, reeking of incense. A huge bleeding Jesus hung from a cross in spotlight. I left Marianne murmuring in a pew, circled the entire place twice but couldn't find anyone about. I returned to her to discuss what to do. She'd taken off her trash bag cape and was all wrapped up in a rosary. Didn't respond when I said her name. Twice. My irritation grew. I had gone out of my way to help her and now I was being ignored. I felt possessed to reason with her. Say something that would shake her. Wake her to the reality of the situation.

"Marianne, prayer didn't get you out of there. There was no sign from above. No electrical interference by deities. No church approved capes. You rescued you."

Marianne turned and smiled at me. "They're looking after you too. You were supposed to find me. So I could save you."

My laughter echoed off the walls. "If that's what you want to believe—'

"You were looking for me. You just didn't know it. Couldn't see. The tights were a sign. Green means go."

I stared at her. How did she know I coveted her tights? Goosebumps pimpled my arms. I shivered. The smell of incense cloyed. This place was infecting me, smothering me. Messing with my brain. This non-stop nonsense was getting too deep, going too far. I had no intention of believing that some higher power, anything other than me, was in charge.

"I need some fresh air," I said and left quick. As I walked, the skies turned ominous. Fat drops fell and I took shelter under shop awning. Wished for a cigarette, that I hadn't left my phone in the car. I don't know how long I waited for the storm to pass. My thoughts were elsewhere. When the sun broke through the clouds, I caught my reflection in storefront glass. Didn't like what I saw. Headed back to the church.

Marianne was gone. I supposed the Catholics found her. Hoped they'd look after her well. The trash bag cape remained on the pew. I sat down next to it. I can't say that I prayed, but I took that bag and folded it into smaller and smaller squares until it fit inside my fist. On my way out of church, I threw it into a litter bin. Felt freed from a heavy load.

I didn't return Jackass's calls. Changed my number. Then changed jobs. Moved house. It was all part of the deal I made sitting in that pew.

When I think back on it now, I can't help but shake my head. I thought I had all the answers. Knew how everything worked. But life threw me a curveball—right out of the blue. Or green. And showed me a way forward that left me a bit stunned by its simplicity. Sure, there's self-determination, but sometimes there's something else. Call it what you like: chance, fate, luck, religion. I call it Green Tights.

previously published in *With Our Eyes Open* anthology, March 2017.

FROM THE EDITORS: *This short 4-page story really affected me. Some stories just climb inside and stay there. When you breathe emotions into inanimate objects, it can go horribly wrong and either sound like a children's book or just sophomoric, but when done right, it's tear-jerkingly powerful. Slusarcyk's Erase Every Plate, was a surprising beauty, where the greater story of life and death, resonates and affects the reader profoundly as we are asked to consider essentially, the value of things and our ultimate mortality. An incredible piece of writing that utilizes emotion in a really raw, honest way. -CLD*

ERASE EVERY PLATE
by Dominik Slusarczyk

I

The cliff knew his time was almost over. Soon the sea will claim him. Soon he will be down there at the bottom with all the other rocks. Soon he will be under the water that defeated him. He will be drowning, coughing and spluttering, remembering the sun on his skin and knowing he will never feel that feeling again.

For years he'd thought he could win. Every day the tide came in. He gritted his teeth as he watched the sea approaching. It would be here soon. The battering will return. Soon the pain will engulf him again.

He stood strong. The waves were tall and frightening but however rough the sea got he did not falter, did not even consider collapsing. His bright white skin remained standing in the same place however hard the sea hit.

A couple of weeks ago everything changed. The sea wasn't particularly strong that day but the lower half of his body had just had enough. It had had enough of being battered every day. It had had enough of the fear, the worry, the knowing that the sea would return and hurt it again.

It broke off. It was just a little bit, just a couple of metres, but that was enough. The rock above it will never be able to stay in place unsupported for very long. A small section of rock broke off so now the whole cliff will come crashing down.

The cliff will just be replaced with a new cliff, of course. When he falls the rock behind him will take his place. But that cliff will not be him. He will be at the bottom, under the water, far away from the sun.

The cliff watches the sea approach. It is never very far away - low tide is only a couple of dozen metres further back than high tide. At the base of the cliff there is a selection of rocks forming a slight slope. The cliff does not know how far that slope goes downwards but he suspects it is a long way because it goes under the sea even at low tide. The part of his body that broke off rolled all the way down the slope and disappeared under the sea. He hasn't seen that part of his body since.

Maybe I will roll forever, the cliff thinks. Maybe the slope doesn't have an end. Maybe I will collapse, enter the sea, and spend eternity getting deeper and deeper into that cold beast.

II

The cliff doesn't have to wait long to find out how far the slope goes.

The sea was particularly rough that day. Waves rose high into the sky and slammed their bodies against the poor cliff's face. The pain was so immense it made him wince. The cliff realised something he should have realised long ago: the pain ends the second he collapses.

Sure, there is no sun under the sea, and there will be no happy birds strutting along his head, but if he is under the sea the waves cannot get him. If he is under the sea the waves will be far away on the top of the sea.

He gives up, gives in, concedes defeat to the awful gravity that has been trying to drag him downwards ever since the rock at his base broke off a few weeks ago. In the end the cliff chose to die. It was either that or be murdered.

There were a couple of loud cracks then his whole body slid downwards into the sea. There was a bird on his head when it happened. As soon as the cliff started moving the bird leapt upwards and flew off into the blue sky. He will find somewhere safer, the cliff thought. He will find firmer ground to stand on. I haven't been firm ground in years.

He felt no pain as he collapsed. He was aware of his body breaking up into a billion pieces, but the pain that fracturing should have caused never appeared. All he felt was a strange numbness.

He took one last look at the sun before his eyes rolled into the sea.

The sea was cold, but it was also refreshing. The water under the sea was not rough and violent like the top of the sea; rather it was calm and soothing. As the cliff came to settle at the bottom of the slope, the slope that only went 20 or so meres past the edge of the sea, he realised that the sea stroked his body in a nice, pleasant, way. There was no violent hammering. There was no pain. The sea caressed him like he was a hamster.

The cliff could still see the sun reflecting off the top of the sea but he could not feel its warmth. The days when the cliff was warm are over.

That night the cliff dreamt of the sun. When he woke up the world was dark and scary.

III

There are no birds under the sea. Instead there are fish.

The stone is permanently underwater so the fish can visit him anytime they like. They do not visit often, though. The stone regularly goes days without seeing any fish, but when the fish do come it is spectacular. They always come in numbers. There is never one fish there are always dozens of fish.

The stone watches the fish swim around him. Sometimes they come very close to him but they never touch him, He curses his body. It is hard, uncomfortable, not the kind of thing you would choose to touch. He wishes he was soft like the sand, or warm like the sun he used to know.

There are other animals too. Sometimes there are turtles. Once the stone even saw a seal. He watched the seal rotate calmly as it propelled itself through the water. I did that, the stone thought. I moved once. It was a great movement, an impressive movement, a movement with strange power flowing through it. I moved, but I only moved once. I moved from where I was to where I was destined to be. Now I will never move again.

The seal swam straight past without paying any attention to the stone. The stone though him wise for knowing it was not worth wasting time on a stupid stone.

When the sea goes in the stone's world gets a little darker. He finds it harder to see the other stones, the stones that were once part of him. He knows they are there, though. He knows they are there even when it is night. Stones cannot move. Stones cannot swim away and go somewhere else. All stones can do is fall.

IV

Years pass. The stone starts to notice that he is getting smaller. He is only a tiny bit smaller than he was when he originally came into the sea but that tiny bit is still noticeable.

He sees the sand all around him. He understands that one day he will be a grain of sand.

He understands that all the grains of sand used to be stones like him.

He was a cliff once. He was tall, mighty, so strong he could stop the sea advancing further inland. Now he is a stone. He is still large, still strong, still something worth mentioning, but he knows that one day he will be a grain of sand.

There are billions of grains of sand on every beach.

The stone remembers his old life. He remembers how the sun felt on his skin. He hasn't felt warmth in years. The sea is always cold, but it strokes, and because it strokes, we welcome its touch on our bodies.

Years pass. The stone gets smaller. He remembers he used to have a pointy bit on his head. That point is gone now. The sea smoothed it away. Finally the stone understands: the stroking of the sea is almost as destructive as the violence of the waves.

V

The grain of sand likes its life. The sea, his best friend, picks him up and throws him about the place. He is sat somewhere, bored, surrounded by other grains of sand, then the sea picks him up and chucks him to his left. The grain of sand flies through the sea. It is exhilarating, exciting, so much fun.

However hard the sea chucks the grain of sand he always ends up sat on the seabed eventually. When he is on the seabed he is surrounded by his friends. He talks to them in his mind but they do not respond.

The grain of sand never stays anywhere for long. Every couple of minutes the sea picks him up and chucks him. Again he is flying. Again he laughs in his mind, relishing the feeling of the rapid movement.

Again he comes crashing down to the seabed.

The grain of sand does not remember being a stone, let alone being a cliff. The grain of sand does not remember everything the sea has taken from him. Once he was a mighty cliff, reaching high into the sky, so tall and so impressive that the people who stood at his edge felt fear flutter in their hearts at the sight of the drop.

His days as a cliff came to an end. The sea saw to that.

Then he was a stone. He was still big, still impressive, still something worth mentioning. The fish swam around him. His body was so large it dictated the movements of the things around him.

The grain of sand does not dictate anymore. He does not affect. He is nothing, nobody, forgotten, unnamed.

The grain of sand does not remember. He does not remember how he was a cliff until the sea killed him. He does not remember how he was a stone before the sea killed that too.

The sea picks up the grain of sand. The grain of sand is sat there minding his own business then the sea comes along, grabs him, drags him upwards, and chucks him far away from where he was.

The grain of sand laughs as he flies through the sea. He always feels immense joy when he is flying. Any other child would feel that same joy. Like the other children who populate this land he does not feel hatred because he is not advanced enough to hate. He is not advanced enough to get angry. He is an infant, a baby, a being living for this moment and this moment alone.

We must be like the grain of sand. We must learn to forget. Memories can only ever lead to hatred and anger. A life lived in the past is no life at all. You must live in the moment you are in now. Smile as you fly through the sea. Never cry about how your body has deteriorated as time ravaged it.

Every time the sea picks up the grain of sand the grain of sand was surrounded by his friends. The sea took the grain of sand out of his happy life and threw him off into the distance. Then, miraculously, as if God has designed the whole thing, the grain of sand settles back on the seabed and again he is surrounded by friends but all those friends are new and interesting.

FRESNO FOG
by Terry Sanville

Martha shouldered her backpack, grabbed the guitar case, took one last look around the room and stepped outside. The December tule fog drifted so thick that she couldn't see the Sierra Motel's neon vacancy sign. She made her way along the two-story building to the front desk where Julio sat hunched behind the counter, reading the morning edition of the Fresno Bee.

"You want some coffee?" he asked.

"No thanks. It just makes me pee."

"At least it's not raining."

She grinned. "Yeah, I should count my blessings."

Martha laid the room key on the counter. She lived at the Sierra for three weeks of each month, stretching her Social Security money to cover the cost. Julio gave her a good rate. But by the fourth week she had to clear out and live on the street until the Feds deposited her SS funds in her bank account. She'd find some place in the warehouse district to hole up, eat meals at the rescue mission, and panhandle if weather permitted.

"So what's with the kid?" Martha asked and pointed to the black boy down the walkway, squatting on the concrete next to the ice machine.

"He comes and goes. Been doing it for a couple weeks. Had to chase him off. Found him sleeping in the laundry room."

"Runaway?"

"Who the hell knows? But having him around isn't good for attracting customers."

Martha frowned. "Having me around probably isn't either."

The boy looked about ten, dressed in a flimsy windbreaker and jeans. His tennis shoes lacked laces. Fog dew dusted his mid-length Afro.

"I'm thinking about calling Social Services," Julio said, "but I hate to dump the kid into the system. He seems polite enough and never gives me any lip."

Martha removed her pack and leaned it against the counter, her mind spinning. "What if he stays with me?"

Julio laughed. "An old white lady shacked up with a black kid?"

"You have a dirty mind, Julio."

"Yeah, guess I do."

Martha cleared her throat. "What if... what if we helped out around this place in exchange for a free room?"

"You know the owners would never go for that."

"But you're never more than three-quarters full and the vacancies are just sitting there."

"Yeah, they've been bugging me about that. Want me to straighten this place up, make it more presentable, attractive. How the hell am I gonna do that?"

"Look Julio, give us a free room with two queens and we'll pick up the outside trash, clean the breakfast room after it clears, garden those weed patches you call landscaping, and do our own housekeeping. When one of the maids gets sick, we can fill in. And then there's cleaning up after those assholes from Bakersfield trash their rooms."

Julio grinned. "You've been thinking about this a while, haven't you?"

"Yeah, but now I might have a strong kid to do most of it." She chuckled. "I just hope he goes for it."

"All right, go ahead and try. But if the owners find out or somebody complains, you're outta here... for good."

"Sure, Julio, sure."

Martha approached the boy as she would a stray cat that she wanted to befriend. As she got close, she could see him shivering, his eyes squeezed shut. *He's probably dreaming of clear skies and summer heat,* she thought and coughed. The boy stood quickly.

"You okay, son?" she asked.

"Yeah, I'm cool."

"It's cold out here in this fog. Wanna come inside? I can get you some hot chocolate from the lobby."

"No thanks." He smiled but looked ready to run.

"Look, are you out here on the streets or do you have a home to go to?"

The boy eyed her threadbare clothes and wrinkled makeup-free face. "The rescue mission takes me in at night. My Mom lives in Sacramento."

"Why aren't you there with her?"

The boy said nothing.

"Hey look, I'm not gonna run you in or anything."

He shivered again and stared at his shoes. "Same ole story. Mom's new boyfriend doesn't want me around. Told me to take a hike. So I did."

"Yeah. I've been living on the streets myself. But the manager of this place offered me a free room."

"Why'd he do that? You're old and..."

"And what?"

"Forget it."

"Look, he'll give us a free room if we help out around here."

"What do you mean *we*?"

"You and me."

"Why?"

"He's tired of chasing you off."

The boy grinned. "Yeah, I can tell I'm getting on his nerves. But that laundry room is so warm with those dryers spinnin' 'round."

"The motel rooms are just as warm."

"What kind of help is he looking for?"

"Easy stuff – picking up trash, cleaning the breakfast room, weeding the landscaping, maybe a little housekeeping, you know, windows."

"Can I keep all the old donuts they throw out?"

"Sure, no problem. But I'm gonna buy a toaster oven at Goodwill and we can cook anything we want in the room. I got money coming from Social."

"And I can leave any time I want?"

"Yeah, sure. But after the Christmas break you should go to school."

"Yeah, I'd kinda like that. They should give me a free lunch. They did in Sac."

"So it's a deal?" Martha asked.

"Can I think about it?"

"No, if you don't say yes I'll lose the room and we'll both be looking for a place in this damn fog."

"Okay, okay. But don't start bossing me around. I can make it out here by myself, you know."

"Sure you can kid. What's your name?"

"Luke."

"Ah, a good biblical name. My name's Martha. Come on, I've got a sweater you can wear."

"I ain't wearing no old lady's sweater."

"Call me old one more time and you'll be spending the night locked in the ice machine."

Luke smiled, showing off even white teeth. Everything about him screamed *youth*!

Julio gave Martha keys to the motel's worst room, the one out back of the second building, right next to the dumpsters. The whine, bang and clang of the garbage trucks woke them twice a week. They spent the weekend before New Years holed up in their new home, doing chores, and eating the continental breakfast leftovers.

Once Martha's Social came in, they went shopping at Goodwill. She bought Luke clothing, a warm jacket, and a toaster oven and kitchen stuff to cook with. Luke enrolled himself in elementary school as a homeless student.

"Yeah, they gave me a test and said I could join sixth grade. I'll be in middle school next year."

Martha smiled. "You know, I used to teach sixth grade in private schools."

"Really? You can help me with homework."

"Ah, that was a long time ago. Everything's probably changed."

"Why'd you quit?"

"I didn't. I kind of retired. When my husband passed, I took it hard, burned through our money and more than a few cases of Jack."

"You still drinking? My Mom's boyfriend's a drunk. I don't think I can stay here if you're a drunk."

"Relax, Luke. I can't afford to drink anymore. The Doc said it will kill me if I do."

"Good. I mean, ya know, stopping drinking, not dying."

Their days fell into a pattern – each rose early to pick up trash before Luke caught the bus to school. Martha cleaned the breakfast room in mid-morning, bagging the leftovers, and helped the housekeeping staff with particularly messed-up rooms. After school they both gardened in the plots of landscaping across the motel's street frontage and around the buildings. As winter morphed into spring, Martha convinced Julio to pay for annual flowers for her to plant. By Easter, the frontage blazed with colorful petunias, zinnias, cosmos, marigolds, and snapdragons.

Julio told them one day, "I'm getting compliments from the customers about those flowers. One lady said she decided to stay here because the front garden looked wonderful."

"See, it's good for business. Now give me some money for fall flowers."

Martha spent more time introducing new plants and color arrangements, splurging on some flowering perennials. Most afternoons, motorists driving Blackstone Avenue could find her wearing a sun hat, sitting on a tiny stool and stuffing weeds, dead leaves and shriveled flower blooms into a paper bag. Some locals honked as they sped past. Martha always looked up and waved, the sun having tanned her face as brown as a field worker's, her fingers blackened with soil.

When the sun warmed her so that her joints didn't ache, she'd close her eyes and think back to her childhood in central Washington and the family's apple farm in the Wenatchee Valley. During the spring, the trees would be full of white flowers whose petals blew in the wind like fragrant fake snow. Later, Martha and her brother would go into the orchards and help with the picking, dumping full buckets of Red Delicious into the bins. Then came the long rest in autumn's slanted sunlight, when school started and excitement over Halloween, Thanksgiving and Christmas filled their hearts.

In her mind, Martha could see her brother on the ladder picking apples and singing. He was still on the farm, by himself, his wife gone long ago with their kids; she couldn't stand the isolation. Martha sent Christmas cards, none with return addresses. She felt guilty at her own escape, her abandoning him and anything to do with family. It's what people did at eighteen. But what do they do at eighty-four?

Martha busied herself pulling weeds and thinking only of their meal that night and what to do in the morrow. She figured that as life became short, so should one's thinking. Anything else just brought confusion and regret. But she wondered what Luke was thinking and how long he would hang around with some ratty old lady in a cardigan.

One evening, a couple days after school let out for the summer they sat watching a TV program on the science channel.

"That guitar in the closet, can you play it?" Luke asked.

"I haven't played for a long time. It was my daughter's."

"Does she live near here?"

"No, she's in Fresno Memorial Gardens."

"Sorry. What... what happened?"

"Cynthia died of cancer twenty years ago. Her husband and my grandkids moved back to Kentucky. I've lost touch. The kids are all grown by now."

"Jesus, you've got grandkids? Just how old are you anyway?"

Martha smiled. "A gentleman never asks a lady that question."

"Well I'm no gentleman and you're no—"

"Watch it buster."

"Hey, you know *my* age."

"All right, all right. I'm eighty-four... and don't say anything."

"So that guitar, can you play me a song?"

"Why?"

"I've got a C-harp and maybe we could figure something out."

"The neighbors will complain about the noise."

"We can go to the breakfast room – nobody's around there now."

And that's how it started. Clumsy at first, they tried playing old folk songs and the blues. As the days passed Luke proved to be a good harmonica player. And for an eleven-year-old, he had an adult-sounding voice. Martha splurged on a new set of guitar strings and strummed and picked away on the ancient Gibson, her brown-spotted hands and fingers searching for the right notes.

After a couple weeks, the word got around to the motel's patrons about the live music in the breakfast room in the evenings.

"Should I put out a tip jar?" Luke asked Martha.

"Sure."

"If somebody asks about us, what should I tell them?"

"You're my grandson, just in from Nashville after a world-wide tour."

Luke laughed and blew a bunch of quick notes that caused the small crowd to quiet down – a lot of them white-haired with canes. They seemed glad to have something to do other than watch bad TV and applauded loudly after each song. Luke and Martha made more in tips than any day panhandling downtown. Some guy left a twenty in their jar. They gave a part of their tips to Julio and turned the lights off before the ten-o'clock news started on Fox.

Julio didn't complain. "Yeah, you guys are great. Some of these folks will come back. You're good for business."

The summer passed all too quickly and, for Luke, the prospects of middle school loomed. When Martha tried to talk with him about it, he'd clam up, or would talk about skipping school for a while and traveling, maybe even taking the music show on the road. Finally, Martha cornered him one night and clicked off the TV.

"What's going on with you?" she asked.

He ducked his head. "My... my mom quit her boyfriend."

"You've been calling her? Why didn't you tell me?"

"I... I just wanted to keep what we have here separate from that mess."

Martha sighed. "Is it still a mess?"

"Not so much... and Mom wants me to come home. She's got a pretty good job and has moved into a new apartment."

"Do you want to go?"

Luke stared into her eyes. "I kinda do... but I don't want to screw it up for you."

Martha forced herself to give a false laugh that hurt more than a cry. "Hey kid, I've been surviving out here longer than you've been alive."

"Yeah but how you gonna do all the work?"

"Don't worry, I'll manage... I'll manage. Always got my Social to keep me going."

Luke came into her arms and they hugged, the first and only time they touched.

Tule fog came early that year with a vengeance. Luke dressed in his best thrift store clothes and stuffed everything else in his school knapsack. They ate breakfast in their room, not speaking. Martha craved a drink, a longing that had lain dormant for years. She shuddered to think it might return.

She finally broke the silence. "It... it'll be good for you to see your mom. She probably worried about you a lot."

"Yeah, it'll be cool."

"Just cool?"

"She told me she's got a computer. So... so I can play games, listen to tunes, do Facebook with my cousins – I've got a bunch that live in Sac."

"That'll be nice," Martha said. "Having some family to be with may give you... may give you strength... comfort."

"Yeah, I hope so. And I'll be in middle school. How great is that?"

Martha smiled.

Luke stood, pulled on his jacket and shouldered his knapsack. "Well, I'll see you."

"Probably not, Luke. But write me a postcard. Sorry I don't have a cellphone or computer."

"I will." He slipped through the motel room door and walked out into the parking lot.

Through the curtained window she watched him disappear into the thick fog before he even reached Blackstone. In her mind she followed him along the sidewalk, on his long trek to the Greyhound pickup at the train station. She could almost feel the slow bounce of the bus as it rolled out and trundled off northward toward Sacramento. She knew his new life would consume him. He would never write.

Martha struggled to keep up with the chores but couldn't. Julio noticed and threatened to charge her for the room.

"Hey, it's only fair," he said. "There's no more music and you can barely do the breakfast room and the gardening."

"I know, Julio, I know. I get tired so easily."

It rained Thanksgiving week. Martha packed her things and put on her almost new slicker that she'd bought at Goodwill. She felt sad and excited at the same time. Julio had called her an Uber and a Toyota Prius pulled into the parking lot and stopped outside her door. She checked the room one last time, shouldered her pack, grabbed her guitar and stepped outside, leaving the door open, the room key on top of the TV. She stowed her things in the back seat of the Prius and climbed in front.

"The train station, right?" the driver asked.

"Yes, please."

"Going on a trip for the holidays?"

"Yeah, something like that."

Their car hustled along Blackstone Avenue, making all the green lights, and turned down a side street then into the station's parking lot.

In Martha's mind she had already boarded the Greyhound, a big fish swimming in a school of cars and trucks that pressed northward. As they passed through Sacramento, Martha would wave, hoping by chance that Luke would stare out his bedroom window and wave back. Then onward through rice fields and into the mountains, past towering Mt. Shasta and across high plains into Oregon. Darkness closed in. She would wake in Washington to painfully-blue skies, change buses to a local that ducked into the Wenatchee Valley and let Martha off at a driveway that led to her brother's apple farm. He would be surprised to see her and overwhelmed, old, bent from years of hard work, barely recognizable except for his sweet voice that could still carry a tune.

She would fix them a pot of coffee, the house hardly changed. They'd talk for hours, the demon booze never raising its ugly head. She'd lie in her old bed and enjoy the quiet and comfort of home.

The Uber driver screeched to a stop in the train station's parking lot. The old woman slumped in the seat next to him, her head resting against his shoulder. Her unblinking eyes stared into the distance. The driver hesitated, then with a trembling hand reached across and took her pulse. Nothing. He stretched her out across the seats and tried CPR. Nothing. He drove to the nearest hospital where she was pronounced, her belongings confiscated. The driver hurried home through thick fog to be with his family.

DOUBLE WIDE
by Nathan Alling Long

My grandma lives in a double-wide trailer on an acre of land her husband left her. My family lives a few hours south, but I don't get along so well with my dad, so I'm spending time up here.

She bought the doublewide from a family whose father died of throat cancer. They had to sell the place because they couldn't afford to rent the land they were on or to move the trailer. The widow and my grandma bonded over losing their husbands and when they sat down to figure out a price, they each argued for the other one's side, worried what my grandma could afford and what the widowed woman needed.

My grandma moved the doublewide down the road to her acre of land, then had septic, water, and power hooked up, and a pond dug. She was the only one in the area to set her house perpendicular to the road, so the bay window faces the pond and only the window over the kitchen sink and the small one in the bathroom look toward the road. It isn't the road so much that's the problem—there isn't a lot of traffic. And the house across the street is neat and well kept. It's what lies a half mile beyond the house, just sticking out over the woods, quiet and calm: the top of the cooling tower for the Tom's Bay nuclear reactor.

Day and night, the tower exhales a thick soft cloud of steam. On sunny days, it's the only cloud in the sky, and on cloudy days, the strange vertical plume sticks out against the layers of natural clouds. But on a rare day, the steam rises until it touches a low cumulus cloud, making the tower look like it's a cloud factory—as if without it, there wouldn't be any clouds in the sky at all.

I sit outside sometimes in summer and watch the ducks my grandma named Donna and Lydia swim around in the pond. They try to make friends with the Canadian geese that visit for a few weeks every year, but the geese aren't friendly—they squawk, ruffle their wings, and chase the ducks away. Sometimes I get up and run after the geese, just to show them what it feels like to be chased and to remind them this isn't their land.

Other days, like today, I turn my chair and look out across the road, at the thin rim of the tower poking up behind the trees. I'd never seen a cooling tower before coming up here, except on a page in a social studies book which compared different sources of energy. When I first saw the tower as a kid, I told my grandma that it looked like a giant coffee cup with steaming coffee. I'm older now—I just turned fourteen two weeks ago—and I think of it like the tip of a cigarette, filling the air with smoke.

My grandma said the family that had lived in the doublewide all smoked—even the three kids, because, as the mother said to her, 'It'd be hypocrite to tell them no." Grandma says they packed up quickly, leaving behind the greasy pans, mildewed rags and dirty socks, forgotten boxes of baking powder and rat poison, but worst was that the trailer smelled like it'd been scorched by fire. "The walls were sticky and yellow with nicotine," Grandma said. "It was like walking through a smoker's lung." I don't know why the kids in that trailer ended up smoking. In my house, you can't see or smell what Dad uses, but you can feel it in the air. That's all I could think of when someone tried to hand me a cigarette in fourth grade. It's enough to make me never want to take anything.

Sometimes when I see the cooling tower, I imagine it exploding, huge pillars of fire. I get lost thinking about what I'd do if that happened, how I'd grab my backpack and my picture of my sister Alice, yell for my grandma to get out, pick up Donna and Lydia and stuff them in the car while yelling, "Goodbye suckers" to the geese. Then I'd drive the four of us West as fast as I could.

I imagine it happening like that, as though I'd be the one who'd get us out of there, who'd save us, though I'm not old enough to drive. I know enough to know we should drive west. I've watched the weather channel with grandma at night enough to see that all the winds come from the west—that we don't want to be east of the fallout.

Of course, deep down I know if an accident happened, we wouldn't have time to gather things up, to grab the ducks, and drive away. If the thing exploded, there wouldn't be time for any of it.

The other day, I asked my grandma about the reactor, if she was scared living so close.

"Not really," she said.

"Then why'd you turn your house away from it?" I get angry sometimes when things don't make sense to me.

"Well, it's only scary when you think about it," she said, "and I only think about it when I see it."

I think about the reactor all the time, whether I see it or not. At home, in my locked room, I sometimes dream I'm at Grandma's and the reactor's exploding. In the dream, I see a fire over the trees and it's so mesmerizing, I start walking toward it. I can't turn away. I tell myself to get out, but I keep stepping closer. I want to see the whole building on fire.

It isn't that I don't have enough things to worry about already. My dad takes drugs I don't even know the names of, and my mom lies to cover it up. She works extra jobs to bring in enough money for food, because Dad's addiction is always first. Mom is always telling my sister Alice and me that Dad's sick and he needs his medicine, but taking his medicine makes him sick, so he's trying to get off it, and we all have to be patient with him. But I'm the one who goes to bed hungry, who has to explain things to Alice, who locks my door at night like Mom tells me, in case things flare up. "There's a fire inside your pop," she told me once, "and it's important you don't add any fuel."

But I guess I did anyway. Last fall, Dad told Alice and me that this was it—he was going to quit once and for all. For us, for his family. He stayed in bed for almost a week, Mom making him food and bringing it to their room. Alice and me were on our own, which meant I made lunch and dinner for the both of us. When Dad was finally up and out of bed, he sat on the couch in front of the tv and drank beer from cans all day. We were told we could help by not disturbing him, by giving up our tv shows so he could watch whatever he wanted. I was mad. He was turning into even less of a dad than he had been, and we were giving up more and more.

Then one day in November, he called me from the living room. "Jaycee!" He yelled it strong, like I'd done something terrible. I didn't want to come out, but a part of me did. I knew I hadn't done anything wrong, and I wanted to see him try and accuse me of something.

"What?" I yelled back, slamming my door and marching out into the hall.

He looked angry, but also scared. He was holding a sandwich bag with about twenty bright red pills in it. I wondered if he was going to accuse me, say that they were mine. He looked at me like he hated everything about his life, me included. "Take these and hide them," he said. "Don't throw 'em away. They're worth too much. But I can't know where they are right now. Put them somewhere I can't find."

He handed the plastic bag to me and walked out of the house. I guess I should have done what he said. But I was tired of doing things for him, of giving up my life, of being the adult when I was only thirteen, and all my friends were able to be normal kids, worrying about themselves instead of their parents.

I held the bag stretched out in my hands there in the living room, trying to figure out what to do. And that's when I sort of left my body, floated up and looked back down and saw myself in some clear way I never had before. I was a thirteen-year-old girl holding a plastic bag with drugs. They were illegal, for sure, and if the police walked in right then, I figured I'd be the one who'd go to jail. But I hadn't done anything wrong. I only had them because my dad had given them to me. He was the one breaking the law, and he had dragged me into it, made me a criminal.

"A criminal in my own house," I heard myself say aloud before I floated back into my body. And that's when I knew what I had to do. I threw the bag of pills behind the sofa, grabbed my cell phone, and left the house. I ran in the opposite direction I'd seen my dad go and I didn't stop until I was in the woods behind the shopping center. When I caught my breath, I called 911 and told them that my father had given me a bag of drugs to keep and I didn't know what to do.

The police put Dad in rehab and then in jail. My mother was so angry, she wouldn't talk to me for a month. Everything she needed to say, she said to Alice instead. And in April, just before my dad was released, she told me I should go back up and live with Grandma for a while, because it wouldn't be safe for me to stay in the house.

"I thought Dad was sober now," I said.

"Oh, he is," she said, though I couldn't tell if she was telling the truth. "He's sober enough to know what his daughter did to him, just when he was trying to come clean."

It was still a month before the school year ended, but my mother worked out something with my teachers. I had to e-mail them my homework on my phone since Grandma doesn't have internet. I left without telling any of my friends, because I knew they'd ask why I was leaving, and I'd have to tell them or lie.

"We need you to be strong," my mother said when she took me to the bus stop to come up here. "Okay," I said, and got on the bus. Then I cried all the way up here, but cleared my eyes before I got in Grandma's car.

Here at my grandma's, things are quiet and safe. She doesn't drink or smoke. She just works in her garden in the day and watches tv at night. We always have enough food, though sometimes, I get bored. I bike up and down her road looking for other kids, but all I see are men older than my dad cutting their grass on riding mowers and old women watering flowers or walking out to the post box to check the mail.

And always in the distance is the cooling tower puffing out its steam, a distant, quiet threat. To get to it, you have to go down the road a couple miles then turn left on a lane that doubles back to Tom's Bay. There's nothing else on that lane, no reason to go down there, so I've never seen the power plant up close, though I want to. Only seeing the top of the tower, with its plumes of steam, makes it seem far away, not quite real. Like something that only lives in dreams.

Still, it's better here than being at home. Grandma has fixed the double-wide up nice. She said she had to tear out the carpet and paint two coats of primer on the ceiling and walls, just to get rid of the cigarette smell. There's a spare bedroom in the back, but I sleep on the sofa. I don't like being stuck in a room with the door shut. "You don't have to close it," Grandma says, but I tell her I prefer the sofa. I like being near the front door, in case I have to get out.

Sometimes I wake in the middle of the night from a nightmare about my father. In one, he's sitting beside me in my bed with a syringe in his hand. He's already so high that when he goes to shoot up, he puts the needle in my arm instead of his. I'd begin to pass out and claw myself to stay awake. I try to tell him to stop, but my speech is slurred. "It's okay," he says. "This way I don't feel the pain."

Last month, I finished school and turned fourteen. My grandma baked me a strawberry cake. I even got a card a few days later from my parents, though I could tell it was just from Mom—she'd signed both their names.

Now it's the Fourth of July, and Grandma and I are sitting by the pond, watching the neighbor's fireworks from across the street. The sound scares the ducks, who huddle in the middle of the pond, as if all that water will keep them safe. I think about my sister, Alice, and if anyone is taking care of her.

"I hate firecrackers," Grandma says. "They scare the hell out of Donna and Lydia."

"But you stay out here and watch them," I say, angry at her for some reason.

"I suppose there's a little pyromaniac in us all."

Not me, I think, but I keep watching them. She's right, I can't really turn away.

After they are done, Grandma goes in to watch tv in the living room, so I sleep in the bedroom because I'm tired and don't want her to feel like she can't stay up and watch because of me. I dream my mother calls me and tells, "Your father's gone." I can't tell if she means left or died—and she wants me to come home. I end up biking to the bus station, but when I get there, the driver says my ticket was only one way, north, not round trip. And it's expired.

I wake up in the room I don't recognize and think I'm nowhere I know. Then I go out to the living room and see Grandma sleeping on the sofa, in my spot.

As I make her breakfast, she tells me about the shows she stayed up watching, as though it's a sin she's confessing. "It must have been almost midnight before I fell asleep," she says. I don't tell her about my dream. Instead, I do the dishes while she goes back to sleep in her bedroom.

I'm looking out the kitchen window, wondering how long I'll live in this doublewide with Grandma, if I inherit the place when she dies. I wonder if I'll end up here all alone, like her. I stare up above the trees then, at the bright blue sky for a few minutes before I realize there aren't any clouds—in the sky or rising from the tower. Without them, the tower itself is hardly visible above the trees.

Something must be wrong, because reactors can't just turn off like that. *This is it*, I think. Instead of flames, there's just nothing.

My head grows fuzzy and I feel something race through my body. I drop the sponge and call out to Grandma. I scramble to think what I need to grab and if I should first wake her, and if there will be enough time to get Donna and Lydia.

No, I tell myself, there isn't time for any of this.

But still, I have to try. Isn't that what creatures do, even if it's pointless?

I yell for my grandma again as I grab my bag in the living room and stuff it with my phone, a journal Alice got me for Christmas, and a few clothes. Then I rush into Grandma's bedroom and tell her to wake up quick.

"What's wrong?" she says, sitting up, drowsy.

"The reactor," I say. "It just stopped."

"Oh, honey." She stares at me a moment. "You know, it does that sometimes. They turn it off to check the system. It's called an outage."

I look at her like she's not making sense. Then I drop my bag and run outside. I have to see for myself that nothing's wrong. The flowers in my grandma's garden are in full bloom, vibrant in the morning sun. The ducks are gliding peacefully across the pond. They'd sense something was wrong, wouldn't they?

I look at the tower sitting silently behind the trees, and I listen for an explosion, for anything. But the day is quiet. It's late enough in summer that even the geese, with their angry squawking, are gone. There's only the sound of a lawn mower, far off, like the hum of a bee.

I'm safe, I tell myself. I can just sit here and enjoy the day, which doesn't have a cloud in the sky.

published in issue 15 of *Qu* (Winter 2022)

PASSENGER
by E.J. Brady

I rode the Santa Ana winds through the canyon for one hundred years. The canyon, a 17-mile swath of asphalt and oak trees and towering yuccas, connected Santa Valenda to the Mojave Desert and was my home even before I died—before the Helenus Dam collapsed and twelve billion gallons of water buried me in my sleep. I roamed the canyon, a soul without a body, until I met her.

I tried to contact the living many times before. Most recently, a boy who was hiking with his mother and yelped with glee when I rattled the shrub into which he was kicking rocks.

"Coyotes," the boy's mother had muttered. She snatched him by the elbow and they hurried back down the trail the way they'd come. But the boy fixed his gaze over his shoulder where I, invisible to human eyes, hung in the air.

The woman was different from the boy and his mother and the others before; her spirit called to me—a tremor in the dry grass, a hum in the air. I followed it and found her at the wheel of her silver sedan for the first time. Curious and lonely, I settled into the passenger seat. Unlike the people before, she was not afraid when we met, although I am not sure she knew that we had.

Yellow sunlight streamed through me onto the passenger seat. "Can you see me?" I asked, but the veil between the dead and the living absorbed my voice.

She removed her foot from the gas and stared at the space I occupied. The car slowed. She looked to the road and back to me. She shook her head and raised her hand to the dashboard, and a splash of piano and strings flooded the car. Medtner, I noted, and our shared taste in piano concertos warmed me. We rode together until the canyon opened like a yawn onto the desert floor, at which point I drifted to the nearest outcropping of rock and watched her car shrink toward the horizon.

* * * * * *

I wished I had woken up right after the dam broke, if waking is what I did. A few minutes to hover over my body and gather clues is all I would need (my face, my age, whether I died alone). That would, I supposed, make it more difficult to cross over, but I still wanted to know.

When I woke up, mud painted the world around me ashy brown. The flood waters were gone, and I was surrounded by crumpled automobiles and skeletal trees. A motorcycle perched in the branches of a half-broken pine and the body of a deer slumped over a chunk of sandstone. Only a few glowing orbs—spirits of the dead like myself—drifted low between the debris.

I watched the sun set over the desert for the first time that night. A stream of souls slipped through the canyon, through the valley, and into the light. I felt the current too; it swelled behind me and prodded me toward the sun, but the connection to the canyon and my past self was stronger. I decided to stay in the canyon for a while longer, at least long enough to see if the yuccas would bloom again in the spring.

* * * * * *

What remained of the dam was a slouching wall about twelve feet high and covered in decades of sun-bleached graffiti. I was watching teenagers, three of them, add a fresh layer of paint when I felt the woman in the canyon again—a familiar buzz in the pine needles and air.

I found her parked in a shady turnout. She leaned against the hood of her car with a sandwich in one hand and a brown paper bag at her elbow. I moved closer. She took a bite and chewed, unaware. I moved closer and she wiped the palm of her hand against her jeans. Only when I stopped a few paces from her did her gaze, previously fixed on the treetops across the road, snap toward me.

A tug, gentle at first, pulled me toward the veil. It felt like a vacuum had opened on the other side and wanted me to fill it. The tug became a yank. When I looked down, two claws clutched the earth; at my side, black feathers cascaded down folded wings and a curved beak tilted between my eyes.

The woman blinked with bland curiosity. Real crows filled the canyon; the fact that one appeared out of thin air was easy enough to explain—a trick of the shadows, perhaps. To me, however, the abrupt reentry into the world of the living was jarring and obtuse. I tilted my head to one side, a greeting. She tore a small piece of crust from the sandwich and lobbed it toward me.

"You want a bite?" She asked.

I didn't know if I could eat food so I lifted my wings in what I hoped was a welcoming gesture. Her eyebrows shot up, skeptical. I squawked and nudged the bread with my beak.

"No one's forcing you." She crumpled the paper bag in one hand and fished her keys from her pocket with the other. "I'll bring you a menu next time."

The car door closed with a thump. Tires kicked bits of dirt into the air. When the car disappeared around the corner, the sounds of the canyon—the wind in the trees, the birds, the chirp of a squirrel nearby—became unbearably loud. The rocky soil and odor of pine stung my senses. I felt myself sucked across the veil again, back to where I was invisible and alone.

* * * * * *

The woman drove through the canyon five days a week with me in the passenger seat. She never spoke but occasionally glanced in my direction, which I took to mean she sensed me there. The invitation to shift into crow-form remained, but I feared the sudden appearance of a bird in the car would scare my new companion. We listened to music during our rides, sometimes podcasts, and occasionally rode in silence, but always together.

Once, as I waited for the woman, two cars came barreling down the road driving so close to each other their bumpers almost touched. When they reached an open stretch, the second car attempted to pass the first. At the same time another vehicle, this one going the opposite direction, appeared around the upcoming bend and, before anyone's foot could reach the brake, a resounding bang echoed through the canyon like cannon fire.

As I watched the sun set that evening, two spirits dipped into the valley. Shadows carved dark circles where rocks and tumbleweeds dotted the landscape. The souls cast a pale light that caused shadows to dissolve and reform as they passed. They gained speed and in a matter of minutes swept across the valley floor into the reddening sun. I wondered what they found on the other side.

* * * * * *

I found the woman parked in a gravel turnout a second time. She sat with her back against the tire of her car. Head back, she stared into the sky. Above us, branches stirred and cast a shifting patchwork of shadows across the ground. Her face was clenched and her eyes were red.

I felt the shape of a crow drawing me toward her and rushed into it. She met my gaze and a trace of recognition passed between us; her face softened into an almost-smile. I wanted to ask what was wrong, but instead plucked a pebble from the ground and dropped it next to her shoe. I would have quipped something about a menu if I'd had a voice.

"For me?" she said, and stuck out her palm.

I played along and plopped the stone in it.

"Here." She slid the rock into her pocket and produced a ring. In the center, a clear stone caught the light. "I'll trade you." She set the ring in the dirt and stood in an abrupt motion, dusted herself off and got in the car.

My connection to the woman's world—the world of the living—stretched and waned, and I was shoved back into my original form.

I hovered over the ring for a moment and decided to follow her car. She was making a phone call and the dial tone resonated loud enough for me to hear it, even before I slipped through the windshield into my usual spot beside her.

The phone rang once, twice, then clicked and went dead. She called again. The phone rang. Silence. She redialed. The call went straight to voicemail. She brought her hands up and slammed them down hard on the steering wheel.

* * * * * *

The woman didn't drive through the canyon for three days. Loneliness stung me like an ant and, in her absence, I roamed the canyon and pretended I was behind the wheel of a car. But the game grew rote and I grew restless. Restless until I found something on which to focus my unease: a coyote carcass in the middle of the road.

There was no blood but it was obviously dead. Its neck and one leg splayed at odd angles and its face twisted into a sneer. A shadow passed overhead. A red-tailed hawk settled on the coyote's shoulder and began to peck greedily; I crouched near in the shade of a nearby tree and watched.

A car came around the nearest bend, distorted by ripples of heat from the asphalt. The sound of the engine, at first a purr then a growl, grew louder as the car drew near. The hawk pecked, a scrap of flesh hanging from its beak. I shouted (some part of me hoped it was a wandering spirit like me and could hear my voice) but the hawk continued. Finally, taking notice of the car, it pulled at the coyote's leg: a futile attempt to drag the carcass to the side of the road. The car honked but showed no sign of slowing down, the bird no sign of giving up. I shrunk away.

The car horn blared, and the bird launched into the air and flipped over the windshield in a flurry of feathers and dust. The car straddled the coyote and disappeared around the next turn. The coyote's fur trembled in the wind. The bird landed, rattled but alive, several yards away and sat there stunned until another car passed and scared it into the sky.

* * * * * *

The next night, the woman drove through the canyon much later than her usual time.

"What are we listening to?" I said to myself as I drifted into the back seat of her car.

In the rear-view mirror her face was drawn; a tight frown pulled her mouth into a thin line. The loud pulse of a baseline vibrated the car (not our usual music) and a haze clouded her eyes.

Hidden in the back seat, I slipped across the veil into the mantle of a crow. Something felt wrong; I sensed it the moment my claws sunk into the upholstery. The music was too loud, the car too fast.

Slower, I thought. *Please, slow down.*

The woman muttered to herself. She was angry, and I could feel it seeping through her skin and into the air around us. The car wobbled for a moment when she lost—and quickly regained—control of it. Most people drove the canyon fast, even at night, but this was different. This was dangerous. Fear heightened my senses.

The road narrowed into a curve. A yellow sign rose in the dark and glowed: 35 MPH with a big black squiggle underneath. The woman pressed her foot into the gas pedal. I shouted, a blaring squawk. Her eyes darted to the rear-view mirror and caught me in it. I stared back, my eyes like small round stones, wings braced for impact. She yanked the steering wheel and instead of smashing into the canyon wall rolled the car over the opposite edge into the darkness below.

A surge of panic thrust me out of my body and I watched the car tumble down the embankment. Metal squealed against rock, and the car came to rest in the belly of the canyon twenty yards below.

Headlights appeared around the nearest bend. Another car, close. As if in response, orange flames appeared beneath the woman's crumpled sedan. The approaching headlights stopped; high-beams cutting through the dusty air.

Two silhouettes emerged from behind the headlights. The first took a timorous step off the road, down the embankment toward the fire.

"—get yourself killed!" The second silhouette said, prompting the first to stop a safe distance from the wreck.

I spurred myself toward the flames. The woman was alive; I could feel it. A vacuum, much bigger than a crow this time, opened on the other side and pulled me toward the veil. As I reached for it, I felt my connection to the living world grow stronger than ever. Invisible threads wove into cords. I tightened my grip, the world rushed into piercing focus around me, and I wondered what shape I had taken on the other side.

Smoke burned my nose and throat. I found the woman slumped over the center console of her car and reached through the window in search of the seat belt buckle. The fire ate at the passenger seat. The buckle seared my hand—a human hand—as I released the clasp and hauled the woman through the window and away from the car.

I dragged her away from the car until the force of an explosion, a flash of heat and light, pushed us to the ground. Illuminated, I saw her face was covered in rusty streaks of blood, and the flesh of my own hands was pink and blistered.

Sirens blared, and thick smoke blurred the flashing red and blue lights above. The heavy footsteps of firefighters sent a trickle of gravel and stones down the embankment. The feeling that I should go, that I didn't belong, breathed down my neck but I couldn't bring myself to stop looking at her face: the slope of her nose and the asymmetrical slant of her eyebrows that I hadn't noticed before.

Her eyes opened, and I wondered whose face she saw above her own. She brought a blood-slicked hand to mine. Her lips parted and moved without sound.

"—you," she said.

Over my shoulder, headlamps bobbed dimly. I felt the woman's spirit retreat, and my connection to the living snapped like a cord.

Bodiless, I watched firefighters subdue the flames and EMTs remove the woman on a plastic stretcher. The canyon carried me away, and I let it pull me to the outcropping of rocks above the desert where, for the first time in a hundred years, I fell asleep.

* * * * * *

A week passed and she did not return. I needed to be sure she was alright and wanted nothing more than her car, accompanied by the comforting buzz of her presence, to come around the corner.

Eight days passed. I decided to check on the ring. A fine layer of dust covered it, but the diamond peaked through. I felt an echo of my friend, the feeling that beckoned to me every time we met. Then I heard it: The faint sound of a car entering the canyon, the warm tremor in the wind that had signaled her arrival so many times before. At first I thought the echo came from the ring, but the shape of a crow formed vaguely on the other side. She was here. In a flurry of excitement, I leapt across the veil, swept the ring into my claw, and took flight.

I'd expected to find the silver sedan, but the car was different. *Of course,* I thought,

The accident. The new car shone like enamel. It rounded the corners of the canyon easily, cautiously, and I followed above on the dry wind.

The car stopped at the site of the accident. I found a small, scrubby tree and perched in its branches. Dirt and ash, a burn scar, was the only clue that anything happened there.

When she stepped from the car, I sensed the woman had changed. Her hair, a lighter shade of brown; her clothes, too tailored and formal. She held a bouquet of flowers in her fist and a picture frame under one arm. I watched as she knelt and placed the picture and flowers against a rock then stepped back, crossed her arms, and stared into the blue-brown horizon.

I thought she might recognize me by the ring, so I flapped my wings and cawed. The woman whirled around and, to my surprise, was not my friend.

She had the same pointed chin and tilted nose, but the eyes were wrong. Her jaw, more angular. The woman—the new woman—stared at me without recognition. I swooped down and placed the ring next to the picture and came eye to eye with the image in it: my friend. The meaning of the objects struck me. She was dead.

The ring lay in the dirt next to the picture frame, unnoticed. I fluttered away and the woman got back in her car. Tires spit gravel as she turned onto the road toward the city. Before the veil could take me, I retreated to my side of it and skimmed through the canyon—the tall grass, the shrubs, and the trees—until I reached the rocks that overlooked the valley.

The sun was low in the sky and cast deep red shadows across the valley floor. The space between the mountains and the canyon seemed to shrink, and a warm wind nudged me toward the sun. The tide grew stronger, the canyon cold and empty behind me. The sun swelled and a tense and dissonant harmony—the familiar call of my only friend, loud and reverberating—sang from beyond the horizon.

I began to slide toward the edge of the rocks, toward the valley. I turned back to the canyon, half hoping it would ask me to stay. Shadows darkened like bruises under the trees, and the canyon was silent. I let go. Caught in the thrall, I faced the horizon and flew into the setting sun.

THE SNUFFING OF MINOR FIRES
by Jeffrey S. Markovitz

She puts peanut butter on toast, then scrambled eggs on top.

I sit across the table and think about the totality of life, how it is first an endless ocean from shore riptiding to horizon and then it swiftly becomes the dribble of a faucet you're backed against.

She's two bites in before a kid calls.

When I think about the totality of life, I'm bored at how boring I am.

Also: the further away you get from something, the less real it ever was. This goes for all things, including but not limited to: the face of your Kindergarten teacher, objects in the rearview mirror, mornings where nothing aches, the first years of marriage.

Before long, one kid angles the bony part of its arm into the fleshy part of her thigh and eats her eggs while the other kid says her name (the name the kids have made her into; not the name I knew her by) at escalating volumes and the photo of us, above her shoulder—a beach somewhere, thinner bodies, full racks of teeth, coronas emblazoned on all of the ignorant royalty of the world—nailed through the drywall into an innocent stud, lies.

That is: fails to tell the truth. Like all photos do, trapped inside their own greater context.

And even if the thirty-year-old woman on the train seat next to me, yesterday, with the slim body I couldn't distract myself away from and the endless hair with only occasional grey and minimalist tattoos that were both incomprehensible and interesting, who read a hardcover book with no discernable title while I stole glances like grand larceny because whatever feed I scrolled through wasn't nearly as arresting, and even if I risked everything and suggested benignly: coffee or radically: dinner, and even if she could get beyond everything incompatible with who I was then and who she was then, I still wouldn't have had any idea what to say to her.

It's really not as bad as my histrionics. Things are essentially fine, better than most. My therapist even says my feelings of impending doom are just Panic Disorder—in the DSM—as if my existential crises from the air-conditioned living room in the suburbs are actually just misfiring synapses that I can mindfully journal away. Phew!

She carries a lot; she chooses them. I'm glad.

The youngest says *I have a tape measure. Do you want me to tape your measure?*

I wonder how you could even hope to calculate the scope of a middle-aged man. How to stick him back together. It's tougher than you think to find where a kid peed in the house. And I used to walk the city, looking for sky beyond the roofline and wondering about the wondrous beauty of the universe.

What I want most (I think) is to get rid of one of the comforters on our bed, so we can share again, and we can cuddle up for the five minutes before contact feels restless, and be the binary star; instead, when she's sleeping, I just look at her hair and only cry when she's asleep enough to snore.

I was going to write "weep" but I bet your patience is already thin.

The kids play in falsetto voices. I can't tell if they're mimicking one another or if kids play in falsetto voices.

In Thailand, during our honeymoon, she accidentally paid for an extra long massage and when she didn't return at the expected time, I thought I'd lost her, and I wandered around Bangkok until she was limber and I was scared.

I feel swallowed, gulped, which wouldn't be too bad if it digested me already.

Instead I sit in the humid stomach.

I tell my therapist that metacognition is ruining therapy for me. I explain how I feel like I can't complain, that no one wants to hear about the sadness of middle-class middle-aged men. That I feel like a fraud who DNF in the Olympics of Suffering. She says *I wonder if other men feel this way and think they don't have the license to express it.* I ask why it hurts more to pull out a hair than to break a bone. She says *That sounds like someone who's never broken a bone.* She doesn't actually say any of the above. She really says *How does that make you feel?* For $200/hr.

On her orders, I keep a journal. But rather than inscribe therein rites of panic...I mean...passage, I keep a list of my medical ailments. Not the little colds but the more pressing concerns. Is this neurodivergent? Anyway, eventually, the big one will come and I'll write: END OF LIST.

The word *passion* means *to suffer*. Think about that for a second.

If you've ever been through an elementary school morning, I could follow you around all day genuflecting and still wouldn't be able to bless you enough for your tribulations.

She talks to me. Mostly lists and plans. The snuffing of minor fires. Each day a wave. Some pummel some to surf. All crash. The trick, I know, is to breathe or hold breath or dive or swim or go limp and to know when to do which. She talks to me. Pharmacy refills. Oil change. Math homework. This is how she says *I love you* now and it's just the slightest bit different from when she wore dresses and I shaved and the towers of the city were our stage prop backdrops and the spotlight was bright but we didn't damn it through our squinting, but I know she means it still.

Where were we? Eggs on peanut butter on toast at the kitchen table. A meal only a nostalgic husband could love.

I tell my therapist that I don't actually want to be with other women. That I want the passion back in my relationship. That love evolves in a way that is essential to life. That the routine coasting is in itself a deeper form of love but doesn't snuff the major fire. You know? That her distance makes me love her more, like, than when we were young. That I worry my belly repulses her even though I don't have evidence. That the kids have vacuum-sucked all of her focus. I'm glad, really. That the passion of young love is irresponsible anyway. That it is self-destructive. Unrealistic. Unsustainable. That I want her to look at me the old way again. That I don't feel I have license to talk about it because, really, I have the ideal marriage. The ideal family. That therapy sure seems like a safe place to bitch about innocuous problems but it is a simulacrum of pressure release. She says *So, um, same time in two weeks?*

I'm honest every fortnight.

An abandoned house in the neighborhood was torn down recently. Two days and an excavator, and something that stood for 100 years ceded to patted down dirt. Thinking of my own home going that way some day makes me lonely like a complimentary hotel breakfast dining room.

The breakfast table is round and I sit on one side and she sits on the other and the kids sit on either side of her close by so we look like an unbalanced gyre. They form a parenthesis and I feel like a period but I know not to actually take it personally.

We give older people too much credit in this department.

I'm drinking a health shake with essential vitamins and nutrients: protein and prebiotics and probiotics and kombucha matcha extract that tastes like shit because that's where I am now. What phase.

In college, I studied literature. And the one lesson I learned from all cautionary tales is to never think back on good things too severely. No good can come of it.

A kid says *You're the worst daddy in the world* and I know not to actually take it personally. Maybe I made a face after a sip. But we give older people too much credit in this department: not absorbing the slight of a child into one's notion of self-worth. I mean, just because my hair is thinning doesn't mean I'm more mature.

The medieval steel helmet with vulnerable visor slots for the eyes.

There's a tunnel between the suburbs and the city and being born in the one all I could see was the other and after growing up I crawled through the tunnel into the other and lived but the tunnel existed still and through it I could look back always with disdain and then the kids had to go to school and so I crawled back through the tunnel to the very same place and the tunnel exists still and through it I can look back always with longing.

I'm trying something new with my hair. I bought pomade. It's stupid, but I like to keep joking with people that this is my midlife crisis. Joking makes it (feel) less true.

I walk groggily to the sink to deposit my breakfast dish, then move toward the living room where we stashed, the night before, the kids' clothes, so it would be easier to dress them before school—it's the little things—and ask them to come get dressed—which they never, ever, do—and she passes on her way to the sink and brushes, purposefully, my hand with her hand and we're off in opposite directions but both turn back and she says *I like your hair that way.*

Getting old feels like a long way away up until the moment of its arrival. It's the only gradual thing that's sudden.

All the clichés are eventually right. We are ships passing in the night. At least it is our ocean.

No one, and I mean no one, cares about your pain. The way teeth crumble; how using the armrests of a chair to rise can sprain a wrist. The younger don't believe you; they don't have the imagination for empathy. The older just have it worse. To them, your pain is a pun from the mouth of a clown.

In Thailand, I took photos on which I look back now and marvel.

On the day of the death of the dog we got as a puppy, on the day of an icon's conviction, on the day of a national tragedy, on the day of the announcement of the long list of the National Book Awards, on the day of a found lump, on the day of the lost Super Bowl, on the day of the humbled buzzing of ancient trunks, on the day of a folded hand; she was there, next to me on the couch, with a full plate of nachos, and we watched a show we'd seen enough to quote the lines in time.

Humans don't know what to do with their trash, so they build big piles of it where people can't see. The man who picks up my trash from the front of my house always waved at my son when he was little, who loved watching the truck compact all of the discarded things that wrapped what I truly wanted. On Christmas that year, the man stopped by my house with a toy garbage truck.

I tell my therapist that my ego termite-splintered when waitresses stopped flirting with me and now I'm pretty sure she hates me, or because I talk about women so much, thinks I have a crush on her. The waitresses were never really interested. They just knew they could use their power to get a better tip, which because it was directed at me suggested I had something of a power too. Man, this stuff looks worse than it feels when you write it down and reread it. I guess there's a reason voices drift into a distance. I tell my therapist that my vasectomy still hurts. I tell her I got a vasectomy because I'm a feminist. Jesus, maybe I *do* have a crush on her.

I'm not strutting; I'm limping.

When the eldest first went to school, I knew then the totality of losing control. This was a soft thing going into a windowless cave of teeth.

I help him with his shoes.

Journaling is a sham built into its own construction; ersatz privacy that you hope someone will, someday, pick up and read. Or is it just me? Is this an attention thing? I imagine myself zen in the center of a WD-40'd wheel nose-thumbing samsara and tripping on transcendental blues but am starting to think I just want to be clapped at on a stage.

Housefly, whole life, trying to get through a screen, to the outside.

I don't collect dandelion clocks; I've had realized sufficient wishes. Enough friends have tumbled in a deadbolt shaft to warrant a simmering hypochondria; every abdominal pain a cancer; she turns the heating pad to my preferred setting.

Hours constrict like young skin.

Though it may take evolution millions of years, it still stands to reason that our children are further on than us. Perhaps we look for gills when we should be looking for lungs.

The youngest jump-spins to a song and says *look daddy* and I watch her thinking of the blubbering moron I'll be dancing with her at her wedding and, sometimes when I've topped off my tumbler, I watch him sleep and know my house will one day be without him and it will be clean and quiet and ordered and I would accept abdominal cancer for just one more week of the chaos he brought (is this injustice or irony?) and the missing will grow like an unchecked forest and I'll be gone and an excavator will come and level this space of ours, where we shared, and all this time will be the effort of a wisp and the weep feeling rises inside but I restrain it in wonder and joy at the preemptive sadness of a loss of something had here now.

My therapist reads my journal and asks *How often do you top off your tumbler?*

High blood pressure medicine leads to an enlarged prostate. Enlarged prostate medicine leads to chest pain. Samsara everywhere.

The downspout is caked with tree droppings despite the wire mesh and so rain collects and falls from the porch awning in sheets. This isn't a metaphor.

I tell my therapist that moments are all we have. That I'm working on this theory that time *isn't* relative. Me, countering eons of physics and philosophy. I tell her I'm not a narcissist, really. Right? That no one reads Einstein but we all think he was a genius because that's what we're told he was. That no one really understands his theory anyway but he's still the high watermark of brilliance. Where's the healthy skepticism? So, yeah, and, uh, anyway, this theory that moments are all we have. That we should do our best to focus on each moment as if it were momentous and that at the end, at that final moment, we'll have a string of pearls even with nothing to buy. I tell her that there is no future, nor history, nor progeny, nor grand rollout of your endlessness, that we are more infantile than infinite, that time does not become slower as we travel faster; it speeds as we do, toward the less real of the further away. I can tell I've lost her. She has that look. Sympathy mixed with the clinical training of never telling your patient that he's crazy. Quotidian idiot.

If we gave birth like spiders—like sea turtles—would we be raptured with the ones loose in the web—still in the sand—would we care less about our loves that didn't live?

Here is a thing I did not know could be a thing: he coughed so hard that he broke bones in his back. This man. Pneumonia. Something else. A distinct memory of mine— one that I return to when dire, dour, pressing on the nerve of patience—a lift, his lifting, me above and surrounded by pines, that woods near our house where they bought the house to be near, my crown brushing the soft needles that would fall to brown and scent the nearby, my nose in the locus of it, his hands on either side of my ribcage, gently squeezing, the lift, his thumbs on hands so big wrapped around and printed into the small of my back. His back, fluid cough, shattered. Now.

His phone call a wheezing ghost from this side of the Ouija Board.

I hang up the phone and the table is cleared. The kids still aren't fully dressed: two legs through one leg hole, breakfast stains on a newly laundered shirt, where the hell is the other sock? But our eyes return to our seeing each other and she knows even though I haven't told her, and I warm my wet hands on the campfire of her.

There are some things I won't tell my therapist. These things, I tell her. I say, I can't lose him. I can't I can't I can't. Over and over like it makes sense. Like any of it makes sense. Like I've ever had a choice, really, about anything. I say cosmic histrionic things like the world can't exist without him and how can I be a father without my father and what kind of God blah blah blah. It's a big scene. This crush of the world. I'm so alone. I'm not alone.

I have always felt watched: spy cameras, an omnipresent God. I've also always defined individuality as being genuine against the rush of external pressure to act. But I acknowledge that, in being watched, everything I do is for an audience; the running film of my life, where I am the titular protagonist, prevents me entirely and totally from being me.

My therapist's chin slips from her shelved palm.

There's another Middle Eastern war. Children in the city won't eat today. A troll will create another handle. The mayor will sleep in. Tires screech through the new stop sign. Another pharmaceutical company will dump another poison into another river. Dogs will shiver chained in yards. A book will be banned. In the Middle East, a parent will pick up the parts of his child. Context.

Family like taffy.

When the school bus pulls away it's the kind of silence that seemed impossible seconds before and I turn back to the living room and there is the debris of plastic, the flotsam of kidspill, and I sit on the chaise part of the sectional with no back and so round my spine with elbows to knees and call out of work and she calls out of work and she sits adjacent and close, dunes eroding, but her eyes have never changed; we don't talk much but eventually get up and she makes a grocery list and I pick up the plastic destined for a landfill and we do the abnormal cleaning things: mop, bleach tub grout, edge lawn, dust dust from fan blades, change air filter, change basketball net, change batteries on everything, idle the furthering apart of our atoms—minor fires. We clip toenails; hedge hedges; settle debts; take stock of the stocks, cabinets, bucket lists; wipe the sleep from each other's eyes; spread the skin wide on each other's foreheads where we've made one another laugh; eat the leftovers; right the frames; think of the children when they were younger. I think about them; every stitch of pain worth it. Then the bus returns and another day is gone but they come and we're all in the living room and we tell them about it and their arms reach out pliable and flex like taffy, stretch and extend and so too do their legs and torsos and the slim necks and their bending forms elastic and resilient surround me and hold me, their forms connect airtight around, together we bend and mold to one another, blend, together all of our limbs and bodies swirl, rubbery, taffy, pull and extend and in the middle of our living room we live, this blob of a thing, contorted toward one another, swirled colors to grey, warm, the most precious evidence of the divine, and in the center we breathe a common breath and know the only thing we'll ever have is to share.

Together.

To get her. A comforter falls from the foot of the bed and the old wood slats crack and protest as old backs edge toward a border that is as imaginary as all borders; binary star, major fire.

THE LAST LETTER
by Dianne Taylor Dunham

"Dear Mr. Adams,

That's all I have. After an hour of staring at this paper, I can't get any further than that. I didn't expect to have to write this letter. I didn't expect to spend all afternoon in this garage surrounded by the shards of my grandmother's life – the wooden spoons, the stamps and stationery, the hatboxes. These things hold the essence of my grandmother like the fading notes of a concerto. They linger until you can't tell if you can still hear them or if you only remember hearing them. Tomorrow what's left will be whisked away to a charity or the dumpster. I just came for the Japanese tea cup.

I didn't expect a lot of things.

Gram died unexpectedly a week ago. It was a shock, but not a surprise. Pembroke women have been unexpectedly dropping dead for four generations. It's easy on the one who dies – no lingering, no sad good-byes, no regrets – but tough on those left to pick up the pieces. Unless it's Gram. She took care of everything. It wouldn't be right to leave her family in chaos. The funeral was planned, right down to the songs, the scripture readings, and the luncheon menu. Her will was signed and clear. All details were taken care of. She had long lists of who got what: my mother got the carved walnut bed in which (we were always told) she had been born two months premature. My unorganized sister, the aspiring author, got the maple roll-top writing desk with its honeycomb of pigeonholes and compartments. I got the oak kitchen table where Gram and I used to make lemonade and cookies.

I just came back for the Japanese tea cup. The one without the handle. The one Gram kept in the canister and always used to measure sugar for the cookies and lemonade. For Gram, there was a right way to do everything, and you were expected to do things the right way. You went to church every Sunday, and women wore hats. Beds were made – always -- with ironed sheets and neat hospital corners. There was a right way to make lemonade – two Japanese tea cups of freshly squeezed lemon juice (she wouldn't hear of powdered mixes), two teacups of sugar, and three slices of lemon in the cut glass pitcher filled with water and stirred with a *wooden* (never metal) spoon. There was always a pitcher of it in the fridge. You could expect it. You could depend on it.

Gram lived next to us in a big Victorian house that she had expected to fill with children. But one day when my mother was two, the foreman came to the door and said there had been an accident at my grandfather's plant, and she had better go to the hospital right away. They didn't expect him to make it until morning, so she stayed by his bed all night wiping his brow and talking as if nothing had happened. The next morning, they were surprised to find him still alive, but they repeated that there was no hope; so she took him home where she cared for him for ten years. For ten years, she fed him, changed him, turned him, bathed him, and talked to him every day as if nothing had happened. He never responded. People told her to put him in a home and get on with her life. She was young; she had a child. Some even suggested that she get a divorce, but she said she had promised to take care of him "in sickness and in health." She had made a vow. It wouldn't be right to break it.

Gram was the reason I went into psychiatry. Without a degree, without so much as a college education, she knew more about how minds work than anyone I have ever met. I could walk over to borrow a cup of sugar, and Gram knew immediately what was on my mind. She'd suggest that whatever I was making, we could make together, and in the process of mixing, measuring, and waiting, she'd draw out the problem, slowly and steadily, like pulling taffy. We talked about my spoiled little sister, fickle friends, unfaithful boyfriends. It was those conversations over Gram's kitchen table that inspired my thesis: *Culinary Therapy for the Treatment of Depression*. I suggested that for some people, cooking and baking might prove to be therapeutic. The topic was well received, and I was allowed to set up a test group which proved successful. I now use the method in my own practice. I've refined it to match patients' needs with specific culinary techniques. Some patients need the calming rhythm of kneading bread; some need to practice the discipline required to decorate cakes; others need the repetition of stirring soups to draw out their problems. Dad calls it "Cookie Therapy" and refers to my patients as "Cookie Kooks," but it works. Gram was right. You can get to know a lot about someone from across a kitchen table.

So I came to find the Japanese teacup. I was weaving my way over and around boxes of books and bric-a-brac, making my way to the kitchen utensils, when I knocked over a very large box. Postcards, greeting cards, and letters fluttered over the garage floor. As I scooped them up, I noticed a postmark from London. Gram had sometimes spoken of a former classmate, her "friend from London," who sent her postcards from exotic places. Gram would slip them under the glass on her coffee table. I remember pictures of the Taj Mahal, pyramids in Egypt, temples in Japan. She must have been saving these for decades. Tomorrow they would be gone. Any insight they held into my grandmother's life would be lost.

I picked up one letter and read:

"Dear Lil,"

Lil? Gram's name was Lillian. Not Lil. Not Lilly. Lillian. The neighbors called her Lillian. Her closest friends called her Lillian. She signed her name Lillian. No one *ever* called her Lil. It just didn't sound right. Only her grandchildren were allowed to call her by an abbreviation. The letter chatted on about work (Gram's friend worked for a very prestigious firm and traveled all over the world), family, books they had read, movies they had seen, their gardens, the weather here and there. Nothing of note. It was signed "Love, Warren."

Warren? Warren was Gram's "friend from London"? I had always imagined another very proper lady on the other side of the ocean, sipping tea and writing letters on flowery stationery. I never expected Gram's pen pal to be a man. I sifted through the letters. There were hundreds! The earliest was written thirty years ago. It seems Gram was in charge of reservations for her 25th class reunion, and Warren had written to send his regrets. He had never attended; however, he noted that there were a few people he would like to see again – one of them Gram. There were letters about holiday celebrations, about children and grandchildren, about family joys and tragedies. Although I had none of Gram's replies, I could fill in the spaces like a one-sided phone conversation.

I picked up one of the postcards. "Dear Lil," it said, "Today we drank rosewater at a little café in Bombay. You wore the blue silk sari we bought at the market. It fell like a waterfall from your shoulders and made your eyes shine like sapphires. You smelled of jasmine."

Gram? Bombay? She had never been out of the country. And if she were there, why would he send her a postcard? I picked up another. "We saw the opera last evening. La Boehme. You were stunning in black satin against the red velvet seats. The chandeliers danced rainbows through your hair. Your hand was cold, so I held it in mine. 'Que gelida manina.'"

In letters and postcards, he took her everywhere – to Japan, Egypt, China, Rome, Bali. They visited museums, attended concerts, the opera, and the ballet. They sipped lemonade in a café in Madrid and drank tea in Tokyo.

He sent her a teacup as a souvenir.

He was gentle, romantic, even solicitous. He reminded her to check her tires, to have the furnace cleaned, to be careful driving in the snow, to wear her hat and gloves. He worried about her and fussed over her from four thousand miles away.

The sun was slanting low in the garage windows and it was growing chill. I had to get home. I never meant to stay so long. I scooped up the letters and put them back in the hatbox. Should I take them or leave them? They were just letters from a man I didn't know. What sense was there to keeping them? I picked my way back to the door. I wanted to take just one more walk through the house. I stood one last time in what would never again be Gram's kitchen. I closed my eyes and thought I could smell cookies, but the notes were fading. The concert had ended.

On the way out, I noticed letters in the mail slot. Someone had forgotten to notify the post office, or the paperwork had not yet gone through. I picked them up. A phone bill, a catalog.

And a letter postmarked London.

The last letter.

I opened it:

Dear Lil,

I've been trying to call you, but you've been out. Probably spending time with those beautiful grandchildren of yours. I know I should say this in person, but it can't wait. I've waited too long already. I should have said this fifty-some years ago. Sit down, Lil.

I'm sorry.

I'm sorry I left you. It wasn't right. Not while you were expecting. Not ever. I'd ask you to forgive me, but I know you already have. You don't write to someone for thirty years while holding a grudge. I want you to come to London, Lil. Please don't say no. Come. I need you. I know – you'll say it wouldn't be right, that we don't know each other well enough. Lil, you know more about me from across the ocean than most people know from across the kitchen table.

Please, Lil. Say yes.

I'll get the tickets and call you soon.

Love,

Warren

So I've stared at this paper for an hour. I have to tell Mr. Adams - my grandfather - that Gram has died.

It's only right.

I WON'T LET THIS BUILD UP INSIDE OF ME
by Chris Cochran

We cross the street and I'm intoxicated.

One hand grips hers; the other, an unopened bottle of wine we've snuck off with from the wedding reception. Mason jar lights flicker in the distance. The reckless abandonment of inhibition from the dance floor has become a faint, buried bass line.

My uneven canter stamps the soil still soft from this morning's rain as we make our way across an unlit field used for overflow parking. "It's definitely the next row," I insist before hearing a chirp in the opposite direction.

"You sure about that?" Rae flashes a flirtatious smile, having just used the fob to locate her car like a sensible person.

I tuck the wine bottle under my arm, dangerously, in order to hold both her hands. "You know that—" The wine bottle slips and I instinctually try to catch it with my foot, punting it a short distance instead.

Amused with my drunkenness, Rae laughs as she turns around to pick up the bottle of wine. "Still intact! For a second, I thought you ruined everything," she jokes, handing me the bottle. I stifle any professions of love, fearing she's right.

Canopy lighting brighter than the sun interrupts my passenger seat stupor as we pull to a stop at a Shell station. Against Rae's protests, I pump the gas; chivalry trumps inebriation when you're in love. A modest gesture to show her what I can not tell her.

Rae heads inside and I'm looking for a place to swipe my credit card, oblivious to the new chip reader, when a gold Honda Accord rolls up beside me. It's a decades-old model in pristine condition. The driver steps out and leers at me from over the top of her car, her close-cropped red hair ablaze under the gas station lighting. Her large, square glasses rest precariously on her button nose, one shake of the head away from toppling over. She's wearing a denim skirt belted at the waist. A stack of books adorns her plaid top with the letters "A-B-C" forming an arch above.

"It's a chip reader, honey. Do you need me to show you how it works?"

I roll my eyes and insert my card, turning away from Mrs. Deprecor, my first-grade teacher. I can feel her eyes boring a hole in the back of my head.

She says, "I was just trying to help, no reason to be—"

"Would you just leave me the hell alone?"

* * * * * *

I may have kissed a girl named Marcy in first grade during recess. I suspect she propagated the rumor herself, however, having no memory of the kiss. News of our alleged affair inundated the school. Mrs. Deprecor took me aside for interrogation as our class returned from the playground. She leaned over, hands resting on her knees, and delivered a look of incredulity.

"Did you kiss Marcy during recess?" she said.

"I don't know," I said.

"You don't know?"

"Yes."

"Yes, you kissed Marcy?"

"No. Yes, I don't know if I did." I didn't learn about "Pleading the Fifth" until high school.

Mrs. Deprecor stood up, sighed heavily, and decided on a different approach: "Look, you can't kiss girls. Do you understand?"

"Like, ever?"

"Not on my watch. Go have a seat." I hurried away, more confused than before.

Like most first grade teachers, Mrs. Deprecor became relegated to the inner recesses of my brain, a memory that only resurfaced as an occasional answer to a security question for an online account. So when I saw her reflection in a dance studio wall of mirrors at a community college fifteen years later, it was surprising. I was watching a classmate interpretively dance to "Vermillion" by Slipknot for an English class project. This was not surprising and only sounds so to those unfamiliar with community college.

For over five minutes, our class watched a horror movie unfold. If memory serves me correctly, she began her dance by writhing out of television static. As singer Corey Taylor growled, this talented demon conjured spirits through a slow, disturbingly seductive crawl across the vinyl flooring. Every guy watched a reflection of the performance in the dance studio mirrors, fearful of looking straight into her eyes and either being cast into the underworld or, worse, aroused.

Perhaps I watched the performance a little *too* attentively—a fact evidenced by the reflection of my scowling girlfriend. Our eye contact was a different type of horror movie altogether.

With traps laid all around, my eyes desperately sought refuge; instead, they spotted Mrs. Deprecor. She was standing amongst the reflection of students at the crowd's edge. She shook her head disdainfully, her glasses slipping down her nose. A colorful arch of letters began and ended just above her crossed arms. She hadn't aged a day since first grade.

I looked away from the wall of mirrors to see the source of the reflection without luck. When I looked back, her reflection was gone.

Leaving campus that evening, I spotted Mrs. Deprecor sitting on a bench in the commons. She looked exactly as I had remembered, her crimson hair not showing the slightest hint of gray—an impressive feat for someone who should have been well into her seventies.

As I approached, she was carefully applying glue to the back of a heart she had cut out of pink construction paper. She began pasting the heart onto red cardstock paper, then looked up to meet my perplexed gaze.

"It's getting chilly. Did you forget to bring a jacket to school today?" she asked as she continued her project, interrupting my rumination.

"What is this? Are you—"

"Have a seat." After confirming no one was in our general vicinity, I sat down beside her, still acknowledging her authority all these years later. "Sit up straight, you're slouching."

"Why are you here?"

She grabbed a pair of scissors and started cutting a larger heart around the one that she had just pasted. "Your guess is as good as mine. Which makes sense when you think about it."

I slowly slid my hands down my face, pushing my closed eyelids with my fingertips, and let out a long sigh. "My eyes wandered a bit. So what?"

"They didn't use to." She finished cutting out the heart and held it up to admire before reaching over and throwing it in the trash can beside the bench.

"Well, that was...not subtle." I watched as Mrs. Deprecor gathered her crafting supplies into a giant satchel, stood up, slung the bag over her shoulder, and walked away.

I spent the following two years trying to fix a hopeless relationship, unwilling to accept the notion that sometimes people just grow apart.

Although never in the same location, Mrs. Deprecor arrived when feelings of self-doubt and vulnerability crept in. Her visits were sporadic at first; however, as my relationship neared its end, she appeared often, and we settled into a comfortable routine. Our conversations felt like free therapy, which explains why I initially mistook her intentions as helpful rather than sinister.

She would ask me to pinpoint exactly when things went wrong, to consider what I might have done differently. She framed the relationship in a way that suggested mending was possible, that things could get back to what they once were—I just had to fix it.

I had just clicked send on a regretful text to my now ex-girlfriend because the internet told me she was *in a relationship* but that had to be a mistake because how could *she* be *in a relationship* since *we* were just *in a relationship* that ended like yesterday and didn't what we have mean anything? Surely, I communicated my concerns in a respectful and rational manner.

"I told you not to look!" My new roommate. She had moved out, and he had moved in. No time to mourn in private when rent is due.

They had met once, my roommate and ex-girlfriend. She came by a week after we split to pick up the last of her things. When she left, his only comment was that "she smelled like dead flowers." These words were the on-ramp for my long road to recovery. He was right, of course, about her perfume and about avoiding social media.

I was staring vacantly out the window of my second-story apartment, which sat above a grocery store, perhaps looking for a way to escape the mortification I felt after transforming into the type of crazy that only heartbreak can evoke. Mrs. Deprecor was loading groceries into the back of her Honda. We locked eyes for a moment; she shook her head, almost apologetically, closed the trunk, and drove away.

What purpose had Mrs. Deprecor served? Was she trying to help, or was she simply delaying the inevitable? For the first time, a splash of bitterness washed over me.

My ex-girlfriend had the decency to never respond to my text and my roommate had the decency to take me on as a third wheel most weekends and time had the decency to drag me along, but Mrs. Deprecor was not as accommodating. Eventually, I began dating again, and she was there every step of the way, reminding me that everything I had ever done in the presence of women was bad and that I should feel bad.

* * * * * *

"Applebees for a first date?" Mrs. Deprecor slid into the booth previously occupied by someone I had allowed my mother to set me up with. "How do you expect any woman to take you seriously when you order mozzarella sticks?"

I looked over my shoulder to make sure my date was not on her way back before whisper-shouting, "Are you crazy? You can't be here—she could return any minute!"

"Honey, she took her purse and coat with her to the restroom. She's not coming back." She was right and seemed smug and satisfied delivering this revelation. "Why did you keep talking about that time you dunked a basketball?"

"I don't know. I was nervous. But it is impressive. I'm not even—"

"It's not, and she didn't care."

"There was a lull in the conversation. I had to say *something*. Besides, I'm not even six feet tall. And look at how short my arms are," I said, my voice becoming more animated as I reached toward the ceiling. I noticed a few sidelong glances, so I lowered my arms and the volume of my voice to an almost inaudible hush. "What am I supposed to talk about?"

"Literally anything else."

Our server came over with the check and failed to notice Mrs. Deprecor, but definitely noticed the absence of my date. "She had to leave early. She, uh, works a night shift," I explained for some ungodly reason. What was wrong with me? I handed her my card and waited until she was far enough away before turning my attention back to Mrs. Deprecor. "Can I ask you a question?"

"*May* you ask me a question."

"Why am I so bad at this?"

"Beats me," she replied. "From what I remember, you were quite the adonis at recess. Of course, you were a mumbling idiot back then, too."

"Well, thanks. This has been helpful."

The server dropped off my card mid-stride and continued walking toward another table. I signed my name quickly and stood up to leave. As I was walking away, Mrs. Deprecor called out, "That's your signature? I can't even make out any of the letters. Did they not teach you cursive in third grade?"

* * * * * *

It was an early morning after a late night. I watched a scattered fog wind its way around saggy clotheslines and broken lawn furniture from my kitchen window. Through the haze, I noticed Mrs. Deprecor sitting on an old, rusty swing in the abandoned playground across the street from the double-wide that two friends and I squeezed into shortly after college. I walked over begrudgingly, having at this point already learned the futility of avoidance. Better just to confront her, get it over with.

"You were out late last night," she said as I sat down in the much lower swing beside her. "Remember our talk about the importance of routine?"

"What do you want?" I asked curtly, but I knew. I always knew.

She stopped swinging, looked down at me, and said in an accusatory tone, "You kissed a girl here last night." I followed her eyes as she looked over at the trailer that was in the lot diagonal to our own, and then I looked down at my feet as they scraped the dirt gouged away beneath my swing.

"Technically, she kissed—"

"Do you really think it wise to start a relationship with a girl who still lives with her ex-boyfriend?"

"Well, it doesn't sound great when you say it out loud," I admitted with a short laugh. "Look, this isn't what you think. I won't feel guilty—"

"And yet, here I am." Mrs. Deprecor jumped off her swing and adjusted her denim skirt. She surveyed our surroundings and shook her head. "Just look at this place," she said in disgust before disappearing into the morning mist.

* * * * * *

My first few steps exuded confidence, but then my lower body turned to lead. My friends noticed the hesitation, which confirmed what they already knew: there was no way I was going to go through with this. Their playful jeering, however, was enough motivation to keep me trudging along.

She looked up from her drink, and we made eye contact as I approached. This was it—the point of no return. Why were my only two choices dying alone or experiencing extreme discomfort and rejection?

I hadn't even considered what I was going to say, but it ultimately didn't matter. Mrs. Deprecor was lurking at a table in the back corner. She shook her head, reminding me that my actions were both unwanted and inappropriate.

So I mumbled an awkward apology to this poor woman as I walked right past her and straight to the restroom, my friend's laughter in the background playing me off the stage.

"Well, that was embarrassing," Mrs. Deprecor said as she lifted her denim skirt at the urinal beside me.

"Jesus, what are you—" I looked over, regretfully, attempting to understand the logistics of what was happening. My eyes quickly redirected to the wall above my urinal. "You really shouldn't be in here." I zipped up and stepped toward the grimy sink, got a modicum of soap from the dispenser after mashing the button several times. As I rinsed my hands under the warm water, I heard Mrs. Deprecor from behind me.

"Have you ever considered just giving up? How do you expect to make someone happy when you're so miserable?"

I looked up and stared at her reflection in the mirror. While her vitriol's intent was harm, it actually had an inverse effect; for the first time, Mrs. Deprecor had actually passed along sound advice.

So I gave up. Until I discovered happiness on my own. Then I met Rae.

* * * * * *

I fumble with the gas tank cap until it finally spins off. I shove the nozzle inside, enraged. Mrs. Deprecor begins her belittlement.

"That is *not* how you talk to an adult." I'm suddenly six again, running up the concrete walkway to get in line at the end of recess. Being pulled aside for a private scolding.

I close my eyes and let her rancor fade into a muffled hum, but I can only fend it off momentarily. Her words emerge a cacophony of self-inflicted criticism.

"You would have told her by now if you were so sure she'd say it back," she hisses.

Enough is enough.

"Why didn't you pull Marcy aside and ask her if *she* kissed *me*?" Mrs. Deprecor scoffs and turns away.

"Please don't tell me you're still thinking about—"

"We didn't even kiss! I mean, we probably didn't. We might have. Either way, it's beside the point." I'm rambling, but I refuse to let my drunkenness interfere with this sudden moment of clarity. "I blamed myself because you blamed me."

I stop and take a few breaths, letting the anger subside. "My whole life, you've been a constant reminder of how bad I am at all this. Never here to help, just here to criticize." I notice a subtle shift in her expression—not quite remorse, but a lesser hostility. "You've made it impossible for me to believe that anyone could ever love me. But, of course, you're me. So what does that mean?" I say.

Mrs. Deprecor puts her pump nozzle back in its holder and, for once, is speechless. She huffs angrily, climbs into her car, and quickly pulls away. I watch her taillights shrink into the evening until the clicking of my gas pump brings me back to reality. I turn back to the pump and notice Rae approaching.

"Here you go, drunkie," she says as she holds a literal gallon of water out in front of her with both hands, pretending the weight is almost too much to bear.

"I love you, Rae."

"Are you serious?" she asks. "You're telling me this now? If I would have known a jug of water was all it took, we could have gotten past this months ago."

"Ugh, I'm sorry."

"No. God, no. That was not—" Rae looks horrified. "Sorry, tell me again. Do over."

"What?"

"Say it again!"

"I love you!" I blurt out again, saying now twice in ten seconds what I could not say over the past eight months.

"I know," she replies. "I love you, too." We kiss. I'm sure of it.

AGAINST ALL ODDS
by Kevin Novalina

The FOR SALE sign is staked through the goat's beard inside the Sigil of Baphomet that's spray painted bloodred across the yard. What was our home is gutted, everything stuffed inside the U-Haul backed up the drive: appliances, furniture, TVs. Clothes in piled trash bags and pillared totes of toys. Porcelain whatnots wrapped in several weeks of daily crime coverage with glass knickknacks in police reports and obits.

A gust blows the sign over. I grab a stone edging my wife's flower garden and drive the stake deeper through an inverted point of the Pentagram, then step inside where Michael's zipping his Hot Wheels the length of the hall floor. Masking tape stretches, rips in our old bedroom where Melissa's packing the rest of her things and sobbing. Still.

What remains of our lives is in the few bags and boxes scattered around the living room. I grab a duffel of photo albums and a Scooby-Doo "Mystery Machine" pops the baseboard between my legs with a hollow thump. I snap my son a wink, but he doesn't see or he isn't looking.

Back outside, I wedge the bag beneath an armoire. Fanning my collar, I trowel sweat from my forehead with the blade of a hand. This heat's like a pillow pressed over the face, but the wind's picking up. The sky bleeding the color of soaked newspaper, a storm quaking in the distant thunderheads.

Melissa's slamming things around the front room and I holler to be careful with the white box. "That's your good China!"

I hop up on the loading ramp to adjust her Cheval mirror, and in the glass see the box of dinnerware wheeling out the open door. It hits the ground and flips upright on one of the circling Hebrew symbols spelling: LEVIATHAN.

Her second anniversary Bone China. I already miss her.

Not bothering to look, I force the dented box between mattresses, the shards of crockery clattering within.

"Spiked Christ," Hewitt shouts, crossing our yard in a wifebeater and striped socks yanked to the shins from his old "McNamara" boots. "Hotter than a blistered pisser in a pepper patch." He's slashed in white paint, carrying two beers to a hand with extras in each pocket of his cutoff trousers. He passes me one, cracks another open, nods toward his place next door. "So what you think about her?"

"About who?"

"My old fence," he says. "Finally finished her off."

I nod, open my beer. "Might wanna cover it up."

"Cover what up," he says, "she's still wet."

"She's about to be soaked."

He squints up, flings a hand. "Shit'll miss us," he says, then nods at the family mess in the moving truck. "See we're about finished."

Yeah, I tell him. "Just about."

"Well look, me and the fellas," he says, swatting a mosquito on his hairy leg. "All that yellow shit at the cookout." He stares up the street, rimming the beer can over his underbite, then says: "We get to sipping, we get to ripping's all."

I tell him I'll live.

"Bygones, by God."

Michael rushes outside, slashing a Matchbox Blue Angel through the air.

"Mighty Mike," Hewitt says. "What're we flying today?"

"Boo Angel!"

"A *Boo* Angel," Hewitt says as the boy banks and dips the jet back inside. He leans close. "Still getting the froze shoulder?"

I nod.

Something crashes in the kitchen. "God*damn* it, Michael," Melissa yells. "Out!"

The boy starts crying and Hewitt whistles, hits his beer.

I tell him she's taking Mikey to her parents' house for a while. Maybe a long while. "Ever hear of a wife leaving her husband for thinking he's a coward?"

"Hell," he says, "mine left me for telling her to get outta the car." He crushes his empty can. "Course, I was hitting fourth gear when I told her." He nudges my side and points up. "Rain's going around us, you watch."

* * * * * *

After a few more loads, I lean on the back bumper with a sweating beer to my temple. Hewitt opens another and stands peeling paint scabbed over his shoulder tattoo: a lightning bolt behind a scythed reaper. A 1 near the blade and a 9 at the end of the snath with THE WALKING DEAD in crested scrollwork above.

After we first moved in, at one of Hewitt's barbecues I asked him what Vietnam was like.

Flipping a T-bone, he rubbed his shoulder and stared at his worn fence. "At times," he said, "like having a second to live every second you're alive."

The breeze chills my shirt, the realtor sign wavering.

A pickup passes, the driver rubbernecking.

Hewitt nods at the Pagan insignia. "Heard anymore from the boys in blue?"

"Said they'd keep their eyes peeled," I tell him, chuffing. "They're dead set on it being a prank."

What local police have their eyes peeled for is a phone call I received at 3:15 a.m., five weeks ago tomorrow. What I was told on said call was the occupants at 611 Oak Street had been commanded for slaughter. "Ritual sacrifice," the man said, "by His people to our Lord and Savior, Jesus Christ."

A family offering in display of unflinching faith and loyalty to God.

My family.

"A martyr's disembowelment is the noblest way to die," the voice said, as if quoting auto insurance while I still wiped sleep from my eyes. "You should feel blessed."

After my statement, the investigating officer asked if we had any known enemies. Disgruntled coworkers, neighbors. "Anyone who might have cause to do something like this."

And no, I told them. Not that we're aware of.

They asked if the man used specific language, like calling us by name.

He just said the occupants of this house. But he said *this* address.

They asked if we'd recently lost a purse or a wallet. Any mail gone missing, charges on a credit card we didn't make etc.

The answers, all no.

We learned the call came from a burner phone, the signal pinging off a tower in Everly Mills. Given the location, the officer said, it was safe to assume it's just some prep school shitdicks screwing around. "Ninety-nine percent of the time," he said, smiling what could be reassurance or mockery, "these things are just a hoax."

At the next cookout, I told Hewitt about it.

"Sacrifice," he said. "Like in the Abraham sense?" He smoothed his Fu Manchu. "Gotta be a joke, I mean, I'm taking someone out I sure as shit don't call and forewarn." He closed the grill, downed his beer, and said: "Even Isaac didn't know what the fuck till his ass was altared on Moriah."

The first week after the call, I couldn't sleep. I poured through every newspaper, never missed the 7 o'clock news. Looking for something—*anything* possibly related.

Every time the house settled, I was peeking around corners. When the phone rang, my body went dead. Once Michael woke screaming from a nightmare and I puked up Melissa's lasagna.

"Just install a burglar alarm," she said, watering her gloriosa daisies and sunflowers.

"I can't believe you're not more concerned," I said.

"I made the same calls in high school, except I'd be AT&T or the IRS." She cupped my cheek with a gloved hand. "On the phone," she said, "you're whoever you wanna be."

The next day, I began researching alarm systems and security lights. I bought a revolver and a .22 rifle, but I've never even held a firearm, let alone shot one. And while bright lights and loud noises might deter burglars or rapists, that caller sounded different. I mean, if Christ endured the Passion, what would passionate nutzoids endure proving obedience to God?

By the second week, I suspected garbage men and joggers, landscapers and dog walkers. In my periphery, I watched mail carriers, linemen, even Girl Scouts selling Thin Mints and Do-si-dos. Every staring eye was someone anxious to see our insides out. Each passing car, a potential Crusader. This world anymore, even Hewitt could be an Abraham.

"Maybe we should move," I told Melissa one afternoon.

"You lost your goddamn mind?" she said, pruning her grandiflora roses. "It was *one prank call!*" She told me it isn't just a house, it's our home. That we'll take a bath in this buyer's market. Not to mention Mikey adores his teacher, so do we really wanna risk landing in a different school district. Deadheading her floribundas, she said: "You're not uprooting our lives over some trust fund fucks messing with your head."

I tried explaining how I come home from work and can hear the puddles of my wife and son's blood squishing underfoot. I turn a light on, the walls are sprayed red. They may be in my head but it's our bodies they're after. "You can't have a second to live," I said, thinking of napalm and Bouncing Betties, "every second you're alive."

One morning the third week, I stepped outside to the official insignia of the Church of Satan like a crimson WELCOME mat spanning our yard.

Standing in the drive, the officer called back to our house said: "You ever hear of the Tag Gag?"

"The what?" I said, watching Melissa walk out the Pentagram's contours.

He opened a memo pad, then told me about this thing the department had gotten wind of called the Tag Gag. Where these bored rich kids go out on random nights performing various acts of vandalism. "*Tagging*, if you will, fine folks such as yourselves just to mess with them." He clicked his tongue. He yawned. "Kinda like a Boujee type of terrorism."

Melissa stopped beside the officer. "Either way he was worried for nothing," she said, nudging him. "It's Aleister Crowley, not Abraham after all."

They laughed.

At work, I called the listing agent and put our house on the market.

There's a fine line between being a pussy and being a news segment.

Eight years ago, on vacation at Martha's Vineyard, I stepped on a nail jogging barefoot on the beach. Miles of sand and my foot finds that nail.

I told Melissa to start packing. "Ninety-nine percent," I said, looking up Moving Trucks, "is not my kind of odds."

* * * * * *

Last summer, the bodies of two newlyweds were found dumped off I-90 near Spokane, Washington.

In Salt Lake City, a family of five was tortured and burned alive three Christmases back.

Returning from his carport with more beer, Hewitt crosses Baphomet's horns, watching the scudding clouds above.

Melissa steps out with the last box of her stuff.

"How do, Sweet Melissa," Hewitt says. "We're looking beautiful as always."

"Not hello, Hewitt," she says, watching me from a tragic mask of running mascara. "Goodbye."

Biting down, my fillings throb. "Just set it anywhere," I say. "I'll make it fit."

"You ever wanna be neighbors again," she tells Hewitt. "House next door to my folks got TP'd last week." She heaves the box up, cracking the flatscreen under its bedsheet covering before pinballing off the ramp to the ground. "They'll for *sure* be moving soon."

She mopes off, stopping beside her garden to toe her wilted bleeding hearts. Then gets in her Xterra parked before the U-Haul, slams the door, and cranks it.

"Women." Thunder growls and Hewitt cocks an eye up. "Can't live with them," he says, "by God it's gonna rain."

Three Octobers ago, an adoptive family of six was slaughtered while vacationing on the Cape, their bodies washing up along the shore days later.

"Know what she said?" I nod at the lawn art. "Said it was probably me painted this shit to force the move." I jam the box in until it holds. "She didn't hear that voice," I tell him. "The guy's either Marlon-fucking-Brando or he meant what he said."

Hewitt says fear's a powerful thing. "Operation Buffalo, lots of boys considered burying their KA-BAR in a thigh or blowing off a toe," he says. "Anything to get medevacked home." He tips his beer, trailing the can from his mouth and crushing it as it empties. "Course none of us followed through."

Fingering foam from the walrus tusks of his mustache, he says back in high school, someone started strangling heavy women around his area. Seven in a two-year span. About the third death, posters began popping up everywhere with a tape measure coiled around a red cross reading: BE SAFE. LOSE WEIGHT. "After that women started getting in the best shape of their lives." He wrangles another brew from his hip pocket. "Fear," he says. "It can be healthy as Slim Fast."

Somewhere sometime ago, seven obese women were strangled by the Waistline Waster.

The door opens and Melissa steps up on the Xterra's running board, her face over the cab. "Hewitt, remember to keep your head on a swivel," she says. "Bigfoot exists, aliens make crop circles, and God?" She stink-eyes me, pointing up. "Bearded old white man in the clouds."

"Roger that, Sweet Melissa."

She drops from sight, slams the door again, leans against the windowglass sobbing. Still.

And Hewitt says, "I'd might not sleep on Bigfoot."

Hotter within than without, I bubble my beer and say, "Whatever she decides, I'll never *not* be the patriarchal pussy."

"Home is where the hurt is," Hewitt says, catches a belch in his cheeks. "It's where you hang your head."

Lightning chromes the sky, thunder snapping like bone in the afterburn as rain begins spattering the driveway.

I roll the door down, latch it.

"So," Hewitt says, sliding the ramp in the slot. "Gonna keep following the news?"

Years back, three young boys were found hogtied and mutilated in a drainage canal of some wooded area near the Mississippi River.

Last Saturday morning, a teen girl went missing in Everly Mills, her Keds and a single bloody earring found behind the Sunoco on Third and Main.

"What for?" I say. "We're gone."

Watching the grainy sky, he tells me during the war, if you dodged the draft or got some college deferment type bullshit, officials just drew again, bumping the next poor bastard up to take your place. "Then," he says, "someone fills the slot of the guy filling yours, and so on and so forth." Mikey tears between us with the Boo Angel and Hewitt high-fives him. "What I'm saying's if you move out, someone'll move in after you." He slings the dregs from another empty. "Isaac might be spared," he says. "But the ram's fucked."

A family of three or seven or thirteen was slain in a ritualistic manner at 611 Oak Street one month after moving in.

Yanking at my hand, Michael says, "Can I ride aside you?"

Hewitt chuckles. "Mighty Mike," he says, mussing his hair. "Let's take care of your old daddy here."

Closing one eye, the boy smiles up. "Kay, Mistu Hooeey."

We stand in silence beneath the gathering storm. "Tell me," I say. "How'd things turn to shit like this?"

The rain picks up hissing and Hewitt smiles, arms raised to the heavens. "God works in delirious ways." He extends a hand and I shake it. "Let's don't turn stranger on me," he says, then heads back across the yard cursing the sky.

I heft Michael into the truck. Trot and knuckle Melissa's window.

She lowers it a crack.

"He can ride with me if you wanna go on ahead," I holler over the roaring pour. "I'll drop him off with what stuff you want."

The crack closes. She drives away.

"Love you," I shout, but she doesn't hear or she doesn't care.

I duck inside the house for one last walk through. Stop by what was our room and look at the four bedpost scars in the carpet. "Nothing left," I holler, and it repeats off the bare sheetrock. I head out and lock the door.

Turning at the intersection, a black RAV4 starts down the street, slowing as it approaches me stood frozen as a garden statue inside the emblem. The window slides down, my insides numbing into helium balloons, and a man leans out with shielded eyes, jots down the realtor info, then drives away.

When I was little, we were on a family trip and Dad took a wrong exit. Turned left instead of right, zigged when he should've zagged. We hit a rough neighborhood and got robbed by two armed thugs. Money, jewelry. They groped Mom's chest, cracked Dad's jaw. An approaching squad car spooked them away or who knows. Thing I remember most though, is them laughing as he cried and begged them not to hurt us. Here's our protector reduced to mush, but with a pistol to your son's temple, it's no time to let your nuts hang.

Melissa'll never get that shit because shit like that could *never* happen to her. And for most, it won't.

But reality is, we're all of us one zig from zagging straight to Hell.

So those old adages about being blinded by fear, they're bullshit. It's not fear, it's indifference. Fear illuminates. It shows you real monsters exist. Ignites their eyes in the dark, and if you don't see them, you're not looking or you're too arrogant to bother.

Better bet they see you though. And no deadbolt or alarm or prayer can save you. Their teeth are always inches from the vitals. Ready to mark your heart, infect your mind. They're the voices on the other end of witching hour phone calls. The growls of mocking laughter.

They lie between you and your wife at night, your backs facing.

They're that one percent everyone ignores, the strapped thugs in bad neighborhoods. The nails in the sand waiting to scrape the arched bones of bare feet.

Standing in the squall, I think about the next family here. Like the Vietnam draft, the next soul queued fills your slot. You dropping from the line of fire puts them in the crosshairs.

You could've been responsible for hundreds of dead soldiers without ever knowing how to hold a firearm.

Next door, Hewitt scampers through the slashing rain yelling, "Shit, shit, shit!" A beer in one hand, the other working an old tarp over his fence, the grass blanched pale beneath.

"Told you so," I say, but he doesn't hear because no one ever listens.

Thunder booms like gunfire and I hop in the U-Haul where Mikey's singing: "Wain, wain, go away..."

Peering back at the house in the passenger side mirror, I can almost picture the door latticed in crime scene tape, different bodies outlined in police chalk.

Objects in mirror....

"...come again another day."

I ease down the drive, up the road watching the sigil grow smaller, then smaller, then gone.

I wish I could say I hope it's all a hoax. That the next family will live safe and sound in their new house. Together and happy in their new home.

But the truth is, I can't.

There's a fine line between being the villain and being the hero. Between cowardice and courage.

So every night I'll be watching the news, each morning scanning all the papers. Then one day it'll be there in black and white print or HD video, and the look on everyone's face will say everything. *You were right,* their pale dropped jaws will say. *You were right all along.*

JOHNNY EISEN MAKES GOOD
by Angus McLinn

Conventional wisdom would indicate that the 42nd floor of the Salesforce Tower doesn't exist. You can stand right here in Bryant Park and count, and you'll run out of stories to tally at 41. But these days, smart guys don't trust their lying eyes, right? So, you check Wikipedia. 630 feet tall, 41 floors. Municipal buildings are closed anyway this time of night, but if you insist on wasting your money making copies just to prove that I'm right, tomorrow you can go down to the DOB and take a look yourself. You won't learn anything I didn't just tell you.

So, the question, my friend, should be obvious -- would you put money on it?

Don't answer that.

You look like a nice guy, so I'm gonna do you a favor and let you in on a little secret. It's there alright. I know, because I've been there.

I was about three quarters of the way into a premature mid-life crisis, and at that point, it was safe to say that gambling hadn't exactly done me a boatload of favors. I'm in this very park, waiting in line for one of the only above ground public restrooms in Manhattan carting around a brown-bagged, half-empty Straw-Ber-Rita and a full bladder, when the guy in front of me takes a nip out of the pocket of his fleece vest and comes on over.

The vest had some bullshit embroidered on it -- "Igneous Conifer Capital Partners" maybe, or something like it – the important part is the guy tells me he's got a line on a new kind of action, if I'm game. Now, I've heard this one before from guys like that, so of course I'm skeptical. He either wants to screw me or get me on one of those day trading apps, which is just screwing me with extra steps. I know, because I've been there before too.

I'm halfway on my heel about to pull a classic get-the-fuck-out-of-there when Fleece Vest puts his hand on my shoulder, and I see his eyes for the first time. I'll tell you right now, I'm happy I did, because guys like us, we recognize each other, right? You've got the itch too. You wouldn't be talking to me if you didn't.

I'd bet you've never bet a gambler who didn't believe in serendipity, so it shouldn't surprise you that the second I realized I actually had an angle on the action, I was in. Not that I told Fleece Vest any of this. I don't think he would have listened anyway. You've never seen a guy more excited, rambling like he's on back half of an 18-hole coke binge about how it's the end of history, labor vs. capital by way of man vs. machine -- what he could get me in on was set to be "The Ballad of John Henry" for Web 3.0. I was steadily tuning him out when he said the magic words.

"You ever read anything by a guy named Johnny Eisen?"

I had, indeed, read something by a guy named Johnny Eisen.

"No," I told him, "And what's that got to do with anything?"

Fleece Vest lays it out for me. Him and his buddies – a bunch of finance guys, techno-geeks, and just for the hell of it, a few interested randos such as myself – were gonna catch one of the most storied hacks in New York City going toe-to-toe, blow-for-blow against the latest and greatest probability machine to come out of Silicon Valley, FactotumGPT. It was purpose built for the content creation competition of the millennium. Factotum had been steeped in the canon of *Buzzfeed*, *Cracked*, *Ranker*, and thousands of other content farms alongside the archives of every newspaper in the nation with a circulation greater than 1,000, all of Wikipedia, and every book they could get their filthy hands on a digital copy of. After six months of testing and training, it was ready to rumble.

In the opposing corner, Johnny Eisen, a prolific staff writer and pavement pounder who had been kicked off more editorial boards than you could name in a minute if I gave you the first five free. Johnny was a published polymath, an editor at large who had also authored works of non-fiction ranging in focus from the history of pickleball to forgotten battles of the 1838 Mormon War. He'd been around the block – back in the old days, if you caught him on his way out to the smoke deck, he'd regale you with tales of the Friday afternoon drinks cart and bitch about how in his day, you could still have a gagger at your desk – but Johnny was more than just a cartoon newspaperman ambling around like a bizarre fossil animated by nothing more than nicotine and bitterness.

What a lot of people didn't – and don't -- know about Johnny is that his real name wasn't his only byline. I had the inside track. Fresh out of school, I'd gotten an internship at The Times on the copy desk, and I'd edit his articles. See, layoffs were coming in heavy at the time, and every couple of months another beat was getting clobbered with the corporate axe. But Johnny, Johnny was the secret weapon of a dying industry. He could write a hell of a feature, everybody knows that – the acerbic wit, the endless and ever apropos anecdotes of old New York, and that iconoclastic impulse he chased half the city's politicians around with for decades – but, as anybody who has worked at a company on the outs will tell you, the more people get cut, the more hats you wind up wearing.

Nobody ever really noticed, but around that time, a lot of the new bylines that started showing up in the online edition were just Johnny stretching his legs. I couldn't tell you how the hell he even did it, just in terms of hours in the day, but he was cranking out recipes, advice columns, air fryer reviews, you name it, imitating ten or fifteen cub reporters at a time some weeks. As a member of the peanut gallery, I chewed on in approval.

So I figure, Fleece Vest and his cronies have done their homework, sure enough, but guys like that, their idea of background was probably a couple of Google searches and putting some interns on dossier duty for a day or two. They didn't really know Johnny, and that means they'd all be betting on the machine. That's the only reason to bring in guys off the street like me. Randos vs. technogeeks, finance guys handing out folding chairs. The kind of fellas who will take long odds just because they think they know something. Problem for me was, I thought that I did.

Next thing I know I'm cooped up with Fleece Vest in the executive elevator of the Salesforce Tower, and he's pressing buttons and whispering some voodoo into the call box. It was quiet the whole way up to the 42nd floor, but when the doors eased open at the end of the line the rumble of the crowd hit me like somebody had clocked me with a beer bottle. Everybody was buzzing. The whole place had a sort of circus-comes-to Wall Street vibe, like it had been double-booked for both Coachella and SuperInvestor and everybody just decided to go with it, Instagram be damned. Fleece Vest had some surprisingly sharp elbows, so I followed him through the crowd to get a better look at what everybody was mobbed up around.

I don't really know what I was expecting to see – I'd thrown a lot of money around a lot of different competitions, though never one like this – but I sure wasn't expecting anything like a surgical theater, which is the best I can describe the alabaster and inoffensive gray arena Johnny was set to be competing in. They'd set him up with a workstation in the center of the thing. Pretty standard stuff, a computer with a couple of monitors, a charging bank, and some creature comforts for Johnny like a pot of coffee, an ash tray, and a bottle of Eagle Rare, next to a cooler full of sandwiches.

I'd somehow gotten it into my head that Johnny's competition would be represented by a physical robot, or a hologram of Mark Twain, or something actually worth looking at, but the only sign anybody other than Johnny was competing was a gadget that looked like a Wi-Fi router sitting on a black box about the size of a small filing cabinet a few feet behind his chair. I didn't have much time to be disappointed.

Soon enough, the pulse of the crowd eased into a dull hum, and a guy who looked like his main job was to wear a suit walked out on stage to get the thing started. He announced Factotum first, to thunderous applause, although that son of a bitch of a machine didn't even have the decency to blink a light or something in response. Next comes Johnny, whose reception was a bit more muted, although what it lacked in volume it sure made up for in passion. Even some of Fleece Vest's buddies gave him a whoop or two. I guess it's hard not to root for an underdog, even if you're a short seller.

Now, you might be thinking that a thing like this, play-by-play, couldn't possibly be that exciting, and you'd be right. It wasn't. The game was a race to 100 million page views, digital platforms only, no social media, as long as it takes for somebody, or something, to win it, which is about as thrilling as it sounds. You could follow what was happening on a pair of screens up on the back wall showing what each contender was writing, and overlays popped up every once in a while with statistics on views, SEO optimization, geographic penetration, and what have you. It was sort of like judging an essay contest but if you had to watch each kid write the thing, start to finish, before you could read it. The shape of the whole thing though, when you look at the peaks and valleys of it, that was must-see TV.

Whatever anybody wants to say about Johnny now that it's all over, I'll tell you he was crafting that night, and on into the next. He wrote listicles that would break your goddamn heart, tying the populist rout of the '76 World Series with Joycean references and withering invective. Allusions to antediluvian lore were effortlessly linked to post-monopolistic music distribution and the top five beach songs of the summer. For the first few hours, he hadn't even turned on his second monitor, and the crazy bastard was just doing all the cross referencing from memory. A chant broke out among the crowd, "Multiple screens! Multiple screens!" and even Fleece Vest took a break from autocompleting emails and got into it for a beat or two.

Thirty-six hours in, blood was flying from Johnny's fingertips, and he was living on pastrami sandwiches and rage between belts of Eagle Rare chased with black tar coffee. Johnny had eked himself out a bit of a lead over Factotum, but that infernal machine was closing the gap, and you could tell Johnny was wearing out just looking at him – stripped down to his undershirt, wheezing like the old man he'd grown into since my days at the copy desk.

Looking back on it, Johnny must have noticed too, probably even before I did. Factotum was getting better. More views per article. More most viewed. More human. And the more Johnny wrote, the more it was becoming just like him.

Small stuff at first, references to Roger Clemens, which Johnny always liked to pepper in whenever he had even half the chance to, anecdotes about an apartment down on Bleecker Street in the 80s – Johnny had lived there once, but the Factotum sure as shit hadn't – and other bits of biographical debris from Johnny's past. But it just kept on growing. Soon this thing is scoring top-of-page placement on op-ed pages with articles on the opioid crisis anchored around the death-by-overdose of its late wife, which sounded an awful lot like the ones Johnny wrote after his daughter died, although distinct enough that I don't know if you could call it outright plagiarism, legally speaking.

I wouldn't go so far as to say I'm lucky things turned out the way that they did. A great man died that day, and I'll always regret that, but at least all of our bets got voided.

If Johnny had made it to the end, with the money I had riding on things, I'd have been finished, but that's the thrill, right? They say it was stress induced cardiac arrest that got him – a day-and-a-half of no sleep, liquor, and hard work after a lifetime of the same was just too much for the old man. If you asked me, I'd say they're half right. There's another name for that condition. They call it Broken Heart Syndrome, and when Johnny realized that after everything he'd done with his life, everything he'd written, all that was left for him was to feed the Factotum, he caught a mean case of it. From what I remember of Johnny, he wouldn't want to be a part of a world like that anymore. The thing of it is, if that's what he was betting on going into this, even dying wasn't enough for him scratch one last win into the old Black Book.

Try it out. Read yourself some Johnny Eisen, whatever you can find -- it shouldn't be too hard, check the books on your coolest friend's coffee table and you're bound to find something. Memorize it. Then, next time you scan across a byline that doesn't seem quite right, maybe mentions Roger Clemens, shift your eyes. Look at it real close, squint just the right kind of way, and think of Johnny. You'll see it then, whether you're glad you did or not – a requiem carved into the kerning, its ghostly refrain embedded in HTML on a digital mausoleum: *There lies a steel-driving man, Lord, Lord. There lies a steel-driving man.*

WASTELAND SURVIVORS
by Kevin Novalina

The daddy spits on the whetstone and grinds the blade up its surface. He flips the Buck knife over and scrapes it back down, the steel over silicon carbide rasping like slow-peeled duct tape.

Sitting at the kitchen table, he thumbs the blade's edge and sets it down. He twists his whiskey glass back and forth in the water lipped around the bottom, then drains it to the ice and pours another.

The son sits beside him eating a butter and syrup sandwich. Whenever the daddy nudges the glass of rye toward him, he takes a sip to wash it down, his face contorting as he swallows back the gag. He's buzzing, though he doesn't know what buzzing is.

The small wastebasket on the table is still smoldering, the room shrouded in a dark haze that smells of burnt hair and old cigarettes. Outside, lightning fractures the night sky as wind rocks the trailer on its blocks and rain begins clicking on the tin roof.

The daddy grabs the knife and grates the edge over the grit again, his eyes bubbled slits. "Don't go repeating this," he says, "but your mother sure cunted us over."

Spread over the wall behind him is a large map of the United States thumbtacked to the faux wood paneling. On it, the geography's been reduced to rubble: different cities and states demolished by deep gashes and wide gapes. Crosscuts in bridges and highways. Mountain topography sheared away, paper rippled over various waterways.

There's a big tear through Texas.

A break in the Mississippi River.

Every time the daddy wipes a new location off the map, he has the son repeat the name aloud.

There's Manhattan laid to waste, Michigan in ruins.

California's broken away from the mainland.

The daddy finishes honing the knife and shaves a smooth strip down his hairy forearm. "She's keen enough to carve a heart out," he says, then slams it on the table and spins it blade—handle, blade—handle, blade—handle, the light and their reflections slashing in the steel with each rotation.

The daddy downs another glass and moves before the kitchen sink, each heavy step shifting the single-wide and tinkling the dishware. His back to the son, he stabs the blade into the countertop beside the mommy's crumpled note.

The son sees the daddy's reflection in the window over the faucet. Since he can remember, he's seen his reverse face in that same pane, but the mommy's had always been beside it. Eating butter and syrup sandwiches at the table, he'd watch them wash dishes, splashing water and blowing soap bubbles in each other's hair. Then their images would pause and smile, their mirrored eyes closing as they smeared in a kiss.

"Takes a real bitch to do this," he says, thick raindrops popping the glass and sliding down his replica cheeks in clear streaks. Lightning whitens the window, erasing his face, and when it reappears, the backward daddy's head is down.

The son speaks his name with no voice. Swallows and says: "She's really gone?"

The daddy looks up at the low ceiling and chuffs a long breath. Swiping a cheek with his forearm, he nods, drinks. "But it's none of it your fault," he says. "Remember that."

At length, he turns to the map and studies the mess of a land. Pops his jaw and rolls his neck. Prying the knife from the counter, he flips it in the air and catches it by the bolster. He flicks it up again, snagging it by the handle.

The son rises, backing hard as he can against the refrigerator door, turning his head with clenched eyes and seized breath.

Rearing the knife like a tomahawk, the daddy steps forward firing, and the son jumps when it slams into the wall. After a second, one eye unfolds, then the other.

"We stripped Vegas," the daddy says, head cocked at the map.

The son traces his gaze to where the blade's buried to the hilt. "Vegas."

"*Las* Vegas," the daddy says, and the son repeats it.

In the Mojave Desert, the daddy tells him.

Sounding it out, the son steps before the map. Wrapping hand over hand over handle, he braces a foot against the baseboard, tugs, and torques. The knife whines, lifting the paneling with it before ripping free, splintered dust swirling around the new hole in the Mojave Desert.

Snapping his fingers, the daddy says, "Let's go."

The son hands him the knife and backs against the fridge again. Looks away tensed as the daddy throws, growling: "Heartless—"

It was a day ago the mommy left, and though he hadn't realized it, the son had been watching her leave for months. Starting back when the mommy and daddy stopped smiling, then speaking. When their reflections no longer smeared together in the glass. When they stopped being in the window at the same time altogether.

After the silence came the yelling, and it never stopped. One night, she slapped his head and clawed at his face. Another morning, he dragged her down the hall, throwing her on the couch. Both screaming curses and curse words as they broke furniture and lamps. The TV and fish tank.

Then yesterday, the son came home from school to find the mommy gone and the daddy at the kitchen table with his head in his hands. Propped against his whiskey bottle, a note and her ring.

The note said: I TRIED.

The ring engraved: *Ever & Ever...*

The son jumps at the knife's impact.

"Just murdered Mickey Mouse," the daddy says. "Disney World, Florida."

The son repeats him, digging the blade from the large chunk of Florida sunk into the insulation.

Eyes crazed with raw blood vessels, the daddy squats on his haunches. "Think it's your turn," he says, passing the knife. "Bitch left *you* too."

The son closes his fingers around the warm handle as the daddy faces him toward the target, saying this distance is perfect for non-instinctive full spin throwing. Since the edge is sharp, he says to hold it by the spine, and that the key here's optimal balance, grip, and wrist-flick. "Then any rage you have," he says, nods at the map. "Just take it out on the world."

The son rolls his wrist, frail as a wren's wing. He wants to make the daddy proud, but he's almost certain that drink's making him sick.

Leaning against the counter, the daddy downs a shot and says: "Now flip it."

The son's arm jellies, the knife going tons heavier. "I can't."

"Try," the daddy says. "Can't never could kick ass."

"Please, you do it."

The daddy shakes his head. "This is *your* anger."

His insides light as helium balloons, the son sees his eyes in the blade, bleared by his quaking grip.

"Flip the fucking thing," the daddy says. "Get *pissed*!"

The son bites his jaw square and hefts its weight a couple times, then lobs the knife in the air. Dropping tip-first, he shies away, and it hits the floor as he hops astride its carom.

The daddy toes it toward him and says: "Catch it."

Jouncing it in his grip, the son captures his breath and slings the knife high, wheeling blade—handle, blade—handle, in what seems like slow-motion. It drops and he catches it along the edge, flailing his hand back as if burned, the tip lodging in the floor at his feet. He stares cross-eyed at the rent meat along his thumbpad going white to pink to crimson, then veining down his wrist.

"Had worse than that in my eye," the daddy says, wets a paper towel, and presses it to the son's thumb, blood soaking through in a puckered bloom. He pulls it away and the cut goes white, then pink, then crimson again and he lifts the wound to the son's mouth and says, "Taste."

Swallowing the nausea, the son tries to back away but he's stopped. "To take pain," the daddy tells him, "you gotta beat it."

The son looks at the gash, closes his eyes, slides his thumb in his mouth. It tastes how the blade looks, and pulling it out, blood strings like stretched Hubba Bubba from his lips.

"Now, back to my fury," the daddy says, twisting the knife-tip from the floorboard. "You still got a lot more hate to grow."

Though she's gone, the mommy left pieces of herself all around the trailer. Just small remnants of the whole her, scattered and lifeless. Her smell and long strands of flaxen hair in the furniture. Fingernail parings and lipstick-stained Virginia Slims in the ashtrays.

A bra in the dryer. An earring in the carpet.

A two-word goodbye letter and her wedding ring on the counter.

The only real proof she was ever there.

Swilling hooch and weeping, the daddy went around gathering up every piece he could find, then threw it in a tin wastebasket and tossed a lit match inside. He hit it with a spit of lighter fluid, and they stood watching as all the mommy's abandoned waste went up in flames, dark smoke curling across the ceiling.

Everything save the note and several strands of her hair the son'd snuck and bound with string.

Now, his wrapped thumb touches the frizzy lock in the shirt pocket over his heart.

The daddy chunks the whiskey tumbler in the sink, bubbles straight from the bottle several times, and lowers it with teeth bared, hissing. He smooths the note flat on the counter, shakes his head. "Know she's your mother and all," he says, sniffling. "But I pray she gets cancer of the fucking face." He runs the blade through the center of the page, then winds up and fires, snarling: "Tried my ass!" The momentum hops him forward, the whole trailer shunting as the paneling explodes leaving the note pinned over a razed Oregon.

I TRIED.

He snaps his fingers. "Again," he says, and keeps throwing.

There's a gorge in the Grand Canyon.

The Atlantic curled back from the Eastern Seaboard.

Grunting harder with each throw, he takes snaps of whiskey while the son retrieves the knife one-handed, the walls shuddering with thunder the while.

Then Yellowstone's cratered.

The Mexican Border's obliterated to the tangled white and green electrical wiring.

The daddy chokes the bottle and stumbles to the map. Large sleevings of paper coiled on the floor, dusted with shredded kindling. "All's left," he says, voiced croaked. The son takes his side, and both study the one state still untouched. A bullseye somehow clinging to the laminate panel marred around it. "Toto," the daddy says, "we ain't in Kansas anymore."

"Kansas," the son says, tranced on Dorothy's home.

The daddy staggers toward the sink singing "Over the Rainbow" before slurring into "This Land Is Your Land." His image forming in the window, he spins and hurls the knife, the son dropping from danger just before the burst of shrapnel.

"Good instinct," the daddy says, resumes singing. "Again."

Still cowering on the floor, the son looks up.

"Now goddammit."

The son rises on newborn foal's legs. Shimmies the blade free, hands it over.

Another throw misses high. Another, a hair to the right.

He fires again.

And again.

Then again.

Overhand, sidearm, before he even takes a firm grip. Kansas never grazed as each throw grows wilder and harder, the son trying to retrieve the knife, then clear its path quick as he can.

A shot misses low, then wide left.

Another clips the baseboard molding.

Eight throws. Fifteen, twenty.

"Mother*fuck*!" he yells, and shatters the whiskey bottle over the floor as the son scampers away. He swats a chair across the kitchen, then flings the knife blind and the butt ricochets off an exposed wall stud, the spine cracking the son over one eye. He drops limp and balls fetal as the daddy flips the table, the wastebasket spilling smoke and the mommy's charred remnants along the dry-rotted linoleum. He slips kicking the icebox and crashes down, the trailer wrenching under the violence, picture frames flipping from the shelves. The daddy pushes against the cabinet beneath the sink. Wrists draping his knees, his forearms flakked with bloody glass. "Why'd she?" he slurs, shoulders tremoring. "Tell me."

Outside, the storm sweeps hard over the corrugated tin.

Heart booming in his wounds, the son crawls and hugs the daddy's arm at the muscle. He kisses his raw knuckles, his dropped head.

Then he rises.

With the ridge over his socket knotting the shape of a chimp's brow, he wants to cry but doesn't. *To take pain,* he thinks, *you gotta beat it.* He stands before what's left of the map, the country, the world. A ravaged wasteland from Redwood Forest to Gulfstream Waters, Sea to Shining Sea. All save one place. "Kansas," he whispers, and peels it from the mangled flinders, the paper foxed and delicate as goldfish flakes. He eases it into the pocket with the mommy's lock of hair and presses a hand over his heart. Protecting the only survivors left to brave the new world.

ANGELS IN THE ATTIC
by Amaria Stone

The angels like to be checked on.

I don't really know why. They just do. Kinda like how you always have to ask teachers if you can use the restroom. I don't know why I have to; I just do.

So we have to check on the angels. Daddy always does when he comes home from work.

"Did you check on the angels today?" he asks when he comes in the door.

"Yeah," I nod, looking back at the TV. I'm watching PBS.

"Good, good..." I hear the creak of stairs behind me. He's going to check on the angels. It's what he does every day. He'll be back down shortly.

"What time does your brother get home from school?" He asks when he returns. His breathing is heavy from the flights of stairs.

I shrug. Shouldn't he know? I don't pay attention to such things. Sometimes he has hockey, sometimes not.

"It's his turn to check on the angels tomorrow."

"I know," I say. That's how it works. Billy goes to school one day; I go the next. Someone has to be home to check on the angels.

"Spaghetti for dinner?" Daddy asks.

"Yes!" I nod vigorously.

"Sure, sure." He wanders into the kitchen, and I hear the clatter of dishes as he sets to making supper.

Soon, my show ends, and I join Daddy in the kitchen. Water is boiling on the stove, and he's got meatballs in the oven.

The front door opens and slams. I wince.

"I'm home!!" Billy cries from the entryway. He sets his hockey bag down by his shoes and strides into the kitchen. "Spaghetti? Again? Agh."

Daddy sighs and says nothing.

"How was school today?" I ask excitedly.

"Eh, fine, you can look over my homework if you want. We started studying The Revolution today."

"Yes!" I love to look at his homework.

"It's your turn to check on the angels tomorrow, Billy." Daddy keeps his gaze fixed on his cooking.

"Yeah, yeah, I know," he says. He's just going to play videogames all day tomorrow, when he's not checking on the angels.

"You know how important it is, Billy."

Billy gives Daddy a funny look, "Yeah, I do..."

I don't really know why Daddy is looking at Billy like that.

"Good, good..." Daddy leans over to pull the meatballs out of the oven.

"Who wants a meatball?" Daddy grins, forking a few onto a plate for us to eat before the rest of the meal.

I love spaghetti and meatballs.

* * * * * *

The bus hydraulics hiss as it comes to a stop, and I scamper to the front of the bus to get off. School was epic today; I'm learning long division right now.

I throw open the front door and rush inside, "Heyyy! I'm home."

"In here," Daddy calls.

I follow the smell of pizza to the kitchen. He's just pulling one out of the oven.

"Oooh!" I say.

He flashes me a smile.

"Where's Billy?" I ask.

He looks toward the stairs, "In his room, playing games." Indeed, I hear the sound of simulated gunfire coming from upstairs.

"Oh," I say.

"Billy!" Daddy calls, "Dinner's ready!"

"Gimme a minute!" Billy yells back.

Daddy turns back to me, shaking his head, "Here." He hands me a plate.

"Pizza!" I slide a piece onto my plate.

"Careful, it's hot-" Daddy says just as I chomp down on the slice and burn the roof of my mouth.

"Ah!" It *was* hot!

Daddy rolls his eyes. "It just came out of the oven, silly."

I giggle.

Billy never joins us for dinner.

* * * * * *

"Billy?" I peer into his room.

He's on his phone, scrolling on some app or something. "Hmm?" he asks, looking up. "What's up?"

"You didn't have dinner. Aren't you hungry?"

He shrugs, "I had a big lunch."

"Too many PB 'n' J's?" I joke. It's all we have in the house.

"Not exactly," says Billy.

I furrow my brow, "What?"

He leans forward conspiratorially, "If I tell you what I did today, you have to promise not to tell Dad."

My eyes widen, "What??"

"I'm serious. You have to promise."

"Okay... I promise."

He opens his mouth to speak but pauses when there is creaking on the stairs. We glance toward the hallway where Daddy walks by.

He's going to check on the angels.

Billy starts talking again once we hear the *thump* of the attic stairs, "I went on a date today."

I gasp, "A date?"

"Yes, with this pretty girl from my class. Andrea. I ended up having dinner with her and got home before Dad."

I blink, "What about the angels?"

Billy rolls his eyes, "The angels aren't gonna miss me for *one day*."

I frown, "I really think you should have stayed to check on the angels, Billy."

"Bah," he says, "And I thought you'd care about my date."

"No, no," I say quickly, "Tell me about your date."

He grins.

* * * * * *

The next day is my day to stay home from school.

I spend the day watching PBS and reading from the stack of books in the corner of the living room. Daddy says I should read as much as I can, because I can't go to school every day like all the other kids since I have to check on the angels. That's how I know about things like the electoral college and nuclear energy, even though I never learned about that stuff in school.

Daddy gets home from work, and he looks *tired*.

"Just TV dinners tonight, kid," he says as he takes two out of the freezer. Billy would make his own when he got home.

Mine has a brownie in it! I settle down with a book at the table, and a few minutes later, Daddy sets the meal in front of me.

"What are you reading today?" he asked, glancing at the cover.

"Hunger Games," I proclaim, "It's about a girl who is forced to fight other kids to the death."

He nods slowly, "No worse than what I was forced to read growing up." He takes a bite of mashed potatoes.

I scarf down my food and then glance at the clock. I frown. It's almost six-thirty.

"Daddy, where's Billy?"

He doesn't look up from staring at his food, his forehead held in one hand while he stirs the cold potatoes with a fork, "Billy won't be joining us tonight."

"Oh." I say, "Where is he then?"

"Away." Then he sighs, "Look, kiddo, you're going to have to stay home from school for a while. Billy won't be here to trade days with you."

"Oh." I say, "For how long?"

"A while," is all he says. Then he stands up to throw away his uneaten food. He walks out of the kitchen but pauses on the threshold, "I'm going to bed. Goodnight."

"Goodnight, Daddy..."

* * * * * *

Billy doesn't come home the next day. Or the next. Or any of the days after that.

I throw my copy of *Tom Sawyer* to the side, already bored of it. It's my fourth time reading it. It used to be one of my favorites. Now, I've outgrown it. I want to read more of *The Hunger Games* series now.

I've already read through most of my stack of books for the month. Daddy is going to have to take me to the library soon. All I have left now are history books. Boring! I'm not *that* desperate.

Some rerun of a show I've seen a gazillion times is playing on TV, but I turn it off. I'm bored. I want to go to school. I *always* want to go to school. No fair Billy gets to be gone this long and I'm stuck at home.

"Ughhh." I've even checked on the angels today already. Four times.

Maybe I can convince Daddy to finally let me have a phone if I'm going to be bored at home like this all the time. Of course, we have a landline, but I want a *smart*phone.

The front door opens, and I glance up at the clock. Daddy's home from work!

I rush to greet him, and he gives me a quick embrace.

"Did you check on the angels today?"

I nod, "Of course."

"Good, good..." He ruffles my hair.

"What's for dinner? I'm starving!"

"I'll order Chinese," he says.

"Ooh!" I love Chinese food.

"Will Billy come home tonight?"

Daddy shakes his head, "Not tonight."

"Well, I'm gonna need some new books if I'm gonna be stuck at home like this all the time."

Daddy scratches his chin, "I suppose you do. Well, we'll go to the library this weekend."

"Neat!" I say.

* * * * * *

The weekend came and went. I had new books. I read them. I checked on the angels. I watched TV. Another week passed. Then another. More books. More TV. Billy never came home. I stopped asking when he would.

* * * * * *

Daddy looked at me sharply over dinner one night, "Kiddo, I'm staying home from work tomorrow. You've got to go to school for the day and pick up whatever homework you've been missing."

I perk up, "I get to go to school?!"

He nods gravely.

"Oh, yay!" I cry, "But that means I gotta go to sleep early tonight." I glance at the clock, "Oh, gosh, it's almost time for bed."

"Finish your food and then go brush your teeth."

I nod and then start shoveling bites of cheesy broccoli into my mouth.

Daddy gets up and starts up the stairs. Checking on the angels, per usual. Except, Daddy's starting to get more tired. He's... he's getting old. The trek up to the attic is getting hard for him.

That's okay, though. When I finish schooling, I can take over for him. I'll sure miss school, though.

I always miss school.

* * * * * *

I trudge off the bus to the front door.

School *sucked* today. All my friends acted like they didn't even know who I was. They're mad I've been gone so long. And the teacher sent a note home to my daddy. I hope it doesn't make Daddy angry. I shove open the front door and discard my backpack nearby. I'll have plenty of time to get caught up on homework with Billy being gone 'n all.

Except...

"Yes, father." I hear from the kitchen.

Is that... Billy? Yes, he's in the kitchen talking to Daddy.

"Oh, Billy! You're home!" I sprint into the kitchen and embrace my brother. I'm so excited he's home, I can tell him all about the books I've been reading *and* I get to go to school again.

"Hey, kiddo," Billy says.

I look up at him. His hair is shorter, like really short, and there are bags under his eyes. What in the *world* has he been up to?

"Billy, where have you been?!"

"Camp," he says, "Just camp. An extracurricular thing." He glances at Daddy, "It was last minute. Sorry... sorry I've been gone." He looks away.

"No matter, you're here now!"

"Yes..."

"Oh, I've got such a cool book series for you to read!"

"Do you, now?" Billy smiles. It doesn't reach his eyes.

"Kiddo," Daddy says.

I look over at him.

"Since Billy is back, you can go to school for a while without having to trade off days. Catch up on your missing work and whatnot."

"Oh. Okay."

Daddy frowns, "Just okay? I thought you loved school."

"Oh, well, I do. But my friends were being weird today. And the teacher gave me a note to give you."

A dark look passes across Daddy's face, "Well, bring it here."

I oblige.

He opens the note and reads it over and his expression turns angry. Uh-oh.

"Nevermind. You're not going to school tomorrow. We'll talk about the next day after I get home from work tomorrow." Daddy turns on one of the burners on the stove and sticks the corner of the letter in it. It goes up in flames in seconds.

"Did... did I do something wrong?" I swear, I've been good lately.

"No, kiddo. *You* did nothing wrong." Daddy gives Billy a look.

"Oh," is all I say.

I don't know how I feel about that.

* * * * * *

Billy goes to school the next day. I do not.

He doesn't talk to me when he comes home. He doesn't eat dinner with Daddy and me. I carefully step into his room. Daddy is downstairs washing dishes. "Billy?" I ask.

He jumps, and looks up to focus on me. "What is it?"

My gaze finds his phone on the floor, like he's just tossed it aside haphazardly. He has a book in his lap and he reads by the waning light from his window.

"How was school today?"

"Fine." He shrugs.

"Daddy said it's my turn tomorrow."

"Sounds good."

I bite my lip, "Do you have any homework I can look at?" I like looking at his math problems. Especially when I can figure out how to do them and he can't!

"Not today," he turns back to his book.

"Oh, okay." I linger a moment longer, "Whatcha reading?"

He's silent for a moment, "Nothing. Look, just leave me alone, okay?"

Oh.

"Um. Okay." I blink before leaving his room. I glance back from the hallway just in time to see him shift enough so I can read the glossy, golden title of the book he's reading. *The Holy Bible*. Oh, fuck.

* * * * * *

I'm anxious at school all of the next day. It isn't the kids or the teacher this time.

I get off the bus and am cautious when I enter the house.

It's quiet, but I hear water running in the kitchen. I approach the threshold and Daddy is making spaghetti. My favorite!

And nothing seems amiss. But I don't see Billy anywhere. Daddy notices me standing in the doorway.

"Hey kiddo!" he says, more jovial than normal.

"Hiya Daddy."

"Dinner's just about ready. How was your day at school?"

"It was fine," I shrug, "The teacher is reading us Charlotte's Web. I've already read it twice." I wrinkle my nose. Not that it's a bad book.

"Oh, I remember reading that. So sad."

"Yeah," I say, shifting from one foot to another, "But I've read sadder."

"I'm sure you have." Daddy sets a few plates down on the table, "Billy!" He calls, "Dinner is ready!"

A few moments later, Billy arrives in the kitchen. He's quieter than usual, none of his rushing-through-the-house nonsense. I'm worried about him.

My anxiety eases slightly when we all sit down to eat. Daddy forgot to make meatballs this time, though.

But at least everything else is okay.

* * * * * *

It isn't until the next day that everything goes wrong.

I stay home from school, of course, and check on the angels. And read. I don't hear Daddy come home from work. But I see him walk by my door. I see him walk down the hallway. I see him enter Billy's room. My throat falls and lodges in my stomach.

I quickly return to reading *The Lord of the Rings*.

When Billy comes home, I creep out of my room and settle on the staircase. My heart thumps in my chest. Daddy is making dinner in the kitchen. Everything is too quiet. I can see through the door of the kitchen from my vantage point. I can see Billy approach the threshold. I see him stop in the doorway. I see him glance at Daddy, and then at the kitchen table, and then back at Daddy.

"Father?" he asks, quietly.

Daddy stops what he is doing. He slowly turns to the kitchen table.

On it sat *the* book. Billy's book.

"Where did you get this?" Daddy asks, his voice low.

Billy inadvertently takes a step back, "From a friend. At- at school."

Daddy fixes his cold gaze on Billy, "Was it from that girl?"

"No- no."

"Don't lie to me, William."

"I'm not lying-"

"Kiddo." Daddy interrupts Billy and looks up through the kitchen door to where I am hiding on the stairs.

I let out a little gasp.

"Go to your room."

I oblige immediately.

All I hear is the sound of a belt unbuckling as I rush up the steps.

Daddy doesn't say another word, not even when Billy starts screaming.

* * * * * *

I shut my door as quietly as I can and cover my ears. My heart is slamming against my ribcage. *Fuck, fuck, fuck.* I try to slow my breathing. Should I read something, should I read something? I don't know what to do.

Though my hands cover my ears, I still heard the thump from the attic. Oh, no. The angels can hear everything. The poor angels.

I know what I have to do. Slowly, I pull my hands away from my ears. I try to block out the sounds from downstairs. Tears well in my eyes, but I wipe them away.

I open my door, walk down the hallway, and pull on the tether that lets down the attic stairs. I have to check on the angels.

I climb the last step into the attic. The angels are restless.

"Don't worry angels," I say, "It's going to be okay. I'll take care of you."

I put on the biggest smile I can muster.

The angels' chains clink as they settle back down.

NIGHTCRAWLERS
by Nick Young

The cigarettes winked in quick succession, like two orange fireflies in the deep July night. Hotter than righteous holy hell, it was. That's just the way grandpap would put it, Lanny Wedron thought. Wet-wool blanket heat.

"What time is it, I wonder? Eleven or so?" Lanny asked, his words sounding flat, affectless in the oppressive air. Another cigarette flare next to him, followed by a long, hissing exhalation.

"Hell if I know," Beau Stanger answered, annoyed. "Why you asking me anyway? I ain't got a watch."

"Well, I figured you'd know."

"How would I know, Lanny, if I ain't got a watch?"

"For one thing, I didn't know you didn't have no watch."

"You ever see me with one?"

"Well, hell, Beau, I don't exactly spend my time gazin' at your wrist."

"Which, if you'd looked, you'd see did not include a watch."

Lanny took a last drag on his smoke and flicked the butt arcing toward the canal where it died with not so much as a sputter. Away to the west drifted the low, dull thrum of water cascading through the Lock 37 sluice, kicking out spray and foam. But by the time it had traveled the quarter mile to where Lanny and Beau sat on the bank, the current was nothing more than a sluggish crawl.

"Okay," Lanny began with a shade of exasperation, "so you got no watch. But I figured you're good at figurin' things out, so you might know, you know, about what time it is."

"And just how would you expect me to do that, Lanny?"

"Well, I guess maybe the moon and stars or somethin'. Maybe the planets."

"You bothered to look up at the sky since the sun went down? You see any stars? Moon? Any sign of a planet?"

"I can't see nothin'. It's too cloudy."

"Bingo, genius." Beau Stanger felt the cigarette burning hot on his fingers and flipped what was left into the small fire that was dying a few feet down the weedy bank in front of them. I swear to Christ, he said to himself in wonderment, in thirty years of living I never meant anyone more ignorant. Dumb as a fuckin' post.

"Guess I'll throw a couple more sticks on our blaze."

"Why don't you do that? And get me another beer. We got any more left?"

"Yeah. Should be. In the truck." Lanny caught his boot under him as he tried to stand, causing him to stumble forward. He narrowly missed planting a foot in the middle of the dwindling fire. "Shit! Goddamn!"

"For Christ's sake, Lanny. Keep it down. Wake the whole goddamn county."

"Sorry, man." Lanny, muttered, and kept it up all the way to his pickup a few yards beyond the lip of the embankment. Beau shook his head, lit another Camel and checked his fishing rod, which was propped up in the vee of a small branch he'd broken off, fashioned to its use and stuck into the earth. It was the way his grandmother had shown him to place his pole—it was always a "pole" to her, never a "rod"; that was for those fancy fly fishermen from the big city in their Army-green waders. He was only six or seven then, and she'd taken him to fish the first time as the early-morning mist rose without purpose or care off the Illinois River.

"You get a bite?" Lanny was back, boots crunching the dry grass, beer bottles clinking together. He tossed a few sticks of dry wood onto the fire.

"A bite? That'd be the goddamned miracle of the night."

"You change out your bait?"

"I have not."

"Fresh worm might help."

"I could put ten of them on the hook and it wouldn't make no difference. It's too damned hot. Wasted trip."

"Aww, come on, Beau. At least we got ourselves some beers. Here." Lanny was carrying two; he passed one over, heard the cap twist off.

"Jesus Christ, Lanny, it's warm."

"Yeah, I know."

"What the hell, man?"

"I forgot to put the top back on the cooler."

"You're shitting me? No, of course you ain't."

"Sorry." Lanny caught sight of his own stupidity, but like many of his thoughts, it was gone as soon as it was there, a flash of electric discharge against an empty sky. He sat down beside his own fishing rig, a cheap six-foot steel rod and Zebco spinning reel. He thought about re-baiting his own hook, but decided it probably wasn't worth the effort. Instead, like Beau, he cracked the cap off his beer and took a healthy swallow. Pretty nasty shit this warm. Still, it was alcohol.

"I don't suppose you thought to bring down the sandwiches?" Beau's voice hollow, without hope.

"I'll get 'em. Won't take but a sec."

Times like these, Beau wondered why in hell he even bothered with Lanny. He was twenty-two, without the brains and sense of a five-year-old. He'd started at the Zippy Lube at the beginning of the summer and latched onto Beau right off. At the time he was open to the younger man's obvious liking for him. It wasn't as though Beau's life was rich with prospects at that moment. Six months before, he'd been let go at the tool and die plant, forcing him to take the Zippy Lube job. Not exactly taxing work, changing oil and checking tire pressures all day. It paid the rent. And it helped him keep his mind off Wanda.

She had moved out in the spring declaring that she had higher aspirations for her life than "shacking up with a grease monkey." That was rich, he'd thought. Still did, considering her aspirations led her to promptly put her hooks into Steve Brenner, whose rung on the career ladder was pushing a broom at the local high school.

Mainly, he was pissed at himself for not realizing clearly where the road would end the night he'd picked Wanda up at the Tiki Torch. She wasn't exactly the bring-her-home-to-Sunday-dinner kind of girl. Not the way she first caught his eye with a few drinks in her doing Jello shots off her girlfriend's belly, egged on by the crowd gathered around them. Beau had a keen appreciation for the sort of sluttish skill she displayed, and within an hour they were going at each other on the faded shag carpeting of her living room floor. That had cemented the deal for him, and within two weeks she'd moved in.

"Here's the bag with the sandwiches," Lanny said, depositing a brown paper sack between them. "And I got me two bags of chips, if you want some."

"What did you get?"

"For me, a liverwurst with ketchup and pickle on white bread— "

"Jesus, how can you eat that shit?"

"—and a yellow cheese on a bun for you." There was a long, labored sigh from his companion.

"I told you—a ham and cheese on rye."

"You said 'or'."

"What?"

"'Or.' You said a ham or cheese."

"Chrissakes, Lanny, I goddamn well know what I said—ham and cheese."

"I coulda swore you said you wanted a ham or cheese."

"And, Lanny, 'and.' Just three little letters. I guess that's pushing the fucking outer limits for you."

"Well..."

"And what happened to the rye?"

"I forgot that part." Beau could see there was no use even responding, not even to tell Lanny what an ignorant son-of-a-bitch he was. There was nothing left to do but unwrap his cheese on a bun and eat and drink in silence.

Time passed, enough so that the two men were able to finish their sandwiches. Lanny had attempted to make amends by offering Beau his extra chips— "the real crunchy kind you like"—but the olive branch was snubbed without a word.

Overhead, a fissure in the thick bank of clouds widened enough so that the half-moon's dull ivory light shone through. The two men sat and smoked in silence. From time to time, Lanny shot a sidelong glance at Beau, whose face in profile was hard, implacable, though Lanny would never have known such a word to use it. He knew his friend had been going through a lot, what with Wanda splitting and all, so he could understand why Beau was as tetchy as he was. He himself had never been snared into a real relationship with a woman. Those waters were much too deep for him, so he stuck to the shallows, quick one-nighters with whatever he could land. It was a lot like fishing he had realized in one of his very rare moments of reflection. What he was counting on in the end was Beau's understanding, such as it was, and his willingness to forgive and forget, just like at the Zippy Lube when he would get the customer's order confused in his head and put Pennzoil in the car instead of Quaker State.

When he'd finished his cigarette, Lanny judged enough time had passed for Beau to have moved on from the fucked-up sandwich order, and he cleared his throat and spat a hocker down toward the water.

"What do you think about that other thing, Beau?" There was a pause as the other man shifted his weight, boot scraping back against the dry dirt and grass.

"What 'other thing' are you talking about?"

"You know, the thing we talked about last week while we was drinking at my place?"

"You mean knocking off the ATM?"

"Yeah. That."

"Well, why in the hell didn't you say so?"

"You told me not to talk about it, so I didn't want to say nothin', you know, to give it away, you know, until you give the say-so."

"Well, you can talk about now, Lanny. For Christ's sake, we're out in the middle of fucking nowhere."

"Okay. So what do you think about it?"

"I don't."

"No?"

"No."

"Why not?"

"Why not?"

"If you ask me, Beau, it's a helluva plan."

"Bullshit."

"No, man, I mean it."

"I was shooting my mouth off when I was drunk. Nothin' more to it."

"But this is really somethin' the two of us could pull off, and then our troubles would be over."

"They would, would they?"

"Sure as we're sittin' here fishin'. We could kiss the fuckin' Zippy Lube goodbye."

"Let me ask you a question, Lanny."

"Shoot."

"Have you thought for two seconds how we're supposed to pull off this crime of the century?"

"Well, like you said at my place—we drag the cash machine out."

"Drag it out?"

"Yep."

"Right out of the Midwest Federal branch?"

"Right. Like you said at my place."

"I said I was drunk, Lanny."

"But we could do it."

"No, we couldn't."

"We could."

"With our bare hands?"

"No, Beau, with my truck!" Beau's barking laugh shook the midnight quiet.

"Please, God, tell me you're shitting me."

"No, I am not. And there ain't no reason you gotta laugh at me."

"I've sure as hell gotta laugh. Your truck?"

"Well, why not?"

"You taken a hard look at it lately?"

"Okay, well, yeah, it's got some pitting—"

"Some pitting? Christ, Lanny, you can look through the chunks that are eaten out of one fender and see straight through the other side."

"Okay, Beau, but you're talkin' cosmetetics. It's still got the muscle under the hood to get the job done."

"Pardon me for playin' the skeptic on that one. But let's just say I agree with you. What's your plan for pulling it off?"

"Okay, well, so here's how I got it figured: we roll up with the truck at Midwest Federal about two or three in the ayem. We head for the drive-up behind the building where the machine is. We loop this logger chain I got around it, hook it to the rear axle and then we drag the whole goddamn thing away."

"Just like that?"

"Just like that. Sweet, hunh?"

"You have the slightest idea how much that ATM weighs?"

"Probably a couple of hundred or so."

"Try a thousand."

"No way, Jose."

"Some of 'em even more. You think they want anybody to just waltz in and waltz out with it?"

"Well, okay. But we could still do it with the truck."

"You'd better get real, Lanny. You hook that machine to your truck the way you say and all that's gonna happen is that you're gonna leave the rear end of your shitbox pickup layin' in the street as Exhibit A when they arrest your ass."

This possibility, which Lanny had obviously not accounted for, generated a long pause. He looked out over the water that reflected dull and brown in the meager moonlight. He saw his vision of the future wither from Easy Street back to his single-wide sitting on a dusty lot in a trailer park bereft of even a name.

"So this big plan of yours that you were goin' on and on about wasn't no real plan after all?"

"No."

"Well, you had my ass fooled."

"That don't take much."

"So you was just drunk?"

"I told you that."

"So what's it mean then, Beau?"

"What do you mean 'what's it mean'?"

"Well, I'm askin'."

"Don't mean nothin', just alcohol talk. Means that bright-and-fucking early on Monday morning we'll be back drainin' pans at Zippy Lube." It was a hard truth that Lanny continued to fight. He shook out a cigarette and lit it, then tried to muster up some hope and bravado.

"I'll bet we could do it, Beau. I'll bet we could."

"Just shut up, will you, and fish?"

Lanny drew on his cigarette and considered reeling in his line to apply fresh bait. Aww, fuck it. He reclined against the slope, and, looking up, saw that clouds were once more moving across the moon.

"Beau?"

"What now?"

"I didn't eat my other bag of chips. You can have 'em, if you want."

"Nightcrawlers" first appeared in the *Green Silk Journal*.

AN ODE TO THOSE WHO BELIEVE IN LUCK
(And All that Lovey-Dovey Stuff)
by Sherry Morris

I fancied myself a rugged, Roving Roustabout, too busy dodging Cajun Queens for mundane things like homework, hobbies or friends. In reality, I was a gangly teen, bored and biding my time in this one-horse, deep-fried southern town. Once forever released from my school daze, I'd bid adieux to everyone I knew.

I'd been careful not to trip up with a temptress. These Bayou Babes had ways of keeping the adventure-struck stuck in the swamp. Dawson Delareux, older than me by a mere year, spelled it out.

"They cast hoodoo on you. Before you know it, you're caught."

"You mean voodoo?" I asked.

"Nah," he said. "Hoodoo. When you're weak they ask, *Who do you love?* You say their name, that's that. You're caught in a honey trap. It may sound strange to an outsider like you, but that's how it works here in the bayou."

Seeing my look he added, "It's not so bad – hoodoo can do you good."

I dismissed Dawson's words. This town was not my final stop. Papa's muddled mind brought us here five years ago but I didn't have to stay. I was my momma's boy, a wanderer. She made the mistake of getting tied down, putting down roots. I watched her wither away. Swore I'd live the larking life.

My awkwardness and Northern Newbie ignorance of bayou ways had proved a repellant against these Southern booby traps. But at the beginning of my final school year, a Delta Darling rested her derriere against my Reno Supremo. In that drawl they all have she said, "My name's Juicy Lucy, what's yours?"

She knew my name. Just like I knew hers. And what folks said about her: *That Lafayette girl thinks she highfalutin', she ain't nothin' but low-down, brash trash that'll crash and burn out young.*

And: *She's looking for a Big Bucks Sucker to tease. Squeeze for all he worth, then leave without saying goodbye.*

"I don't need a tag-a-long," I told this femme fatale. She smiled and said to take her for a drive. I wasn't gonna oblige, then she sashayed my way, fixing me with her bright green eyes, shaking her hips, licking her lips, and tossing her long dark hair. Her perfume filled the air. Such beauty was difficult to deny.

"How about a partner in crime?" she replied, getting in on the passenger's side. "One with new places and spaces in mind."

"I work alone," I said, but complied, sliding behind the wheel and taking her for that drive. Wondering if there was a type of hoodoo a man could survive.

We drove around the town square in circles, staring at the same old scenes. Then, from Lookout Point, we listened to cars whiz past. Watched streaks of plastic, steel and wheels race along highway byways.

"Forever on the move," I said. "That's my dream."

"I dream too," she said. "'Bout where everybody's going."

"Gotta do more than dream, Juicy."

She grinned. "I dream about my Daddy. Momma says he's either in Heaven or Las Vegas. Then she cries a bit."

I contemplated these two locations.

"I looked them up on a map," she said. "They aren't that far apart. Both seem like good places for those who want to lark."

I wasn't sure what to make of her talk. Did she have wanderlust too?

She moved my hand up high on her thigh and the world fell away. There was only the green of her eyes, the black of her hair and the heat radiating from her glorious white thigh. She looked me in the eye and said, "Or we could just sit tight here..."

The *whoosh* of cars broke the spell, sounding like alarm bells. I removed my hand from her thigh.

"Come June I say goodbye," I said. "Nothing's changing my mind."

Patting my knee and adjusting her skirt she said, "Don't sour on me being sweet on you, sugar. You do what you need to do. Till then, where's the harm in us having final school-year fun?"

I nodded. Wary, but determined to resist her charms.

We settled into a routine of cruising through town, then sitting in Lookout Point Park. She'd come up with stories for the cars that passed as we sat holding hands in the dark.

"That's a family going to look at a new house."

"That's a man rushing home to see his new wife."

"That's a couple heading to Las Vegas to elope and start a new life."

I'd shake my head and she'd say, "What wrong with letting love and luck decide your fate."

"Love dries up," I replied. "And I don't believe in luck. I plan to make my fate."

"Do you?"

"I do," I said. And Juicy smiled.

A breeze stirred the leaves just then. Their rustling whispered *hoodoo*. On guard, I peered at Juicy. Her placid face revealed no trace of mischief or malarkey. Gesturing towards the cars, I asked, "Where'd you go?"

Without hesitation she said, "Lady Luck's dealing my hand. I'll go with her plan. See what treat she has in store for me. I've told her what I want is right here – to hold my Yankee Doodle Crackerjack near."

I got confused being called a kid's sweet. She laughed at my look, said I was mistook. She wasn't saying I was the chewy caramel popcorn or the salty peanut hook.

Leaning in she said, "You're the prize hidden inside, the best bit in the box, the only real destination I got."

She squeezed my hand and kissed my lips. A deal, it seemed, was sealed.

And just like that, it was the end of June. Me and Juicy sat in the parking lot of Daddy D's Donuts, watching cars dawdle past, waiting for a breeze to move the heat that shimmered off the road. Summer stretched into the distance blurring sky with sun. It was 10am. The day was sticky and old, like a sweet forgot in a pocket. Heat clogged the air, my throat, and my thoughts. It was time to think of something to do, somewhere to go, but my head wasn't working. Thoughts floated in slow, hazy-lazy circles, like beach balls in swimming pools. I had a memory of wanting to leave, but the effort felt too great. Juicy sat next to me fanning herself with a deck of cards, looking cool as a mint julep, while I melted away.

Laying down her cards she said, "Now that schools out, Daddy-O, I been thinking."

I turned and saw her hand was full of hearts. It gave me a start. The sun shone directly in my eyes, making me half-blind. I blocked the light with my hand and saw stars dancing round Juicy's head. A voice came through then, loud and clear. A chant of words: *Why not stay here?*

An idea came to me then, floated in from outta all that hot, heavy air. I wanted to open that idea, like a cold bottle of sarsaparilla. Drink it down. On my own. But Juicy was right up in my face, invading my space. Asking me a question.

"Who do you—"

"No." I yelled, turning away. I switched on the radio, held my hands to my ears. I had to keep the hoodoo at bay, wouldn't let it cloud my thoughts and make me stay. I took a deep breath, then looked Juicy's way. She had that lopsided smile on her face.

"You gotta relax more honey," she said. "Try a change of place."

I declared that idea mine all along. Juicy looked pleased, unsurprised when I proposed we head out west for some poker-chip kicks under the lights of Las Vegas. I didn't look at her legs or her thighs, used the sternest tone I could find.

"Don't get up to any tricks. Pack light. Don't take white, there'll be none of this 'I-do' hype."

She chuckled with delight, threw her arms around me and said, "Alright."

Her Mama held onto her tight. They quarreled late into the night.

"Two Vegas wrongs won't make it right," she cried.

But I knew who'd win that fight.

I didn't bother talking to Pappy. He was still lost in a maze of grief and booze. I used the money that came to me from Momma's passing and when we left that bayou, Juicy cheered. I didn't know if it was for this new start or ending that old life. Maybe it didn't matter.

We cruised for weeks through cloudless skies, pedal to the floor, eating doughnuts, sipping soda pops, caring less about the cost. We country crooned with the radio up and the windows down, finger-snapping Dollywood ditties and Johnny Cashola tunes like loons. At night we'd sit together, holding hands drinking Southern Comfort while looking at the moon.

Just outside Heaven, Juicy turned to me and said, "I could sit right here forever. Couldn't you?"

I shook my head, folded my arms, sighed. "We keep moving Juicy. I've said it all along."

She gave her crooked smile. "Las Vegas, it is then. Where all good men go to get mar—"

"Juicy, I swore I'd not get tied down."

"I swear too," she said pulling out a small, clear tube. Inside something sparkled.

"Brought stardust luck," she said, sprinkling it over us. "Now we're larkers, letting luck and love decide our fate. Committing ourselves to wanderlust, cavorting through life 'til we turn to dust."

I laughed. "Sounds good if it's true."

"It's up to you!"

I couldn't reply. A funny feeling was filling my insides.

"To lifelong larking," she said, clinking my glass.

Something gently encircled us. Something soft, warm and right. Looking up, I saw the stars shimmering that shade of Juicy thigh-white. If this was hoodoo, maybe there was no need to feel affright.

Las Vegas is a funny place. Full of people making desperate bets on money and love that decide their fate. Wanting to be winners, wanting love to last. But under its glittery, glamorous surface, I smelled desperation and misery, the scent of losers and loners. Maybe these were warnings sent from Momma, to avoid her mistake. All those Vegas neon signs shrieked *Stardust turns to rust in a blink*.

Down to the last of our dough, a sudden urge came over me to go, to leave Juicy to her own means. Keep her Daddy company. She'd get mad, feel had, but in the end we'd both be glad we'd gone our separate ways. I'd told her from the start I wasn't one to give my heart. She hadn't listened. That wasn't my fault.

At the craps table, she held the dice. Maybe saw leaving thoughts tumbling round my head. Pulling me close she said, "Darling, don't be afraid of the roll. It's all part of the thrill."

I shook my head. "Juicy, it's time for me to go."

"No!" she said, jabbing a finger into my chest. "It's time to throw."

She set our remaining chips on the Queen of Hearts. A waiter splashed down two Mint Julips. Looking at me, he warned, "Only fools bet the house on love."

Juicy didn't hesitate. Looked me straight in the eye.

"We're a sure thing. Not a fling. We sealed a deal with Lady Luck. Daddy's blessed us with kiss. Says when we get hitched, we'll be Mr. and Mrs. Larker -- of love and bliss!"

Her words held me in a trance, floated 'round me in a strange dance. I swayed unsure to stay or to go.

"Honey," she said reaching for me. "Don't fret or fight. The hoodoo's right."

She blew on the dice, handed one to me. "We throw on *three*. You'll see."

Then she winked. "Here's to a good life!"

Whatever it was luck, fate, hoodoo, she was right. All those years ago, when we were young, we threw the dice. And won.

previously published with *Firewords*, Issue 16, November 2023

A BOY AND THE FOX WHO ATE HIS MOTHER
by Jess Weixler-Landis

She and I lived in the woods, away from everything. She liked it that way, no one around. There were men from time to time, dull lights eventually swallowed by my mother's fire. The ashes always returning things to the two of us. It was the seventies – if you weren't running a cult, you might be part of one and you didn't know it. This happened long ago. Before the Manson killings and the Kool-Aid drinkers. For all my history we were two, my mother and myself. I turned twelve that year, her twenty-six. Our birthdays tied to the same day, fourteen years apart. We shared the name Myer. A family line bred in the Pennsylvania Dutch since our ancestors moved from Germany. We also shared the same father. That is why she took us to the woods.

We lived off the land. Tucked into the Blue Ridge Mountains, beside a green artery pumping out brook trout. Surrounded by thick laurel, white pines, and the breathing beings of small game. The cabin came from her grandfather, an old hunting retreat without electricity or running water. We made do, and when we couldn't, she got the walnut box from under her bed. The one she stole from our father the night she left. Filled with silverware from the old country. She'd spend the five-mile walk to the pawn shop in town shining forks and spoons with spit on the hem of her shirt, cursing the capitalist pigs who required cash for trade.

Our tract of land ran straight up to the ridge of the mountain. At the top, a hull of polished stone jutted out like the teeth of a goblin king gritting in the wind. An old fox lived in the crevices of those stone teeth. Picking its way on black velvet paws. The confident tail an orange flame licking at the air. I played alone in the woods those days and being the only other creature around, I took the vixen to be my friend.

A week before my mother died, we spent a day collecting elderberries. Their overripe flesh breaking between our fingers, staining our hands purple. She licked her coated wrists and the viscous innards of the berries pooled on her tongue. Uncooked it is poisonous, but she believed in her own righteousness. In the purity of the two of us. She liked proving how strong we were.

We skipped through the woods, hand in hand back to the cabin, our bowls filled. I thought I saw a flash of orange and begged her to wait so she could meet my fox friend. We were in too much of a hurry, she said, "against the dark."

With the pot of black liquid bubbling over the fire, she painted my face with the remnant of berry juice in the bowl. "A warrior," she said. "Braver than any other." She held the bowl up, pretending to tempt me with the rest. "Drink up Dionysius, god of these woods." I lifted my head and opened my mouth. She poured it into the dirt between us and we both laughed. She believed in living by our godhood. Actualizing things by claiming them.

We watched the fire bite at the pot while the sky darkened, our backs settled against a mossy log. Something cracked in the brush behind us, and I turned to look. She pressed the tip of her nose to my cheek stopping me. "Don't be afraid, little one. There's nothing in this world that can touch us." She was like that, always knowing my thoughts even before they fully clarified in my own mind. I leaned into her warmth. Tried to suck the heat of her into my bones. A moth soared over the flames, its wings transforming from white to gold in the firelight.

That night I heard her crying. I crawled into the bed beside her. She lay on top of the quilt, her hand at her throat. I realized she was crying in her sleep. A ray of moonlight from the high window illuminated the mood ring she always wore. It gleamed at me like an opaque blue eye. As she cried, I whispered to the eye. "Don't be afraid. Nothing in this world can touch us."

Every day my fox friend came to me when I whistled, followed me through the woods. Keeping close enough we could easily talk. Not that there was much to say. Mostly I liked to tell her about my mother. I wanted them to meet. I often tried leading her with bread, little nubs of my crust balled up and scattered in a trail. But the fox never came past the gully behind the cabin, like there was an invisible line dividing her from my mother.

One evening I returned earlier than usual, driven home by hunger. When I got to the cabin, I heard low moans coming from the porch. I crept closer, careful as a mouse, pressed up against the rough-hewn logs. Peering around the saddle notch corner I saw her under the thick body of a man. Her arms slung over her head, hand resting on the mildewed porch planks. The mood ring stared blankly at me. A calm blue ocean.

The man's face contorted in a grimace. His shoulders roped with muscle in his effort. My mother moaned again, and the man threw his head back grunting. He saw me then, watching, and his grimace twisted into a smile. "I delight myself in the Lord and He grants me all the desires of my heart." His lips brushed my mother's forehead as he spoke, but his eyes were on me.

I ran. Through the woods. Hopped the stones of the creek. Up the bank to the crest of the gully. I dropped to my knees, my heart thrumming like the wingbeats of a hummingbird. I whistled for the old fox. Whistled and waited. At dusk, the shadows across the gully moved. Her sleek pelt shone in the moonlight. We stood like that in the darkening. Eyes casting out each other's fear. When the stars clicked on, I got up. "I have to go," I said, "hurry against the dark." Her green glowing irises seemed to say, "But it's already dark."

The man remained. Hunched into our small cabin like an unwelcome giant. Talking and talking about his colony of believers, living on free love. He told me to call him Father Shine. After dinner, my mother pointed the sauced ladle in her hand at me. "Be a good boy. Get my silver." I brought the walnut box out from under her bed. Dutifully carried it to the table. The man selected a silver spoon, my favorite one. The stem shaped like an hourglass, ornamented in honeysuckle and shell motifs. He held it over the candle sending off a curl of black smoke. I reached for it, my thumb a perfect fit in the curved metal, the heat burning my skin.

"Please, that one is my—."

Father Shine stood, his chair toppling behind him, and grabbed the hair fringing my nape. "The earth and everything it contains is the Lord's." He pulled my head back. His face so close I could smell the yellow plaque fleecing his teeth. "Give it to me." I strained my neck against his grasp, searching out my mother. She turned back to the stove, her square shoulders folding down. A tear squeezed into my eye, fracturing the image of her. A thousand mothers all turned away. I didn't blame her though; we both understood the hierarchies of power. That is how we survived. With my eyes closed and her ladle ticking in the cavern of the empty dinner pot I released the spoon. A chided dog I retreated to the corner. Sat with my knees tucked up to my chest, my back against the hearth, sucking my burnt thumb. Father Shine filled the spoon and held it over the candle. His eyes flicked at the bubbling tar. "Communion for the true believers."

My mother echoed him. "True believers."

Father Shine stayed three days. I begged her to make him go, afraid he would get all the desires of his heart. She looked at me with pity and told me we all must do things we don't like, sometimes. I whittled away the time in the woods. The first day I whistled till my throat was hoarse, but fox never showed. The second day I gave up. I spent my time smelling moss, licking the wet meat of broken walnuts, pulling the slick bodies of worms through my fingers feeling for their heartbeats.

The third night Father Shine told my mother it was time to celebrate our move with him to the colony the following day. "Then nothing can keep us apart." He said it like it was a forgone decision, his gaze on me. My mother rubbed her blond plait between her fingers, her tiny knee bobbing up and down under the table next to mine. "Two spoons," he said to my mother, "one for me, one for you." My cot in the corner wasn't far enough away to escape the pitch of my mother's laughter growing higher and higher.

Go ahead, I thought, *be a twosome with him at his colony, I'll stay here with fox.*

Late into the night, I twisted in my blanket. She came to my cot. "Settle love. Everything will be okay." Her cool hand rested on my forehead like she was cleaving open my nightmare. "Nothing can touch us." The man called from the porch. She kissed me where my hair met my forehead, her breath filling my lungs.

Morning came with damp oak cracking in the hearth. Splayed on the floor, Father Shine snored, air rattling through a chamber too tight. The fish belly white of his inner thigh glistened with sweat. My mother looked like a mountain, her quilt mounded around her, peaked in the middle. I wanted to become the mountain with her, huge and strong. I moved across the cabin, the floorboards keeping silent under my sparrow weight. Father Shine's snore snaggled in his throat. He grabbed me by the ankle digging his unclipped nails into my skin. "Leave your mother sleep. Go play."

I didn't know it then, but they say trees can talk to each other through the ground. They communicate with chemical signals. Whisper warnings of things coming. Help each other. When one is dying, they can pump sugar through their network to save a fellow tree. Mother Earth's way of looking after her own.

Father Shine let go of my ankle, the bite of his nails releasing. He tugged at my mother's quilt pulling a corner over himself, spreading her mountain to encompass the two of them. "Kid, throw more wood on."

The split log I tossed landed in the grey ash of the sleepy fire. It knocked against the firebricks, and rolled back out, a trail of soot in its wake. Father Shine held his fingers to his lips and mouthed the word "quiet." He closed his eyes and buried his head under my mother's quilt. I kicked the log back into the hearth and left.

Outside the cabin, blackbirds filled the trees. Thousands squawking. Feathers rustling like leaves. My sneakers crunching in the dirt set them alight. Overhead the sky darkened with their spread wings. When I got to the gully the old fox was already there like she had been waiting. That day I followed her. Fast up the mountain. Calves biting. A stitch in my side. At the stone teeth, she ducked under a fallen pine. Powdery soil caked the webs of hanging roots and when she slipped through the curtain a cloud of dust erupted. I shimmied down and peeked through. In the den, the old fox stood over three orange cubs curled together.

"Your babies." The fox's opal eyes shone. The cub's tiny forms nuzzled and shifted in the cozy pile. My body pulled down, wishing itself tucked into the den, safe in the vixen's refuge. Her fierce wild a steady protection. Instead, I whispered to the cubs, told them they had nothing to fear, that their mom was good, that she would look after them.

I reached into my jeans and pulled out my empty pocket. "I'm sorry I forgot bread today, but I'll go get some. I'll get extra for your babies too, and I'll—" my words tumbled into each other. "And I'll bring my mother." I thought I saw the fox's wet snout tremble. "Don't worry, not the man, I won't tell him." I climbed down the stone teeth. Looking back only once. My friend stood outside the den, her determined chest heaving like a stationed guard. For the first time in my life, my adoration for my mother soured.

I raced down the mountain, branches slapping at my skin, roots tripping me. My twelve-year-old heart bursting with the news. Through the trees, our cabin looked illuminated by the sun. A palace of gold, fit for gods.

Coming out from the dark canopy I saw the cabin was so bright it could have been the sun itself. The walls flaring red. The eaves crowned with flames. Everything burning.

The next fall my foster mother drove me out. I cradled the blue ceramic urn in my lap, keeping one hand on it as I pointed the way. The sight of the burned-out cabin collapsed into itself, trapped my breath in my chest.

She waited in the truck with the engine on, let me go up the mountain alone. I whistled as I went, scanning the woods. At the stone teeth, I felt like the goblin king gritting at the wind in my face, bearing the weight of the mountain. I climbed on the felled pine, stood at the splintering crack where it broke, and opened the urn. Into the gaping dark mouth of the abandoned den, I sent her. Wishing her in the next life a guardian mother of her own. The ashen powder caught in the wind and whipped around me. I heard a creak behind me, but I did not turn because I wasn't afraid of anything when I was with her. I threw the empty urn against the stone teeth and screamed to the valley below, "You can never touch her."

A warm snout nuzzled into my palm. I looked down to find the old vixen returned to me. She stood guard, licking my mother off my hands.

CASEY'S CRICKET FACTORY
by Chez Bratache

"Hey there, it's a happy hoppin' day at Casey's Cricket Factory. How can I help you?" said Blake. She twirled her pen in her hand and pressed her ear to the receiver to make sure she could hear the customer's order. There was a warbling clicking sound coming through the receiver and she rolled her eyes. *Ugh, it's Marvin.* Marvin Skinner was her least favorite customer and she could always tell when it was him over the phone.

"Sorry, sir, I'm having trouble hearing you," said Blake. She doodled circles on her notepad waiting for Marvin's line to clear up.

"Can you hear me better now?" said Marvin.

"Yes, sir," said Blake, impatiently. She preferred the warbling clicking sound his phone made over his actual voice. It was a wet sticky voice that sounded like he needed to spit. She shuddered as she suddenly imagined him whispering in her ear and getting saliva in it. She gagged inaudibly as he spoke.

Finally placing his order, Marvin said, "500 Superworms, 500 roaches, please."

"Sure thing, Mr. Skinner," said Blake. She wrote down his order then drew little disgusted faces next to his name on the notepad.

"Is that you, Little Miss Blake? How are you today?" said Marvin.

"Oh, I'm fine. Thank you for asking. So, should we go ahead and charge the card on file for this order, sir?" said Blake. *Please let me charge the card, please let me charge the card.*

"The card on file is fine, Little Blake," said Marvin.

Oh, thank goodness! "Okay, great! We'll chirp with you later!" said Blake.

"Bye B–" Blake hung up the phone before Marvin could say "goodbye". She felt bad for hanging up on him but consoled herself. *It's okay if I hung up on him, as long as I read from Mr. Casey's stupid script he won't care, he won't mind.* Duncan Casey was the owner and founder of Casey's Cricket Factory. He kept a plaque of the company's logo next to a picture of himself on the wall across from Blake's desk. In the picture, he had two thumbs up, smiling his signature gap tooth smile situated under a heavy mustache. Although he had plenty of cheesy sayings and slogans, he liked to use to keep his employees motivated and "customer focused", the plaque read his favorite motto: *Treat all creatures with kindness, big and small.* Blake often referred to the plaque on the wall when dealing with difficult customers. She especially looked at it when dealing with Marvin. As much as she hated to talk to Marvin over the phone, she hated having to see him in person even more. She especially didn't like that stupid nickname he had for her. "Little Miss Blake". As if she wasn't self-conscious enough already about her small stature, he certainly didn't have to remind her of it every time he came in. If that wasn't bad enough, there was her coworker, Marrissa. She was a busty brunette with thick curly hair and thighs. Fortunately, charging the card on file meant he would only be in the office long enough to pick up his order and Marrissa was usually around to deal with him then.

"Another order?" said Marrissa coming from the warehouse. She said she was preparing an order for 50 crickets but that was an hour ago and by the looks of her messy hair and wrinkled shirt she was probably texting explicit photos of herself in the bathroom again.

"Yeah, your favorite person, too," said Blake.

"Oh?" said Marrissa, putting a cheap grin on her face. Debauchery clouded her eyes as she wondered who Blake was talking about.

"Skinner," said Blake. She handed her the sheet of paper with Marvin's order on it.

"Oh!" hummed Marrissa.

"I don't know why he calls in every week. I wish he'd just do an online order like all the other regulars so I can stop hearing his voice!" said Blake. She dropped her head back and blew out a breath of frustration.

"What did he order this time?" said Marrissa.

"Roaches and Superworms, 500 each," said Blake.

"Oh, maybe he got a raise? That's way more than what he usually gets," said Marrissa, with a smile. The idea that one of her prospect's had money was always exciting to her.

"And that's another thing, like, what does he even have? You're personal with him. What is he, like a breeder or something?"

Marrissa shrugged and leaned against the desk. "I don't know. Maybe he owns a pet store or something. Either way, I better go get his order ready for him," said Marrissa, twirling a finger in one of her curls. She winked at Blake then headed towards the warehouse.

"Just be sure to wash your hands first!" Blake called after her.

"What, why?" said Marrissa.

"Well, if he does own any pets, we don't want them getting sick from bugs you've touched with your filthy hands."

Marrissa licked her middle finger and shot it at Blake. *Ew.* Blake shuddered and pumped some hand sanitizer in her hands.

A few hours later, the front door chimed as a tall man with long dark hair down to his waist slithered in. He was a pale man with deep green eyes in his early to mid-30's. Though she never tried to look directly at him, Blake noticed he was a little paler than usual.

"Hi, Little Miss Blake," said Marvin in his sticky voice.

"Hi, Mr. Skinner," said Blake smiling. *Be polite.* "Here is your order, sir."

"How many times do I have to tell you to call me "Munchy"? Everybody does." He grinned, showing dingy, yellow stained teeth that seemed to be sharper than normal teeth.

"I keep forgetting," said Blake feigning forgetfulness. She rolled her eyes internally and shuddered a little but not enough for him to see.

"Oh, had you processed my payment already? I meant to call back and say I'm going to have to pay differently. That's okay, isn't it?" said Marvin. He approached her desk and leaned on it, still grinning that sharp dingy grin of his.

"Oh I–" she frantically looked for his invoice on her desk, then on the order. She double checked the computer. *Shit! I must have forgotten to process it.*

"Looks like I haven't, and it's no problem!" said Blake. *Ugh! Damn it!*

Marvin reached for his wallet. "Great. Part cash, part card," he said.

"Of course!" said Blake, she composed herself while throwing the world's worst tantrum in her mind. Marvin took forever to pay in person. The longer she had to sit there with him, the worse off she was. She glanced past him at the plaque of Mr. Casey with that heavy mustache and gap tooth grin. She exhaled and gritted her teeth. *Patience.*

Marvin opened his wallet with long dirty fingers, "40 in cash," he said. Blake noticed there was soot under his nails as he handed her the cash. His money looked as grimy as his fingers.

"Put the rest on this card," said Marvin. His fingertips left a black greasy film on his card as he handed it to her. All Blake could think about is how she needed to wash her hands and wipe her desk down with disinfectant wipes when he left.

"Hey Munchy!" said Marrissa. Blake can tell she must have stuffed bubble wrap in her already fully occupied bra again. *Of all the weirdos, what does she like about this one?*

"Sweet Rissa, how are you? Always good to see you," said Marvin. His gaze was situated exactly where she intended it to be.

"I've got what you want right here," said Marrissa. She held his order positioned perfectly under her bubble wrap boobs.

"That you do. You are so sweet," said Marvin. He licked his sharp teeth. His voice sounded extra sticky and wet as he spoke to Marrissa.

Blake, currently trying not to vomit over this dirty exchange, processed the payment and handed him his receipt. His grimy fingers touched hers as he took the copy from her. His hands felt clammy and gritty.

Marvin nodded to her. "Thank you, Little Miss Blake," he said.

Blake smiled politely. "Sure," she said. Marvin and Marrissa started to chat; Blake took this opportunity to excuse herself. She thought he would be completely distracted by Marrissa, but she could feel his eyes watching her as she went to the bathroom. *What does she see in that creep show?* She washed her hands then her arms all the way up to her elbows. She rinsed her mouth with water and washed her face with paper towels. By the time she got back to her desk, Marvin was gone. She went ahead and started wiping her desk with disinfectant wipes then sprayed it down with disinfectant spray. *Can never be too careful.*

"I'm sure they have a pill for that," said Marrissa. "By the way, Marvin says I should treat you to lunch. You know, make sure you eat well," said Marrissa. She wrapped her index finger and thumb around Blake's dainty wrist.

Ignoring her jests, Blake asked, "tell me, honestly, what do you see in that weirdo?"

"Mr. Casey wouldn't like you talking about his customers that way," said Marrissa, dodging the question.

"Whatever," said Blake, "all I'm saying is he looks like he has fleas."

"You know why they call him "Munchy", right?" said Marrissa.

"You call him that. Nobody else calls him that."

Marrissa leaned in close to Blake, she could smell her dollar store perfume.

"C'mon, 'Little Miss Blake'. Why would they call a guy like that "Munchy"?"

In an instant, Blake imagined Marvin's long greasy hair in between her legs, smiling up at her with those sharp grody teeth. She actually vomited a little in her mouth.

"You two are made for each other," said Blake, as she ran to the bathroom.

The next few weeks were much more relaxing for Blake. Things were pretty slow around the office, and she hadn't seen Marvin in weeks. His orders were a lot bigger, but he had been placing his orders online, so she didn't have to see, hear and especially not touch him. She had just finished processing an order from him then called Marrissa to the front.

"Your boyfriend put in another order," said Blake. She handed Marrissa the invoice.

"Aw," said Marrissa. She pouted her lips. *She looks genuinely upset about not seeing Marvin again today, maybe she really does like him. Yuck.* About an hour before closing, Blake was cleaning off her desk. The last customer of the day had just left about 30 minutes ago with a box of crickets for their baby bearded dragon. Blake thought about how excited the little girl was to show off her new pet.

"Feed him several times a day for the first few months and he'll grow to be this big!" said Blake. She spread her arms about two feet apart.

"How will I know when he's growing?" asked the little girl in her tiny voice.

"He'll start to shed," Blake told her.

"Shed?" said the little girl.

"His skin will turn white then it'll come off!" said Blake.

"Ew!" said the little girl excitedly, "I can't wait!"

Blake smiled remembering this exchange as she wiped down her desk. She started spinning in her chair as the last hour crept along, as it always seemed to do. She noticed Marrissa appear with a large order.

"What's that?" said Blake.

"Oh, just a little delivery," said Marrissa. "I figured it's slow and we can go drop this off before we close for today," said Marrissa. She smiled that cheap smile of hers at Blake.

"What delivery? I thought you shipped everything off for today?"

"Oh, I did, except this one."

"One? That's one order?" said Blake.

"Sure, now let's go while it's slow and we'll be back in time to close."

"Who does it belong to?" Marrissa grinned and made her way to the door before Blake could look. Blake intercepted Marrissa at the door, her small frame blocking the exit she looked at the invoice. The tag read, *M. Skinner 200 Crickets, 500 Dubias, 500 Superworms, 50 Black fly larvae.* Blake felt her face flush and she looked at Marrissa with horror and fury in her eyes.

"Listen! I–" Marrissa pleaded, but before she could say anything Blake cut her off.

"No, no, no! I thought you sent this out earlier!?"

"I was going to," said Marrissa, trying to defend herself, "but you know he's one of our best customers and, listen, it will look really good to Mr. Casey if we deliver it!"

"I hate it when he comes in here! Why would you think I want to go to his house!"

"You don't think it would look good to do a home delivery for one of our best customers? Just this once?" Blake thought about it, she hated it, but Marrissa was right. Blake's eyes darted to the plaque on the wall of Mr. Casey. *Treat all creatures with kindness, big and small.* But Mr. Casey never had to deal with Marvin and now Blake and Marrissa were going to go to his home.

"You don't even know where he lives!" said Blake.

"Of course I do. I do the shipments, remember?" Marrissa knew she was wrong for springing this on Blake at the last minute, but she couldn't help but think how cute it was to watch Blake flounder.

"Do you even know *why* he hasn't shown up here in weeks?" said Blake.

Marrissa put the boxes down, pulled out her phone, and opened her messages to a chat between her and Marvin.

"Look," said Marrissa.

Blake instinctively shut her eyes. "I don't want to see any sex pictures of you!"

"Shut up and look!" Blake opened one eye cautiously to peep at the messages, they read:

Haven't seen you around the office lately said Marrissa with the anime sad eyes emoji.

Busy molting Sweets, you should come by said the message from Marvin.

"Molting?" said Blake.

"Moving! That's why he hasn't come by, see?" said Marrissa. She pointed her index finger at her head as if it was common sense.

"We should be nice delivery girls and give him his order, just this once, please!" said Marrissa. She begged Blake with those same large anime sad eyes. They didn't work on Blake like they probably worked on 99% of the men Marrissa talked to but reluctantly she agreed. Marrissa did have a point. Mr. Casey would be impressed to know they made a delivery to a valued customer no matter how freakish he was.

Blake rolled her eyes. "Fine," she said. Marrissa bounced and giggled happily.

"And I better not have to see his creepy face again!" said Blake. She pointed a tiny finger at Marrissa.

"I'm sure you won't," said Marrissa.

"Hey," said Blake, "and if you guys get all weird and flirty I'm leaving you there and he can take you home!"

"Deal!"

Blake picked up the order and they headed to the company van. They packed the bugs in the back and Marrissa plugged Marvin's address in the GPS.

"He lives pretty far," said Blake. She strapped herself in the seatbelt and lowered the height of it to get it off her face.

"Good thing we're using old Mr. Casey's gas then, huh?" said Marrissa, winking at Blake. They arrived at Marvin's house, and it looked exactly how Blake thought it would. It looked like an older house that was way overdue for renovation. The porch was dilapidated, and Blake could see that blinds were haphazardly thrown up with drapes covering what the blinds missed. Blake shuddered; *it's going to be filthy in there*. "There's no way he keeps animals in here," said Blake, looking at the order. She unpacked the bugs and held them close as they approached the door.

"Well, maybe this is why he's moving. Stop being so judgmental," said Marrissa at a whisper. She knocked on the door and rang the doorbell. The doorbell made a lazy chime.

"We should just leave the bugs here. He's obviously not home. Let's just go." said Blake.

"No, they might die out here," said Marrissa. She tried turning the knob and the door opened leading to a living room area.

"Oh? We'll just leave it inside, then," said Marrissa.

The place was certainly disheveled. There was food and trash everywhere but no moving boxes. The only boxes that could be seen had Casey's Cricket Factory on them. "If he's moving where are all the boxes, where are the animals?" said Blake. She looked around the home nervously, afraid to take another step.

"They may be in a back room, he's probably in the back," said Marrissa. *She's got an excuse for everything*. Blake heard a crunch and felt a squish underneath her foot. She stepped right into one of their boxes.

"There's stuff in here!" said Blake. She shook her foot and Superworms went across the floor.

"Let's go!" said Blake. She found a spot on the crowded couch and placed the bugs down gently.

"Sorry guys," she said to the bugs and headed for the door.

"Oh, hey Marvin!" said Marrissa. Blake whipped around to see that Marvin had been sitting at a computer just around the corner the whole time. She craned her neck slightly and saw his long greasy hair draped over the back of the chair.

"Hey, Marvin we don't mean to startle you, but we dropped off your order," said Marrissa. He didn't say anything but continued sitting in the chair looking at the screen. Marrissa and Blake stepped closer; they could see the logo of the website he was looking at– Casey's Cricket Factory. He looked as if he was in the middle of placing another order. *So weird*.

"Hey, Marvin," said Marrissa. She touched his arm, and his head fell back; his eye sockets were empty, and his mouth was wide open. Marrissa jumped back accidently pushing the chair. The chair whipped around as if Marvin weighed nothing sitting in it. There were hundreds of thousands of Superworms all over him eating away at his clothes, his hair and his skin. If the floor wasn't so dirty, Blake would have fainted. Marrissa screamed and suddenly they heard a heavy thudding and clicking sound coming from one of the back rooms. What emerged from the hallway was a giant beetle as long as Marvin was tall but much wider than he was in his human shell.

"Ah, Sweet Rissa," said the beetle. Its pincers clicked together as it spoke. Blake recognized that wet sticky voice as Marvin's.

"Thank you for coming by. I've been so busy with my molt, I haven't had a chance to come see you and here you are," said the beetle. Marrissa was frozen, she looked at the carcass in the computer chair then back at the beetle.

"Yes, that old skin was getting pretty tight but now I'm finally free of it and it feels good. Though, Sweet Rissa, I am so hungry, starving actually," said the beetle. It came a little closer to Marrissa, its antennae feeling over her body frantically.

Marrissa pointed to the couch. "We– we brought your order," she said.

"Oh, how kind. But those little things simply won't do anymore. I need something bigger," said the beetle. In an instant, the beetle lunged at Marrissa. Blake watched in horror as the beetle started from her feet, and she slowly disappeared wailing and screaming into the beetle's mouth. When the crunching sounds stopped, the beetle clicked its pincers together satisfied.

"Ah, Sweet Rissa, what a delicacy," said the beetle. It turned towards Blake, its antennae twitching and jerking frantically around her body.

"Little Miss Blake, you're all skin and bones. No good. Do indulge a bit more, won't you?" The beetle turned around knocking over boxes and garbage as it made its way towards the back of the house.

"Good day, Little Miss Blake," said the beetle. It disappeared around the corner and back down the hallway from which it came. Blake realized she was holding her breath then gasped out loud. She really *really* didn't know what Marrissa saw in such a weirdo.

RITES
by Shane Camoin

Cole stood in the backyard tossing rotten pears over the fence, aiming for the neighbors' birdfeeder, when he heard Myoko scream his name. He found her on the kitchen floor cradling Kayli. Kayli was limp in Myoko's arms, her yellow muzzle stained with blood. Cole stared at them for a moment, unable to move or breathe. He kneeled behind Myoko and placed his hands on her trembling shoulders. She dropped Kayli and twisted around burying her face in his chest. He held her and rubbed her back. Her shirt was backless, tied around her neck and waist. It was one of the shirts he'd told her not to wear in public.

"Are you okay?" He closed his eyes and pressed his face against the top of her head. Her hair smelled like mangoes

"No," Myoko said. Her tears soaked through his thin t-shirt.

"Are you hurt?"

She shook her head.

"What happened?"

She looked up at him with mascara-streaked cheeks, her bottom lip quivering with guilt. "She was chasing a squirrel." She pushed her face against his chest and clawed his back with her sharp nails. Her voice was muffled but loud. "I tried to stop her and the car almost hit me too. It didn't stop or slow down or nothing. We should call the cops. It was a red Bimmer. The license was W-R something. There was an eight in it."

"I'll call them." He glanced at the microwave on the counter next to the fridge. It was a little after five. Myoko wheezed and trembled in his arms.

"I need my inhaler," she said.

"I'll get it." He kissed her forehead and headed for the living room, but after two steps he slipped on the blood-streaked linoleum and landed with all his weight on his ankle. Myoko was too busy crying and gagging to notice. Tears welled in his eyes as he limped into the living room. The front door was open and there was a trail of blood across the white carpet.

"I don't see your purse," he said.

"It's in my backpack."

Her Hello Kitty backpack was on the couch. He unzipped the front pouch, found her little black purse, limped back into the kitchen and handed it her, couldn't help but glance at Kayli, her eyes bulging. Myoko was bright red and heaving. She shook her inhaler and sucked off two hits.

"Better?"

She shook her head and spit on the floor.

He sat down facing away from her and Kayli, lifted his corduroy pant leg and examined his ankle. It was already green and swollen. He pulled off his sneaker and sock to let it breathe.

Myoko stood in front of him and unbuttoned her blood-soaked jeans.

"You should close the door first," he said. He tried to bend his ankle but it hurt too much.

"You close it. I can't wear these anymore."

She slipped off her jeans, pulled the panties out of her crack and walked down the thin hall to the bedroom. Cole sighed and tried to think of something other than Kayli or fucking Myoko. His ankle felt like a water balloon. Myoko came back carrying Kayli's blanket. She'd taken off her shirt and was only wearing panties. She held the fuzzy blanket out to Cole.

"Wrap her in it."

"You wrap her in it."

"I can't touch her again." She shoved the blanket in his face

"Stop it." He tore it from her hands and dropped it over Kayli, not covering her at all.

"My stomach hurts." Myoko slumped against the counter and held her belly.

"My ankle hurts." Cole picked the yellow hairs out of his mouth and scratched his nose.

"What happened to your ankle?"

He lifted his leg to show her.

"That doesn't look good." She reached out to touch his ankle but he pulled it away. She cuddled next to him, laid her head on his shoulder and they both stared out the front door.

"We should bury her," he said.

"Where?"

"I have a place."

* * * * * *

Myoko parked across the street from Cole's old house. The new owners had painted it maroon with dark green trim. He wanted to see how the inside looked and if they'd finished the downstairs bathroom. Lawn gnomes guarded the front stoop. He leaned his seat back and stared at the headliner. The roof light was busted and he'd stuck candy wrappers and a little plastic ninja in the casing.

"Are you tired?" Myoko sat beside him wearing a short yellow dress with matching sandals, white stockings and fuzzy bee clips in her shiny black hair. She looked nine years old.

"A little," he said.

She turned down the radio. Freddy Mercury was singing about big bottom girls.

"When are we going to do it?" She was anxious and picking at her lip.

"When it gets a little darker."

"Should we take a nap?"

"Maybe."

"Keep your leg up," she said. "It'll help with the swelling."

He rested his foot on the dashboard. Myoko had wrapped his ankle with a bandage and tied an ice pack around it.

"Where's the ice pack?

"Your foot will fall off if it keeps swelling." She leaned her seat back and stared at him.

"Stop it," he said.

"Stop what?"

"Staring at me."

She rolled over and curled in a ball. "I like looking at you," she said. He rubbed her back. The car smelled like Kayli, probably from all the times she'd pissed on the backseat. He closed his eyes.

"Are you happy with me?" she said.

"For the most part."

* * * * * *

He woke up a little after one in the morning. Myoko was snoring loudly and all the lights were off across the street except the one in what used to be his dad's den on the second floor. Cole took the keys from the ignition, the shovel from the backseat and shut the door trying not to wake her. She was a heavy sleeper. He yawned, stretched his arms and cracked his neck. After struggling with the key in the dark he finally opened the trunk and gently lifted out Kayli. He'd wrapped her in her favorite blanket and then in a trash bag. The smell made him gag but he held her tightly.

He dropped the keys on the passenger seat and limped across the street carrying Kayli in one arm and the shovel in the other. His dad had built an eight-foot-high redwood fence around the backyard that the new owners had decorated with vintage Volkswagen hubcaps. He limped the length of the fence but couldn't find the door handle. There was no way into the backyard.

Cole tossed the shovel over the fence. The metal clanged against something hard like concrete and he froze. After waiting a minute, he placed the bag over his shoulder and climbed the fence using the hubcaps for support. As he straddled the top of fence, he lost his balance and fell into a rose bush. Thorns stabbed his ass and thighs as he rolled himself out and picked up Kayli, trying not to tear the plastic. The shovel lay on a stone path. He'd have to come back for it later.

The backyard was different than he remembered; it had more plants and smelled sweeter, like spiced cider. He followed the stone path through stalks of bamboo carrying Kayli to the back of the property, where he laid her under the big elm tree and felt the trunk for the names of other departed pets. The last had been his sister's flop-eared rabbit, Dizzy, after she'd dropped a gallon jug of milk on his head eight years ago. He couldn't feel any names and limped back through the bamboo for the shovel.

The kitchen light turned on as he hop-ran back through the bamboo to the elm tree, was pretty sure no one had seen him and started to dig. The dirt was moist from three days of rain. He stopped digging every few minutes to peer through the bamboo at the backdoor and kitchen window. He wondered if he'd find some remains of the previous animals, but there were none. The earth had swallowed them up. After what felt like an hour, he decided the hole was big enough and placed Kayli in it. He petted the trash bag and tried to think of something to say—his sister always had something cheesy and endearing to say at such times—but his throat felt funny like something was caught in it, so he covered her with dirt, padding the soil gently. He plucked a rose from the bush and rested it on top. He considered leaving the shovel next to the tree but Myoko had borrowed it from her dad and she'd make him come back for it.

The kitchen light was still on as he made his way through the bamboo. The kitchen looked pretty much the same except the wall now had a unicorn painted on it, with a forest and a castle in the background, and there were fairies with butterfly wings painted on the cabinets. He didn't notice the woman sitting at a small table in the corner until she stood up and walked over to the window. He was afraid she'd spot him but he couldn't take his eyes off her. She filled her cup from a coffeepot next to the sink and wiped the tears from her eyes. Her bronze robe was open and Cole was oddly drawn to her exposed breasts, tan and wrinkled. She stood by the sink, drank her black coffee and cried. He envied her, wanted to cry himself but couldn't. Another woman in a matching bronze robe came up behind her, embraced her and kissed her cheek. She was almost a foot taller, bald and smiling. The first woman cried harder, spilled her coffee and placed the cup in the sink.

As Cole climbed the fence, the untied sneaker on his swollen foot snagged a rose bush. It was harder without the hubcaps. He crossed the street to Myoko's Camry using the shovel for a crutch. The radio was blaring death metal and she turned it down as he got in the car after tossing the shovel in the backseat.

"I saw the light on downstairs." She rubbed her eyes and yawned, didn't look like she'd been awake for very long.

"Let's go," he said.

"Did you do it?"

"Let's go." He reached over and turned the ignition key. The lights went off in the house, first downstairs and then in his dad's den.

MAGIC DOORS
by John Raisor

On the mornin of April 28th, day of our lord 2024, I limped my crippled ass up to them big glass lunium framed doors, and they slid apart like magic. The whole store's magic. Magic like how me and my wife was magic. 'Fore they opened the magic store I'da had to go to two differ'nt stores in two towns clear across the county from the other to get my subscriptions, and my ammo.

Used to be I was just takin Traima-doll after some lady run a red light and T boned me. But I got bad nerves on account I couldn't work. Ain't no man worth his salt can sit at home on his dead ass alla time. I went to the only doc in town and he put me on all kinda pills. But I quit takin 'em a while back. My old lady didn't like me not workin neither. I come back home from a specialist for my hip and the house was plum cleaned out.

The lights was so damned bright in the store reflectin offa them white tile, I kept my sunglasses and ball cap on. But I took em off when I showed my ID to the pharmacy girl. She went back to the walla stapled bags. They put me on Booze-Par at first and it didn't do a damn thing but make my eyeballs jiggle around in my head on their own account. Then they put me on Sarah--Quill after I shot the neighbor's dog in the ass. I'm on three hunnert milligrams a day.

They upped the dose after I shot 'eem again. It keeps me outta trouble, but makes me awful tired. I tolt the doc and he give me some Add-rall. That and the Traima-doll's the only stuff I took that day. My hip hurts like hell.

I didn't know which end was up on account of the doctor givin me all them pills. I quit taking all that shit and seent that my ass end was up and the doc was behind me. He put me on that shit to make me stupid and steal my woman. Got everythin a man could want and had to take what little I had that's worth stealin.

The pharmacy girl handed me the stapled bag and I broke it open in front of her and them magic cameras. Everybody's lookin to take what little I got left. All the Sarah-Quill was there.

They give me Zan-Axe for 'mergencies. I ain't took a single damn one, but my neighbor sure likes em, and I need the money on account I cain't work. My antidepressor was in there. They give me all they was spose to so I stuck the bottles inside my jacket and left the instructions and the bag on the counter and walked to the huntin stuff.

Asked the boy for as many boxes of five five six rounds as I could get. They didn't always have 'em. He give me three. So I asked for a buncha thirty aught six rounds, and seven six two, too. He give me three boxes of thirty aught six, but they was out of seven six two. Ain't nothin wrong with cheap Chinese ammo. You just gotta polish your brass, or them dirty bullets'll gum up the works the same way them pills gummed up my brain. I took off my shades and my ballcap and showed the boy my ID and paid 'eem with the money I got from my neighbor for the Zan-Axe subscription and he double bagged em for me. Got my pills and my ammo under the same roof. Magic.

Limped over to the jewelry counter and sit my weddin band down on the glass case with the receipt. My sister in law was workin and kept talkin to the bag I was carryin insteada me. She said it'd been too long to return the ring, said to take it down to the pawn. I told her to keep it.

She hollered while I limped away but I didn't pay no attention.

Went over to the grocery and got a case of beer and had to take everything off my head and show my ID again. I limped out of them magic doors all leaned over. Used to carry hod all day with my back straight as an arrow. Now I cain't hardly carry a case of beer on account of my hip. My wife had that lady hit me so's she could get ridda me.

Got in the truck and cracked one. Sucked it down. I sucked down another'n tossed the empty in the floorboard. Just needed a couple to calm my nerves. When I quit takin my anti depressor I couldn't get outta bed and I got shit to do so I started doublin down on the Add-rall. Ain't nobody wants to live forever, but everybody wants to do somethin that does, and I'm fixin to.

That goddamned doctor. If he knew the ground from a hole up his ass he'd know I ain't crazy. Same with my wife. She works for 'eem, but she hides in the back when it's time for my pointments. Ain't nobody round here who wants to understand. They all got their heads and their asses screwed on the wrong ends.

I pulled the thirty aught off the rack behind my head and dug a boxa shells out. Pawpaw's M1 Garand only holds eight rounds, but I only needed two. That rifle didn't have a single spotta rust or any pits in it and it was older'n Pawpaw. He took good care of it, and took good care of me. I took a rag and cleaned all the gunk off the rounds and put em in the clip. Took down the AR and loaded it up too.

Got me an appointment to take a drug test I'm gonna fail, but I don't need no more pills no how. Drove to the strip mall, to the doctor's office end, not the pawn shop end, that's where I bought my AR from. Parked in the handicapped spot and hung my blue tag so's I didn't get towed. My hands still shook from the Add-rall. I cracked another beer and sucked it down.

Got out and slung the thirty aught across my back, carried the AR. A five five six round breaks up and bounces around inside a body. The thirty aught blows a hole out the back. AR does more damage. I had to make sure they knowed I wasn't just gonna lay down and take it.

You better believe that hard headed ass dog don't come on my property no more. He gotta do a handstand to get around nowadays. Shoulda listened the first time. I don't know why I bought so damned many rounds. I only needed two. Same reason I bought a case of beer and drunk three, I reckon.

Coulda took my gun back down to the pawn. Coulda took my pills an forgot about it.

Guns and doctors in the same strip mall. The magic store's got it all under one roof. How come they ain't got a doctor in there too?

Pulled the door open and wadn't nobody at the front desk, or in the waitin room. So I walked on back and started pokin my head in the other rooms. Pulled the knob on the break room door. There's a half eat Lean Cuisine on the table, still steamin. My wife's.

Sound like a damn herda mules come in the front door stompin and kickin. I knew'd what was comin. Walked over to the chair in front of the Lean cuisine. Slung my rifle behind me, and knelt down to get my nose close to the seat. The chair smelt like her, back when we was still magic. The deputies slung the door open and started hollerin to get down, but that was as down as I could get with my hip the way it is. I turned to grab the table and lift myself up.

Pop.

First she had that lady T bone me, then she had the cops shoot me, same hip too. My ass meat was burnin from that round tearin through it. I fell over onto the chair and they come and pinned me to it. One of the deputies got down so I could see his face, it was my cousin.

"You quit takin your pills again?" he asked. "I have the right to remain silent."

"Darlene didn't leave you for no doctor, dumbass, she left you cause you quit takin your pills. Now you got yourself shot in the ass cause you won't listen."

Me and the neighbor's dog ain't so differ'nt. So, yeah, I done it, and that's bout how it went.

Forever Yours, Darlene.

Jerry Jeff Holcomb

THE DUST OFFENSIVE
by Harriet Radford

I'm at war with the lint trap in my dryer, or more accurately, I'm at war with the people inside it. I didn't think much about the lint trap when I first moved in. Didn't think much about the laundry at all. No one puts on a wash their first week in a new place. But two weeks in—and an unholy accumulation of socks later—I opened the dryer for the first time. The lint catcher looked like it hadn't been emptied in months, years maybe. I pulled out the mesh trap and peeled away a thick carpet of lint from within. The slot behind the trap was a deep black. I could only see an inch inside, and the space beyond was inky darkness. Odd, I thought. But for now, I was just happy to spin my socks dry without setting the house on fire. Priorities.

Then we started to notice the dust. It crept out of the laundry cupboard in small guerilla teams, gathering in the second-floor hallway and making sallies into the spare room. Within a week it came in more brazen waves, whole battalions rolled down the stairs and made camp in the cracks between the couch cushions. I vacuumed and wiped. Twice. Perhaps I had just missed the dust when we first moved in. Finally, on our third weekend in the house, I washed our sheets and emptied the lint trap again. The gray covering inside was already so thick it was as if the trap had never been touched. I told my husband. He pointed out that our sheets had been in storage, maybe that was just how much dust they had on them.

But soon the dust was laying waste to every room. It floated into pots bubbling on the stove and rode the air-conditioner like a rapid transport system to our master bedroom at the far end of the house. My husband developed one of those coughs you attribute to old smokers. I developed a healthy suspicion about the lint trap.

One evening, I got up to get a glass of water. It was a still night, but when I opened the bathroom door a swirling storm of dust motes danced in the fluorescent light as if caught in a strong breeze. It was time to act. I went upstairs, propped open the laundry cupboard, and angled my phone light into the dryer. The trap came out easily, and with it a haze of gray that flew straight into my lungs. Spluttering, I thrust the light further into the deep hole behind the trap.

There was no missing them, though I couldn't quite understand what I saw. Three little dust men the size of my thumb looked out at me with narrow gray eyes. They held tiny, dusty spears in their thin hands and waved them at me in a way that might have been menacing. I reached forward with my free arm and another cloud of dust flew from the hole. Definitely menacing. I rubbed my eyes and stepped back. The dust abated.

This gave me an idea. I picked up the trap and held it in front of the little men to show them that I hadn't yet cleaned the dust from inside it. Then I slotted the trap back into the hole. Immediately the lint settled, and I could breathe more easily.

At breakfast the next morning our orange juice was suspiciously clear. No gray sprinkles floated down to join the icing sugar on our pancakes. I told my husband about my strange encounter with the little people behind the lint trap the previous night. He shrugged, seemingly uninterested, but then managed to get through a whole session on his exercise bike without needing his inhaler.

We don't empty the lint trap anymore. We just dry our clothes and pray nothing ever ignites in the laundry. I haven't poked around behind the trap since that first meeting, but sometimes I think I see the lint people in the corner of my eye; hovering in the first shafts of sunlight through the bedroom blinds, or tumbling down to earth when I shake out the winter blankets from the linen press. I imagine them padding softly through their felt city, deep behind the dryer, hoarding all the dust in the house like defiant gremlins.

I may be at war with the lint trap in my dryer, but for now a ceasefire suits us both.

THE GIRL UPSTAIRS
by Chris Cochran

In my lost years after college, I lived briefly in an old Victorian home that was carved into four separate apartments. It sat behind a used car lot that doubled as a coffee shop, and I would sit on an Adirondack bench on the house's stone porch and catch whiffs of pine air freshener and caramelized sugar. *Just pick one thing*, I thought. *You can't be both.*

Despite having already graduated, I spent the previous two years living with my college roommates, pretending to still be in college without the hassle of having to attend class. I would stay up all night playing drinking games and then work an eight-hour shift selling sporting goods to soccer moms and distracted dads. I was masquerading as both student and adult, unable to fully commit to either. Trying to have it all without having much of anything. When a girl at a party scrunched her face and asked me how old I was, I knew it was time to grow up. I started packing my meager belongings the next day.

After years of stagnation, I suddenly found myself in a hurry. The Victorian apartment was close to work and affordable, so I signed a six-month lease without deliberation.

I met her the day I moved in, the first day of fall. I was fumbling with the worn brass doorknob of my new apartment, balancing my bulky television on my thigh. "Seems heavy," she said, and I looked up to see her at the top of the staircase leaning against the banister. Instead of offering to help, she revealed a playful smirk that sent the television sliding down my leg. I recovered and, spurred by embarrassment, got the door unstuck. I attempted to kick it closed behind me as I waddled inside, but it bounced back open off the warped frame.

After centering the television on its stand, I turned to find her already inside, surveying my apartment. I had never let her in. "It's like a mirror image," she said with a sense of wonder. She walked past me, through the living room and into the kitchen. Before entering the hallway that led to the bathroom and bedroom, she looked at me and raised her eyebrows. I gestured, granting her what would become the first of many permissions.

She lived opposite of me upstairs. Her apartment was exactly the same as mine, she had said, except the layout was reversed. When I told her how much I paid in rent, she shook her head and tsked. She gave me the lowdown on the other residents, warned me of the occasional nightmarish house centipede, and asked me if I owned a shovel—the previous tenant had cleared the porch of snow each winter.

I was painfully shy; if not for her boldness, I would have settled for a quick hello in passing and hated myself for it. The girl upstairs had shoved me outside of my comfort zone before I could retreat.

We became friends in the way proximity makes friends of neighborhood kids with little in common. She loved old black and white films, and I loved the attention of a woman, even if I had to share it with Clark Gable. We would sit a safe distance from each other on my couch and eat Chinese takeout from the family-owned restaurant down the street while watching movies late into the evening.

After a month in which we never bothered getting to know each other, she would lie back and prop her legs on my lap. I consciously had to remember to breathe. One night, she fell asleep in this position, only to be awakened by the swell of the orchestra that marked the beginning of the end credits. This was, in a sense, the beginning of the end to the relative safety that existed between us. She came over the next night with a bottle of wine and never made it back to her apartment.

We never talked about us. I assumed our arrangement was as much one of convenience for her as it was for me. We were enjoying the perks of a relationship without actually being in one. Trying to have it all without having much of anything.

Months passed, and I learned that even casual relationships can fall prey to routine and the burden of expectation. The initial excitement had dwindled. I dreaded seeing her car parked in the driveway when coming home from work.

It was late afternoon. We sat on my couch as the first snow settled on our front porch. Her hair was in a messy bun and she had on the same gray sweatpants she always seemed to wear.

"Did you buy a shovel?" she asked. When I shook my head, her typically stoic expression betrayed a subtle hint of disappointment. That sinking feeling returned, the one I had sought so desperately to avoid.

"You shouldn't expect me to buy a shovel," I said. "What, because the last guy shoveled means it's now my responsibility?" Her expression shifted from disappointment to disbelief.

"You said you'd buy one, so I didn't. What are you even talking about?" Before I could use the shovel to dig myself deeper, an odd shuffling sound from outside, followed by a high-pitched series of distressed chirruping, interrupted. I got up and looked out the front window, but the swirling snow made it impossible to see anything. She stepped into a pair of my boots and went to investigate. A few seconds later, I heard her panicked scream.

I hurried outside. She stood frozen, her face creased in disgust. I followed her gaze to the Adirondack bench where a bluebird was frantically flapping its wings. It had somehow got its leg caught between the bench's wooden slats.

I cautiously approached the bird, which triggered a flurry of activity as it fought to loosen its leg. Its efforts were in vain, as were those of the girl upstairs; she pleaded with me to do something, but I stood paralyzed as drops of blood punctured the snow beneath the bench.

"Can you free its leg?" she asked.

"I...I don't know." I looked behind the bench to see a leg that was badly broken. Getting closer exacerbated the problem, for the bird would resume fearfully flapping its wings in futility. "I don't know what to do."

"Please! We can't just leave it here!" She twisted her head, attempting to hide her tears, and I knew, at that moment, that whatever we had was over. I walked back inside despite her continued protests. After a few minutes, the sound of heavy footsteps signaled her return to her apartment.

Why had this bird not migrated for the winter? Was it too scared to venture into the unknown? Too stubborn to admit there was nothing left worth staying for?

I turned on the television to drown out the sounds of distress. The snow fell relentlessly.

The next morning, I found my boots carelessly abandoned outside my door. I slid them on and stepped out onto the porch. The bluebird was gone. Blood trailed from the bench down the concrete steps, accompanied by a small set of footprints.

I wondered if the bluebird had still been alive when the cat had come in the night.

The girl upstairs and I never talked again—it was easy enough to avoid her until my lease expired. There was one evening, however, not more than a couple weeks after the incident, when I heard her door open upstairs as I was entering my apartment after a closing shift. A man came jogging down the steps with a big cat-like grin, and I thought it curious how most problems eventually take care of themselves.

END.

LIST OF CONTRIBUTORS

AHONA DAM is currently a student at Vassar College studying neuroscience with a minor in English. who loves to write, create art, and spend time with friends and family and has always enjoyed writing and other forms of creativity.

* * *

AIMEE R. CERVENKA is a writer, climate activist, and professional baker. Her poetry has appeared in more than a dozen publications, including *Poet Lore*, *Slab*, and *Ascent*, and won the 2022 Briefly Write Poetry Prize. She is also the author of the micro-collection *(Not Quite) Political Animals* (Rinky Dink Press, 2023). She currently lives in Spokane, WA.

* * *

ALEX BASKIN is a graduate of Harvard Divinity School. Rooted in over a decade of Buddhist practice and his upbringing in an orthodox Jewish family and community, he works as an interfaith hospital chaplain. His poetry appears in *Gulf Coast*, *Lucky Jefferson*, *poetry.onl*, *Redivider*, and elsewhere. He has an essay in *Refuge in the Storm: Buddhist Voices in Crisis Care* (North Atlantic Books, 2023.) Originally from New Jersey, he lives in Massachusetts.

* * *

ALISON STONE (no bio given)

* * *

AMANDA TROUT is a Kansas poet with a love for sound and form. Her work has been published by Yavanika Press, Raw Earth Ink, The Common Language Project, and more. Find Amanda on Instagram @atrout2972.

* * *

AMARIA STONE (no bio given)

* * *

ANDREW NICKERSON's originally from Massachusetts, and has studied military history/tactics/strategy for almost 30 years. He has a BA in History (English minor) from UMASS Lowell and JD from Mass. School of Law. He can be found daily on Twitter (AndrewNickers19@), analyzing pop culture characters via Sun Tzu.

* * *

ANGELA CUMMINGS writes poetry, fiction and micro-fiction which explores how identity and grief are connected to the continual evolution of the natural world. Her early work appeared in *Cobalt* and *Slightly West* magazine. In 2012, her story, "Humane" was a finalist for the *Aspen Writers and Esquire* magazine's Short-Short story contest. She lives in the mossy and mushroom-laden Pacific Northwest with her husband and dog.

* * *

ANGUS MCLINN is an investment researcher and author based in Chicago. His award-winning short fiction has been anthologized in *Writers Digest's 17th Annual Short Short Fiction Competition Collection*, *Songs of my Selfie: An Anthology of Millennial Stories*, and the 2013 *Saint Paul Almanac*. Other stories of his have appeared in various literary journals in the US and abroad including *High Shelf*, *Millennial Pulp*, *Antithesis*, *The Other Stories*, *Blue Monday Review*, and elsewhere.

* * *

ANN KATHRYN KELLY writes from New Hampshire's Seacoast region. She's an editor with *Barren Magazine*, a columnist with *WOW! Women on Writing*, and she works in the technology sector. Ann leads writing workshops for a nonprofit that offers therapeutic arts programming to people living with brain injury. Her writing has appeared in a number of literary journals. https://annkkelly.com.

* * *

ANNE MARIE WELLS is an award-winning and Pushcart-nominated poet, playwright, memoirist, and oral storyteller. She is the author of *Survived By* (Curious Corvid Publishing, 2023) and *Mother, (v)* (Cinnamon Press, 2024). She is a freelance copy editor, poetry coach, and creative writing instructor. Find her @annemariewellswriter or annemariwellswriter.com.

* * *

BRADY KENT - I am a retired, sixty-seven-year-old man living in Bishops Stortford, twenty miles north of London. I am very fit, very tall and vary bald. I have a partner and two grown up children. I have lots of sporty friends, some from school and lots from my university. I spent my working life in the world of business travelling around the world. I always promised myself that I would write a book or two when I retired. I like to look at subjects from a different point of view. I have now written about ten poetry books and then produced a' Best of the Poems' edition'. I also written two books of country song lyrics. I've had all had the books printed, but only for friends at this stage I cover a variety of subjects but particularly like political poetry.

* * *

BRAEDEN MICHAELS is an American author and the creator of Deconstructive Literature. He won first place in the prose poetry section of the 2023 Northwind Writing Award and has been featured on several podcasts and anthologies. He is a Pushcart Nominee. Braeden's creativity never stops. Constantly observing human nature and analyzing their depth, he continues to write every day.

* * *

CAMILLE HILTBRAND (no bio given)

* * *

CAROLYN MARTIN is blissfully retired in Clackamas, Oregon and a lover of gardening and snorkeling, feral cats and backyard birds, writing and photography. Since the only poem she wrote in high school was red penciled "extremely maudlin," she is amazed she has continued to write. Her poems have appeared in more than 200 journals throughout North America, Australia, and the UK. See more at www.carolynmartinpoet.com.

* * *

CHARLOTTE CROWDER lives and writes on the coast of Maine. An accredited editor in the life sciences, she is a medical writer and editor by day. Her publications include, among others, stories in *Tamarind Magazine, Present Tense, Intima, Branching Out: International Tales of Brilliant Flash Fiction, Maine Character Energy, Maine Standard*, and a picture book, *A Fine Orange Bucket* (North Country Press; Unity, Maine. 2019).

* * *

CHEZ BRATACHE here! I am a fiction author from Augusta, Georgia. I write novels and short stories in the realm of fantasy, magical realism, horror, and science fiction. I am happily married to my amazing husband, and a proud parent of two bouncing bearded dragons! When I'm not writing, I'm painting and reading all the stories that inspire my imagination. My goal is to create a diverse space within and outside the walls of my books. Here's to better days, and better books, ahead!

* * *

CHINA BRAEKMAN is a dancer and writer living in Jersey City, NJ. She was raised in France and has been living in New York / New Jersey for the past ten years. She currently works for the International Rescue Committee, a organization that supports refugee resettlement in the US and delivers humanitarian aid in crisis-affected areas around the world.

* * *

CHRIS COCHRAN is a high school English teacher who writes first drafts on an old typewriter in a small nook beneath his basement steps. He lives in Michigan with his wife and son, where he spends most evenings drinking tea and falling asleep to comedy podcasts.

* * *

COLM O'SHEA (no bio given)

* * *

DANIEL MORESCHI is a poet from Neath, South Wales, UK, who found solace in writing amid his ongoing struggle with severe M.E. His approach to poetry entails crafting a phonetic symphony where sound, rhythm, and meaning intertwine to create art that transcends the sum of its parts. Daniel has been acclaimed in over 100 competitions to date and featured in anthologies of prize-winning literature. His writing has been published by *Lunar Codex, The Lyric, The Sunlight Press, Formal Verse, Society of Classical Poets, Reach Poetry, The Dawntreader, Autumn Sky, 14 Magazine, Spirit Fire Review, WestWard Quarterly, The Chained Muse, Every Writer Resource*, and many others. Additionally, he has received nominations for both Best of the Net and the Pushcart Prize.

* * *

DAVID SUMMERFIELD has been co-editor, columnist, and contributor to various publications within his home state of West Virginia. He is a graduate of Frostburg State University, Maryland, and a veteran of the Iraq war.

* * *

DEBORRAH CORR is a poet residing in Seattle, WA. She is the author of the chapbook *Naked Rib* coming out in February 2025 (Finishing Line Press). Her poem "Night Vision" was awarded an honorable mention in the Connecticut River Review 2024 contest. Another poem, "The Red Onion," received honorable mention in the Streetlight Magazine contest. Other poems have appeared in several journals and anthologies including, *Sunlight Press, Catamaran, The McNeese Review* and others.

* * *

DEVON JEFFERS VALDES grew up in the rural suburbs of Savannah, Georgia where her roots instilled in her a love for the American South and its rich culture. She holds a BA in English from Valdosta State University and an MA in English from Arizona State University.

* * *

DIANNE TAYLOR DUNHAM I am a former teacher of English and French and have always loved to write. I started with poems that I trudged across fields to present to our local author for critique. She was kind and encouraging. I continued in grad school with a professor who was tough, but supportive. He liked this piece.

* * *

DOMINIK SLUSARCZYK is an artist who makes everything from music to painting. He was educated at The University of Nottingham where he got a degree in biochemistry. His fiction has been published in various literary magazines including *moonShine Review* and *SHiFT – A Journal of Literary Oddities*. His fiction came first in *The Cranked Anvil Short Story Competition* and was a finalist in a number of other awards.

* * *

DONNA MYERS is a mom and regenerative farmer who recently returned to America after raising Bretonne Pie Noir cattle in France. She has a master's in writing and her work has appeared or is forthcoming in *The Ecological Citizen, Milk House, Avalon Literary Review*, and elsewhere. You can find her on Facebook and Instagram at The Happy Homestead.

* * *

E.J. BRADY lives in Brooklyn with her husband and their two children: a calico cat and a retired racing greyhound.

* * *

ERIN ROBERTSON is the founder of BoCo Wild Writers, outdoor nature writing classes (@bocowildwriters). Her poetry has been published in the *North American Review, Cold Mountain Review, Poet Lore, Deep Wild*, and elsewhere, and has been performed by Ars Nova Singers and The Crossing choir. Past honors include being a guest artist hosted by the U.S. Consulate in Kazakhstan, Voices of the Wilderness Artist in Residence at Koyukuk National Wildlife Refuge in Galena, Alaska, Boulder County Artist in Residence at Caribou Ranch, and awards in the Michael Adams Poetry Prize and Columbine Poets Members' Contest. She lives in Louisville, Colorado with her remarkable husband, two sons, parakeet, and pup who teach her about wonder every day.

* * *

FIONA RITCHIE WALKER is a Scottish writer now living in England. Her poetry and short fiction have been widely published, with work in over 100 collections, magazines, and anthologies. In 2024 she won the Scottish Poetry Library's Julia Budenz Scots Poetry Prize and the Neil Gunn Poetry Competition. She is a Hawthornden Fellow and has an MA in Writing Poetry from Newcastle University.

* * *

H PETERS (no bio given)

* * *

HARRIET RADFORD is an Australian writer living in California. A recovering lawyer, she is currently completing a Masters in Creative Writing and Literature at Harvard Extension School. When not writing (or reading), she can be found happily button mashing her way through video games with her husband.

* * *

HARVEY SILVERMAN is a retired old coot who writes nonfiction primarily for his own enjoyment.

* * *

HEIDI LASHER writes from a refurbished goat barn near her home in Spokane, Washington. Her creative nonfiction essays have been published in several literary journals and magazine, including *Orion Magazine, Cagibi, Litro Magazine, Cream City Review*, and in Allegory Review's nonfiction anthology, *Allegheny*. One of her essays was a finalist for the Michigan Quarterly Review's 2024 James A. Winn Prize in Nonfiction. She is currently working on a collection of essays about her exploration of the Spokane River. More of Heidi's work can be found at www.heidilasher.com.

* * *

JACK HARNESS (no bio given)

* * *

JEFFREY S. MARKOVITZ is a writer and educator living in Philadelphia. His fiction, non-fiction, and poetry have appeared in a number of online and print publications and his books include: *Zero Day Blue Jay* (forthcoming 2025, Tartt First Fiction Award), *The Sharpest End* (2021), *US VS* (2020), *Permanent for Now* (2018), *—for Olivia* (2013), and *Into the Everything* (2011). He has been nominated for the Pushcart Prize, was published in *The Best Short Stories of Philadelphia*, and was a finalist in the Inkwell Barbaric Yawp contest. He can be reached via his website: www.jeffreysmarkovitz.wordpress.com.

* * *

JESS WEIXLER-LANDIS has lived in Canada, England, and Burkina Faso. She currently lives and writes amongst three acres of beloved trees in rural Pennsylvania. Jess has fiction in *Lone Mountain Literary, Mag Pie,* and *Beloit Fiction.*

* * *

JESSICA NATASHA LAWRENCE writes about chronic illness, realistic hope, and the beauty and trials of ordinary life. Her work has appeared in places such as *ONE ART: a journal of poetry, 50-Word Stories,* and *To Write Love on Her Arms,* and she can be found on Instagram and Medium @typewriterbird.

* * *

JOE LABRIOLA is a Professor of Writing at Stony Brook University in New York, where he is also the Environmental Club's Faculty Advisor. His fiction and nonfiction usually focuses on issues relating to nature and the environment. He is an avid beach cleaner and sustainability advocate, hosting regular cleanup events, lectures, and even a TEDx Talk. When he is not writing, you can usually find him cleaning up his local beach—and enjoying a swim once the water is clean.

* * *

JOHN RAISOR can be found on Substack at occamsraisor.substack.com.

* * *

JONATHAN CHIBUIKE UKAH (no bio given)

* * *

JOSEPH WILLIAM VASS has been writing poetry for over fifty years, won several poetry contests, and been published in a number of literary journals. He has recently completed a memoir, *In the Found Embrace of Your Hope.*

* * *

JOYCE FROHN has been published in *ClarkesWorld, Dirty Magic,* and the anthology, *Leadership Gone Right*; among other places. She is married with an adult daughter. She also shares a house with two cats, a guinea pig, and too many dirty dishes.

* * *

J.R. WOODS is a Pacific Northwest-based writer of poetry and fiction. His work examines society and human nature through a unique and satirical dark lens. He is of the belief that art is meant to be experienced and felt, not merely observed. While the topics are often quite heavy, he strives to provoke profound thoughts in his readers.

* * *

K. S. DEARSLEY's fiction has appeared in various publications, including *The Binnacle Ultra-shorts and Diabolical Plots.* She lives with her husband in the middle of England, and when she is not writing they borrow other people's dogs to take for walks. Her novel, *Discord's Shadow,* was nominated for Best Novel in the British Science Fiction Association Awards 2021. Find out more at http://www.ksdearsley.com.

* * *

KAIT QUINN is the author of five poetry collections. Her work appears in *Anti-Heroin Chic, Exposition Review, Reed Magazine, Watershed Review*, and elsewhere. She received first place in the 2022 John Calvin Rezmerski Memorial Grand Prize and in *Sad Girl Diaries'* 2023 Fall Poetry Contest. Kait is an Editorial Associate at Yellow Arrow Publishing and a poetry reader for *Black Fox Literary Magazine.* She likes repetition, coffee shops, tattoos, and vegan breakfast. Kait lives in Minneapolis with her partner and their very polite Aussie mix. Find her at kaitquinn.com.

KATIE MOINO received her Bachelor's in English with a Creative Writing concentration at the University of Vermont. Moino's poems have appeared in or are forthcoming in *Humana Obscura, Isele Magazine, Vagabond City Lit, Book of Matches,* and elsewhere. She serves as a poetry reader for *Atticus Review.* You can connect with her on Instagram @katiemoino.

KELLY J. SULLIVAN is the author of numerous novels and books of non-fiction. A longtime journalist and writer – who regards William Shakespeare, F. Scott Fitzgerald, and Truman Capote among her teachers – she resides in Rhode Island.

KEVIN NOVALINA has published two short story collections, *Death Roll* and *Ink on Wood,* and has had Fiction, Non-fiction, and Poetry published in over 200 literary journals, magazines and anthologies. He won numerous writing competitions and was nominated for multiple prizes and awards, including three Pushcart Prizes.

KIM KIEDAISCH Journaling since her teens, it is within these pages that Kim lived abroad, traveled the world, struggled with depression, loved and lost and found happiness within her own skin. Considering herself an amateur writer, Kim gathers a lot of inspiration from her journals. She has written several essays, but has yet to be published. At the age of 60, Kim is still trying to find her niche, but enjoys writing personal essays, drawing from her experiences.

LAURINDA LIND lives in New York's North Country. Her first chapbook, *Trials by Water,* is forthcoming this year from Orchard Street Press.

LOWELL KLESSIG led a life of action, ambition and accomplishment. He directly participated in the Civil Rights and Peace Movements. In addition, he became a celebrated conservation leader and environmental advocate in Wisconsin, the nation and around the world.

MATT DENNISON is the author of *Kind Surgery,* from Urtica Press (Fr.) and *Waiting for Better,* from Main Street Rag Press. His poetry has appeared in *Verse Daily, Rattle Bayou Magazine, Redivider,* and *Cider Press Review,* among others. His fiction has appeared in *ShortStory Substack, THEMA, GUD, The Blue Crow (Aus), Prole (UK), The Wondrous Real,* and *Story Unlikely.*

MEI DAVIS A former Angeleno, Mei Davis currently resides in the cold wilds of Metro Detroit with her husband, children, and an oft-neglected laptop. She has previously been published by *prairiefire, Translunar Traveler's Lounge, Sans Press, Parsec Ink,* and others.

NATHAN ALLING LONG grew up in a cabin in western Appalachia, worked several years on a queer commune, and now lives in Philadelphia. Their work appears in various publications, including Best Small Fictions 2023, Best Microfictions 2020, Electric Lit, and Witness. *The Origin of Doubt,* their 50-story collection, was a 2019 Lambda Award finalist.

NEIL VINCENT SCOTT is an accomplished poet. His most recent works were published in *Wheelsong Anthology* 4 in the UK. His poetry writing dates back to 1979, with his first publication *Midnight Sunshine.* Neil is a producer/host at *iHeart Radio* in Seattle, hosting *Men's Health Matters* on 93.3 KJR-FM, as well as the national podcast, *Recovery – Coast to Coast.*

NICK YOUNG is a retired award-winning CBS News Correspondent. His writing has appeared in more than thirty reviews, journals and anthologies. His first novel, *Deadline,* was published in September. He lives outside Chicago.

P.T. McALLISTER studied English Literature at The University of Cambridge and was awarded a Distinction for his MA in Creative Writing. He is the editor and co-founder of *Inkfish Magazine* and a committee member for the Penzance Literary Festival. He was recently shortlisted in the Hammond House International Literary Prize and the Ironclad Creative Awards. His short stories and poems have appeared online, in print journals, and in numerous anthologies and his debut book is slated for publication.

* * *

PATRICIA DOYNE (no bio given)

* * *

RACHAEL IKINS is a 2016/18 Pushcart, 2013/18 CNY Book Award nominee, 2018 Independent Book Award winner, & 2019 Vinnie Ream & Faulkner poetry finalist. 2021 Best of the Net nominee, 2023 2nd place winner Northwind Writing Competition. A Syracuse University graduate. Author/illustrator of nine books in multiple genres. Her writing and artwork have appeared in journals worldwide from India, UK, Japan, Canada, and US.

* * *

REBEL BROWN hopes, through poetry, to bring understanding, wisdom, empathy, and curiosity to the world. They have been a lifelong peace activist, writer, musician. They work full time as a spiritual leader, and write a column about migrating birds for the local paper.

* * *

ROBERT B. ROBESON's 968 articles, short stories, and poems have been published in 78 anthologies and 334 publications in 130 countries. This includes the *Reader's Digest, Vietnam Combat, Writer's Digest, Official Karate, Positive Living, Soldier of Fortune,* and *Writer's Yearbook 2014,* among others. After retiring as a lieutenant colonel from a 27-year U.S. Army career as a helicopter medical evacuation pilot, he served as a newspaper managing editor and columnist. He has a BA in English from the University of Maryland—College Park and has completed extensive undergraduate and graduate work in journalism at the University of Nebraska—Lincoln. He lives in Lincoln, Nebraska with his wife of 55 years, Phyllis.

* * *

S.G. (SANDY) BENSON is a retired forester and journalist. She published *My Mother's Keeper: One Family's Journey Through Dementia* in 2021 and, in 2024, a collection of her father's letters home during World War II. She is currently working on a memoir, *Girls Can't Do That: Stories from a Female Forester.*

* * *

SHANE CAMOIN, a second-generation American, was born in Los Angeles and raised in Salt Lake City and Las Vegas. Along with winning awards for creative writing and visual arts, Shane has lectured on the concept of identity at symposiums and conferences throughout Asia, Europe, and North America.

* * *

SHERRY MORRIS (@Uksherka & @uksherka.bsky.social), originally from Missouri, Sherry writes prize-winning fiction from a farm in the Scottish Highlands where she pets cows, watches clouds and dabbles in photography. Her first published story was about her Peace Corps experience in 1990s Ukraine. Read more of her work at www.uksherka.com.

* * *

SHOSHAUNA SHY is the author of five poetry collections, two of which won Outstanding Achievement awards from the Wisconsin Library Association; her poems have recently been published by *Change Seven, Poetry Breakfast, Black Coffee Review, Creative Wisconsin* and the *San Pedro River Review.* Her poem "This Is You in the Sundance Catalogue" was longlisted for the Fish Publishing Poetry Prize 2022, and in 2023, her poem "Not Wanting to Meet My Birth Mother" was a finalist in the annual contest of *Naugatuck River Review.* Her poems have been made into videos, produced inside taxi cabs, and even decorated the hind quarters of city buses.

* * *

SUMMER CHAMBLEY is an American writer based in London, UK.

* * *

SUSAN MASON SCOTT lives in Madison, Indiana, a small town on the Ohio River. Prior to settling in Madison, she lived in other Midwest states, on both coasts, as well as Sierra Leone, Nicaragua, and Italy. She is a mathematics instructor serving adult education students. Her poems appear in *Flying Island Journal, tiny wren lit, Thimble Literary Magazine, Heartwood Literary Magazine,* and elsewhere.

* * *

SUSAN MAYER BRUMEL began writing poetry upon retiring from a thirty-five-year career in hospice social work. Her poems are inspired by her patients' journeys, the beauty of nature, and the human condition. She is grateful to be published in several journals, including Verse Virtual and Lothlorien. She lives near the Jersey Shore with her husband and Bernese Mountain Dog, Dottie.

* * *

SUZETTE BISHOP has published three poetry books and two chapbooks, including her most recent, *Jaguar's Book of the Dead.* Her writing has appeared in many journals and anthologies and received an

Honorable Mention in the Pen 2 Paper Contest from the Coalition of Texans with Disabilities. She lives in Laredo, Texas with her partner and two cats.

* * *

SVETLANA LITVINCHUK is a poet and permaculture farmer with degrees from University of New Mexico. She is the author of a debut poetry chapbook, *Only a Season* (Bottlecap Features, 2024). Her work has appeared or is forthcoming in *Apple Valley Review, Sky Island Journal, Plant-Human Quarterly, ONE ART, Apocalypse Confidential, Union Spring Review, Longhouse Press,* and elsewhere. Originally from Kyiv, Ukraine, she now lives with her husband and daughter in Cape Girardeau. She is a reviews editor with *ONLY POEMS*.

* * *

TERESA K. BURLESON's book *Redefined* is the 2024 recipient of the CLA Henri Award in the devotional category.

* * *

TERRY SANVILLE lives in San Luis Obispo, California with his artist-poet wife (his in-house editor) and two plump cats (his in-house critics). He writes full time, producing short stories, essays, and novels. His stories have been accepted more than 550 times by journals, magazines, and anthologies including *The American Writers Review, Bryant Literary Review,* and *Shenandoah*. He was nominated four times for Pushcart Prizes and once for inclusion in Best of the Net anthology. Terry is a retired urban planner and an accomplished jazz and blues guitarist – who once played with a symphony orchestra backing up jazz legend George Shearing.

* * *

TOM CONLAN lives on a small farm in the highlands of Northern Michigan. His prose and poetry has appeared in numerous literary journals, including *Walloon Writers Review, QU Literary Review, UP Reader,* and *Michigan Trout Magazine*. Find his lyrical memoir - *My Journey Begins Where the Road Ends...* and his novel, *Gentle Spirits* at: www.thomasfordconlan.com Amazon and Ingram Tom holds an MFA from Queens University and an MS from the US Naval Postgraduate School.

* * *

TOM WADE is a retired state government employee. He lives in the Atlanta area and volunteers with the American Civil Liberties Union. His essays have appeared in *Canyon Voices, Dr. T. J. Eckleburg Review, Lunch Ticket, Inlandia, Harmony Magazine, Rivanna Review, The Dead Mule School of Southern Literature, 805 Lit+Art, William and Mary Review, Black Fork Review, Bookends Review, Ilford Review,* and other publications.

* * *

TYLER MARTINEZ is a writer and student living in New York. His work has previously been published in the *Olivetree Review* and in *Major 7th Magazine* (August 2024).

* * *

VIDYAROOPINI NAIR is a recent graduate from Durham University, where she studied law. Her creative work often explores life in Singapore, capturing the fast-paced nature of city life and the importance of savoring small moments. Through her poetry, she seeks to celebrate the beauty of everyday experiences and encourage others to pause and appreciate the world around them.

* * *

WINTER ROSS has published in literary journals, magazines, two anthologies, and has written, illustrated, and published a chapbook of visionary prose, *4 Warnings: Shamanic Journeys*. She was awarded First Place in Short Story by the New Mexico Press Women's Association and the National Federation of Press Women for *Orienting Heaven*. Winter lives near Taos, New Mexico. Her websites are: wintersweb.journoportfolio.com and www.ceremonialvisions.com.

www.ingramcontent.com/pod-product-compliance
Lightning Source LLC
Chambersburg PA
CBHW080743250626
47162CB00010B/3004